"DON'T YOU WANT TO LEAVE TESTAMENT?"

Mead grinned and went into a fighter's crouch, the knife she'd previously offered him now held at the ready.

"Stupid Gray," she said. "Mother guessed what you were at the end. She died disappointed."

"That's a lie!" Gray shouted, glaring at his sister in disgust.

Mead walked closer, holding the knife between them. "You're so gullible, you're almost entertaining." The knife glittered in her hand. "I'll free us both since you don't have the nerve."

"What do you mean?" Gray asked.

"I'm doing you a favor. There won't be blood on your hands." And then she lunged at him. . . .

TESTAMENT

Valerie J. Freireich

A ROC BOOK

ROC
Published by the Penguin Group
Penguin Books USA Inc., 375 Hudson Street,
New York, New York 10014, U.S.A.
Penguin Books Ltd, 27 Wrights Lane,
London W8 5TZ, England
Penguin Books Australia Ltd, Ringwood,
Victoria, Australia
Penguin Books Canada Ltd, 10 Alcorn Avenue,
Toronto, Ontario, Canada M4V 3B2
Penguin Books (N.Z.) Ltd, 182–190 Wairau Road,
Auckland 10, New Zealand

Penguin Books Ltd, Registered Offices:
Harmondsworth, Middlesex, England

First published by Roc, an imprint of Dutton Signet,
a division of Penguin Books USA Inc.

First Printing, August, 1995
10 9 8 7 6 5 4 3 2 1

Portions of the first three chapters of this book, in altered form, appeared in
The Magazine of Fantasy and Science Fiction, December, 1993, as "Testament."

Cover art by John Jude Palencar

 REGISTERED TRADEMARK—MARCA REGISTRADA

Printed in the United States of America

To the one I will become,
To my mother

Chapter 1

I. Stone Town

Shortly after learning he was married, Gray Bridger realized he might need to kill his wife.

"I'm sorry, Mr. Bridger," the Dispatch Office clerk said, her bureaucratic indifference belying the formal expression of sympathy. "You're confined to Testament by the quarantine."

Gray's fingers tightened around his hard-earned money. The paper counts used on Testament by the Harmony of Worlds felt damp in his hand; he wished he'd exchanged the thick wad of accumulated tips and venturing profits for a few larger, more dignified bills down in Edgemarket, but now it was too late. "What do you mean? I'm not quarantined. I'm human, like you. Not Altered."

She frowned as she looked into what appeared to be blank space; it was a secured display, visible only from her side of the desk. Typical Harmony secrecy. "You automatically forfeited the right to leave the Protectorate of Testament when you married a native. You can't purchase a ticket to Darien, or anywhere else within the Polite Harmony of Worlds."

"I'm *not* married." He thrust the Harmony counts across the desk at the offie woman as though if he forced her to accept the money, he might persuade her to deliver his ticket. One of the counts dropped off the far side of the desk onto her lap. The offie woman glanced at the paper counts—Harmony citizens used paper only for dealing with the natives of Testament—then at him. Her washed-out blue eyes narrowed as she weighed his appearance. He'd taken time dressing before coming into the Exchange District. His Harmony-styled black suit, although not imported, was handmade to the finicky standards of offie travelers seeking Edgemarket bargains; his long brown hair was pulled tightly

back into an acceptable Harmony fashion. Although his face
was typically Bridger to anyone who knew his family line,
he was tall enough to pass for an offie; however, he was not
one of the occasional offie workers trapped by unkind circumstances on Testament. Gray hesitated, disliking surren-
der of his camouflage, then said, "Marriage isn't even one of
our customs here. There must be a mistake. Please look at
my file."

"Oh," she said primly. "You're a native." She no longer
met his eyes.

"Gray *Bridger.*" Heedless of the fastidious off-worlder
protocol, and resisting her natural authority as an older
woman, he tapped his fingers on her desktop; she leaned
away from him. "I'm approved to leave. I passed every
test."

She grimaced and looked back at her invisible display as
though it were the script for obstructing him. "It doesn't
matter. Local marriage cancels your eligibility, and you are
registered in your Compound Council's datalog as married
to a native 'far cousin' named Dancer Bridger." She snapped
off his file with a finger motion. Nothing detectable
changed. She glanced over Gray's shoulder at a man who
had just entered the Dispatch Office, then bowed to him,
very deeply. The newcomer was apparently important.

"But I'm a singleton," Gray insisted, without moving
away. "I want a ticket to Darien." The offie behind him
crowded too close. Gray noticed an emblem on the man's
right sleeve; he was an official of some kind, not just a tourist.

The clerk lifted the dropped bill from her lap, holding it
between her thumb and middle finger; she placed it with the
rest and nudged them all back to him with a flick of her fingertips. "These are yours. Take them, Mr. Bridger. I'm
sorry."

Dazed, Gray reflexively picked up his money. The man
behind looked as if he intended to speak to Gray, but Gray
wanted no more meaningless, patronizing offie platitudes,
and he rushed from the office, brushing the man aside.

Once outside Dispatch, his rejected Harmony counts still
clutched in his hand, Gray hesitated, trying to think. He'd
been married by fiat of the Compound Council of Testament.
That meant his grandmother was behind it, since she was
Bridger Dome's representative on the Council, and a power

there. He hit his fist against the wall, into the middle of one of the Harmony window screens lighting the interior corridor. The window screen's view disappeared when his hand smashed into it, then immediately resumed. It showed a sunny seashore. No doubt because of the information quarantine, every Harmony window screen he'd seen showed scenes from Testament itself; this counterfeit window gave a view of the famous beach at Rose, in the Kolor Islands. A cloud passed over the warm, sparkling water; it looked as real as if nature had made it, but the corridor was fifteen hundred miles from Rose, where it was still winter.

The door opened behind him, and Gray strode off toward the outer exit.

Married. He imagined his wife, a woman like his sisters, like all the Altered women of Testament, with ghosts staring at him from behind deceptively young eyes. She would have a soul a thousand years old. One of *them*. "No," he whispered. He would kill his supposed wife before letting one of those scornful, hag-ridden women trap him on Testament.

Gray hurried out of the Transit Building, glad to be free of its muggy offie atmosphere. Once in the clear, crisp air of Testament, where he could think, he stopped again. The paper Harmony money fluttered in his fist, ruffled by the irregular gusts of wind coming down from the mountains beyond the Exchange District, as if the counts were struggling to break free of him, or of Testament. He stuffed them into his jacket pocket. The outer door opened, bumping Gray. He grunted and turned. It was the offie VIP from the Dispatch Office. At Gray's glare, the man said, "Sorry."

"You all apologize too much," Gray said testily, "and it never means a thing."

The man bowed in the deepest Harmony style; Gray suspected irony. "But I do apologize," the man said. "The impact was entirely unintentional." He didn't smile, which made his steady attention uncomfortable. "You're a native. I'm looking for a guide."

"Not interested." Gray turned away.

"I'll pay well," the man said to Gray's back.

Wind swirled around the corners of the angular offie buildings, spinning dust, like miniature tornadoes, across Amity Square. Gray lowered his head and started across the square's broad, empty expanse toward the lifting lines that led out of the hilltop Exchange District and down into the

domes and blocks of Stone Town proper. The sound of footsteps following him made Gray increase his pace. The frigid
wind from the ice-covered mountains was worse in Exchange than on Stone Town's plain below, but the offies'
view was magnificent. Gray paused at the tunnel entrance,
staring out from the overlook at Stone Town and the sea beyond it, glittering in the afternoon light. He wondered, not
for the first time, if the off-worlders had built their enclave
here just so they could look down on the natives.

The persistent offie caught up. Gray waited for him to
speak, hoping for another opportunity to snub him, but the
man stood silently at the overlook, his big hands holding the
railing, his feet spread wide apart, as if he commanded all
he surveyed.

"Testament," the offie said eventually. "You should call
this world Entropy; it's one huge monument to the dead.
Even the capital is a cemetery."

Gray faced the other man, uncertain whether or not to be
offended—he had thought much the same thing himself—
and said nothing.

The stranger gestured at the domes and rainbow light
caught on the facets of the gemstone ring on his right hand.
"Magnificent engineering, though."

Even from a distance, the family domes were huge. The
First Comers on Testament, and their descendants, had built
on a massive scale, trying to outdo each other. Immense
half-spheres of golden stone, some with bands of diamond
glass, the domes rose in a cluster along the shore of the
Stone Sea, on either side of the river, dwarfing the pastel
grid of blocks forming the living city. Bridger Dome was the
largest intact dome, the only one with an opening at its apex,
visible even from this distance as a shadow. The opening
was called Eye on the World, and was six hundred feet
above the ground. The sight didn't inspire pride in Gray,
however, just resentment. Bridger Dome—all of Testament—was his cage. "I'm not interested in acting as a
guide," Gray said. "I don't need Harmony money if I can't
leave."

The man turned to him. "Your marriage is unfortunate. It
is legally valid inside the Harmony, since it's registered with
the proper local authority, and if the woman is like the rest
of them here on Testament . . . The Harmony won't let you

abandon a spouse, and won't authorize emigration for one of these freaks."

Freak. Gray had heard the word often enough—applied to him—and hated the sound. "Who are you?"

The offie bowed again, less fully. "My name is Martin Penn. I'm a visitor here. I overheard your conversation."

Gray nodded, not deigning to bow in the Harmony manner despite the intimidating authority of Penn's tone. Instead of the standard tourist outfit of clearsuit and ready alarms (although offies often commented on how little crime occurred on Testament—at least, crime affecting them), Penn wore well-tailored brown pants and a Harmony-styled long tunic-jacket made of a soft, rich material that looked capable of becoming wet and rumpled; somehow that made him appear more important rather than less. He was taller than Gray, and huskier, but with the symmetrical muscles of a man who kept in shape, not someone who had built them by physical labor. His feet and manicured hands were both large, giving him a gangling, proletarian look in conflict with the rest of his appearance. Oblivious to Gray's uneasiness, or unconcerned by it, Penn looked out at the city and pointed. "What happened to that dome, the broken one?"

Gray didn't look. "Shak Dome fell shortly after the Harmony's quickships found Testament, a hundred years ago, standard. Until then it was the largest. The Shak still use it, though, what's left of them." He frowned, reminded of the Shak's most recent attack. One Cohen and two Bridger men taken.

"For interment of the dead?"

"Yes." Gray sighed and glanced at his city. From this distance, it seemed an abandoned ruin from the antique past. Much of Stone Town's activity was underground, in tunnels and caverns that protected the inhabitants from the frequently harsh weather; none of the ships anchored in the harbor was under way, and the midday wind blew too vigorously for the zeps. Stone Town looked dead.

Somewhere down there was his wife, Dancer Bridger. He didn't know the woman, but he knew what to expect. Her line memories would stretch back in time like a mentally fossilized heredity, all the way to Earth and the founder of the Bridger line, Janet Bridger—although, unless she was a precaster, her recall of more than a few generations past would be unconscious. He had to get away from her, away from Testament, to where he could be free of that. Of them and their contempt.

"I want to get inside one of those domes," Penn said. "To meet a precaster, but not one of the Edgemarket fakes that prey on Harmony visitors. The real precasters have refused to see me so far." He waited for Gray to respond.

"The domes are generally just for the line," Gray said.

"I'll pay 150c," Penn said.

That was half the fare to Darien, a fortune for an hour's work, so easily accomplished. Gray studied Martin Penn. The emblem on his sleeve—a black stick figure of a man on a golden background—meant nothing to Gray, except that this man was no ordinary visitor, nor was he one of the inexperienced Harmony administrators ordinarily posted to Testament. Maybe this insistent off-worlder was influential, and Gray could use an influential offie friend. "All right," Gray said slowly, still reluctant to agree. "I'll guide you to Bridger Dome. No guarantee you'll get inside, though."

Martin Penn smiled condescendingly, but with satisfaction. "You're main line in the Bridger family, a direct descendant of the founder through the youngest daughters. You'll get me inside."

II. Not Quite Come

Three old women were talking, their low voices a braid woven around Janet Bridger, a ribbon of sound holding her fast to the bed. She listened without troubling herself to understand, as though their voices were noise from a television kept on too late and she'd dozed during an old rerun. Vaguely, she noticed their lilting accents. Jamaica?

Her eyelids felt heavy. The anesthesia's residue, she supposed. A woman had patted her hand: nurse or anesthesiologist? The egg-harvesting operation must have gone well, because while she felt lethargic, there was no pain, no cramping, no sensation at all that would have inhibited movement, had she been inclined to move. Dr. Bennett had promised there would be nothing, but Janet had assumed that in her eagerness to collect eggs for her experiment, Emily Bennett would lie.

It was time to appear to awaken, to let them know she was aware and alive—it was curious that they hadn't checked on her already—but she wasn't eager to be recalled to life, es-

pecially while feeling so comfortable. Hooray for pain-
killers, she thought. Surreptitiously, she stretched her legs.
Her usual accumulation of aches was gone; she felt young
again.

One of the three voices was, if not precisely louder, then
stronger than the other two; it seemed familiar. She tensed
her shoulders against the stiff hospital mattress to listen better.

". . . necessary, for gray to trust her . . ." the voice said,
fading out, then in. ". . . to enhance the encounter."

Janet shifted position slightly. The peremptory tone, the
timbre of the voice, reminded her of Grandmother Tillie.
Janet recalled the long, boring drives through unrelieved
flatness, until the Mississippi River, then a banquet of heavy
food on the buffet table at Grandma's Iowa farm, followed
by the usual after-dinner adult slump. Surprised at the clarity
of the memory, Janet remembered the time Grandma Tillie
had taken her upstairs to explore her old clothes, her jewelry,
and her powders, viewing her long life in the reflection of its
physical traces. *For you,* her grandmother had said, *my
daughter's daughter.*

Janet would leave only paltry traces behind, and no one to
remember; that was the real reason she, a forty-six-year-old
spinster, had been secretly overjoyed to be asked to donate
eggs to Bennett's strange project. It was the only possible
way she would ever have children, if these things Emily
planned to make were real and could survive. HSU, the Hard
Science Underground, would help, but . . .

Janet gasped as sudden head pain disoriented her; her
memory of that time deteriorated like fireworks extin-
guishing themselves as they burned brightly, then out, in the
night sky.

She dozed, then gasped as the sensation of falling awakened her again. She opened her eyes and blinked at the unexpected brightness of the light and the unfamiliarity of
what she saw.

Instead of artificial lights in a cold, tiled room with hulk-
ing pieces of medical equipment, there was a wall of slightly
curved, sun-lit windows. The quality of the light was wrong,
and the walls were whitewashed, like those of a peasant cot-
tage in a fairy tale. A nightstand and a rocking chair were
the only furniture.

Three old women, outlined against the pale blue sky outside, stopped whispering and turned toward Janet. A peculiar sensation overcame her, an intuition of old nightmare, of many voices speaking all at once inside her mind. She struggled to lean her weight against her elbows and sit, but her body felt disconnected from her mind. Janet glanced across herself, then opened her mouth to scream. She couldn't make a sound.

One of the old women had come to her bedside; she took Janet's hand and patted it, in a comforting gesture that steadied Janet. "It's all right," the woman said, soothing Janet's fear. This was the authoritative voice she'd heard earlier. The woman was tall and wrinkled, but she stood straight, and wore a sparkling shawl of a fabric Janet didn't recognize.

"What . . .?" Amazed at her own soft voice, Janet closed her eyes. Even her breathing felt wrong.

"Hush." The woman stroked Janet's hand. "Be calmed by my touch. All is well. We have a bit of work to do together—though you won't remember it. Poor freak." Janet heard humor in her nurse's tone, and then a sigh. "Poor Gray. Well. You will be good to him." It was an order. "But first, Elene. *Your* time is not quite come."

Who is Elene? Janet wondered. *Who am I?* The question faded even as she did, a light turned dimmer on its switch, then gone.

III. Not Prince Hamlet

The air in Bridger Dome had a parched quality, as if something had been burned a long time before. It was dim inside the immense rotunda, the light limited to that provided by the tough, diamond glass bands high on the wall and the Eye. At night thousands of tiny bulbs—and at that, only a fraction of those available usually lit—would be set aglow. Forty floors of rooms and ever narrowing galleries went up the dome wall, and above them the bare inner surface loomed like a stone and glass sky. Although few people except precasters lived inside Bridger Dome, on February 17 of every Testament-local year more than a million Bridgers celebrated Janet Bridger's birthday inside. Next to Gray, his arms behind his back, Penn stared up through the Eye, then gawked at the intimidating volume of interior space that could hold them all. "What happened to the people who could build this?" he asked. "Why is Testament such a back-water?"

Gray shrugged. Presumably every precaster remembered precisely how the domes had been built—a precaster remembered everyone in her direct motherline, and had the intelligence to use the information—but Testament's vigorous human expansion had ended when the Harmony announced itself and its quickships arrived. After the Harmony established its "protectorate," Testament's precasters no longer built and planned, they tended the dead. "They're different," Gray said, suspicious of this offie who pretended they were chance acquaintances and yet knew so much about Testament and Gray. "They take a longer view; they see connections that we can't."

Penn shook his head as if freeing it from the grip of his distance vision. "Inertia," Penn said, answering his own question while ignoring Gray's response. "All they do is reminisce. This ancestral memory Alteration was a dead end, designed for a single purpose—the generation ships—and an impediment to achievement after their arrival here. Perhaps Swan is right that it's a flaw, an appendix that should have been removed."

Gray started at Penn's careless, slightly dismissive reference to Governor Swan, the Harmony's oppressive agent. Meanwhile, Penn studied the levels of galleries, watching a group of adolescent Bridger girls waiting for medical checkups on level three, and then higher, to the honor guard's training gyms. He ignored Gray's favorite area, the Earth garden, where species of Earth plants unable to survive on Testament's windy surface, or incapable of adapting to the short year, had been preserved inside the dome for centuries.

The honor guard at the entrance arch through which they had arrived, eight women and two slightly older men, had followed them indoors and appeared exceptionally vigilant. Gray glanced up at the first gallery, called Command Level. Virginia Bridger, his eldest aunt of first degree and chief of the Bridger Dome honor guard, had left her office. He quickly looked away—he remembered her exasperated refusal even to accept his application for the guard: *You're a singleton!*—because she was standing at the railing, watching him. Gray, wearing his long, Harmony-styled tunic-jacket, a man and a freak, abruptly felt as much an outsider in Bridger Dome as Penn; he didn't belong here anymore, not since he'd decided to leave Testament, and he wished he hadn't brought Penn inside. They'd allowed Penn in on Gray's endorsement—singleton or not, Gray was main line—and if Penn made trouble, Gray could be fined in family court. "You've seen it; let's go." Gray jerked his head toward the arch.

"Not yet," Penn said. "Is that a precaster?" He gestured behind Gray, and took a determined step in that direction.

Gray looked around. An old woman approached across the rotunda floor. She was thin, tall, white-haired, and elegantly draped in a long white dress and fringed icesnakeskin shawl. She walked directly toward Gray and Martin Penn, moving regally, merely nodding a greeting to others she passed.

"Yes," Gray whispered, turning away from the woman. "Reed Bridger, chief precaster of Bridger Dome. We should leave."

Penn ignored Gray's advice and went to meet the precaster. Gray felt Virginia watching. He followed Penn, one step behind. The offie bowed when Reed Bridger stopped in front of him; his foreign gesture looked peculiar and seemed dishonest inside the dome. It was said that Harmony citizens bowed to prevent people from seeing into their eyes. "Lady precaster," Penn said, "I've tried to get official permission to visit, but the domes won't answer me. I want a precast. I'll pay." He reached into his pocket, then stopped at her upraised hand.

"No. Not everything can be forced or bought." She tilted her head, observing him. "You're no tourist. Who are you, friend of Gray?"

Penn bowed again, as deeply as he had first to Gray, but without the implicit sarcasm. "I am an Ahman of the Academy, from Center, the Harmony's capital, lady Bridger. My name is Martin Penn. I have questions to ask a precaster, important questions. If I may speak with you privately?"

She shook her head, chuckling softly. "I won't answer any *important* questions now."

Penn lost his smile. "Lady precaster, I am not accustomed to being refused."

"A terrible problem, I agree," she said, "but stay on Testament longer. It will be remedied."

Penn observed her—she winked at Gray, but he turned

aside so as not to seem to take her part against *Ahman* Martin Penn—then Penn said, "This is not wise."

She smiled. "Wisdom isn't always useful; sometimes ignorant courage is better. But I'll tell you something that may be of use." Without awaiting his response, she closed her eyes and swayed, slowly picking up speed. The shawl dangled loosely in her hands, around her narrow hips, and across her lower back. The wrinkles almost vanished in her entranced face. Gray stared, amazed. Penn was wide-eyed, fascinated by her every move. Bubbling sounds came from her lips as she quickened her pace, then the sounds changed pitch and became sharp, brief screams, like those of a wild creature in urgent pain. Her voice echoed in the rotunda; Gray felt chills down his spine, but he also had to suppress an urge to snicker. He looked up. Virginia had returned to her office, but on the fourth level a small group of Bridger women stopped their exercises, came to the railing, and gawked at Reed Bridger. Gray took a step forward, intending to stop her, but just then she finished, opened her eyes, and poked Penn's chest with her rigid index finger. "All truth is faith. Your doubts have an answer. Now go. Go!" She laughed.

Penn took a single involuntary step backward, then sternly observed the old woman like a judge preparing to pass sentence. She defied whatever opinion he may have intended to deliver by turning away and waving far across the rotunda to some women of her own age who were leaving the garden. Gray guessed at Penn's outrage, a Jonist Ahman being teased and ignored by a native, and hoped Penn wasn't entirely certain he had been teased.

"Sir?" Gray said obsequiously. He needed Penn's help in his application to leave Testament. Gray gestured at the arch.

"Gray, stay here!" Reed Bridger said, turning her attention back. "A prince of Bridger Dome doesn't grovel before an offie."

Gray gawked at her, speechless. *Prince?* It was a joke at his expense. Testament would only have princesses.

"Prince?" Penn said, looking speculatively at Gray.

She waved her hand, reclaiming Penn's attention. "Prince Hamlet since his marriage—do you see the hesitations? Or perhaps he's only Prufrock."

Penn regarded her for a moment, lips pressed together, hands behind his back, then he bowed curtly. "Lady precaster, it would be best for you to speak more soberly with me. I am *not* simply another visitor. The Polite Harmony of Worlds governs the Protectorate of Testament with a light hand, but we do not enjoy becoming figures of fun."

"Fun?" She grinned at Gray, who wished he could be elsewhere, anywhere but with Penn inside Bridger Dome, but Gray smiled slightly, so as not to let his strain show. Reed continued. "And I suppose an Ahman of the Academy had a better mind than that of the governor of Testament—ah, what an ugly-minded man is our short-necked Swan—but here is that light hand getting heavier, and I'm an old woman who only wants an open hand, or perhaps a slow hand, if any hand at all." She clapped her hands together as if chasing dogs away, and did it nearly in Penn's face. "Go on!" she said, grinning. "Go! A precast cannot be an entertainment—for either participant. Go!"

The members of the honor guard were indecisively drifting closer. "You'd better leave," Gray said uneasily.

"Another time, then," Penn said with dignity. He bowed curtly at Reed. "Come, Gray Bridger." He expected to be obeyed.

Reed grabbed Gray by the wrist. "He stays."

Penn's gaze traveled around the rotunda. The honor guard was close, and many other members of the Bridger line had watched their chief precaster's encounter with an offie. Gray saw Penn realize that, whoever he was off Testament, however eminent or powerful, his influence did not reach inside Bridger Dome. Penn faced Gray, awaiting Gray's decision.

Gray shrugged and didn't leave, although Reed had released her grip; he felt a certain pride at his rebuff to Penn, just as he had enjoyed slighting him in the Exchange. He wanted to get away from Testament; he needed Penn, but he was a Bridger. No arrogant offie would command him, like a dog, to heel.

Penn hesitated but didn't protest. He straightened his back, then turned and strode out of Bridger Dome, passing the honor guard without a word, looking nowhere but directly ahead.

"Well, grandmother, what was that show?" Gray asked as Penn reached the entrance—the honor guard following close behind, hurrying him as if herding an independent-minded animal. It hadn't seemed politic to admit their relationship in front of Penn.

"Impressed?" she asked, chuckling to herself. Some precasters were preoccupied with their dignity, but never Gray's grandmother. "I decided to give him a memory worth recalling, since you were the one to bring him here. You've always been my favorite grandchild." She gazed fondly at him, then glanced in the direction Penn had taken, and her voice lost some of its gaiety. "It may have been a mistake. He seems astute. We know so little about the universe off Testament. They censor everything, and none of us is allowed to return, of the few allowed to leave." She brightened again and lowered her voice as if sharing a secret. "But then, they don't know us, either."

"Why not precast for him?" Gray asked. "An Ahman is high in the Jonist hierarchy, just below their six Electors. I thought the Compound Council wanted to hear off-worlders' questions, because of what they implied about the Harmony of Worlds."

"Policies change." She shrugged, glancing around the rotunda. Gray followed her gaze, but saw nothing important. She pulled her shawl higher on her shoulders and turned back to him. "Well, Gray, are you visiting your mother's necropolis or have you come to be introduced to your bride?"

Gray stepped backward, seeking distance between himself and his grandmother's eyes. She grinned and he clenched his fists. His *bride* was some far cousin coerced into marriage with the notorious Bridger main line singleton because Reed wanted to keep him on Testament; he would have nothing to do with his *bride*. Gray mastered his hot, hostile wave of anger, forced open his hands, and smiled, as dealing with offies had taught him. "You can trap me on Testament for now, grandmother, but sooner or later I'll get away. Let me go. I don't belong here; I can never be happy."

"Sloppy thinking, Gray," she said. "Happiness is no measure of a life. Happiness is an illusion created from the recognition that you're useful; anything else is selfishness."

"So you want me on Testament, unhappy and unselfish."

She grinned and studied him. He stood as motionless as the honor guard at formal inspection on Janet Bridger's birthday; his grandmother was alien and frightening at the same time that she was lovingly familiar. The combination left him feeling lonely.

"Gray," she said, "singletons don't remember their mothers' lives, but we're within you, in your heart. You need us;

you need Testament; if you leave now, you'll die alone in
that black void of stars and strangers, extremely unhappy."

He held up a hand as if to ward her off. "I didn't ask for
a precast!"

"I can't control what I know," she chided him. "I tell you,
Gray, this marriage is for the best." She hugged him quickly,
ignoring his stiffness.

"Whose best?" He pulled away. "Bridger Dome, so you
won't be embarrassed when a member of the main line
leaves Testament? It can't be for my good. I want to live
where I'm like everyone else, where I'm normal."

"That will never be." She shook her head and made a
half-unconscious clucking noise he remembered from his
childhood scrapes; she'd been his mother after his own
mother had died. "I hurt for you, Gray," she said. "It's difficult to be a singleton, notwithstanding that every family
line begins with one. I watched your frustration when your
mother's memories didn't come in at adolescence, as did
those of all your friends. I watched your shame when you
stayed a child in the only way that matters, in the mind.
You're not like the rest of us, but you can still serve your
people. Come with me. Meet Dancer." She gestured farther
into the dome, toward the nearest bank of elevators and up
toward the galleries.

"No. I'm leaving, grandmother." Even to himself, Gray
sounded like the stubborn child she'd just called him.

Reed put her arm through Gray's and tugged him toward
the garden with wiry strength. "Walk awhile with an old
woman. What harm can it do? You've obviously forgotten
the Earth literature we taught you, though your friend seems
to remember well enough—interesting—but do you remember your lessons of how we came to Testament?" She didn't
wait for his answer. "Our ancestors were altered for their
journey here—'Altered' wasn't a noun then, or a dirty
word—given a mini-racial memory tagged into our mitochondrial DNA in order to prevent the loss of information
and the memory of Earth. Since mitochondrial DNA is inherited only from female ancestors, only female memories
are passed on. Men know it, which is why so many of you
are sour."

Gray gently tried to pull away again, but she tightened her
grip. "Listen. We all know each other. Men and women of
a line have generations of memories in common, shared life-

times and attitudes, except for the occasional singleton, like you. And the lines also understand each other from those same generations of living side by side. But we don't know the Harmony, and those people are afraid of us, Gray, no matter how they disguise it with disdain. They're afraid of what we could do if they let us learn what they know. So they keep secrets. They tell us as little as they can."

They had reached the garden's outskirts. Small plants with large flowers lined the path, but the glory of the garden, the trees, were still ahead: tall, gracefully branching shapes that would barely survive, stunted and twisted, outside the dome, grew here, precious and proud. The humidity increased, and the air was scented more than was usual on Testament, though it was quite unlike the bland mugginess inside the Exchange District. The sweet fragrance didn't remind Gray of anything except this garden, but his grandmother stopped and smiled. Her eyes unfocused slightly as momentarily she reminisced.

"Do you think these flowers are exactly what we brought from Earth?" she asked. "Or by planting them, selecting among their seeds for generations, have we changed them? A thousand years is a long time."

"Grandmother . . ." He moved away from her.

She resumed walking and he followed, annoyed that she was, as always, controlling the conversation, turning it in directions she chose, but unwilling to interrupt. The garden's floor was not tiled, like the rest of the rotunda floor; it was bare soil. Unlike the alluvial soil of the Red River plain in the fertile Eastlands, this was dark, filled with centuries of the closest care and humus, the growth and residue of alien Earth plants. When damp, the garden smelled like nowhere else on Testament. Once, when Gray was a child, a special boy to be living inside Bridger Dome, Reed had said it smelled of distant Earth.

The shawl slipped lower on her shoulders. The icesnake-skin shimmered first blue, then lavender and red, and finally deep green, echoing the garden colors. She smiled, noticing it, then her smile deepened as she looked at Gray. "I've always liked this best of all your presents. You killed it yourself, didn't you? This was the one you took alone, with just a knife?"

He nodded, remembering the camphor stench of the approaching icesnake, the tearing fabric of the tent, the feel of scaly skin against his bare arms as he struggled to keep it off, then the cool, sticky blood on his hands and chest as he managed to slice into the beast's throat, turning away while stabbing at it so its acid breath wouldn't damage his eyes. The beast had been far south of its normal range—lost and drawn to heat in a fatal misapplication of its normal instinct—and was the lucky first kill of the hunting venture. Some said Reed Bridger was equally dangerous, and she was in her optimum habitat. "You precasters never talk in a straight line," he said.

"Is this straight enough?" she said. "You are what we are not: a man, a singleton, and acceptable to the Polite Harmony of Worlds. That can be useful."

"How?" he burst out. "What can I do that everyone else can't do better?"

Swiftly, she answered, "You can marry Dancer."

"You've already married me to her."

"Don't pout, Gray. It's unappealing in a man. I mean that you can marry her properly, bind yourself to her. Come meet her. You'll be pleased. She's beautiful. I'm sure she'll love you, too."

Gray stopped. He suspected that ahead, in a hidden recess of the Earth garden, Dancer Bridger was waiting. "I don't want any wife from Testament," he said. "If you take me to her, then I swear I'll kill her, grandmother, just to be let alone."

She laughed, sounding almost young. "I don't believe that, Gray. You have too much heart to kill anyone. You're only being melodramatic. All right. Go home. Next time you visit me, you can meet Dancer."

"She lives inside the dome? Then she's a precaster." Appalled—they were the worst of the knowing women of Testament—he scowled and finally turned to leave.

"No." Reed grabbed his arm. "She's not a precaster, Gray. You'll see what she is when you're in a more tranquil mood. Now go home." She released her hold on him.

They were in the midst of vegetation so thick that it was impossible to see they were inside Bridger Dome; even the closest voices were muffled. He hesitated. Since adolescence this had been the place he considered his true home, because there was nothing of Testament in it. It was the promise of his future, the single place he was always reluctant to leave. Without a word, Gray turned and walked away.

IV. A Street-Corner Oracle

Martin Penn was lost. The Altered precaster and his own surly native guide had amused themselves at his expense, and he, an Ahman of the Academy of Center, had been furiously impotent. With barely a thought to the direction he should take, he had stalked out of Bridger Dome and then lost himself in the maze of parks, plazas, and circular streets that serviced and surrounded the cluster of Stone Town domes.

Penn stopped and looked around. The icy wind off the mountains penetrated his finewave jacket, and he shivered. Women were everywhere, women with parcels, or women going busily about their jobs. A gang of them, all pregnant, chatted nearby. From their sideways glances, they were talking about him, an obvious outsider; he turned away.

The worst of it was, he suspected the old woman had manipulated him into just this agitated state. Why?

Penn started moving again, to an open area between two huge domes which had blocked his view of others. He thought that if he could sight Bridger Dome, which was unique for its open Eye, he could find his way to the Exchange District. He had seen that Eye, and noted the challenge inherent in its stare, as he'd shuttled down on a tender from the quickship *Belle*. He'd asked the Harmony governor of Testament, Cevan Swan, about it; Paul Ruben, a bureaucrat on Swan's staff, had recommended Gray Bridger as a guide, saying he might get Penn into Bridger Dome. Penn had expected a native man to be servile, vaguely feminized. Instead, Gray Bridger was touchy, careful of his pride, and impudent, but not marked by any obvious difference from young men in the Harmony, nothing that correlated with the relative unimportance here, numerically and politically, of men. Penn was shocked, however, that a native, a would-be Harmony immigrant, had behaved so rudely.

Penn felt women watching him as, with his longer stride, he passed them. He was heading nowhere very quickly. Perhaps they knew.

Penn had assumed he would be interested by the Testament precasters, and had even anticipated being impressed by them, but he'd only hoped, without truly expecting, that they had special knowledge. Reed Bridger had enlarged that hope. She was shrewd; it showed in her eyes and her attitude. *Your doubts have an answer.* She also made him wary.

Penn was the chief aide to Elector Jeroen Lee, yet he'd abandoned Elector Lee and left Center to avoid the repercussions of Elector Lee's unmasking: Jeroen Lee, one of the six most important persons in the Harmony, was an Altered. Obscurely grateful that the deception was finally over, guilty for his part in the lie, yet ashamed that he'd deserted Lee—although Lee himself had insisted on it—Penn now craved truth. Reed Bridger's intelligence meant she might distort facts, or fabricate some fantasy to please him.

Penn stopped again. A young, freckle-faced woman, really only a girl, bumped into him. She smelled of motor oil, and her pretty face was dirty. "Sorry," she said casually, like a man, and continued on with the girl of about six who accompanied her. The child—sister? daughter?—gazed back at Penn, curious where the adult was not. The women on Stone Town's streets were often accompanied by children, or else were pregnant. Testament was an insular world filled by women: young and old, beautiful and plain, tall, thin, short, fat, in groups or alone. Women, but what mattered most was that they were Altered women. Intellectually, he accepted Altereds as equals, but emotionally he perceived all Altereds as freaks. Even Jeroen Lee.

Penn sighed. He admired the Elector, agreed with him on most issues, and wanted Lee to keep his position, yet couldn't help but feel there was a limitation inherent in Lee's Altered nature. Penn hungered for something beyond the search for scientific rationalism prescribed by Jon Hsu's emphasis on order. He sensed something missing from Jonist philosophy. He feared what it might be, and that finding it could destroy his already fragile faith in the completeness of Jonism's exclusively rational approach. Elector Lee tolerated Penn's unorthodox opinions, but he did not share Penn's sense that there was something unexaminable in the universe. Penn secretly supposed that was an Altered imperfection, a change from standard human that left Lee, the only Altered whom Penn knew well, insensitive to the existence of certain Mysteries. Yet, impulsively, Penn had come to Altered Testament, to discover the deep truth he suspected might exist in its Altereds' long memories, seeking knowledge which, by some un-Jonist miracle, might save Elector Lee.

Penn sniffed and turned away from what he hoped was the ocean; therefore presumably heading toward the Exchange District. He tried to recall Gray's offhand comments about Stone Town—guide patter, to avoid silence between them. Stone Town was a "mixed" town, which in native parlance meant it was inhabited by more than a single family line, or closely allied group of family lines. About half of Testament's lines had some presence in Stone Town, a city of several million, but there were only twenty-six major domes; they were proof of the eminence of a family. The largest local lines, such as the Bridgers, had entire residential districts to themselves, a ghetto of cousins; the domes were residences for very few, usually just precasters.

Edgemarket separated the wharves and the domes from the rest of the city; there would be Harmony tourists there, and thus a means of transportation, but Penn didn't see the Edgemarket banners or smell the greasy stench that had impressed him during Ruben's tour. Gray had brought him directly to Bridger Dome in a closed, human-driven coach he'd hired at the bottom of the funicular railway down from the Exchange District. Penn smiled; Gray had also expected Penn to pay the attendant driver. They had traveled on wide streets busy with noisy, multicolored, motorized vehicles of divergent types and sizes moving in chaotic patterns, then gone underground at a large intersection, into the tunnel roadways. The organization of transportation on Testament was, like everything else, archaic and exotic. Penn noticed none of those rental coaches on this street; he had no idea how to call one—no city utility system was integrated into his mind, and the Exchange District utility was much too distant to be accessible.

As he walked, there were fewer pedestrians. Women were continually descending into open staircases leading underground. Already lost, Penn thought it unlikely his situation would be improved by doing that.

At each corner, Penn stopped and looked in every direction, and finally he saw the tower of Governor's House—Swan's headquarters and Security building—visible at cliff's edge in the foothills of the local mountain range; it caught the sunlight and reflected it back like an ancient seaside signal lamp, fending off the mountains and the indigenous city: a lighthouse, first bastion of civilization. The image cheered him. He turned in the direction of the fortuitous beacon.

He should have expected something like the incident in Bridger Dome. Testament was a primitive place, populated by Altereds. Courtesy wasn't the given it was on a Harmony world, and, not being Jonist, they failed in the automatic respect due an Ahman. Testament could even be refreshing.

After several long blocks, Penn realized he was not getting significantly closer to the Exchange District. The city was too large. He hesitated, sensing eyes on him, and turned. A woman, who had been pretty once, before her wrinkles and thinning, graying hair, was seated on a battered chair at a folding table, watching him. On Reed Bridger, old age seemed natural and had added dignified authority, but this woman, who still showed signs of youth, was like overripe fruit, worsened by time. As a medic, it offended his sensibilities to see age exposed on her face, the wrinkles like frost on a badly insulated windowpane, and yet the woman might easily be younger than Penn. On the table, between her folded hands, was a clear glass jar, one-quarter full with Testament coins and Harmony counts. He'd noticed similarly accoutered women throughout the city. Passersby dropped coins into their jars and stopped for brief conversation. Penn assumed these street women were beggars and was scandalized.

"Do you want advice?" the native woman asked.

"No." He turned away, scanning the street for help.

"You're lost," she said.

He looked back. "How did you know?" Though it had probably been simple to deduce.

She leaned back in her chair and smiled. It seemed false, and didn't include her brown eyes. "I'm an oracle."

A street-corner oracle? Of course. This was Testament, where precasters who remembered the distant past foretold the future, and where women who rarely lived even ninety years claimed they never died because their memories continued in their children. Penn smiled. "How do I get back to the Exchange District, then?"

She extended her hand, palm up. Penn recoiled. He first thought that she wanted to shake hands, like equals and friends, and was repulsed at the idea of touching her. She reeked, perhaps from some unfamiliar native food. Then he realized she was requesting money. "You'd charge me for directions?"

"I charge for what I know."

Penn fumbled through his pockets, feeling for local currency, and found a 20c note, his smallest. He stuffed it into her jar.

"Well," she said, studying the paper money.

He'd overpaid. Her largest coin was a brown native "fiver," but with her cold eyes on him, he was shy of asking for change—the money didn't matter—and impatient to get away. "Where do I go?"

She looked up, squinting at him. "Go back to the Loop Boulevard," she said, indicating the main street he'd left. "Cross it and walk down to the nearest yellow sign, then hold your hand out into the street. A cab will stop eventually. Tell them to take you to Exchange. The fare shouldn't be more than 15c, unless they drop you in Exchange itself, onto the loading deck—then the fare's double, 'cause there's likely no return."

"I could have done that myself."

"If you'd known. Knowledge is indispensable."

He had what he needed, but, despite her smell, he didn't leave. A whimsical notion, that their encounter was ordained by a higher source—in which orthodox Jonists weren't supposed to believe—and wasn't mere chance, tickled his fancy. There were no monitors, and thus no need to censor his words or hide his quest for an ethic beyond reason and Order. "Precast for me."

She laughed, slapping the table. "I'm an oracle, not a precaster," she said. "And I won't fake. I'll tell you where your keys were lost, or if your lover is cheating; I usually know what's going on. But I don't play God; I don't precast."

He considered, as she took his 20c note from her jar and pushed it into the deep crevice between her breasts.

"What line are you?" he asked.

"Quinn."

That meant nothing to him, but at least she wasn't a Bridger. There had been a family resemblance among the denizens of Bridger Dome, tendencies toward dark hair and eyes, height, and austere handsomeness, that this woman lacked. Testament would have been an ideal genetics laboratory, since its family records went back a thousand years, if only those official records included both parents, not exclusively the maternal line.

"You've been frightened," she said.

"I was angry, not frightened."

She shrugged. "Anger and fear are cousins."

"That doesn't sound original."

"Oh, you want originality!" The Quinn oracle stood. Her looks worsened as he saw her fleshy middle. "I thought you wanted truth."

Penn moved away from the table, as startled as though she'd read his thoughts. Jon Hsu, in his *General Principles,* explained that truth was the First Principle of the search for Order in the universe. Truth, not faith. The Bridger precaster had been playing with him when she'd said all truth was faith. Reed had known what—and whom—she was disputing. Access to information about Jonism and Jon Hsu was one exception to the information quarantine. Now this so-called oracle had mentioned truth. "This is nonsense." He started back the way she'd directed.

"Wait!"

He hesitated, looking around at her.

The oracle smiled with cautious camaraderie. "You paid enough to get some real advice. Here: the Bridgers know something; they always have. If you really need a precast, go to them." With that, she picked up her jar of coins, clutched it against her ample bosom, and walked off in the opposite direction from the way she'd directed Penn. He watched, fascinated and ashamed; the woman limped. Even Altereds deserved better medicine.

The Bridgers know something. Penn had sensed it, too. *The Bridgers know something.* The woman, a street-corner oracle, met by random chance, had just confirmed his hopes. Penn had the perfect lever with which to pry a precast from Reed Bridger: Gray Bridger, who wanted to leave Testament. Penn watched the Quinn oracle disappear into a building, then he went where she'd directed him, to hail a ride back to rationality, to the Exchange District.

V. Symmetry

"Melany Kane called," Gray's youngest sister, Mead, yelled to him as he came through the back door into the dustroom. Gray tossed his Harmony-styled jacket onto a chair before walking two steps down into the warm kitchen.

Mead was chopping carrots as if each cut were an execution. The counters were strewn with vegetables. Liquid simmered in a large pot on the "new" stove—only two years old—sending a cloud of onion-scented steam into the air. Stew. Gray knew the meaning of stew. It was comfort food for Mead. He looked across the kitchen to where Eris, their oldest sister still living in their mother's house—Mead's house now, by right of being the youngest daughter, except that Mead lacked children—was patiently kneading biscuit dough. Their eyes met; Eris rolled hers and nodded. Mead still was unhappy. She'd been difficult since the preceding week, when she'd had her period.

"What did Melany say?" Gray asked.

Mead looked up from her work. A slow grin spread across her face. "She asked if you wanted a position on her next outland venture, since you have a wife and you're staying on Testament."

They all knew, then, about his marriage. Welcome home. He came the rest of the way down into the kitchen.

"Kanes are never tactful," Eris said. Heavily pregnant, she had difficulty bending forward to hand her four-year-old daughter, Nellie, the ball of dough she'd been begging.

"Too bad they didn't marry you to Melany," Mead said. "Of course, even a stupid Kane woman wouldn't want a freak to father her children, in case the defect passed down. Melany doesn't have any of yours, does she? Despite four outland ventures together?"

Mead knew where the pain was, and went for it. He took a piece of carrot from her chopping block and ate it, just to annoy her, but she didn't react except to gather the remaining pieces and drop them into the pot.

"Leave Gray alone." Eris smiled at him with just the look she might have given Nellie.

Gray frowned. "Melany's all right. She means well." Despite her centuries of memories, Melany was reassuringly gauche. Gray had joined the outland ventures she captained in order to earn Harmony counts on the sale of the skins. Hunting icesnakes required silence, stamina, luck, and quick reactions, but not too much in the way of remembered experience. He was comfortable in the bleak, high outlands, at the edge of the ice.

Gray washed his hands and took over Eris's work. She smiled and leaned back, grunting as she tried to get comfortable long after it had stopped being possible. "I'm glad you're staying." She patted her protruding belly and left a dusting of white flour on her clothes. "She'll want an uncle."

"Or a permanent child to play with." Mead's mouth pinched tight and she resumed chopping vegetables. "Why am I the only one in the family to call him what he is? A freak and an embarrassment. Reed just won't admit she was wrong to school him."

"Memory isn't the same as intelligence." It had become Gray's mantra. "The Harmony people do just fine with what they learn in a single lifetime. They have the quickships, not us."

Mead chuckled. "Keep telling yourself that you're all right, Gray. Maybe someday someone will believe it."

Gray kneaded the biscuit dough, squashing it flat. Educating children wasn't economically productive on Testament, where everyone remembered basic skills, and much more, at adolescence, but a select few Bridger children were nevertheless educated in Bridger Dome, taught to read, stuffed with information and analytical skills. "Grandmother brought me to the dome instead of you—that's your real complaint. A thousand years of memories and you're still petty."

"Or maybe grandmother already knew you were a freak; she brought you there so at least you'd learn to read."

That cut closer to his own fears then he liked.

"Will you go hunting with Melany?" Eris spoke quickly, changing the subject.

"Why not?" Mead said before Gray could answer. "It's all he's good for—killing beasts."

Gray stopped working the dough. Eris touched the back of his hand. He looked at her, and she shook her head. "Hormones," Eris whispered. "Whatever she remembers, she's still only seventeen."

Mead's latest companion, Learner Wolf, sauntered into the kitchen from the front hall, hands tucked into his pockets. She hesitated, then nodded curtly at him and continued cutting. Learner frowned, settling onto a stool without taking up any work to busy his hands. It was Mead's house; Gray said nothing.

Learner glanced at the tense Bridgers. "Arguing with Gray doesn't get you anywhere," he told Mead. "He couldn't inherit even if he wasn't a singleton."

"So? Neither can you," Mead taunted. "Man."

Gray had the pleasure of watching Learner flush. The Wolf line had fair skin and bitter dispositions, but Learner Wolf had fathered seven children; if Mead was dumping him, she was also giving up.

"I'll ignore that," Learner said stiffly, "because I am a man. But no one can make you into a real woman."

Gray looked at Mead, but she had continued working. A tear ran down her cheek, but then, she would have claimed it was the onions. "What's new with the great redactors?" Gray needled Learner. "Have you finished listing the entries under A yet, so some woman can memorize them?" Learner Wolf was a full member of Testament's Human Encyclopedia Project.

"Speaking of A's, I discovered something interesting today about your new sister-in-law," Learner said to Mead, though he clearly intended his words for Gray. "Gray's wife is an alia."

There was a moment's stunned silence, then Mead put down her knife and looked at Gray. Her face was without expression. His own mind felt blank.

"What?" Eris was indignant. "I don't believe it."

"Funny, isn't it?" Learner chuckled. "Pure symmetry. A man who remembers nothing but his own life and a woman who remembers every past life so well that she doesn't exist as an individual."

"Grandmother would never do that!" Eris protested. "Gray, she loves you."

Eris's memories of Reed Bridger necessarily stopped at their mother's conception; Eris couldn't possibly remember Gray, except in her personal memories. Only Mead, the youngest, had prior memories of him, and only through their mother, not Reed. Sometimes it seemed Mead hated him. He looked away from her, pinched off a wad of dough, rolled it like a worry bead between his fingers, then cast it onto the board. The force of the impact flattened the ball.

"It's true. Didn't you know?" Learner asked softly, showing some transient male-to-male sympathy.

It was true. That was why Dancer lived inside Bridger Dome. Gray was not only trapped, he'd been insulted. An alia had all the past lives of her mothers present in conscious memory from birth. Victims of alia syndrome never had an opportunity to become real people, with independent minds. They were immediately bombarded with their mothers' memories; they had no childhood, no adolescence, no separate life. An alia was lost inside those remembered lives; an alia was no one.

"Gray," Mead said, then nothing more. No jokes. No jeers.

Gray felt light, free. An alia was not human, even when she emulated someone else. One person had blocked his departure from Testament with her life and their fraudulent marriage, but now he knew that Dancer Bridger did not exist, that she was only an agglomeration of memories inside a fleshy shell. He knew what he had to do and finally believed that he could do it. It wasn't murder to turn off a faulty recording. He stared at his hands, white from the dough, then wiped them carefully on a dishtowel. He went to the dustroom and took his regular jacket from its peg.

Eris lumbered after him, the good mother. "Where are you going?"

"Back to Bridger Dome," Gray said.

Chapter 2

I. A Time Traveler

"What is she like, this ... *bride?*" Gray asked.

As if an appointment had been set, Gray's grandmother had been waiting for him near the Cityside Arch in the rotunda of Bridger Dome. Reed took his hand; hers was papery-smooth, and she smelled of soil and flowers. She wore a black-eyed Susan in her hair, a circle of narrow petals as orange as the rising sun around a puffy black center; her favorite flower, it even grew outdoors. "It depends on who she is." Reed began walking, drawing him with her. "Come along. Dancer is in her room."

So it was true. If a singleton was a freak, then an alia was an abomination. He didn't want to see the woman; he only wanted her out of his life, but Gray let his grandmother lead him on a diagonal path across the rotunda to the closest bank of lifts. "Does Dancer always emulate someone else?"

"Whenever she's alert. There is no woman 'Dancer' by herself."

The dome was busy, as it always was on fine spring evenings, when Bridgers came to rest and relax among their own line. Gray studied Reed. Every one of her descendants, except him, remembered her as the young woman she had been; the thought gave poignancy to the girlish flower. For him, she would never be young. He had his own fond memories of her, though: reading stories as they cuddled in a wide, red-cushioned rocking chair in her sun-lit study; tending the Earth garden together; Reed teaching him and encouraging his dream of becoming one of the rare male precasters of Testament. He wished he hadn't failed her so miserably, yet wondered how she could do this to him.

She stepped into a vacant lift, turned, and waited. Gray

glanced uncomfortably up to the open galleries where, behind a closed door, his wife waited.

"Gray!"

Gray sighed and followed. He would meet Dancer Bridger. Whatever happened then would be on their hands.

Reed reached past him and pressed the button with a smudged 10 inlaid in rare cobalt hing shell from the Stone Sea; offies paid a fortune for it. The lift jerked to a start, moving up.

Ten. "She lives with the precasters?"

"We take care of her."

An alia. The lift traveled slowly, but Gray wished it went slower still.

"She has no personal memories, Gray," his grandmother said. "If someone looks out from Dancer's eyes, then it's an emulation of a woman who lived before. Sometimes—usually, in fact—the individuals pass through her so quickly, so randomly, that no one grasps cognizance of reality. There is a mental vacancy."

"That's what you've married me to."

She didn't answer. The lift bumped to a stop; she opened the gate herself and went onto the gallery. On level ten it was a wide veranda. Gray walked to the railing, looking down on the rotunda. Trees sheltered people in the garden from view, but the rest—cousins, every one of them—moved purposefully about their business. His line, but Gray was separate. He looked away, then examined the railing. It was beautifully joined, carefully embossed icesnake-skin stretched over metal, centuries old. Dullness along the upper surface evidenced its use by thousands of Bridgers; their hands had left oils embedded in the skin, preventing the color changes which were the essence of icesnakes' value. Gray placed his hand where so many others had been, feeling a moment of rare kinship with his ancestors.

His grandmother touched his arm. "You can have children with Dancer," she said. "The children of an alia are as likely to be normal as those of anyone."

Gray stepped back from her. Reed knew precisely where his heartaches hurt worst—in that, she was like Mead. So far as he was aware, he'd never fathered a child; no woman had wanted to bear a child of his. Some men wouldn't care, since children never remembered their father's life, but Gray did. He imagined intercourse with a soulless alia—masturbation with a warm toy—and shuddered. "Women always overestimate what a man is willing to overlook for sex," he said lightly.

Reed smiled, and drew him forward along the gallery. "There are drugs for Dancer," she said. "We've stabilized her in emulations for relatively long periods of time. She was just given a dose for your meeting." Reed glanced sideways at Gray. "Perhaps she'll be my own grandmother, Freida, your last common ancestor. If so, be kind!" She grinned, as she had when she teased Penn with her outrageous display of supposed precaster powers, then she grasped the knob of an unmarked door, turned, and pushed the door open, moving aside to let Gray pass through first. "Your wife."

The setting sun appeared to be directly opposite the huge expanse of diamond glass that was the outer, almost imperceptibly curved wall of the dome. After the dim light in the rotunda, the sunshine in the whitewashed room made Gray blink. Dust motes floated like flourescing jewels. Gray walked into the room, drawn forward by the wide view of Stone Town. The nearest visible dome was that of the Bridgers' former friends and recent enemies, the Shak; its tumbled, broken edges seemed to enhance the vista rather than obstruct it, like a landscape painting's bright focus on a pastoral ruin. Bridger Dome had a different perspective from the Exchange District, a view from within rather than from outside. Stone Town did not look dead; it was a vibrant shining place. A ship was leaving the harbor, riding low in the water, probably bound for New Angeles with a load of Stone Town–manufactured tractors. Two zeps crossed paths in the calm evening sky. Planted fields on the terraced hillsides gleamed green in the light. Women and men bustled along the nearby avenues. There were vestiges of life even in the Shak ruin: the red-haired Shak perimeter guard; a garden plot. Which view of Testament was accurate? Gray turned to his grandmother. She held a finger in front of her lips, smiled, nodded, and began to close the door, leaving.

"Wait!" Gray said.

It closed.

Gray looked around the room, at the bed, the white-painted table to one side, and the lone rocking chair; there were no marks of personality or signs of use in the room. A slim girl lay between crisp white linen bedsheets facing away from him. Her long black hair and the red-brown of her smooth hands, visible against the sheet, were the room's only color. He frowned at the door in the blank white wall, but didn't leave. On the bed, the girl tossed fretfully, then settled, this time turned toward him. Her lips moved, mumbling something unintelligible. She grimaced, trembled, then was quiet. What nightmares would an alia have?

Gray went to the bedside and peered into her face, searching for a sign there was a real woman inside the body. He touched her forehead. She didn't react. He squatted beside the low bed and watched her breathe, then looked at his hands. An adult's, they were callused from hard physical work in the outlands, even after a winter spent guiding vapid offies through Stone Town. He remembered the rifle, out of reach, his companions away from camp, and the hard, cold steel of the skinning knife in his hand as the icesnake came at him through the tent wall; he remembered a single frozen moment, fearing death. He'd killed. He'd skinned too many untreated pelts to be squeamish. He leaned over the girl and grasped either side of her soft pillow. She turned her head restlessly and mumbled sounds he didn't understand. He listened, still studying her face, then released the pillow and straightened. The imprints left by his hands vanished. He went to the window wall, staying back from the edge. He felt too close to falling.

Was Dancer more than a repository of dead minds? He would not kill a person, but was she someone, or just a human-shaped beast? He remembered the blood odor as he'd ripped soft organs out of icesnakes and northern otters in the outlands; he imagined human blood staining the pale floor. Staining his hands.

Gray went to the rocking chair and sat down heavily to wait. Stone Town spread out before him, the low red sun glamorizing even the bit of shabby Edgemarket visible from Dancer's room. Edgemarket's outer booths, open to the air, made the best of their exposure. Wildly patterned pennants fluttered from the tops of canvas windbreaks, attracting Harmony tourists to the overpriced stalls, as well as business from native outlanders too lazy to shop in the humdrum commercial districts. A ragged line of shouting children on a health march—Bridgers, Cohens, Chens, and Wolfs—ran through the plaza between Shak and Bridger Domes, hugging the Bridger side of the street bisecting it. The Shak were a menace to everyone, but they singled out the Bridger line for their deepest enmity. He'd been nine when they'd murdered his mother. He remembered Reed, crying as she gave him the news. "You must be strong," she'd said. And he'd tried to be.

Gray settled into the chair. It creaked, so he kept it from rocking. Testament was his home, but it was a ghetto of Altered humans and he wasn't one of them. He would leave. He would.

The sun was below the horizon, although the sky was still light, when Dancer finally opened her eyes. She murmured a slurred garble, then stared, unfocused, at Gray. He said nothing, deferring all judgments. Her eyes gradually lost their glazed appearance. She sat up abruptly, then yanked the top sheet across her body, covering her bare breasts. She looked out the window, then wildly back to Gray, obviously frightened. "Who are you? Where is this place?" Hers was an aggressive voice with an awkward accent, though easier to understand than the Harmony speech had been at first, and with a cadence precasters sometimes used.

"You've lived here all your life," Gray answered. He leaned forward, studying her changed face. It was no longer a mask blighted by twitches and tics; she was an individual. For the first time he saw the beauty his grandmother had mentioned. Dancer had classic Bridger features: a narrow nose set between wide eyes and wide, full lips, high cheekbones, and a long neck. Only an emulation, he reminded himself. He'd met an alia once, at Vincent, the largest mixed town in the outlands. She'd been an entertainment for her family, a branch of Smiths, and for anyone they'd cared to share her with, half pet and half burlesque. Her body, its mind occupied by a Smith ancestor, had been available for rent, like a priestess whore of some ancient, dead religion.

"I've been kidnapped! Who are you? What's this all about?"

"I'm your husband," he said, grimly amused. "Don't you remember?" The rocking chair creaked as he leaned back. Dancer flinched.

She was silent, searching his face without a glimmer of recognition, then she turned tentatively to the window, gaping at the town outside as she struggled and failed to identify it.

Gray looked down, ashamed. It was like teasing an animal; there was no fairness in it. "That's Stone Town." He spread his arm wide, indicating the city. "We're inside Bridger Dome on Testament."

"*Bridger* Dome," she repeated, turning back to him. "I remember. I gave tissue and eggs. . . . Have I been asleep . . . or something . . . ?" She stopped. Holding the sheet against herself with one hand like a shy woman-child still lacking the memory of sex, she used her other hand to reach for and then inspect a length of her long, dark hair. She stared at that hand, holding it first close, then at arm's length. She turned again to Gray, and her voice was softer, amazed. "What's going on? I'm changed."

Clearly she was an emulation of someone very early. The alia at Vincent had understood what she was in a curious half-life of quasi-individuality. Dancer didn't. For Gray, reluctance solidified into inability. Emulation or real, there was enough of a person present in Dancer that he could never kill her. "Go back to sleep." He stood up.

"Please help me," she whispered, and reached out a hand to him that she couldn't even identify as her own.

"I can't," he said, as quietly as she had spoken. "I don't know how." For now they'd closed the trap on him; it was pointless to stay with the alia. His wife. Gray sighed and started for the door.

"No! Don't leave. I want to know—I demand to know—what is going on. You! What's your name?"

He smiled at her imperious tone. "Tell me yours."

She hesitated, obviously weighing the merits of doing so. "Janet Bridger," she said finally.

Gray released the doorknob he had just grasped and turned back, staring at her. Janet Bridger! The founder of the Bridger line. She had lived before the First Comers—she had been born on old Earth before the slowboat left. Even the precasters' reminisced image of her was only an echo off the blank wall where memory stopped. The vague tales about her were as much confabulated legends as memory. Curious, he took a step back.

"You know me," she said flatly, watching him with sharp intelligence, but without the frightening depth of a precaster's eyes. "Who are you?"

"Gray Margaretson Bridger." He wet his lips and returned to the rocking chair, gripping its back for an unstable brace, then began a formal recitation. "Gray Bridger, son of Margaret, youngest daughter of Reed, youngest of . . ." He stopped. She stared, uncomprehending. "I'm your husband—husband to Dancer, whose body you're wearing—and a descendant of Janet Bridger in the main line of descent, twenty-seventh generation."

"The generation ship people," Dancer said to herself. "No! It wasn't supposed to work like this!" The statement was a plea.

"It doesn't, generally," he said. "You—Dancer, that is— are unusual." The woman stared at him, more victim than any singleton, and he felt an unaccountable sympathy. "There are disorders that are unique to the Altered people of Testament, to our peculiar memory."

Her hands waved weakly, requesting silence, then she placed them on her lap, staring down at those same hands, shoulders hunched, her long hair veiling her face, hiding her thoughts.

Janet Bridger had died more than a millennium earlier; Dance had never lived. Gray tried to convince himself once again that the death of this body was without meaning, but couldn't. "I'm sorry," he said inanely, and glanced at the door. It was himself for whom he was sorry, not this alia whose Janet Bridger persona would disappear soon enough into the tangle of past lives. Unable to kill her, he was trapped on Testament by their supposed marriage.

She looked up, brushing her hair away from her face. Her lips were fixed in a determined line. She nodded slightly to herself before she began. "Do I awaken like this every day, without a memory of the day before? And why are you here?"

He smiled; there were reasons Bridgers had done well on Testament, and perhaps one had been named Janet. He came around from behind the chair. "No," he said, thinking of the alia in Vincent. "There's continuity of memory within an emulation's awakening, but you—Janet Bridger—share this body and mind with other ancestors of Dancer. She has no thoughts of her own."

She grimaced, then looked at him. Her expression was mildly patronizing—something about her mouth and eyes— but Gray was accustomed to that, and he chuckled, to have an alia condescend to him. She smiled in return. "You're adjusting very well," he said, suspecting that a precaster-administered drug explained her composure.

She shrugged and touched the soft rise of her full breasts surreptitiously, then pulled the cover up to her neck. That exposed her right leg, which didn't appear to bother her, although the long brown curve of her calf and her pale pink toenails were alluring, too. "Multiple personalities?" she asked.

"More like multiple lives. It's been explained to me that the usual sensation is similar to retrieving information from a book. The more rereadings—the more frequently remembered—then the more vivid the memory of the past life. Some things are automatic, without the memory of having consciously acquired the information. But for Dancer— you—there is no reader, just the books, the individual remembered lives."

" 'It's been explained to' you?" she quoted, questioning him.

Gray flushed. "That's right. I don't remember my mothers' lives. It's . . . another disorder."

He knew she saw the wound his admission made, but she smiled. He took a step closer, drawn by the honesty of that smile. "So you're normal," she said, "and I'm a freak."

"No!" He was startled by the vehemence of his own denial. "No," he said more quietly. "You exist, now. And I'm not normal, for Testament."

She looked out the window. "What happened to me, after my memory ends?"

She meant: What happened to Janet Bridger? He didn't correct her. "Precasters might know, from your daughters' memory or other records, but I don't know anything about your afterlife."

"Afterlife?" She sounded fleetingly amused. "I suppose I am dead. . . ."

He liked her changes in mood; they showed that someone was truly present with him. She was intelligent and seemed to have a pragmatic disposition. And Reed was right; she was beautiful. Gray smiled at her. "Afterlife is the time after a woman's last child is conceived. No one will remember those years. Some women have a late child, as late as they can, but others want the freedom. It's like being a man—no one remembers a man's life; there's only fame. All precasters must be in their afterlife, no matter what their age." Through the deepening gloom, he sensed she was growing tense again and wished he could help. He went to the side of the bed. "This is all new to you."

She shrugged, and he understood it as diffident agreement. "But you haven't told me why you were here," she said.

He hesitated, unable to explain that he'd come to kill her.

"You said you're my husband."

He nodded. "But we never met before today. The marriage is a formality, my grandmother's plan to keep me from leaving Testament." She wouldn't understand. She was essentially a woman from a thousand years ago. He added, "As long as I'm married to a woman with multiple life memories, then the Harmony won't let me leave this world."

She continued to gaze uncomprehendingly at him, but he stared just as hard at her. This *wasn't* a woman with multiple life memories; this was Janet Bridger. Just now, like Gray himself, Dancer remembered only one life. She'd appear to be a singleton on any of the psych tests the Harmony had given him.

Gray stared into her startled face as the jumbled threads of his intuition coalesced into a plan. He sat down heavily on the side of her bed. First startled, she smiled and made room for him. "Will you help me?" he asked. "I swear I won't let you come to any harm, and we can leave Testament together!"

"Leave? Why?" She giggled nervously. "I've just arrived, and even so, I'm not really here. Am I?" The question was a challenge, but he heard it as an entreaty for a denial.

She was waiting for an excuse to hope. Maybe he could give her one, and a future. "I don't know how long you'll be Janet Bridger. There are drugs, I'm told, to keep you the way you are now. The precasters must have their methods." He shook his head at her questioning look. "What you need to know is that there's a universe filled with people—at least thirty planets in the Polite Harmony of Worlds, and maybe others outside of it—and the Harmony won't let us leave this one world; we're quarantined because the people here are Altered. No one from Testament can enter the Harmony unless we prove we're standard human, not Altered. I did that. So can you. I know; I've been through all their psychological tests." He stopped. She seemed bewildered. It was too much for anyone to absorb at once, a thousand years of change in a quarter-hour conversation. He tried to imagine what Janet Bridger might want. "We can go to old Earth eventually; I'll take you there, if you like. I've enough saved for two passages off Testament, if we skimp on start-up money, but first we need permission for both of us to leave. That's up to you."

"The ships go faster than light?" She moved closer. "How?"

"I don't know. No Testament native does; they won't tell us. But in the Harmony the people are like me; I'll be ordinary."

"Not me."

He imagined his misery if he hadn't known that inside the Harmony, singletons were ordinary. "If you could be permanently stabilized as Janet Bridger," he began, taking one of her hands between his own. She pulled away, but then looked shyly at him. She was frightened, but lonely, he guessed. She needed him. "You have to decide whether to trust me," he said. "I want to keep you in Dancer's body, staying yourself. No one else cares." That sounded harsh, but it was true. He touched her knee. She faced him. "I promise you, I will keep you alive." He looked into her somber eyes, then had to look away, because he wasn't certain that anything he promised could be made real and she was watching him with desperate hope. "I'll try," he amended. "To the best of my ability."

"If not, then I'll melt away, won't I?" She tapped her hand against the side of the bed, then looked at her hand and stopped. She smiled tentatively at Gray. "Tell me about yourself, Gray Bridger, my son to the twenty-seventh generation and my husband."

He smiled back at her brave attempt at humor. "I can't do much of anything as well as others can. For them, it's as if knowledge is an instinct." He heard the whine in his own words, and imagined his grandmother listening. "Well," he amended, "I really don't do badly, even so. I'm good in the outlands, better than average for sure, and I've made quite a bit of money as an offie guide—they like having a native, but not a frightening one. I can read and write, even though I'm a singleton. The Harmony people are better-educated, but I'm as competent as any of them."

She laughed. It went on too long. He gently touched her cheek, as his grandmother might have done to comfort him. She stopped laughing and turned her head, brushing her lips against his palm. He took his hand away. "I never married," she said. "I'm—I was—a forty-six-year-old childless spinster. When Emily Bennett asked for a contribution of eggs, I thought, why not? It seemed no worse than donating the blood and spinal fluid, or the tissue samples. So here I am, the result of my own thoughtlessness. I know I'm dead these thousand years"—she lowered her voice—"but, Gray, I don't want to die."

He took her hand in his. He'd never thought of Janet Bridger as childless. She was the mother of the entire Bridger line, but she'd never had a child to raise, to love and cherish, to watch grow into a reincarnation of herself. He could give her children, ones she wouldn't reject even if they were singletons, because to her his condition was normal. His thumb caressed the palm of her hand. There were no rough places on her soft flesh. She'd never cooked, never cleaned, never dressed herself, never held a book or walked outside. She'd been washed, fed, and exercised, tended like a delicate flower in the Earth garden, for beauty's sake, for compassion. Gray placed her hand down at her side, on the bed.

"Hold me," she said.

This marriage was a trap he might still manage to pry open. He stretched out on the bed beside her, drawing her close with an arm around her shoulders. She was so thin her flesh felt tight over her bones. Gray stared out the window, surprised to see that the sky had darkened. The Edgemarket lights and those of the city beyond were the only illumination in the room, except for the cold, distant stars and the faint glow of the single one of Testament's three small moons to have risen. They didn't speak. He contemplated the stars like a primitive, as points of light, not distant suns, knowing he might never see any of them closer, but it was a rare, tranquil moment, and, however angry with Testament's women he might be, this was one woman he couldn't blame or resent.

"Gray?"

He rolled onto his side, but saw only her outline and a vague impression of her face. She was observing him, although with his back to the window he couldn't have been more than a shadow against the dark night. In their closeness, from their mingled breath, Gray smelled the musky fragrance of a naked woman, one who was also aware of him.

"Tell me about this place, Testament," she said.

He did, speaking softly as he explained the precarious balance of memory and self that was natural among the Altered residents of Testament. He gave an overview of their history, so far as—without true memories—he knew it. Old Earth had sent the slowboats on a one-way trip, no contact with the homeworld being possible in the then foreseeable future, unlike attempts to colonize anywhere ever before. The slowboats were all experiments, and methods had been experimental, but the memory Alteration had saved Testament from barbarism and disaster when its settlers arrived four long generations later. The First Comers to Testament had settled on the relatively lush east side of the mountain chain called the Spine, which bisected the world's major continent; Stone Town was at the base of the Spine, between the Eastlands and the more sparsely settled west. North and far west lay the outlands. He described the hardships and, unflinchingly, the wars—Testament's matriarchies had not been immune to them—which had contributed to the dying out of some original lines. He sketched the social, political, and economic divisions into major lines, such as the Bridgers, with their dependent and minor lines—often offshoots of an earlier family line—as well as the late lines, the so-called new people, the lines founded by singletons. "Not me, though," he said. "I'm only a man." That made her laugh.

"After the Harmony found us, there were two reactions," he continued. "The Assenters, the majority, believed cooperation with the Harmony was best. Dissenters said we were being conquered and wanted to fight. Bridgers are Assenters. Dissenters, like the Shak, did fight—but with Assenters, not the Harmony; the offies only watched and waited. When it was over, most Dissenters left for the far west, at World's End, or sailed to the South Sea archipelago. They have nothing to do with the Compound Council in Stone Town or the offies. Only the Shak stayed, a thorn in our side." A careless man walking alone in the plaza at night might wake up halfway to Big Red, the Shak's only other remaining settlement, to live there in the outlands for the rest of his life, in service to women who despised him. Gray had minimized the Shak threat, thinking that she had enough worries. The Shak preyed mostly on men, but they'd been aggressive lately; it was best to warn her. "That's their dome, the ruin," he said, pointing. Shak Dome's base was raggedly lit; the rest was underground. No rooms above ground level had survived the war. "It's close, so if you're ever alone outside, be careful. They killed my mother."

She turned her head. "Why?"

"Hatred. They hate the Bridger line, because of the offie war; we won." He sighed. "I think it's hard for people here to let go of things. The emotions hang on in memory, visceral, unforgotten."

She asked about the quarantine, and the terms of their accommodation to the Harmony. He was defensive about those old Assenters; inwardly, perhaps childlishly, he thought them more cowardly than wise. The sympathy he felt for her was equaled by respect for her acute and rapid understanding. He no longer thought of her as Dancer, but as Janet, someone real and alive.

"I've been used to trick you," she said. "I'm sorry."

"You didn't do anything." Compared to hers, his was a mild affliction. "And you've agreed to help me get away."

"Gray, I'm like a time traveler who can never return to her own time. Are you sure you want to leave? You haven't said why it's so important to you. I think you would love Testament if you let yourself. It's your home."

He remembered the pride he'd felt as a child—a boy and chosen for the dome. He could never be proud here again. "I want to leave," he said simply. "Will you come?"

"Yes. I want to live." She put her arms around him, as though he was her source of life.

When she slipped over the edge and was once more the hollow creature he'd first seen, what would he do? He sat up in the bed.

She grasped his sleeve. "Stay," she said. "I don't want to be alone." She let the sheet fall away, exposing her body to him, protected only by the dark. "We're married, aren't we?"

Marriage meant nothing on Testament, but it might to her. "All right, Janet." The name sounded right. He reached for her. He wondered what he had committed himself to, and who, but knew a commitment had been made.

Her thin fingers slid between two buttons of his shirt, brushed against his chest, and then she unbuttoned the top button. Her movements were clumsy, first teasing, then inhibited. She was too indecisive to be alluring in any way he had known before. Like other men of Testament, Gray had only rarely refused an invitation from an interested woman, and had never considered that a woman's overture might be something of which she was herself uncertain. Then he understood. Janet was inexperienced. Her body was adult, but of all the women he'd known, she was the first without a repertoire of lifetimes of sexual encounters. Her hesitations weren't insults, or the practiced allure of knowing seduction to which he was accustomed, they were artless. Tenderness—she knew less than he did—translated into his own indecision; he stopped her hand and held it.

"You don't want me?" Her husky voice was that of a girl on the edge of womanhood, just before her memories came in.

"I do." The damp scent of her loose hair, the fragrance of her skin, her warmth so close to him, her slim hips, and her willing, naked nearness were more than sufficient to arouse him, but whatever women thought, lacking memories of men, physical passion wasn't an irresistible tide for a man any more than it was for a woman. "But we can wait."

"I can't. I might not have tomorrow." She snuggled close, insinuating herself against him in the way a child, playing at the erotic, might have thought to do. "Please." Her mouth was touching his ear; he felt her warm breath as well as heard it. "This is the best way to learn my new body."

With compassion, if less passion than usual, Gray cradled her in his arms, achingly conscious of her personal, unique, and ephemeral existence. By all logic, Janet Bridger was a transient personality inhabiting a vacancy. She had even called herself a time traveler. He visualized her, adrift in a time machine made of her descendant's vacant body. It was an awful thought.

"Gray?" Janet's breasts brushed against him. She kissed him, but missed his lips, placing the kiss on his cheek.

He smiled, closed his eyes, and let his fingertips skim her face. Other women lived inside this woman, waiting to be recalled as she had been, yet he touched only Janet. His hands slid along the line of her neck, to her chest. She tensed but then thrust herself forward, against him.

For the first time in years he wasn't angry with the woman beside him, or reticent because he feared comparisons with sexual athletics going back for generations. That difference alone made the moment meaningful. He kissed her neck while holding her in his arms. He would do this slowly and well. Janet Bridger had been mother to them all, but this Janet, his Janet, was by Testament standards nearly a virgin. Gray wanted her, wanted to erase the misery lurking at the edge of her new, impermanent life. Other men knew, from memory, what it was like to be a woman, but he could only guess, and in that guessing he must sometimes be wrong.

And sometimes right. She sighed and relaxed as he slowly explored her body. She entwined closer against him. "This is our wedding night," she murmured.

His grandmother wanted him to bind himself to Dancer, but instead he had bound himself to Janet Bridger. She might someday bear his child, and his child might remember. Reed herself had said it: *The children of an alia are as likely to be normal as those of anyone.* "Yes," he said, "you're my bride."

II. Her Memory of Herself

Who am I? Janet wondered. She stared at the blank white wall as though it were a theater screen and it might yet show a movie of her life, but no explanation came. Gray had fallen asleep. His soft, regular breathing was unaccountably comforting, and yet she was restless. She needed to do something, anything, although she was amazed and embarrassed by what she had actually done. It was decidedly unlike her memory of herself, and yet, at the time, sex with Gray Bridger had felt entirely right. She rationalized: it would bind him to her. Urgent need, though, and not logic, had sparked it. *What will they think?* kept running though the background of her mind, despite its patent absurdity in this situation. Whatever situation that really was.

Should she believe Gray Bridger's story?

Janet wiggled her arm out from beneath Gray's side, then lay still. Every movement reminded her that her sense of bodily fit didn't square with the memory of self inside her thoughts. She was bisected into mental and physical halves, and only the mental, only her memory, was Janet. Her body was the Other. She blamed it for what had occurred with Gray. Her body was also the greatest proof possible that Gray had told her the truth.

She was dead. She was a ghost, a phantom memory dredged up from the thoughts of a distant descendant, a poor handicapped woman whose mind she had taken over like a demon needing exorcism. Not only that, but apparently she existed as potential in all of her descendants, and this resurrection could occur frequently, over and over, through centuries. She might have appeared before, like a jack-in-the-box in some familial temporal dimension. She shuddered and sought relief pressing against Gray's warm mass beside her, without wondering why that could help. Gingerly, not trying to awaken him, she ran her fingers across his chest, glad of his presence, the one good thing in this new, unnatural life.

It could have been worse. (*Perhaps other times it had been.* She suppressed the thought.) Her experience of men was limited, but Gray Bridger far exceeded her unconscious specifications for a man. He was intelligent, but not arrogant. He was too young for her, of course, at least as she remembered herself—he looked somewhere between twenty and twenty-five—and despite the even greater youth of her own body, that was subtly gratifying; he was handsome. His dark, hurt eyes and unaffected manner made her want to protect him, while his kindness, his air of reticent competence, made her trust him and his ability to protect her. She needed him, and he was there.

He sighed and turned. She kissed his bare shoulder, hoping he would awaken so they could talk again. Or something else. He continued to sleep, however, smiling slightly.

She was hungry, but it was a nagging sensation, nothing compared with the need to act, or at least not to sleep. Sleep frightened her. Had Rip Van Winkle ever napped again? Janet sat up. In that position, she was more aware of the unfamiliarity of her body, and of her nudity. She took a deep breath, trying to force away her tension. *This body is mine, and not the Other,* she decided firmly, but her physical awareness of self was not swayed by mere determination. She could be temporary, just one of forty channels on the TV of Dancer Bridger's life. And why did her analogies derive from fiction? Did her subconscious recognize the absurdity of this existence?

Gray's clothes were on the nightstand. There was a door. She got up, having to catch hold of the bed momentarily to steady herself; her legs were weak. Gray's shirt scratched like wool; there was no label. The sleeves covered her hands, but she rolled them up, smiling because it was his, and buttoned it to the top. He had broad shoulders. It was adequately long.

Outside, the city was brightly lit. Stone Town. A hard name; a difficult place. In the hills, lights were rare. Gray had said that the Exchange District, where the outsiders stayed, shed no visible light at night. That was mysterious. In the morning, they would go there.

Janet went to the door, listened—she heard nothing—and turned the knob. The door opened easily. A column of light brightened the room and showed Gray, still peacefully asleep. Barefoot, she walked out.

He hadn't described the place, only mentioned it as Bridger Dome. She was surprised by its immensity and, after her room's silence, by the noise. The handrail overlooking the dome's floor reminded her of opal: basically white, it sparkled with other colors. It was cool to her touch; she gripped it tightly and looked around. Bridger Dome had a look of frayed grandeur. She was several stories up from the dome's main level, in an atrium of gigantic dimensions, bustling with people. She observed them with no sense of connection. Her descendants? They were no more than exotic strangers. She was lost in unconscious thought for an unknown length of time, then someone touched her hand. Jerked back into cognizance of place and time, Janet turned, smiling, expecting Gray.

It was an old woman holding a cloth bundle. "My dear?" the woman asked. "Are you all right?"

Janet stared at her, trying to resolve the sense of *déjà vu* into an actual memory. "Who are you?" she asked slowly, as the wisp of recognition vanished into doubt.

The woman grinned. "Your mother-in-law. No, that's wrong, even with Gray's mother dead. Well, then, I'm only Reed Bridger." She nodded at Janet's skimpy borrowed attire. "I believe you know my grandson."

This was the woman who'd used Janet as a trap for Gray. "You've hurt him, trying to run his life."

Reed Bridger frowned. "You don't know anything about him."

Janet felt belligerent. It had more to do with her own nameless feelings toward this ostensible stranger than with Reed Bridger's manipulation of Gray, but Janet burned with resentments she couldn't quite recall, all out of proportion to a first meeting and brief conversation. She longed to tell this woman how Gray planned to defy her, with Janet's help, but restrained herself. "I know he's a good man," she said. "I know that we care about each other already, and that he'll never trust you after what you've done."

Reed shook her head. She was smiling—grinning, really—but her eyes glittered ominously as she watched Janet. "A few hours and already you 'care about each other'? I'm pleased your encounter went so well. You can thank me later for my help."

Janet waited, dreading what Reed Bridger would say.

Reed nodded. "Clime. An aphrodisiac. Gray is a favorite of mine, despite what you have heard from him. I want him to be happy with his new wife."

Janet blushed, and nearly turned away, then raised her head and stared back at the nasty old woman. "You act as though we're nothing!" she said, feeling justified in her anger.

"Not Gray," Reed Bridger said quickly. "But that's what *you* are, my dear. A memory of a memory, a dream we've all had, the revision of the story I'm still writing."

"I'm real." Janet blinked hard to keep away tears of anger, frustration—and fear. "I'm Janet Bridger."

Reed sighed and shifted the position of her bundle, balancing it against the railing. "Do you believe memory is immutable, my dear Janet Bridger? Do you believe your memories continued, a discrete, unchanging unit, through a thousand years and, for your line, thirty or so lives? Who are you? You're no one real, merely a figment of thirty minds. And mine."

Janet felt that her mind was choking on an indigestible fact. She couldn't speak.

"I'm sorry to have been so blunt. I didn't intend it, but you need to understand your true position. You are a convenience, my dear, a pawn that I've helped to make. Not a queen for my Gray. And I suggest you don't mention this conversation to him. My gallant grandson might have a different perspective on you if he knew the trouble I've taken." She glanced down at the bundle, then thrust it at Janet. "Clothes," she said. "In the morning, Gray will take you out of the Dome. I'll send a schoolgirl, early, with breakfast for you both. I won't embarrass him by coming to say I told him
so."

Janet took the bundle. Reed went to the open door and looked into Janet's room, where Gray still slept. Reed sighed. When Janet stopped trembling and walked over to her, Reed Bridger merely nodded briskly and walked away, down the long veranda.

Janet entered her room. Gray had settled into the middle of the bed. Asleep and unaware of her, his presence still caused her to smile. An aphrodisiac might help explain her nearly instant infatuation—that was the only explanation for the rush of emotion she'd felt—but she was a rational woman. He *was* a good man, one with a reason to help her stay alive. He wanted to help her; he was the only person in all this new world who did. She walked to the bedside, then reached out and brushed his hair off his forehead. He was a good man. Who was she? There was only one answer that was entirely true: Gray's wife. She removed the shirt and snuggled close to him on the bed.

III. A Generous Offer

"Let me do the talking," Gray told Janet. He waited for her nod, then opened the door to the Emigration Office.

The empty room was uncomfortably dank, like most off-worlder places. The broad expanse of imported wood flooring was scuffed in a single line from the door to a black partition; Gray supposed he might almost trace his own footprints from the last few months. He walked to the partition, trailed by Janet, and only then did a thin, middle-aged man—no one from the Harmony ever looked either truly young or very old—in a long, loose green tunic-jacket appear from behind it. It was briefly obvious in his expression that he recognized Gray, but the offie didn't acknowledge it. "Yes?" he asked curtly, not quite looking at either of them. In this one office, exclusively devoted to dealings with natives, since it enforced the quarantine, the Harmony clerks were consistently rude.

"My wife needs an application."

The man's gaze shifted over Gray's shoulder, then back. "Women need to present a clean DNA scan. Does she have one?"

Gray shrugged. "She's a singleton, like me. Standard."

The clerk became conspicuously wary. "Native males only need symptomatic normalcy or a toxic work permit; females need a DNA scan indicating they're standard human, or else a complete hysterectomy. Full, irreversible sterilization."

Gray gaped at the clerk. He hadn't realized there were different rules for women. "We'll get it," Gray said finally. "Can I have the application?" He asked entirely for the sake of pride; an alia's DNA scan would look as Altered as that of any other native of Testament. In order to leave Testament, Janet would have to be robbed of her ability to bear children. Gray would never do that to a woman—it would end her line—and didn't even want to try to convince Janet. His grandmother's trap had succeeded after all.

"From a certified Harmony medic." The offie snickered. "Not some native witch doctor." He reached beneath the counter and placed a sheaf of papers between them. "The Harmony doesn't want a pack of Altered brats running loose."

"Okay," Gray said, then amended the native idiom. "I understand."

The man slid the papers to him and stepped back, avoiding physical contact, just as the use of hardcopy forms prevented contamination of the Harmony's information system, whatever it was, by Testament's computer networks. Then the offie went back behind the partition.

Janet stood on tiptoes and whispered into Gray's ear, "What should we do?" Gray had warned her that Harmony offices were monitored; he'd discovered it the hard way, after making disparaging remarks about an examiner.

Gray shrugged. "Go home." It was over; he'd lost. Testament would keep him, and the Harmony had kept him out. A part of him resented Janet, but if it hadn't been her, there would have been some other woman. Besides, now that he knew Janet, he couldn't simply abandon her to the harsh mercy of Testament. He tried to smile, and took her hand, leading her outside.

Martin Penn, red-cheeked and dressed more casually than the day before, was just outside the building. He bowed to Gray and Janet, but the gesture was perfunctory, a habit. "Well," he said. "Now that we've run into one another so conveniently, Gray Bridger, perhaps we might talk?"

"I'm sorry, sir, we were leaving," Gray said, significantly upgrading his assessment of Penn's influence with the local Harmony personnel because he'd known so quickly that

Gray was in the Exchange; this encounter was no coincidence. Governor Swan's staff was cooperating with Penn. Gray put his arm over Janet's shoulders and pressed her slightly toward the lifting lines.

Penn didn't move out of the way. Gray considered, then dropped his arm from Janet and remembered to bow. Why not? Penn was a long shot, but with Gray's own plan unworkable, just now Penn was their only possibility for getting off Testament.

Penn scrutinized Gray, taking his time. "Do you know what an Ahman is, Gray Bridger?"

Gray nodded. "Some kind of Jonist scientist-priest." Gray immediately wished he hadn't said "priest." Offies were sensitive about religion. To them, Jonism was always a "philosophy."

Penn smiled. "Some kind." He took the emigration application from Gray's unresisting hands. "I can make this unnecessary. Or I can have you banned from the Harmony, despite the earlier approval." He ripped the papers in half and returned them. "Either way, you won't need these. Now do you have time?"

Gray bowed again, to hide his expression. "Of course, sir."

"Good." Penn never glanced back to confirm it, but Gray and Janet followed him across Amity Square. Penn took long, rapid steps; Gray tried to hurry Janet, but she had difficulty keeping up, so that when Penn reached the multistory residential building that formed one blank-faced side of Amity Square, he was forced to wait for them. He stood impatiently tapping his foot against the shiny fused-clay ground. Gray sweated that distance, with Penn's cold gaze on them. A Harmony soldier—they had recently begun guarding most offie buildings, making Exchange into an armed camp—stepped through the residence's outer door, watching their approach with wary attention. Despite Penn's gesture waving the man away, the soldier stayed.

"All well, Ahman Penn?" the soldier asked when Gray and Janet arrived. His attention was fixed on Gray.

"Fine," Penn answered, preoccupied with studying Janet, whose defect, fortunately, was invisible. He ushered Janet into the building ahead of him. Gray, behind them, was probably the only one who heard the soldier say, "We're watching you, scum."

Gray didn't flinch; Jonists lacked graphic obscenities, and offies had been rude to him before, even soldiers wearing stick guns. He bowed and followed Penn.

The lobby of the residence was entirely empty except for a counter to the side of a bank of lifts. There sat a second soldier, who put down a flatbook and watched as they entered a lift. Once inside the tiny, darkly paneled, claustrophobic box, there was nothing to press, which, Gray assumed, meant either that the soldiers controlled its movement or that the lift determined its destination by Harmony telepathic magic, as Melany claimed, because Penn stood without speaking any order, aloof from them, in front near the door. Janet met Gray's gaze, smiled, and nodded slightly in Penn's direction, rolling her eyes. Irrationally, Gray felt better.

Penn turned to Gray. "You've been here before? As a guide?"

Gray shook his head. "I always met clients in Amity Square."

Penn hesitated. He glanced at the wall behind Gray. The lift door opened. "House Security will recognize you, now," Penn said. Gray had noticed nothing; telepathy for sure.

They exited the lift and were in another lobby, this one furnished, but without guards. It had a low table and heavy upholstered chairs in muted colors, of the type supposed to be comfortable, but too elegant and seldom used for that. There was only one door. Penn walked toward it and it vanished; Penn passed inside, and disappeared. Nothing could be seen beyond the open door, as if fog obscured the region between the lobby and the interior of Penn's suite. Gray used the moment's ostensible privacy to pull Janet close and whisper, "This man is dangerous to us. To you!" He wasn't certain that was so—Penn might have no interest in Janet— but it was the quickest way of ensuring her caution.

"Come!" Penn's voice, more expressive than his face, was loud through the murk, and he sounded irritable.

Janet looked up to Gray. He nodded at the opening and they walked in together.

Inside was only more of the same. Gray was certain this suite was just a superior sleepover, like an outland hotel or a guest room in Bridger Dome. After a large, unfurnished entry zone, the residence opened into a truly huge room decorated in the same overly majestic style as the upstairs lobby. There were closed double doors on one of the two side walls, and a large window—apparently a real one, not a window screen—with a view of the mountains of the Spine. The room was done in neutral, soothing colors, and the air was blandly neutral, too, clean but without scent. No personal items were obvious, unless the red stoneware vase perfectly positioned just off-center on a table or the elaborate gilt thing—Gray didn't recognize its function, although it looked like a giant's headdress—hanging on a wall was from some personal collection of Penn's. Except for the view, there was not the slightest sign, either in style of furnishings or materials, that the room was on Testament. Penn was seated in a low chair, legs casually extended, although one hand was gripping the arm of the chair very hard. He gestured that they should sit.

Gray didn't want to face Penn directly, so he edged past a table delicately balanced on one thin central post, drawing Janet with him; they sat on a wide seat perpendicular to Penn's chair.

"That precaster was your grandmother," Penn said without preamble.

Gray set the ripped application on the dainty table as if it were the last block in a child's tall tower. Then he looked up at Penn. "Yes, sir."

"You didn't warn me that she was amusing herself at my expense."

Gray shrugged. "It was none of my business." Anxious not to sound disrespectful, he added, "You only paid me to bring you inside the dome."

Penn observed Janet. The dark green shirt and narrow pants Reed had sent were flattering. The unaccustomed exertion of the walk had flushed her cheeks and made her eyes shine. She looked lovely, but Penn frowned. He turned back to Gray. "If the marriage was a sham ordered to keep you on Testament, then why is she cooperating with you now?"

"My wife is a singleton, like me," Gray answered quickly. "I was unaware of that until we met."

Penn studied him silently. Gray wanted to turn away from that inspection, but didn't dare, in case it would be deemed rude by Penn, and because doing so might indicate he had something to hide. "I don't believe you," Penn said finally. "If the marriage wasn't designed to trap you here, then you could go to the local authorities and register a divorce, in-

stead of dragging her to Emigration. There was no purpose
to their creating this marriage if she also wants to emigrate."
Penn's voice was flat, even as he called Gray a liar. Before
Gray could make a suitable reply, Penn turned to Janet.
"What do you have to say for yourself?"

"It's true."

Gray was pleased by Janet's succinct answer.

"If she is not one of the usual freaks," Penn said to Gray,
"then I suggest you delve into the question of why you were
married to her more thoroughly, Gray Bridger. But I think
she is Altered, and you persuaded her to collaborate in trying to falsify psych test results, unaware that native females
are held to a more stringent standard. Whatever the truth,
whether she's standard or Altered, neither of you will ever
leave Testament unless you cooperate with me." He stopped.
Without looking away, Penn nevertheless seemed momentarily distant, like a native of Testament engrossed in reminiscence. When his focus returned, he spoke as if there had
been no hesitation, and forcefully, leaning forward toward
Gray. "I want a precast. You can get me one without forcing
me to make an official demand through Governor Swan. Perhaps these women don't understand. Tell them, Gray, that
Swan isn't the only authority they need to indulge."

"I have no influence inside Bridger Dome," Gray said.
"I'm nothing. Here I'm a freak, not them."

Penn turned to Janet. "You?"

"I don't know anyone."

"That's unfortunate for your husband's departure plans."
Penn stood and glanced about the room. He walked to the
window, but didn't look out, staring at its glass expanse as
if the view were as irrelevant as a blank, painted wall.

Gray realized that Penn wanted the same thing he had before: a precast. Maybe Gray could get him one, although not
with Reed. There were Bridger women who might be sympathetic to Gray's situation, or even out-line women who
might help. Melany might convince a Kane precaster. But
Penn hadn't offered anything yet, he'd only puffed about his
own importance.

Gray gazed out the window at the mountains. There were
no settlements on these rough, high slopes, despite their
proximity to Stone Town; perhaps that was why the Harmony had installed a real window and not a window screen:
there were no visible natives to spoil it, and mountain

scenes, like this view of the Spine, were probably common to many worlds. It was a good view from which to pretend that he was elsewhere, already gone into the Harmony. Gray adjusted his position in the stiff chair. He felt Janet beside him and touched her hand.

Penn turned to them. "You have a different accent from the people here," he told Janet.

"She's from the outlands," Gray quickly said.

Penn ignored him. "You walk differently, too. As if the gravity is wrong. I've seen that on other worlds, but not here, where no one travels off-world. Explain."

Janet smiled at Penn while Gray held his breath. "I've been ill," she said quietly, not making the mistake of trying to modify her accent. "I've spent several months in bed."

Penn weighed her answer, then shook his head. "And I suppose you want to leave Testament, too?"

"I want to stay with my husband."

This time Penn spoke to Gray. "I've reviewed your test results. Thoroughly. You meet all criteria for admission to the Harmony. I have no information on your wife, except that the Exchange District Security Office just made a conditional and very preliminary confirmation of your claim that she is asymptomatic for Testament's usual Alteration." Penn walked back to the grouped chairs and stood behind the one in which he previously had sat. "If I obtain what I want—an opportunity to question a precaster—then you'll get exit approval, without further bureaucratic paper shuffling. If psych tests indicate she is cognitively normal, then I won't bother investigating your wife's conformity with the usual Harmony criteria, and she'll receive exit approval, too. One woman hardly constitutes a threat to the Polite Harmony of Worlds. You'll never leave Testament without my help, but if you do as I ask, you both can go. There. A generous offer. Well?"

Gray smiled, and bowed from the chair. Penn had made exactly the offer Gray wanted. "I'll do my best, sir." Gray stood, then so did Janet.

Penn nodded as if Gray's statement had been a commitment. "I'll expect a meeting with a precaster. Soon. In the meantime, Gray Bridger, consider yourself retained as my guide; I'll want you available throughout my stay here, at my call."

It was the offie's petty revenge, Gray thought, for the

events at Bridger Dome, but a small price to pay for leaving Testament—particularly if he was the one paid. Gray bowed. "Of course, sir," he said. "And at your usual rate of 150c an hour?"

Penn seemed nearly to smile. "I've been informed that a generous rate is 15c a day," Penn said. "I'll give you 100c a day, but if you fail me, or ever abandon me again, the way you did inside Bridger Dome, I'm certain I can make you quite sorry. Understood?"

"Ahman." Gray bowed deeply, to placate Penn.

Penn nodded. "You can leave for now; I'll want you here tomorrow, though."

It was a clear dismissal. Gray started to move out from the grouping of chairs, toward the doorway, but Janet didn't come. "What *is* an Ahman?" she asked. "Are you a priest?"

Gray, beginning to sweat, grasped her arm and tried unsuccessfully to maneuver her toward the door, but stopped when Penn bowed slightly at Janet.

"No," Penn said. "Your husband was mistaken. An Ahman can be anything—it's a rank, not a specialty—but no true Jonist is a *priest;* that implies old superstitions. I happen to be a medic—in Testament's terminology, a doctor— although Harmony training is much broader than medicine; you might describe me as a biologist who specializes in humans." He smiled and seemed relaxed. Penn was easier with Janet than he was with Gray, perhaps because he didn't quite take her seriously. Harmony tourists often made that mistake about women, Gray had found, a serious mistake on Testament. Gray started toward the door again, tactfully urging Janet along.

"What do you want to ask precasters?" Janet asked Penn, abruptly halting their departure again.

Penn frowned.

She shouldn't have asked anything so private of an offie. "Come on, Janet," Gray said, low and hard. He stood, frozen, not looking at Penn. How could he have been so stupid?

Martin Penn clasped his hands behind his back and studied them both, then he smiled at Gray, bowed to Janet, and answered her. "I want to ask a precaster about God."

Janet herself didn't seem to have noticed Gray's slip. "You're searching for faith?"

"Not faith," Penn said immediately. "Jonists rely on knowledge. With so many centuries of memories, precasters should know something worthwhile." He looked at Gray. "Although there's always more they can learn. Isn't that right, Gray?"

"Sir," he said, and bowed stiffly while clutching Janet's hand and pulling her into a bow, too. He treated Penn's comment as a dismissal and hurriedly left the suite, with Janet in tow. As they passed through the insubstantial fog barrier and entered the waiting lift, Janet started to speak. He hushed her with a curt "Later, *Dancer.*" And what, he wondered, had Martin Penn made of his calling her Janet?

Chapter 3

I. Talisman

"So, when do you plan to kill the alia?" Mead asked. She leaned back against the cluttered kitchen counter and crossed her arms against her chest.

"What?" Gray and Janet had just come down the steps into Mead's kitchen; he stopped and shook his head at Janet. "I don't know what you mean," he told Mead, but his voice was weak and he wondered guiltily if he had expressed sufficient shock at Mead's question. When he put his arms around Janet, he felt awkward, even fraudulent—not that he would hurt her, but because he had once considered doing so.

"Don't be coy, Gray." Mead yawned. She looked as though she'd had a sleepless night. "That's why you went to the dome. To kill her. I understand wanting to do it away from Reed, but don't leave any bloodstains in my house."

Janet turned to him, seeking reassurances he couldn't give; he *had* intended to kill Dancer. "Mead, this is my wife," Gray said firmly. "I'm not going to hurt her."

"Wife?" Mead said, as if the word were a joke.

"My name is Janet Bridger." Janet extended her hand to Mead, who didn't take it. Janet withdrew it, and the two women studied each other. Janet was classically beautiful, while Mead had too much repressed energy for true beauty, although, highlighted by her dark, expressive, and knowing eyes, her face was more interesting. Mead's hair was pulled into a workaday bun, while Janet's shorter hair was loose and tangled from the wind; Janet was taller and thinner, less voluptuous than Mead. Their real difference, the difference of their minds, didn't show.

"Janet Bridger," Mead repeated, and turned to Gray. "I have to admit, Reed knows exactly how to get to you."

Mead sighed and looked around her kitchen. Strewn across the counters were the contents of the cabinets: pots, plates, cups, glasses, strainers, boards, utensils, silverware, platters—everything imaginable, from all the accumulated sets and partial sets that remained after five long generations of habitation. From the quantity of visible kitchenware, the many open cabinets, and the sharp smell of cleaning solution, she'd been working for hours.

"My room's upstairs," Gray told Janet and began shepherding her across the kitchen, away from Mead. He pressed her arm reassuringly, but her tense, wide-eyed gaze didn't relax.

Mead frowned. "So you're going to play with her first." To Janet, she said, "Gray never has a problem getting laid. Women want to try a man who doesn't have a woman's memories; Gray is better than an offie and more virile than boys who haven't remembered their mothers yet." Mead's laughter was an aural leer.

Janet blushed and looked away.

"Why are you talking to her like this?" Gray left Janet's side to confront his sister. His larger size gave him a sense of power. Mead didn't cringe, but her arms tensed and she turned deliberately toward him, reflecting a satisfying wariness. Then Gray realized that Learner Wolf was gone. Mead's fear that she would never have children was probably hitting her hard. He lowered his voice. "Just leave us alone. Please."

Mead scowled and turned to Janet, who had come close, following Gray. "I suppose it works both ways. An alia is a change for him, especially an emulation of Janet Bridger. No wonder the old bitch did it; she's always doted on Gray."

"That's enough!"

Mead didn't look at Gray. "I bet Reed regrets not having a direct alia descendant. Then she could have called her own emulation to life, and had Gray vicariously."

Gray grabbed at Mead, but she slipped away from him, laughing. "Stop goading me!" he shouted. "One more word and . . ."

"Kill her, not me," Mead interrupted. "Then you can leave Testament and never see me again; I've been counting on it. Oh, don't look so frightened," Mead said, turning to Janet. "He won't actually kill *you;* you'll be long gone by then. Don't expect to wake up next time you fall asleep. Killing you solves all his problems."

"That isn't true," Gray said. He had to deny it, but doing so added force to Mead's accusations. "I'll never hurt you, Janet. Besides, Penn will get us off Testament."

Janet slipped her hand into the crook of Gray's right arm. She smiled, entirely composed. "I see why you're anxious to leave Testament if all my descendants are like her." She looked up at Gray, trusting him, or pretending very well.

Relieved, he nodded, indicating the door into the interior of the house, and arm in arm they started for it.

"You stupid cow," Mead called after them. "Every founder leaves her mark on a line; all Bridgers do is talk. If we had fought the offies a hundred years ago, the way the Shak wanted, then things would be different now."

Gray spun around. "Yeah. We'd all be dead." He was furious at Mead's disloyalty in showing even feigned sympathy with the Shak.

"Our mother *is* dead, Gray. Or didn't you notice, what with Reed spoiling you in every way she can? Isn't that why you haven't killed the alia yet? Because you don't want to disappoint Reed? Push the alia down the stairs; I'll say it was an accident."

Time seemed suspended. Gray imagined how Janet must feel, hearing Mead while being entirely dependent on him. Janet's situation touched him in a way no other had; he'd pledged himself to help her. Mead stared, wearing a viciously victorious grin, a horrible parody of his grandmother's capricious smile. He weighed the insults he'd had from Mead since her memories came in; they were enough. Just once, he would make that grin fade. "You'll never have children, Mead Bridger," he said, calm with a cold anger that left his mind clear. "Grandmother knows; even mother knew it. It's time for you to adjust to the truth. The main line won't pass through you. I was schooled; Irene got a big new house, and Eris stays here, waiting for her children to inherit this one. Irene will be the twenty-seventh link on the main line, not you."

"You're no precaster, Gray." Mead was still grinning, but the expression seemed pasted on her flushed face. Gray felt queasy to see it, but regret was too late.

He wheeled around, bringing Janet with him, and hurried out of the kitchen. There had been a battle, and for the first time, he had won. Victory should have been sweeter, but he was too aware that he had hurt Mead so effectively only because he knew her so well. She was his little sister. She'd been beside him when Reed broke the news of their mother's death at Shak hands. She'd been the only person with whom he'd dared to share his dream of being a precaster. Only to him had *she* confided her need to be the next link in the thousand-year Bridger main line chain, and hinted that her expectation of that honor somehow kept their mother alive inside her heart. They'd shared each other's triumphs and fears for ten years, the only two children orphaned by Margaret Bridger's death, because their sisters had been adults already, with children of their own. Best friends and confidants—but only until Mead's memories had come rushing in. She'd first withdrawn from him, and soon rejected and despised him. A singleton. Her apparent contempt had deepened as time passed and she didn't have children, as though she blamed him, imagining his flaw had affected her bloodline, too. He understood her fears too well.

Gray led Janet into the hall, to the bottom of the steep staircase. "The bedrooms are upstairs," he said.

Janet nodded. "You said."

"Unless you don't want to be alone with me."

"Of course I do. But don't leave me with her." Janet tried to smile.

Eris's two youngest children were quietly playing dolls in the broad room on the right. Noticing Gray, they begged him to join their game, but he shook his head no. "Go on up," Gray told Janet. "You need to rest."

"You?"

He nodded back at the kitchen. "I don't want to leave it like this. She already hates me."

Janet touched her palm to Gray's chest.

Her touch was typically Bridger—or prototypically? He almost smiled, then looked back at the closed kitchen door. "Some things shouldn't be said."

"She doesn't hate you, Gray. She wants your attention, and she wants me dead."

Gray took her hand. "I swear I'll never hurt you, Janet."

Janet met his eyes, hesitated, smiled and nodded, then climbed the first stair. "I'll wait for you."

"Second door on the left." Gray watched her leave. Each

step she took was just slightly too high. Penn was an observant man. Gray frowned and went back to the kitchen.

The room seemed empty, then he heard a clatter as a pan bumped another. He went farther inside and looked down. Mead was kneeling on the floor in front of an open cabinet, putting various-sized frying pans where mismatched plates had been kept. "Mead?" he said.

She looked up, observing him without expression. "You need help killing the alia?"

His first reaction was to leave, but he didn't. "I'm not going to kill her."

"That's too bad. It's your only hope of getting away free."

He squatted next to her. She was staring into the open cabinet, studying the remaining empty space. "What are you doing?"

"Changing everything. We'll be years getting rid of old habits. This will force us to think when we reach for things in the wrong place. It's good to shake up the mind."

He smiled dubiously. She was excising her past, he thought, because she didn't see a future. "It's your kitchen."

She sat back on her heels. "What do you want, Gray?"

"We were friends once. Brother and sister. I haven't changed."

"I have. I could kill you, but it would be too much trouble. Reed would find a way to make me pay for it."

"You don't mean that."

"Don't I? You're mistaking me for you. I can do what you can't. You're never angry enough. I thought I was finally rid of you, then the old bitch in the dome married you to that walking mnemonic device." Mead grasped the edge of the counter and pulled herself to her feet. She looked down at him. "I admit—they surprised me. I've assumed they wanted you to leave, once they were done screwing with your head, but if they're testing you, this is one test you won't pass."

Gray stood, too. "I intend to leave. I'm working on it."

Mead leaned close. "Kill her, Gray. Whatever purpose the precasters have, she's part of it. Break free and run." She was serious.

"I can't, Mead. She's as much used by them as I am."

She smiled and shook her head. "You're such a fool."

"Look, I'm sorry about what I said. It might not be true." He held out his hands to her.

She ignored him, while putting an omelet pan in the cabinet. "You were five when mother had me, her duty child, to keep the main line young. A woman shouldn't care about a son so much. She never really wanted me."

Gray remembered their mother. The memory wasn't of incidents, but a seamless, snug gestalt of emotion, of warm arms, smiles, and confidence. Mead had given him a gift, an unintended gift "of the left hand," the reminiscence of Margaret Bridger. He didn't hate the women of Testament. They were his family, his line. Mead, too. It would be difficult, but she could adjust to being infertile. "I'll never be a precaster," he said.

She glanced at him, then gathered scissors, new shelf paper, and cleaning solutions from the counter and carried them to the next row of cabinets; she set them down. Gray followed. She looked sideways at him. "If you were a daughter, you'd be next after me."

"If I was a daughter, I'd still be a singleton." They looked at each other, and Mead's expression eased.

She surveyed the disarrayed kitchen. "It'll be leftovers for dinner." She sounded displeased; she took pride in her cooking.

They hadn't been this easy together for months. "Have you been to a doctor?" he asked gently.

The line of her mouth stiffened. She knelt, pulled out the shelf, and began removing an old, mismatched set of china—Eris's daughters sometimes played with it—from the cabinet. "All of them," she said. "None would go against Bridger Dome."

"Go to an offie," he suggested, kneeling down beside her. "They don't care. Martin Penn, the one I'm guiding right now, is a Harmony medic, an Ahman."

"How stupid are you?" she snapped. "Ask people who think we should be exterminated for help propagating more of our kind?"

Mead had no contacts with offie tourists; she might never have met one, except for brief, reminisced encounters. "They're not all as bad as Governor Swan. Penn seems okay. He might help; he likes women. He definitely looks at them a lot."

"That's your answer for everything—run to the offies."

He shrugged, irritated, but he knew how to handle Mead. "Give up, then. I don't care."

"I'd have to have something to trade for his help," Mead said. "Does he know about your wife?"

He shouldn't have tried. She was seventeen, going on a thousand, and he only knew the seventeen-year-old. "How can you have all the same memories and be so different from the others?"

She laughed and shook her head, as if at an idiot. "Singleton, you don't understand much. We don't all remember the same things. Even the precasters. It's what we, individually, have an affinity to reminisce. I remember how to butcher people; the First Comers weren't the glory girls they talk about to you children. It hasn't been so long since Shak Dome fell, either, and we slaughtered them, our former friends and cousins."

"I give up." He spread his hands wide. "Look, Mead, I never intended to hurt you."

"Don't lie; you're no good at it."

"How can I talk to you?" he said, and started out of the kitchen, back to Janet.

"Go kill her, Gray," Mead called as he left.

He let the double-hinged kitchen door flap back and forth like a brisk metronome behind him and took the stairs two at a time. The door to his room was open. Janet was standing, holding the black queen from his chess set.

"Testament," she said, turning toward him, "it's too familiar. Because of this memory trick, you're like people from my time, the early twenty-first century, set down in a different place a millennium later. The offies—that's what you call them?—their manners, their attitudes, even the way they talk, are less like what I'm used to from Earth." She put the chess piece back on the board. "I might as well have said 'from the past.'" She glanced around the room.

He followed her gaze and saw the room, his sanctuary, through a stranger's eyes. The painted walls were covered with pictures of faraway places, mostly sketches he'd drawn from eavesdropped descriptions, though a few were posters of the kind occasionally available even on Testament. "That's Darien," he said, indicating a scene of rolling green hills under a cloudy sky, which hung above his desk. "It's supposed to be the most tolerant of the Harmony worlds."

A shelf, bolted onto the foot of his bed, held notebooks from his schooling and knickknacks he'd accumulated over the years: a jagged bit of stone from Shak Dome, taken on a pretend raid he'd engineered with friends on the occasion of his twelfth birthday; a small curved knife, the handle and sheath beautifully inlaid in multicolored hing shell by Kent, his mother's far cousin and Gray's father of record, who now lived in the Eastlands; a black clay effigy pot from Vincent, in the outlands, which had reminded him of his mother; trinkets from various women. Another shelf held a row of printed books, all products of Bridger Dome, which bound hardcopy books as a way of increasing hard currency—they were a popular tourist item.

His battered desk was littered with papers, the copious Harmony documentation of his quest to leave Testament. The Harmony forms were easily distinguished from his submissions made on local paper. The texture of Harmony paper was different, thinner and smoother than that of Testament, and easier to tear. An access to Testament's computer network was pushed to one side of the desk; the mail light was blinking. He turned it off.

The chess set had its own separate stand. His grandmother had given him the priceless set when he left the dome; she claimed it came from old Earth. Only two of the original pieces were missing after a thousand or more years, and their plastic forms had been replaced long before the set came into Gray's possession. He picked up the piece Janet had set down. The ancient plastic was fissured with tiny lines. It had a greasy sheen that was partly from its own material and partly the shine produced by generations of hands. "Was this yours?" he asked Janet.

"I had one just like it." She didn't smile. Her spirits needed bolstering, after Mead.

"Welcome home." Gray set the black queen down. It reminded him of Reed; she always gave him white, and had always beaten him.

Janet nodded listlessly. She picked a book off the shelf. "One of my favorites. Naturally." She sighed.

Gray went to her. "I like the old books best," he said. "The ones with heroes and adventures. Stories written on Testament are hard to understand sometimes, when you don't share the memories."

Janet replaced the book and scanned the other titles. Gray felt embarrassed. The bookshelf was too much like a diary. "I've written some stories," he said, partly to distract her.

She finally smiled. "I tried once, but I couldn't finish it. Did you have any luck?"

He pointed at some papers stacked beneath the desk. "I've never let anyone read them, though."

"I know the feeling." She went to the desk and looked sideways at the papers, trying to read the title page. "Do you think I might?"

He bowed like a gracious offie to hide his shyness, and his pleasure, too. None of his sisters would have bothered. "Of course. You're my wife."

She sat on the side of the bed and put her head in her hands. "I'm afraid Gray. I said how familiar everything is, but that's not true. Testament is horribly different from what I remember. Everything is skewed. Your people remember, but by remembering, they've changed themselves. I'm an alien here."

Gray sat on the bed next to her and put his arm over her shoulders. "I am, too. And it won't be any different for either of us in the Harmony, but at least we'll be together."

She looked up. There were tears in her eyes, yet she actually looked more cheerful. He hugged her. "You should rest," he said. "You'll have to sleep sometime. Don't listen to Mead."

Janet had her own fears. He'd awakened in the dome that morning with Janet sitting upright beside him, staring out the window wall. He had studied her profile and recognized, with an instinctive, pleased assurance, that she was the same woman. He'd shifted position on the bed to inform her he was awake. When she glanced down, her eyes had been shadowed. "The nights here feel so long," she'd said.

"Do you intend to kill me?" she asked abruptly, although her tone kept the question lighter than the words implied.

"No. Of course not." He looked directly into her eyes, willing her to believe. "I thought about it before we met, before you awakened, but even then I couldn't do it."

She nodded slowly, accepting it. "I do need to sleep." Janet lifted her legs onto the bed and deliberately lowered her head onto the pillow. She lay still, like an anxious, unwilling patient in a hospital bed, eyes wide open. Gray stroked Janet's arm, up and down, in a rhythm older than human memory, a comfort to them both. It was as if he'd captured a soap bubble that could burst and disappear at any time, and he didn't know how to save it. Did he really want to? Now, with Penn's help, he might be able to leave without her, but Gray knew he couldn't abandon Janet. He wondered how Penn would react if he learned she was an alia. Would Mead tell him?

Janet had relaxed, pressed partially against him. Her eyes closed, then she shuddered, as if startled from an unwelcome doze, and sat straight up.

"It's all right," he whispered.

"I'm afraid. Stay with me, Gray. I don't want to be alone."

"I'll call you back," he promised. "Probably everything will be fine. You'll rest and wake up, refreshed. Together, we'll figure out something to satisfy Penn." He smiled at her, and touched her under the chin, raising her head. He kissed her.

Janet lay down on the bed; he stretched out beside her, listening to the subdued sounds in the house: children's voices, muffled footsteps, wind blowing against the room's small window, a fan turning in the insulating attic. Her taut expression faded and he was anxiously reminded of the mindless body he'd seen in Bridger Dome. He forced the image away, but was relieved each time she opened her eyes and smiled at him, still Janet Bridger. Finally she fell asleep. He touched her cheek, whispered her name like a talisman, and hoped.

II. The Testament Problem

Governor Swan was a pig. Clearly he ate too much; clearly he didn't care that it was obvious on his person. A pig in a sinecure, Martin Penn thought, while smiling at his host. Fat, sloppy, and dead-ended in this job, Cevan Swan had nevertheless cooperated diligently with the Ahman from Center, given him broad access to the resources of his tiny domain, and this formal dinner was intended as the starting point for Swan's . . . just deserts.

"I've heard Jeroen Lee sets a fine table," Swan said, pushing his chair back and gazing insouciantly at Penn. "And you were on his staff how long?—twelve years?—before this revelation. You must miss his cuisine."

Swan wanted information. "We rarely dined together. Elector Lee tends to treat everyone, even including Ahmen, as servants." It was true, but Penn felt uncomfortable criticizing Jeroen Lee, despite Lee's own order that Penn distance himself from Lee's situation.

Swan sipped his wine, a deep red, too dry for Penn's admittedly unrefined palate. "*Elector* Lee," Swan quoted. "Then you believe he should retain his position as one of the six Electors despite the fact that he's an Altered."

"I use the title because he remains an Elector of Order until such time as a voting majority of Ahmen impeaches or otherwise removes him; I haven't expressed a public opinion on whether or not that should be done, and won't. I'm too close to the situation." By failing to publicly support Lee, his own mentor, Penn had given Lee's opponents substantial ammunition.

"And all those years you didn't realize that he was Altered?" Swan asked, allowing a dash of incredulity into his tone.

Penn shrugged. *What I knew or didn't know, I certainly wouldn't tell you,* he thought. "Elector Lee is an intensely private man," he said.

Swan chuckled, then toyed with the stem of his glass. "I'm only an administrator in a remote, unimportant outpost of the Harmony. You know Center. What do you believe will happen?"

Penn looked directly at Swan. "Never discount Jeroen Lee. I don't know a more resourceful man." It wasn't an answer.

Swan stood, glancing outside. Surprisingly, his window screen was naked, not set for a view off Testament. "But Lee is Altered," Swan said. He extended his fleshly hands wide, indicating Stone Town. It spread out before him, filled with lights. Although wasteful of energy, the lights were pretty, like grounded stars. "Essentially, he's no different from these disgusting people."

"His Alteration is entirely different from the one found here," Penn said testily. The discovery of Lee's Alteration had shocked the Harmony. It would take a miracle for Lee to keep his position, but Penn was hoping for a miracle. Meanwhile, bureaucrats like Cevan Swan had no business judging Jeroen Lee.

Swan waved the objection away. "All Altereds are essentially the same—not citizens. Not human."

In profile, Swan's rotund belly made him look pregnant, like one of Testament's women. Penn turned away to hide his amusement at the comparison. "On the contrary, the Academy of Center has frequently ruled that the differences are significant, and Altered groups have been reassigned to the status of adjusted humans, and citizens. Cevan, human biology is my field, and a matter for the Academies, not government officials."

Swan hesitated, then bowed his acceptance of the reprimand. His beady eyes were bright, like those of a bird, giving no hint of his thoughts. "Testament is an uncommon destination. Our usual tourists are visitors from ships passing through to Rockland or Amacuro, and because of the quarantine, few enough of them qualify to land. There are sights worth seeing, but Testament's only attribute worth *your* interest is the Altered population." Swan walked to the sideboard, where a dish of iced melon pieces, previously ignored by him as he indulged in gooey after-dinner sweets, apparently now tempted him to extend his meal. He ate a handful while watching Penn, who was neither disturbed nor goaded into speaking by the fat man's stare and insinuations. "I only mention this," Swan eventually continued, "because of your expressed interest in a precast. In some circles, precasters have acquired an undeserved reputation for insight. The situation in Center, just now, could make a shrewd, seemingly objective intuition appear valuable." He chuckled unconvincingly. "I myself would like to know the future. But these women are dangerous. I believe that, and the edicts of the Grand Assembly establishing this Protectorate agree. Enforcing the information quarantine is *my* duty. If a precast involves telling these women anything about the Harmony, it would be my responsibility to prevent it."

"I have no intention of telling them anything about the Harmony, or the politics of Jonism, and I would despise their comments on the subject," Penn replied firmly.

Swan looked unhappy at receiving only a bald assertion of innocence, without an explanation, but his power was limited and local, while Penn's potentially was neither, though it lay in the Academies and not the government. "But what of the price of a precast?" Swan asked. "A fertile Altered woman set loose in the Harmony is contrary to the basic principles of our quarantine."

Penn had suspected his suite was monitored—it was only natural—and Swan had just admitted it. Penn frowned, although he wasn't upset. He did wish he hadn't mentioned

God to the Bridger woman, but such a comment by an Academic was not subject to the oversight of Governor Swan. "We are speaking of one woman, who is symptomatically normal. I would take responsibility for bypassing that portion of the quarantine, and as an Ahman, I have sufficient authority. In any event, I have not given my imprimatur to her travel yet."

"You are known as a liberal man; liberals are often also naive." Swan shook his head, preventing Penn's protest. "Very few understand this Alteration's dangers. Whatever these women learn, their daughters remember, and add to that knowledge. They even have a project to distill all knowledge into memory."

"The Human Encyclopedia Project?" Penn shrugged. "An encyclopedia is always out of date, and I've never heard of one that's dangerous."

"These women are devious. They ferret out information, and the more they know, the more they are able to extrapolate."

Precasts could be real, then. There might be answers to be found on Testament, not merely the unending questions that were Jonism's supposed core. "Perhaps I'll understand once I've been here longer," Penn said.

It mollified Swan. "The danger is real, Ahman Penn. No one at Center understands. They send me boys straight from training classes to guard the Harmony from the Altereds of this world. Peter Isaacs, my military commander, is only a captain. He has no experience in combat; except for my Security group, the military here are essentially police. The drones on Center think because Testament is dominated by women, it's harmless. Even my staff has to be constantly reminded. There is, in most men, a tendency to equate sex with friendliness, but on Testament that equation is wrong."

Penn had real difficulty repressing his smile. Swan was a crank, one who probably had peculiar relations with women. "You needn't concern yourself with me on that score," he said.

Swan nodded. "These Altereds are restive, as if they sense the recent trouble in the Harmony and want to take advantage of it. I hope you'll tell the Electors of the dangers here."

"From what I've seen so far, these women are just curiosities."

Swan poured himself more wine. "But why have you come? Why do you want a precast?" Swan seemed genuinely puzzled, and though he had no right to question an Ahman, there was no harm to an edited disclosure to set his mind at rest.

"Precasts as fortune-telling are irrational, unbelievable, and distinctly anti-Jonist," Penn said. "The memory Alteration is useful for one thing only—history. The slowboat which brought the natives here embarked after Jon Hsu's death, but while his immediate students were still alive. The Hard Science Underground was intact, though they hadn't yet formed the First Academy. I'm interested in Jonism's early years, and the milieu in which Hsu's *General Principles* was written. The memories of these women are pieces of that past."

"Of course you know, Martin—if I may call you that?— that the Altereds here aren't Jonist." Swan seemed jovial again, gratified by Penn's disclosure. "They were asked about their historical memory when we discovered Testament. They knew only trivia." Swan finished the melon.

The man had no moderation; he'd eat everything set before him, exactly like a pig. With such habits, he had been lucky to stay off the Academy Flawed List, making his citizenship probationary, or he had important Academic friends. "They may volunteer more, now that they know the Harmony better," Penn said. "Also, if your proposal to eliminate their memory Alteration is ever implemented, all those memories will be lost. Though in the current climate, I doubt the Electors would approve your plan."

Swan grimaced and turned aside. "Only their precasters would remember back so far. I urge you to stay away from them."

When he wasn't eating, Swan's bulk could seem majestic. Penn wondered if there were advantages to a massive body in primitive cultures; perhaps it impressed Testament's women. "Surely you are exaggerating the capabilities of these Altereds. My new guide—a normal enough man, though he was raised here—has managed to trick their Compound Council."

Swan laughed, but it sounded too high-pitched. "Did he? Who really knows, when precasters are involved? You're wrong to take Testament so lightly, Martin. But I won't dispute the point. You are my guest."

Penn stretched surreptitiously. The heavy meal and boredom had combined with the long, pointless walk in Stone Town to stiffen his muscles. Swan seemed naive and paranoid; perhaps he was just afraid of women. Jon Hsu had written in his *General Principles* that alteration of the human genome was unnecessary, but he had never called it *wrong;* technically there were no restrictions on Altereds entering the Academies, only custom—an argument Lee was using. There even were good reasons for some Alterations, such as the filter nose on Gas. The Testament Alteration had once had a purpose; it was vestigial, now, with interesting consequences. Still, Penn wanted an easy relationship with Swan, however backward his opinions. "Personally," Penn said, then paused, "I am personally uncomfortable with most Altereds. I'm from Flute, a Virtual Earth, where there is no need of them."

Swan's face had a greasy glow. His smile looked strained. "You've publicly expressed the opinion that Altereds should be citizens. Isn't that saying that Jon Hsu was wrong?"

Swan was using orthodoxy to conceal a bigot's heart—and he had investigated his visitor. "The traditional interpretation may be mistaken," Penn said. "Mine is not an uncommon opinion among the younger Ahmen on Center. And I stated it before I'd ever met Elector Lee."

Swan went to the window and looked out at Stone Town. With his back to Penn, he said, "You're here looking for something you can use to rescue Jeroen Lee from his Alteration."

Penn smiled to hide his discomfort. Swan was both right and wrong, but it was expedient to get along with him. Swan's cooperation would diminish otherwise. Penn got up and walked over to Swan. He stood beside him, gazing out the window. "If I wanted to 'rescue' Elector Lee, there are more direct paths to take than the long shot of discovering something relevant in this world of Altered women. Cevan, *I left Center.*"

Swan turned, stepped back, and bowed, understanding Penn's implication that he did not support Lee. "I apologize, Ahman. I've been too long among these devious women. I should have realized that, however liberal, no reasonable man could countenance an Altered person as an Elector of Jonist Order. Lee's unmasking must be especially difficult for you. But please be wary of these women; Testament is a real threat to the Harmony of Worlds. Their Compound Council makes regular attempts to circumvent the quarantine restrictions, though as long as I am here, I will keep them out. The safety of the Harmony, and Jonism, is my primary concern."

Penn returned the bow, feeling dirty at having satisfied Swan with a half-truth, essentially a lie.

Apparently pleased by the conversation, Swan gestured at another door, leading to the private rooms of his apartment. "I have an entertainment planned. Something special, in your honor?"

It was early. Penn didn't want to spend the evening with Swan, but a refusal would only alienate a man he'd gone out of his way to humor. Penn nodded graciously. "Certainly."

Swan crossed to the private door and led Penn to another room, which contained an entertainment hub. Penn covered a yawn and wondered what manner of gross frolic Cevan Swan had prepared, suspecting it would be participatory, but he followed Swan inside.

III. A Living Memorial

Gray shook Dancer's body while calling Janet's name, but couldn't rouse her, or anyone. Her face was slack, with occasional brief shudders that vanished before manifesting any personality. He felt that he'd betrayed her, and also, unfairly, that he'd been betrayed. Janet was gone.

Outside, the air whistled as an evening windstorm began in Stone Town. Gray sank onto the floor, his back braced against the bed. Dancer's limp arm trailed across his shoulder, and he held her hand, pretending Janet existed and would awaken soon.

Mead opened the door. Gray replaced Dancer's hand at her side and stood. "What do you want?" he asked defensively.

Mead walked into the room, glancing around curiously; it had been several years since she'd come inside. She held her hands behind her back as if she were skittish or sly and peered at Dancer before looking at Gray. "She's gone? Good—then even you can do it now."

As if in answer, Dancer mumbled unintelligibly.

"Gray." Mead sounded reasonable, a woman pleading urgently for justice. "Killing his nonentity is the best way for you to get off Testament, to where you claim you want to be." She brought her hands from behind her back; she was holding a butcher knife, which shone as if she had just oiled it. "Here. Take it." She extended it to Gray.

"I'm not going to kill her, Mead. Never."

"Stop being naive. The woman you brought here has been dead a thousand years. I am as much Janet Bridger as that useless thing on the bed. I have all those memories inside me, too."

"You're nothing like her."

"Don't you want to leave Testament anymore?" Mead challenged him.

Gray looked at Janet. Though he hadn't admitted it to himself before, the more he knew offies, the less convinced he was that he could live comfortably alone among them. Yet he couldn't stay on Testament. Taking Janet was one answer.

"Don't you hate them?" Mead asked.

"Hate who?" He was genuinely puzzled. "The offies?"

She laughed. The way in which she held the butcher knife changed. She no longer offered it; she held it as if readying it for her own use. "Stupid Gray. Mother guessed what you were, at the end. She died disappointed."

"That's a lie!"

"They made you a singleton, those old crones in Bridger Dome. Grandmother *suggested* that mother have a boy, and made sure she had genetic counseling. Mother doted on you, her sweet-natured son, because she assumed you were special. She knew what a precaster's suggestion meant."

"Shut up, Mead."

She walked closer, holding the knife between them. "Margaret Bridger was as ambitious as anyone that I can remember, and I remember a lot of them. If she hadn't died in that pointless battle with the Shak, even you, a singleton, would have recognized her for what she was. No different from Reed. No different from me. She thought she was mothering Testament's version of a messiah—a man who can be remembered—or at least a remarkable precaster, and look what she got instead." Mead stepped back and examined him from head to toe, sneering. "You're so gullible, you're almost entertaining." The knife glittered in her hand. "I'll free us both, since you don't have the nerve."

"What do you mean?" he asked, but he stepped between Mead and Dancer as if his body understood.

She grinned and went into a fighter's crouch, knife held in two hands, attention riveted on him. "Do you think you have a chance to stop me? Consider what I remember, singleton. I've killed so many times in memory, I can't remember all of them." Mead shifted to the side, to avoid Gray, but he moved to intercept her.

"I won't let you do it."

She shrugged and seemed to study her knife, while looking past it to him. Its edge was very sharp. "I'm doing you a favor. There won't be blood on your hands."

He started to answer, but she lunged at him. Her eyes were bright and her lips were parted with anticipation. Gray jumped aside and realized, only after he did, that it had been a feint. She had switched directions and was nearly at the bed, where Dancer lay, unprotected.

"No!" Gray yelled, and dove at Mead without technique or thought, smashing into her and bouncing her away from the bed by size and the force of his impact, not plan or skill. She should have been off balance, yet she landed on one hand and a knee, and stared at him, ready to get up, yet surprised.

"No," Gray said again, firmly. She had expected ignorance where there was no memory, and imagined combat was based on abstract knowledge. He had the advantage of his life in the outlands. Before Mead recovered her feet, Gray tried to grab the knife. Mead pulled it up and away from him, tumbling the contents of the bookshelf onto the floor as she used it for quick leverage in rising. The blade grazed Gray's right forearm as he stumbled on a book. He'd been cut worse, and barely noticed the gash. He went at Mead with his arms outstretched, reaching to grab her or the knife. His blood dripped onto the carpeting.

The smell of blood, or the sound of their struggle, excited Dancer. She tossed on the bed beside them and muttered like a child being roused from heavy sleep. Mead grimaced at Dancer, then ran straight at Gray. He waited for her, but she grabbed his right arm as he launched himself forward to attack, twisted him somehow—he yelled—and he was on the floor.

"Please!" he shouted as Mead scrambled toward the bed.

Mead hesitated, perhaps not quite so cold-blooded as she had pretended, and looked back at Gray. "It's for the best."

"We'll leave," he begged. "You'll never see us again. Don't do this." He sensed her decision and in a sudden effort at speed dove forward before she moved; he tackled Mead's knees and yanked her down. She tumbled, her arms flailing, but her grasp of the knife was secure. He rolled out of the way, grabbed the edge of the bed, and jumped up to his feet, becoming a barrier Mead would have to cross.

"Come on. Make it easy, Gray," she said. She gestured with the knife, an invitation to attack. "You can't win. Back off and it'll be over quick. One thrust and a twist." She moved the knife, demonstrating.

Gray's arm ached; he was panting. He didn't move. He had ruined his last opportunity to be free of the impediment of a wife. Was it a mistake? Dancer was nothing, except that Janet, his Janet, was inside her.

Mead grinned, and, slowly, watching him for a reaction, she got up from the floor. "Step away."

"What's going on?" Dancer's body asked.

Mead chuckled, sounding unpleasantly like their grandmother.

Gray, not daring to turn completely away from Mead, glanced at the figure on the bed. Dancer wasn't the limp mass of inert flesh she had been; instead, a woman looked out from her face. It wasn't Janet Bridger. This woman—it was surprisingly obvious—was harder, more like the usual women of Testament. She sat up and stared back at Gray, coolly assessing him and the situation. Downstairs a door slammed, but the silence inside Gray's room stretched on until he had to break it. "You're an alia," Gray said.

"So I guessed." The woman's attention turned to the knife in Mead's hand.

Mead shook her head. Slowly, she lowered the knife, and though she didn't put it down, she didn't appear poised for an attack. "Another wife, Gray?" Mead said. "You'll have a harem in one body."

"You're my husband?" the woman asked, frowning. "An alia? Something's strange." She observed them with a calm that spoke of martial training. "Who are you?" Her voice was husky; her diction was nothing like Janet's.

Mead laughed, lowering the knife further, to her side. She was watching Gray, waiting for him to answer.

Gray didn't want to explain anything to this alia, didn't want conversation, didn't even want to know her. He hoped she would vanish—he wished for Janet—then guilt made him say, "Gray Bridger, son of Margaret, youngest daughter of Reed, youngest of Tillie, main line in the twenty-seventh generation from Janet." He forced a weak smile, but it seemed wrong to even mention Janet to this person, who only a few hours earlier had been Janet Bridger.

"Elene, nineteenth," she said succinctly. "On the main line."

Gray recalled the name as one in a long, memorized list. Nothing more. The nineteenth generation was long before the Harmony quickships. She wouldn't understand anything of Testament's current situation.

"Why . . . marry?" Elene said distastefully. She glanced at the oozing wound on Gray's arm and frowned at Mead's knife. Her attention rarely left it.

"This is really too amusing," Mead said. She took a step closer to the bed. Gray let her, though he didn't move away. "I almost regret what I have to do, but the facts haven't changed."

"Mead, no!"

Mead darted at the bed. Gray was too late trying to stop her, but the alia was alert and alive. Elene dodged the knife, coming up off the bed, counterattacking Mead at the same time Gray struck his sister. Elene grappled with Mead and did what Gray had been unable to do: she tore the knife away from his sister. Gray pulled Mead away from Elene and the bed, afterward holding her wrapped tightly in his arms. She contorted her body, trying to wrench herself free, then abruptly she stopped trying. Gray didn't believe in her submission and continued to keep her trapped in the unpleasant intimacy.

"Thanks," he said to Elene. Absurd. It was Elene that Mead had attacked, but she'd saved Janet, too.

Elene shrugged. "Is this a soft time? Peaceful? She lacks experience."

"No." It was another voice, Gray's grandmother. "It isn't soft, but it's very different." Reed Bridger was framed by the doorway. Her black traveling cloak was dusty and her eyes were tired. She seemed smaller outside Bridger Dome.

"Grandmother," Gray said with false joviality, jerking

Mead forward as a kind of shield, "meet Elene Bridger—or perhaps you already know each other."

"Let your sister loose, Gray." His grandmother walked inside the room.

Gray hesitated, then released Mead, pushing her away. His grandmother couldn't want Dancer dead; she must know what she was doing. Mead stood quietly where he'd shoved her. Gingerly, he moved his right arm, feeling pain from the superficial wound Mead had inflicted. His ripped shirt was wet with blood, and blood still seeped out of the cut.

"Men are trouble," the alia, who was now Elene, said.

"Hush. The situation is complicated." Reed spoke to Elene as if she were real. "Give me the knife."

After a long, hard look at Mead, Elene handed the knife to Reed Bridger, extending it hilt first.

Mead was scowling at their grandmother. "Why are you doing this?" she demanded.

"Leave us, Mead."

Mead took an involuntary step backward. "What do you want from me, grandmother?" Instead of angry, she sounded shrill.

"Nothing. Nothing more. You're finished."

Mead gasped, to have it said aloud. Even Gray, an outsider between them and their memories, understood. He had been right and wished he hadn't been; Mead's line was ended. She would never have daughters. Gray held his breath, expecting an explosion from his sister. It didn't come. Mead was unnaturally still, but her expression was composed. If she was disillusioned of her goals, as he had once been, then she had the stoic courage to dominate her emotions.

"Mead," Gray said, proud of her, knowing exactly what she must be feeling. They both had seen the future they'd expected disappear.

"You're still a freak." Mead glared defiantly at Gray, avoiding their grandmother, then she left the room, limping slightly as she went through the door.

"So," Elene said to Reed, indicating Gray with a nod.

Reed didn't answer; she glanced around Gray's bedroom. Gray was embarrassed to have it seen for the third time that day, or fourth, if Elene counted. The pictures of Harmony worlds seemed views into adolescent rebellion, not a man's determination. He'd outgrown them, overnight. He pulled out the desk chair, but only rested his injured arm on its high back, watching the two women.

Reed picked a book up from the floor. She glanced at the title, smiled, and replaced it on the broken shelf. When she saw it wouldn't stay, she set it on the end of the bed. Finally, she looked at Elene. "Remember Gray if you see him again. He's important to me. Help him if he needs help. Don't hold it against him that he's a man."

Elene seemed amused. "His arm needs tending."

"Lie down," Reed said. "Your time is done."

Elene hesitated, showing a strong will of her own. Reed took Elene's hand. Elene lay down, sighed, and closed her eyes.

After a short while, Reed released Dancer's hand. Elene's eyes remained closed. Reed left the bedroom without a word to Gray. Her heavy steps on the stairs were punctuated by children's voices calling to her—Eris's girls.

Drying blood made it difficult for Gray to inspect the cut on his arm, but it didn't seem serious. He turned to Elene. She was gone; no one had taken her place. Dancer was vacant once again, sunk into an alia coma. There were tears in her eyes. Gray sat down, slumped on the bed, and gently wiped those empty eyes, wondering who, so briefly, might have looked out and cried. Dancer's body lay still, without the twitching that, in his limited experience, seemed to signify it was about to house a self-aware personality. "Janet," he whispered, but nothing changed. Testament. There was no need of monuments. Each person was a living memorial to the dead, his wife most of all.

Reed Bridger returned, carrying warm water and bandages on a kitchen tray. Gray removed his shirt one-handed, without either of them speaking. His arm hurt when he moved it. Reed sat beside him, both of them next to Dancer's passive body on the bed, and washed the long cut Mead had made. The water stung, but Gray didn't object.

"Gray?" Reed asked, as she applied white gauze to the wound. "What were you thinking?"

He hadn't been conscious of his own thoughts. "You win, grandmother," he said after a moment. "I'll stay on Testament."

She put the washcloth into the pan. "Why?" she asked, stirring the water with her index finger.

"I can't keep up with you. I can't follow all the twists my

life takes, and I can't hate you the way Mead does. So, I give up. Do whatever you want."

She smiled into the water. "You're usually much more persistent. What did Martin Penn want?"

He looked curiously at her. "You know we went to the Exchange?"

"Of course I do." She wrung out the washcloth, folded it, and put it on the tray. "What did he want?"

"He won't let me leave Testament unless I get him a precast; he'll let us both go if I do."

She stood and placed the tray atop the papers on his cluttered desk. "Ahman Martin Penn," she said. Her voice was a scale weighing the man. "A Jonist from the Academy on Center. Why has he come to Testament?"

He recalled Janet's question and laid his hand over Dancer's closest hand. Its warmth surprised him, then he was ashamed of that surprise; she wasn't dead. "He wants to ask a precaster about God." Gray couldn't restrain a grin, even now.

"Does he? A Jonist?" She nodded to herself. "So have others. What's going on out there, that they come to despised Testament to ask Altereds about God? We don't know; no one is allowed to return here from the Harmony. But old people are patient, Gray. We know that mankind is forgetful, that empires crumble and nothing stays the same. We can make educated guesses—precasts—and I'll make one now. Martin Penn didn't slink around Edgemarket asking directions to a precast the way others have. He's using the resources of the governor to get what he wants. Penn is very, very important, and that makes his visit an interesting opportunity. The Harmony doesn't send official expeditions here to ask about God—at least, not yet." She grinned. "But something interesting is happening at Center."

"What?" Gray was curious, despite his other concerns.

She shrugged and looked at his tumbled books. "They forget what we remember. They need to be sure we're not a danger."

"Testament?" Gray laughed.

Their eyes met. It was like seeing into a deep pool in the middle of the western desert. Her attention on Gray was both chilling and kind. Eyes of a thousand years, he'd called them. There was something to fear in that.

"Testament," she agreed. "What is happening that makes

them insecure? All those questions about God, when Jonism vigorously denies faith in anything not objectively verifiable. What would they really like to find? And what will they do if they decide we are dangerous? We need to know these things."

"And I'm acceptable to them. I'm even male, like most of their administrators." Gray looked at Dancer. Her lips were moving in a soundless tangle; perhaps every one of Dancer's predecessors was trying to control this single body. "You want me on Testament as a liaison?"

"You're clever, Gray. You have enough data to determine what we want."

In just that way she'd encouraged him to reason for himself when he had lived with her in Bridger Dome, but she hadn't been training him to be a precaster; she simply manipulated him, like pruning a plant or training a rose—or a stunted bonsai. Yet he did as she asked, thinking aloud. "You refused to precast for Penn in order to put pressure on him, to cause him to seek out local help—to seek me out—but Penn won't tell me anything, especially not here on Testament. Off Testament, where he might talk, I couldn't return to tell you what he said. You married me to Dancer so I'd work for Penn, but if you wanted me to leave, why saddle me with a wife?"

She didn't answer. He walked across the room and looked out the sealed window, set at an adult's eye level, high above the floor. The window had been his measuring stick. *When I can see out of that,* he'd used to think, *I'll be a man.* Now he looked, but there was nothing to see. Blowing dust obscured Stone Town. In the only way that mattered on Testament, he still wasn't an adult. Gray shook his head and turned to Reed. Somehow, he was looking at this problem wrong. "Why not tell me what you want from me? These guessing games are pointless."

Dancer stirred on the bed. Abruptly, Gray understood. He had assumed *he* was important, that all this maneuvering was oriented on him. That was a mistake. The significant person on Testament was usually a woman—Dancer. "Mead was right after all," he said slowly. "You do want me off-world, but only because you want me to take Dancer."

"Ah, Gray, what a fine precaster you could make, if you had the memory for it. I've always said that you're my favorite." His grandmother was chuckling to herself.

Barely noticing her, Gray was speaking as the thoughts rushed into his head, seemingly from nowhere: intuitive comprehension, such as precasters used. "Penn is an important man. You knew it. He's already offered to let me take Janet—Dancer—off-world with me, which you maneuvered by this marriage. But what use is a woman who doesn't exist? Except"—he stared at Dancer, seeing her body as a vessel of the future, rather than the past—"she's a woman. She'll have children who remember Testament, if she leaves here without being sterilized. It's like what old Earth did, in reverse."

Reed briefly hugged him, grinning. "In twenty years your children will come home to the only place where they'll be normal, for the same reasons you want so much to leave, and they'll know and remember the information we need. I swear it."

He would leave Testament, but any joy of escape was gone. His departure had been intricately planned, and not for his own benefit. "Twenty years is a long time," he said, equivocating.

She laughed aloud. "Not to us. Not even to them; they live longer individually than we do. Ask Penn his age sometime. And matters may need to ripen in the Harmony."

"Ripen for what?"

She shrugged, smiling. "After a thousand years, Jonism is due for a reformation. There surely are inequities, abuses. Jonism needs a Martin Luther."

Gray walked to the side of the bed and looked down again at Dancer. He'd been married to an alia so they could use Janet Bridger to pass the Harmony exams as a singleton, or at least to seem harmless. He was her caretaker, and presumably aside from that, his only role was to father children, assuming they cared whether her children were his. "No."

He saw the startled movement of Reed's hands. He could do something unexpected, then. They weren't infallible.

"No, *what,* my dear?" Reed asked.

"I won't go along with this." He watched her face, but she was once again impervious to his examination. He remembered Mead: *Don't you hate them?* Had they twisted Mead's life, too? "You made me a singleton."

Reed came close, reached up, and patted his cheek. Touch was practically its own language on Testament. "It was necessary, Gray. So many men who leave Testament are bitter.

The Harmony isn't stupid. You had to seem to be one of them; you needed a reason to go. We needed a man who would answer their specifications, but also ours. We raised your expectations throughout your childhood, then thwarted them, bent you so far you longed to get away. But Gray, you never broke. You kept your pride and your honor; you kept the ability to love. I am very proud of you. If we'd told you, the Harmony tests would have discovered your application wasn't honest. Penn would never have approached you. I ached, though, each time I saw you, for what we've done."

She was waiting for him to be swayed by her praise and sorrow into complying with their plan. "I'm not a fool, grandmother. I won't be your puppet. If—when—I leave Testament, I'll leave free from all your manipulations." He thought of Mead's answer: kill Janet. He couldn't then, and was less likely to now. Testament needed her. It needed him. He didn't want to go into the Harmony alone.

"We aren't puppeteers, Gray. We've never done more than set parameters, define your situation; how you resolve your life has been entirely your choice. You might have accepted life as a singleton on Testament; you might have become a bitter, angry man, even one who slinks out at night to hurt women—we would have been forced to abandon this plan, then. You've become who we need. We are depending upon you. You'll be remembered."

"Fame."

"Don't disparage it. Fame is what the standard humans of the Harmony all crave. We will remember you—and so will your children. You'll raise them, not Dancer."

It was something, more than most men had, but it was far from enough to satisfy his wounded pride. He looked at Dancer and, despite the slackness in her face, he saw Janet. However it had happened, Janet Bridger was real. She, and others like her, had created the slowboat population; now they sprang up occasionally in their descendants, a unique and ultimately horrible form of immortality. But he'd promised, and wouldn't abandon her.

"If you stay on Testament, then it will be alone," she said.

Perhaps there was some hope of outmaneuvering the precasters. It was the first time his grandmother's intuition had not been ahead of his thinking. He wasn't as predictable as they were to each other—but that meant neither was the

Harmony predictable; precasters had to guess. They could be wrong.

"You won't leave Testament if you don't provide a precast for Martin Penn." She smiled confidently, imagining he was trapped.

Gray sat on the bed. Dancer mumbled and turned, rolling into him, brushing against his injured arm as she tried to awaken. Reed was waiting for his answer. "Why are you threatening me?" he said. "Why don't you just *ask* for my help?"

She stared, then bowed her head and sat beside him. "You're right," she said softly. "You deserve better. I'm embarrassed, and no one has done that to me in years. My only excuse is the importance of this. We're depending on you to protect our future. Will you help?"

He took her hand. He was needed. For once, he was sure of Reed's respect. "Yes."

"I do love you, Gray. I wish this didn't trouble you so much. There is no one whose happiness means more to me."

Reed seemed like the grandmother he remembered from his childhood, stern and kind, but those memories were lies, part of a plan; Reed was a precaster, too. "You mean I'm useful."

She grinned, looking more like her usual irrepressible self. "How could I not love you?"

He cleared his throat. "You must have a way to make Janet—you planned her appearance yesterday. What is it?"

"You can't discuss this with her," Reed admonished. "She has tests to take, and besides, always remember that Janet Bridger is not a native of Testament. Probably you should never tell her; I don't particularly like her. You'll find she isn't the most useful of your possible companions once the tests are done."

Gray shuddered, imagining the legions of women contained in Dancer's body; he only cared for Janet. "Grandmother."

"All right. I'll raise her for you, but then you must consider what to tell Penn about arranging the precast. He's shrewd, that one. I like him." She removed a dark blue medical patch from a pocket and handed it to Gray; it smelled like aromatic smoke. "Place it against Dancer's throat. It will awaken her deepest memories," she said. "There are other ways. Hypnosis, if she's sufficiently alert. Aural cues. It will be easier the more she is out. She may eventually integrate with other emulations to become a pseudo-personality."

He didn't want to think or plan; he needed to talk again with Janet and know that the only woman on Testament he fully trusted was alive. He did as his grandmother directed, then leaned back against the wall, waiting.

"Gray," Reed said, "it will be all right."

He didn't answer. She wiped her tears with the back of her wrist and touched his leg. "Come to the dome with Dancer if it isn't safe here."

Mead. Her attack seemed to have occurred weeks earlier. "Okay. But leave me alone with Janet now."

His grandmother bit her lip, looked at Dancer, at Gray, then nodded and left the room. Her footsteps, going down the stairs, sounded heavy and slow.

On the narrow bed, Dancer tossed and turned, muttering as she had when he'd first seen her. "Janet?" he said each time she stirred, attempting to bring her to life. He knelt beside the bed and watched her face. Tics raced across it; her hands trembled unless he held them. Her lips moved. He kissed them, hoping her wandering soul would come home soon.

Chapter 4

I. A Tragedy on Testament

The Gateways House utility insinuated itself inside Martin Penn's dreams, waking him from a heavy sleep. "(Apology)," it gushed in the hyper-conciliatory emotional undertone of a publicly formatted system, while informing him that he had a native visitor, who was being detained in the lobby. It offered supplementary information about the visitor. "No," Penn subvocalized—he was that tired—and the tenuous foreign presence withdrew from the connect in his head, leaving lingering sullen traces in his mind.

Gray Bridger had arrived without calling first; let him wait. Penn sat up in bed, rested his elbows on his raised knees, and held his pounding head in his hands; he groaned. He'd been too tired after Swan's lush frolic to arrange for a wholesome awakening, and it was too late now for anything but drugs. His solitude felt grim; the silence was too empty. Swan's figment women had made Penn crave a real presence, a confident woman who wasn't an artfully designed illustration of Swan's peculiar notions of romance. Each of Swan's scenarios had involved an initial flirtation, followed by the slow manufacture of apprehension in the figment. Though Penn had not participated beyond that point, he had shared sufficient emotion through the connect to feel uncomfortable; he would decline any of Swan's future invitations. Penn's own taste in women was simple, and didn't include fear or violence.

Penn stumbled out of bed and dry-swallowed a loaded aspirin, then kept the room dark as he took a hot shower, inhaling the warm mist as though it could clear his lungs of Testament's dry air. Water poured onto him from all directions; he increased its pressure gradually until the water stung as it struck his flesh, enjoying the carnal pleasure of hygiene more than he had Swan's entertainment. With a muted ping in the recesses of his rambling thoughts, the utility reminded him of his visitor, then gave the time: 10:00 a.m. local, late morning by native standards.

Penn didn't mind keeping Gray Bridger waiting, but the day had to begin sometime. He cut the shower and signaled on the sun-stones, wincing as light battered at his recent aspirin-induced defenses. Through the house utility, he ordered the Gateways lobby guards to send his visitor up, cutting them off before they could begin the false-friendly chatter that infested this isolated outpost's staff and seeped loneliness into Penn's mind. He dressed for traveling outdoors, in warmer clothing than he had worn before, and packed a pocket clearsuit, then inspected himself in the mirror—tired, but all right—and walked into the suite's social room. He stopped abruptly just beyond the door.

A very young and quite attractive woman was sitting stiffly upright in the chair Gray and his companion had used the day before. She was alone. Penn didn't know her, but she met his eyes and smiled as though she knew him. The wide chair gave her a tiny, even childlike, appearance. The effect was enhanced by her large, dark eyes and amber-rose complexion. She looked a bit like Gray's impostor wife, but she was prettier, not so sculpted-looking, and she carried herself with startling self-assurance for one so young. He guessed she was a Bridger.

Simultaneously with accessing the house utility for her identity, since, on Testament, no one was allowed in any Harmony building without proper identification, he asked, "Who are you?"

She stood, first having to slide forward slightly so her feet could reach the floor, and bowed gracefully to just the depth proper between new acquaintances. "My name is Mead. Bridger, of course."

The utility also named her, adding that she was believed to be next in the Bridger main line of descent. Gray's sister, then. There was a smarmy undertone to the offer of additional biographical background, including monitor medical readouts. All connects into the mind evoked emotional responses—that was how the human brain worked, not by objective, abstract intelligence—and this public system had picked up sexual innuendo from the Harmony visitors it had serviced over the years. Penn switched out of the system again, briefly wishing for Center's deft utilities and Jeroen Lee's meticulous, sensitive personal house system. He walked farther into the room, but kept the chairs between the two of them. "Where's Gray?"

She smiled with condescension. "At home, last I saw him, waiting for your call."

Penn studied Mead Bridger. Her spread-legged stance was aggressive, but otherwise her posture was playfully erotic. "He sent you?"

"No. I came hoping to take his place. As a guide, I'm at least his equal; as a companion, I'm far superior. I am a woman, and you are both men."

There was nothing coy about her. *Belle*'s shipboard briefing had said as much. Sex had few moral complications on Testament. Mead Bridger removed her jacket and placed it on the chair. Her blouse revealed the soft, rounded curves of her full breasts to the edge of their areolas; her close-fitting pants emphasized her enticing legs. Her expression established that this was intentional. "Are you proposing sexual intercourse with me?" he asked, purposely stuffy, for the psychological distancing it provided.

She laughed. "I'm suggesting the possibility," she said. Her attention warmed into a leer that managed to remain attractive on her. Her mélange of innocent youth and voluptuous craft was alluring, but had a dangerous, hard edge.

He came around the barrier of the chairs. Closer, he was put off by her musky perfume scent, reminiscent of Swan's concept of glamour. Penn sat down across from her, legs outstretched as his final hedge against her; he kept his expression as impassive as decades of training would allow.

Mead barely hesitated, then she sat down in a single, fluid movement. Gray's companion had been awkward. The more Penn watched this woman the less likeness he found between the two, but Mead Bridger's assurance around an Ahman of the Harmony was troubling. "Perhaps I prefer men," he said.

Her profound, immediate disgust was obvious. "You don't," she said, after a moment's deliberation. "Anyway, Gray doesn't."

Testament had inherited some crossman convictions, or created its own; logical, with relatively few men. "No, I don't, but I need more reason than your generous, unsolicited offer before I discard my arrangement with your brother." She grinned at his sarcasm. "I would have to understand why you want to be my guide."

"Why look a gift horse in the mouth?"

"What? I don't understand." The local proverb grated, reminding him she was a native Altered.

Mead observed Penn with a curious smile. "I've never had an offie. You're not bad-looking. For now, leave it at that."

Pique, that he hadn't eagerly accepted her invitation? Penn shifted position, then recognized, by his restlessness, that Mead made him uncertain. Her look was too intense, her alertness was too bright for comfort. She reminded him of Reed Bridger. "Are you a precaster?"

She flushed and withdrew farther into her chair. "Of course not. They're old women, done with raising children."

The house system pinged for his attention. He let the message enter his consciousness, meanwhile observing her as she scrutinized him. They both smiled. "Your brother just voice-called," Penn said. "He's on his way here."

"Poor Gray. Always a day late and a dollar short."

Penn grasped the gist of the odd aphorism. Mead's native accent was stronger than Gray's. His strong, positive reaction to her, despite the reminders of her native status, made it obvious that this woman was trouble. "He's more accustomed to dealing with Harmony visitors, and your motives are too much a mystery. I decline your imaginative offer." He bowed from the chair.

"But Gray is so mundane. Didn't you come here for mystery?"

Penn fought the feeling of having been exposed. The word "mystery" didn't necessarily have religious implications. "No. Thank you."

"You don't trust me," she said. Her voice was huskier; her look was softer. "But you don't need to." Mead left her chair and came around to where Penn was seated, settling beside his legs, on the floor. Her progress was of exaggerated sultriness, but he watched, unwillingly attracted. Rather than a barrier, his legs became her approach to him. She placed a hand on his left knee, but her attention didn't leave his eyes. "I can read Gray pretty well; he thinks he'll be able to leave Testament—*and* with his wife. Whatever you got from him in exchange for the Harmony exit permits, I can get for you, too. The truth is, I want what Gray wants. To escape Testament." She stroked his thigh. It was brazen and amusing, and, unexpectedly, he began to be aroused.

Penn covered her hand, stopping its motion. "You're no singleton."

"Do you think singletons are the only people who are disillusioned here?"

He heard her pain. Even distrusting Mead Bridger, it was difficult to believe her mixture of frustration and unhappiness was fabricated. "How?" he asked, his tone neutral.

"I can't have children."

He understood, intellectually, that infertility was a tragedy on Testament, but his emotions weren't engaged. "If you leave, you won't have children, either."

She hesitated, glancing down. "There would be a reason, then, and compensations. Look." She removed her hand from under his and used it to indicate herself contemptuously. "I'm already seventeen and never once been pregnant."

"As old as that?" he asked dryly.

She didn't pretend to be amused. "True age isn't a condition of the body on Testament. I have a thirteen-year-old niece who's pregnant, and living in my own house. I don't want to still be here at thirty, and barren. That's what will happen, or else I'll be dead."

Reckless pride was something Martin Penn recognized and with which he sympathized, though he'd personally never felt the desperation necessary to create it. "What about Gray? Your brother? How will he get off Testament if you take his place?"

She shrugged eloquently; she didn't care.

Abruptly, Penn stood. Mead was sprawled at his feet like an alan supplicant; she was just as deceitful. Mead didn't need his help to get off Testament, as Gray Bridger did. If she was infertile or willing to be sterilized, then she qualified to leave. He was more thick-headed that morning than he had realized, not to have seen through her ruse immediately.

Penn stepped over her and went to the window. He had purposely left it naked, as Swan did, superstitiously—he admitted to himself—supposing that a sustained view of the physical world of Testament might help him understand its psyche, but these Altered people were unworthy of such concentrated attention. Swan's fears were those of a fanatic.

The longer Penn stayed on Testament, the less remarkable its people seemed. He entered the Gateways utility and ordered the window replaced by a random screen view of Flute. The house warned that a native was present, but Penn overrode its quarantine inhibitions. Like a curtain dropping, the mountain landscape vanished, replaced by a tasteful scene of the famous White Garden of Lemont, on the grounds of the Academy of Flute, where he'd been trained.

Penn turned around. Mead was sitting upright, still on the floor, a disappointed pet. Her skimpy, close-fitting clothes, available body, and attitude had been ample distraction and some excuse for his obtuseness. "You don't want to leave Testament," Penn said. "You want a cure. Gray probably told you I'm a medic. You assume I could give you children. I won't, and I strongly dislike the dishonesty of your approach."

"You're wrong. I do want to leave." Her tone was flat. "Harmony medicine is no better than ours in at least that one specialty; don't you suppose the human reproductive system is something we know?" Her grin was sickly. "I've tried doctors; they could cure me, but they won't. I admit, I did have some small hope of you, but if I could have children, then I'd be dead. My grandmother doesn't want me to continue the main Bridger line. She even discouraged my mother from having me." Her small hands were clenched at her sides and she wasn't meeting his eyes, but intensity made her statement convincing.

Briefly, Penn responded to her heartache, however odd its origin, then suspicion set in. "I will contact you if I find Gray unsatisfactory," he said in conspicuous dismissal.

Mead rose from the floor like an old woman, using her arms for balance and support, moving slowly. Rather than leaving, she approached him at the window. He considered, but didn't call for a guard. She was only as tall as his chest. Her dark hair shone in the artificial light of the screen; he disliked the exaggerated styling of the row of tight curls encircling the crown of her head, but the overall effect was pleasing. "If you want to leave this world, why come to me rather than proceeding through proper channels?" His voice was low, too intimate for what he had said. He was disappointed there was no excuse to see her again.

She put her two hands lightly against his chest. "Let me be your companion on Testament."

"To what purpose?"

"Sex?"

He almost laughed at her earnestness, and did smile. "You are an unnecessary complication, and you didn't answer. Why did you come to me?"

She finally looked directly up at him; her eyes were truly beautiful. "The truth? Because Gray did. I'm following his trail."

It was in no way a complete answer, or even intelligible, but just then the lobby guards sent word through the house utility that Gray had arrived. Penn instructed them to send him up. "Gray's here now," he said aloud.

"Good." She grinned, then slipped her arms around him. Penn let her hold him, enjoying the embrace.

II. Family Troubles

"What are you doing here?" Gray had assumed he'd have more time before Mead approached Penn, if she ever did, given Reed's rejection.

Mead broke off hugging Martin Penn and smiled critically at Gray. "Aren't you overwhelmed by his clever repartee?" she asked Penn. "What an insightful question!"

Penn's lips moved in an aborted smile. Gray didn't react; he was too dismayed by Mead's presence. Blatantly intimate, Mead stood beside Penn at the window, which had changed into a screen view of black brick buildings and white-flowered garden paths, a gentle, alien opposite of Testament's mountains. Mead held her hand on Penn's arm. Against that backdrop, they seemed to be already off Testament, together, and Gray was left behind. Had she told Penn about Janet's condition, as she had threatened? Janet was taking the psych tests in Exchange even as he wondered. Would Penn stop the tests and send Gray home, permanently barred from the Harmony for fraud?

"You're late," Penn said.

"We didn't set a time." Gray wished he'd been less blunt as Penn frowned, then the offie shrugged, acknowledging the truth. "Sir," Gray added, and he bowed. Penn responded to the bow with an indifferent wave; Gray's shock at Mead's presence had made him delay too long for offie propriety. Gray came farther into the room, and tried not to stare at Mead. Her clothing was designed for titillation; he hadn't known she owned such things. "Where's Learner?" To Penn, he maliciously explained, "Her lover."

"Oh, I don't have to put up with *him* anymore if I won't have children." Mead wiggled closer to Penn. "I can find someone more interesting."

Gray shook his head, she was so obvious, but while Penn doubtless didn't take her flattery too seriously, he still looked pleased. Men. His sisters were right.

"It is true that she's infertile?" Penn asked.

Warily, Gray considered his answer. It was his own fault Mead was here; it had been his idea, though he'd mentioned Penn to her before learning the precasters' plan, and before Mead had attacked Janet. "As far as I know, it's true," he admitted. "That's why she's crazy." He lifted his right arm slightly. The bandage wasn't visible through the jacket except as increased bulkiness, so he carefully removed the jacket. "She did this; she attacked me yesterday with a butcher knife. Be careful of my sister, Ahman Penn. She prides herself on remembering how to kill."

Mead chuckled. "I notice that you're not dead. Martin, I remember death, but I remember a few other things, too."

Penn moved away slightly as she tried to stay close. "Why attack your brother?"

"I didn't. I attacked his wife, and he got in the way." She strolled toward Gray. "Where is your bride, my dear?"

Even Penn must have heard the echo of their grandmother Reed in Mead's parody of affection.

"Safe from you. Hurt her, and I'll kill you, Mead." The threat sounded foolish to Gray, but Mead stood and glanced momentarily at Penn.

"I'm already dead. My body just hasn't stopped yet." Her cold, dark eyes rested on Gray. "But at least I'm not a ghost."

Immediately, Gray looked at Penn to see if he understood the reference to Janet, but apparently Mead was just issuing Gray a warning. Even so, Gray feared what Penn's entanglement with Mead could do. Gray, Janet, and the Compound Council needed Penn's goodwill. He had to discredit Mead and discourage Penn's attachment, or else scare her off. "Not a ghost, just a precaster's daughter," he said, suggesting he could tell Penn the unspoken but likeliest reason she wouldn't bear children on Testament—their mother had al-

ready remembered too much when she became pregnant
with Mead, and therefore Mead might be an illicit precaster.

Mead blanched, then raised her head high. "You don't
know a thing about mother, singleton. You need to learn.
Meanwhile, tell the old lady to get you new quarters, or stay
with your *wifey* inside the dome. I want everyone out of my
house: you, Eris, Diane, and all their brats. I want to be
alone."

It was against Bridger custom to evict a son from his
mother's house, but Gray shrugged. He would be leaving
soon for the Harmony, with Janet. "Fine. Live entirely
alone."

Mead had turned back to Penn. Gray saw her shoulders
tense. "You're going to keep *him* as your guide?" Mead said.

Penn walked past them both and seated himself in the
chair he'd used the last time Gray was there. He observed
first Mead, then Gray. "Yes," he told her.

Relieved, Gray bowed again. Penn ignored him.

"Okay." Mead spoke as if the final decision had been
hers.

Penn seemed to need to explain his decision to Mead.
"Clearly, you have more difficulty than your brother getting
along with your family; I want a precast from them."

"A precast." Mead looked inquiringly at Gray.

Penn frowned. "Have you arranged it yet?"

"Not yet." Gray braced himself for a show of temper from
the offie, but he didn't want Mead to know his grandmother's connivance in arrangements aiding Gray and Janet's departure from Testament. Mead knew how to reason, too.
Penn's explosion didn't happen; smiling slightly, Penn was
watching Mead.

"About your other offer . . ." Penn began.

"Should I come here tonight?" Mead finished for him.

They exchanged a long look, then Penn turned to Gray, as
if Gray had a right to object. Mead's sex life was her exclusive concern, but Gray considered using offie ideas of morality to object. He saw Mead, waiting. She hadn't told Penn
about Janet, apparently intending to use sex, not information, as the price of her cure; Gray was sorry he'd threatened
her. Let her have children. He nodded slightly, acquiescing.

"Tonight. Eight local." Penn was curt.

Mead grinned. She retrieved her jacket, trailing her fingertips across Penn's shoulders as she passed behind his chair,

and sauntered out of the suite, plainly aware of the two of them watching her.

Penn was quiet after she left; Gray didn't know what to say. He sat down and waited with his eyes lowered, straining through the nearly absolute silence of the offie suite for some clue to Penn's attitude, trying to deduce Mead's real relationship with him. They couldn't have been together long, but Penn had invited her back. Gray cleared his throat. "I apologize, Ahman Penn, for any disturbance my sister caused, and for involving you in my family troubles."

"You've lied to me, Gray Bridger. The woman you brought here yesterday is not the wife the precasters assigned you. You substituted a friend of yours, a true singleton, and managed to subvert the local record-keeping system. Your sister suspects it, too." Penn looked at Gray for confirmation.

Carefully, Gray nodded. Penn didn't know Janet was an alia.

Penn sprawled out in the chair, unwinding after the tension of Mead's presence, not showing any concern over what he had wrongly guessed was Gray's deception. "Does Mead really want to leave Testament?"

Gray shifted position in the chair. Mead's motive must be to continue in the Bridger line, but she *had* protected him. "She's never said so to me, but we rarely talk. It's possible."

Penn nodded and stood. Gray quickly rose to his feet, too, trying to look properly humble.

"Why did she want to harm your wife?"

"She *said* it was to help me leave Testament."

Penn studied him. "It was the real wife, then?"

This was too convoluted. Janet and Dancer were both Gray's real wife. "Yes."

Penn tapped his fingers against his side. "Why didn't you let her do it?"

Gray stared. "Let her kill someone?"

Penn nodded, as if satisfied, then asked rather too casually, "Is your sister dangerous enough to kill?"

Gray looked out at the open door, where Mead had vanished in the mist. "She's the most dangerous person I know."

III. Butterfly

"Who are you?" the technician asked Janet. He looked up from a display of letters and numbers floating in the air above his desk and smiled more than politely at her, with real interest. "We don't generally do psychological evaluations on women, and we never do any this quickly."

Who am I? Janet wondered. For the first time on Testament, she was alone, which meant away from Gray. That idea had frightened her. She'd half expected that, like the figment of the imagination Reed said she was, she would dissolve outside Gray's presence. She hadn't. Her continued existence gave her more confidence than she'd had since awakening. *Awakening* was what, privately, she called her surfacing, her . . . whatever. She'd died and now she existed again, as if she'd spent the time in hibernation. Continuity meant reality, despite Reed Bridger's comments. She was a butterfly metamorphosing from an ugly caterpillar; she had emerged from her dark cocoon in a different shape, but she was the same creature, the same woman she had been, only better. "I'm Dancer Bridger," she answered firmly, adding her registration number, as Gray had taught her.

"My name is Ruben," he said. "You don't have to be frightened, Dancer." Ruben was of indeterminate age and indecipherable race, as was everyone she'd met in the Exchange District, including Martin Penn. They all had bland, balanced, deracinated features, with innocuous skintones of pale to dusky brown, as if political correctness had been translated into their genes. The Bridgers also were apparently of mixed race, darker than Janet would have imagined her descendants, with a subtle Asiatic cast, but it didn't disturb her as it would have a millennium earlier; none of it mattered. The universe was different, and that issue, at least, seemed resolved; there were other criteria for discrimination, and as an Altered native, she was from the wrong side of the contemporary tracks. "I'm not frightened," she said, smiling back at him in the way a forty-six-year-old spinster could not, but a flirtatious, nubile woman did naturally.

"These say otherwise." He gestured, passing his hand through the figures. They disappeared momentarily. "Temperature, blood pressure, adrenaline."

She studied the numbers as they reappeared, but they

might as well have been code. "I'll try to relax." Ruben was friendlier than Janet had anticipated after their encounter in the Emigration Office; he smiled often and seemed curious. It was a bad combination for someone with so much about herself to hide.

The entire display vanished. At her startled look, Ruben said, "I prefer it in my head."

"Ah." In case this was everyday technology on Testament, Janet thought it unwise to look impressed. She only smiled wider and leaned closer. Really, it wasn't so exotic; nano-technology had been just around the corner for fifty years, a thousand years earlier.

"It'll also be easier to relax if the display isn't hanging between us." He leaned back in his chair. "I don't usually do this anymore; I supervise. We've recently increased our testing staff because of the number of applications; men are fleeing Testament." He chuckled. Janet smiled politely. "Governor Swan asked me to help Ahman Penn by fitting you in. So, how do you know him? Are you friends with the Ahman?"

If Penn hadn't taken this man into his confidence, perhaps she shouldn't either, but it also might be wise to get Penn's promise to Gray on the record. "My husband is working as his guide, and Ahman Penn has agreed to help us leave Testament. We both want to live where we're normal." *My husband.* That had a thrilling, possessive, and atavistic ring, yet she'd never craved marriage before. After her encounter with Reed Bridger, Janet suspected her reaction to Gray, and felt unworthy that she did. He was her only connection to this time and place. She needed him, though he could probably have abandoned her and made a simpler deal with Penn. He hadn't, and she'd begun to believe he wouldn't. He was solicitous and kind; he'd protected her from his spiteful sister. He believed she was really alive. She was in the bizarre position of suspecting both her emotions and her logic all because of the lies told by the witch of Bridger Dome.

"I remember Gray Bridger," Ruben said, as if providing an opening for her to continue.

Janet only smiled. She recognized when she was being pumped, and she knew that only those not legitimately entitled to the information resorted to such tactics.

Ruben shifted in his chair. "I recommended your husband

as Ahman Penn's guide. I'm glad to hear they're getting along."

Janet nodded brightly. This man was no technician, if he was making personal recommendations to Martin Penn.

Ruben glanced at her with kindly condescension. "Ahman Penn says you're not like the others here, and I'm supposed to verify that. I'm going to ask you a few questions, then we'll just talk. The system is very sensitive; Governor Swan likes thoroughness."

"How does it work?" She was curious about offie technology.

He frowned slightly and ignored her question. Apparently she'd tread on a ticklish issue, something to do with the information quarantine. She cooperated fully as Ruben began a series of routine questions. They weren't intended as tricks—her place of birth, her age—but were traps for her, with two different, equally true answers. She imagined a futuristic polygraph: she didn't believe she was only nineteen, but it was true; she didn't remember growing up anywhere but Earth, before it was "old Earth," but obviously she had. She wondered if the tests would declare that she was lying, and their plan would be found out, but Ruben continued as if nothing untoward was happening. The test didn't conform to the peremptory questions and domineering manner Gray had described, but followed the general procedure he'd prepared her for. Soon it shifted into a facsimile of a conversation, except Ruben asked all the questions. "Don't think too much," Gray had counseled, so she answered honestly and quickly.

Gradually she noticed that the central topic was Martin Penn. Gossip? "I scarcely know him," she said, evading questions. "We met only once."

Ruben asked what had been discussed. Concerned, she didn't answer immediately. Penn had offered his help; to reveal anything that could harm him would also harm them. "He wanted a precast, and asked my husband for help getting one."

Ruben leaned across his desk conspiratorially. "Why do you think an Ahman of the Polite Harmony of Worlds would want a native precast?"

Janet suspected political intrigue; Ruben wasn't a good actor. Though she knew nothing about this era's politics, Penn's expressed interest in a precast seemed anything but

political. "He said he wanted to ask them about God," Janet
answered.

Ruben smiled like a man given a surprise party: startled,
then wholly pleased.

Something was strange; Janet squirmed in the chair. She
needed Gray's advice. "I think that's what he said. I might
have it wrong—we were leaving, almost out the door, when
he mentioned it. What difference does it make?"

"None at all," Ruben stated blandly. "Did he refer to Jon
Hsu?"

Jon Hsu. She remembered: Jonism's founder. "Not that I
recall," she said cautiously. Ruben was too eager. Gray had
said that Jonism, the Harmony's quasi-academic/intellectual
cult of order and knowledge, rejected spirituality. Questions
about God might not be proper, even for an Ahman.

Ruben sat back. He pursed his lips and studied her. "But
surely you discussed the need for faith," he said.

She wouldn't be trapped by leading questions. What little
she knew of Jonism sounded like a scientific, or pseudosci-
entific, blacklash against the transcendence movement of her
own time—angels and crystals and similar stuff—and a kind
of veneration of the Western idea of progress. It was supposed to be purely rational, but Jonism, like any religion
(though Gray said never to call Jonism a religion), must
have dogma. Perhaps political intrigue in the Harmony included changes of heresy. Janet smiled sweetly and shook
her head. "I'm sorry. I don't remember anything like that."

Thereafter, Ruben asked additional, unremarkable questions, but essentially the interview was over. Soon she was
free to leave. He stood and immediately ushered her toward
the door.

"Did I pass?"

"Oh, yes," he said, without looking at her or pausing to
review anything. "I'll enter a report to Ahman Penn that
you're fine, symptomatically a standard human, just as he
thought."

She had more questions, but Ruben didn't give her time to
ask; she'd become irrelevant. She smiled to herself, once she
was alone. She'd done all right, given the great handicap of
her unfamiliarity with the local circumstances. She needed
Gray, but she wasn't a useless dependent, either. Then she
recalled that Ruben had never bowed; was there a slight to
her in that?

Janet walked slowly through the hall. The visual monotony of the Harmony building was disorienting. The windows were all false, and often showed the same view, from an identical perspective, as if she were on a treadmill. The air inside smelled wrong to her, or to Dancer's, bodily perceptions. *There is no Other,* she told herself firmly. She was glad to leave the building; inside, she felt watched.

Since they hadn't known how long he'd be occupied with Penn, Gray had instructed her to go to Bridger Dome when she was finished. She was supposed to take a cab at the bottom of the tramway; he'd given her explicit instructions and money. Inside Exchange there was nothing to buy; there were no stores. Janet was hungry; there would be food available in Bridger Dome, both a "dole" (free to all line members) and several restaurants. There was also a common kitchen, where she could cook for herself, had she been so inclined. Janet wasn't, though food was a comfort in this new, second life. Spices were different, and the natives—as she thought of her weird descendants, disconnecting them from herself—drank a pale sweet-sour tea, but bread was still bread, despite the thousand years. Its aroma kept reminding her of Thanksgiving with Grandma Tillie, but she felt as though she were on an exotic vacation. Gray was her only connection here.

She walked diagonally across Amity Square, looking around. The Exchange District was a peculiar place, an odd juxtaposition of functional, nearly identical windowless buildings, similar to low skyscrapers of mid-sized American cities (although the materials were wrong—no stone or glass, only a dull-finished porcelain substance), arranged around a plaza like a Spanish colonial town; the effect was unwelcoming, like being trapped in an empty box. There were no benches, no sculptures, no trees or other vegetation, just a smooth, bare, burnished earth surface that seemed like exposed footings for the buildings. It was busier than when she'd entered, crisscrossed by pedestrians, who, from their clothing, their ingrained acceptance of the wind, and their glum demeanors, were probably natives in Exchange on business.

"Lost, little girl?" a woman's voice sneered from behind. "Or only losing it?"

Janet spun around. Mead Bridger, hands on her hips, was assessing Janet from about ten feet away.

"Don't disappear yet," Mead said, approaching Janet. "It would be a nuisance to have to drag your body home, unoccupied."

This woman had tried to kill her. Janet continued on toward the tram entrance.

Mead followed, and spoke from behind. "We're going to the same place; I'll make sure you arrive in one piece. It's the least I can do for my brother—look after his wifey."

"I'm going to Bridger Dome, not your house. I don't want any help from you!" Janet glanced around, but there was no one who looked like a policeman, or anyone who might help.

"But you're going to get it." Mead came even closer, staying just behind Janet's left shoulder. Her tone changed. "Look, I'm sorry about yesterday. I have problems, too. I'd like us to be friends."

Janet increased her pace, forcing her formerly indolent body to perform. Mead matched her progress easily. "Janet, I think my grandmother is toying with you. The old bitch."

Janet stopped walking. It was necessary—she was panting—but she also wanted to hear what Mead had to say. "Janet?" Janet asked. "Not 'the alia'?"

Mead grinned. "I can't help teasing Gray."

Her actions went far beyond teasing, but Janet was prepared to listen. They might need an ally against Reed. She smiled, surprised how easily she thought of herself as a unit with Gray.

"I wonder why she married him to someone like you." Mead's voice lingered over the uncomplimentary speculation.

"Chance," Janet said, watching Mead suspiciously. *Never forget,* she cautioned herself. *Don't let down your guard.*

"I don't believe in chance, not with precasters involved."

"Just what is it you want?" Janet asked, confronting Mead.

Mead smiled. "Revenge."

IV. Stained by Centuries

Penn glanced around the Stone Town tunnel city: women dragging children, or hurrying hand in hand through the bustling corridor, chatting, browsing, bargaining, buying, and lugging things away; women clerks standing outside their open-fronted stores, or sometimes seated behind tables piled high with representative samples of their sometimes primitive, always exotic goods. There were men, too. One removed a pile of children's winter buntings from a storefront, another strolled beside a woman. The underground was clean but smelled its age, as if the air had been stained by centuries of life. It had a certain innocence; no menace accrued from the low stone ceiling. "Tell me about the Human Encyclopedia Project," Penn asked Gray, turning from contemplating the noisy marketplace in order to catch Gray in any guilty reaction.

"The Project began thirty years ago, to integrate the new information available to Testament from the Harmony with native knowledge," Gray began, launching into guidebook babble.

Penn interrupted. "What's *your* opinion of it?"

Gray regarded Penn a moment, then shook his head. "It's busywork. No one with sense pays attention to it."

"Governor Swan seems to think it constitutes a threat."

Gray hesitated before answering, and bowed slightly as he did. "Governor Swan is wrong. The Encyclopedia is a waste of time. Human memory doesn't work well enough that any one person can remember everything. The Project keeps men occupied; most of the staff are male. They need high-status jobs. Men are rarely ever precasters, and they're never on the Compound Council. The Project prevents more men from leaving Testament; that's been a problem ever since Harmony contact."

They. Gray identified with Testament's women, though he, too, wanted to leave. "You deduced all that yourself?"

Gray shrugged. "My grandmother told me, once when I considered joining it. They have jobs there I could do."

"Harsh of her."

"Honest."

Gray was convincing, and Penn agreed with his assessment. Swan was a fool, imagining clandestine activity to bring down the Harmony where the only plot was to keep the male minority happy.

Penn had mellowed toward Gray Bridger. The native had proved a good escort through Stone Town; he was knowledgeable, sufficiently intelligent, and competent to answer Penn's questions. Certainly he was a more comfortable companion than an Altered native, and it would have been impossible to visit so much alone; with his sister, Penn suspected he would have seen Stone Town without noticing anything but Mead. He was looking forward to eight o'clock. "What is the ratio of men to women?"

"Men are forty percent of the population," Gray said, a bit too firmly. The obedient guide, he waited for Penn to resume walking, but he glanced meaningfully ahead.

The reports Penn had reviewed on *Belle* said men were only a quarter of the population, and that there was constant male/female tension over the fact that women controlled reproduction. They wanted daughters. "That seems exaggerated, judging from what I've seen today," Penn said.

Gray shrugged.

Penn had found Gray reticent on certain subjects, particularly those relating to gender, but he'd made some telling observations of his own. At the Museum of Testament History, from which they'd just come, the displays had been equally balanced between male and female accomplishments, giving the place an air of lifeless, decorous precision. The Edgemarket customers were mainly women, but most advertising included pictures of men—except for the frequent advertisements relating to pregnancy. A study of human social interactions on Testament, where the gender ratio was skewed, would be interesting. Still, Gray was trying; there was no reason to push the issue.

"Some lines don't bear sons," Gray volunteered. "The Shak, for example. It throws the percentages off. But women need men, so cheater lines like the Shak are outlaws. They kidnap men."

Penn smiled at the lurid and entirely fantastic image of being kidnapped for sex, to be used as a stud. "Are we in danger?"

Quite earnestly, Gray shook his head. "Not here in Edgemarket. Most Shak kidnappings are of men stupid enough to be alone at night on the roads outside Stone Town, but the Shak sometimes capture men who get too close to their dome—the ruined one—especially through their underground. They tunnel like bury mice; being so close, they're a constant problem for Bridger Dome." Then Gray seemed to realize Penn had been joking. He frowned and resumed his formal, textbook manner. "I've never heard that they've bothered an off-worlder."

There was an insult to off-worlders implicit in Gray's

tone, retaliation for Penn's failure to take sexual slavery seriously enough. Penn turned away, to keep from meriting even greater disdain from his guide if he started laughing. His attention was caught by a sign stretched across a store's front window. "When you're ready, be ripe: Pergaid, the fertility supplement," it read, accompanied by the picture of a pregnant woman done in muted pastel shades. "That's the third one I've seen like that," Penn said, indicating the sign. "Are children so important?" He remembered Mead's aura of tragedy.

Gray smiled. "Off-worlders never understand how important. Children are immortality, for a woman." Gray changed the subject. "Did you want to buy a passport to any of the family towns near the city?" he asked. "They're available here, which is easier than traveling to each dome or family center. I can recommend some friendly lines."

"Not today." Penn wondered if the Bridgers qualified as friendly, then warmed at the thought of Mead. He stopped himself from joking about her friendliness; she was Gray's sister. Penn scanned the market. Where they were visible through the signs, curtains, paint, and pictures covering most surfaces, the walls and ceiling were tinged with the patina of their age. Stone Town's underground was the original settlement, one of the earliest on the planet; the theory was that the original settlers had craved the enclosed feel of their ship. The heavy air of the tunnels, the uneven lighting cast by electrical lamps, and the echoing din all took on a deeper meaning. "Do you realize this is one of the most ancient human constructions in the universe? The only world with older human remains is old Earth."

Gray Bridger nodded solemnly, but Penn guessed he was bored. A native never appreciated the special nature of his home. They started walking again, aimlessly as far as Penn could determine. Penn studied the way Gray moved through the crowd, without brushing against anyone or meeting the eyes of those women who glanced at him, his manner polite to the point of diffidence. When Gray spoke with women there was an implicit flirtation, usually initiated by the woman. The cultural mores were different on Testament, but not precisely opposite.

Gray hesitated outside a small, bright, cheerful restaurant with red-painted metal tables and chairs and a spotless white tile floor. There were two groups of Harmony customers already inside, and no natives. "Do you want to stop for tea, Ahman?"

Penn felt an urge to surround himself with natives, although hours earlier he had decided they were unremarkable. The day spent in Stone Town, among their accomplishments, had influenced his opinion. The Harmony made raw worlds into comfortable human homes, but on Testament, it was as if the "First Comers" had been castaways. They'd survived and prospered alone. Harmony worlds were minor variations on the same theme of Jonist order and technology. Stone Town had none of the familiarity of the human worlds Penn had visited before. There was a lure in the unusual. "No," Penn said. "This place is obviously for tourists. Take me where you'd go if you were alone."

"The only difference would be the price and decoration; the tea and cakes here are good."

Lunch at the waterfront—an indigenous shellfish Gray recommended—had been gristle and grease; Penn suspected Gray received a kickback from the owner, since he hadn't eaten much of his food, either. "I'm not hungry enough for another native meal," Penn told Gray. "And the poor lighting is giving me a headache. Take me aboveground."

Gray bowed. The depth was too low for mere confirmation from an inferior. Penn wished Gray would stop trying, except that when he didn't exercise the common courtesy of bowing, that annoyed Penn, too. "When will you arrange a precast?" he asked as, at Gray's lead, they changed direction.

"It may be possible to get one tonight; my grandmother will be in the dome."

Gray's few references to Mead had been unfavorable. Now he offered a precast at the time he knew Penn intended to see her. Apparently he didn't want an "offie" to bed his sister. Penn frowned, to let Gray Bridger know he'd been found out, but felt some sympathy for the young man, who, after all, was probably only trying to protect the Bridger family honor. Then, too, Penn wanted the precast more than he wanted Mead. "How do you know she'll precast for me, when she refused before?"

A woman shopkeeper approached them, offering a violently multicolored, shimmering cloth for purchase. Gray gestured at her, a casual twist of his hand, and she went away. "I told my grandmother you were angry because of her behavior; I said you'd threatened to have Governor Swan hold me in the Fort if she didn't precast for you. She said she would."

"I knew you'd find a way." Penn suspected he'd placed too much significance on the precast because it had been unexpectedly denied. How could these Altered women help Jeroen Lee or direct Penn to a fuller understanding of the ethic beyond Order that he sought? Intuition, not defensible logic, had brought him to Testament. Still, the source of Jon Hsu's philosophy might run clearer on Testament, free of the accretions of eight hundred years of Electors and their interpretative Rulings. There were auspicious signs, if he could convince himself to believe in omens: the script in common use on Testament, visible even on the storefronts they passed, was different from that of the Harmony, more curvilinear; it was the style of Hsu's original manuscripts. The quaint native spelling was the same spelling as the original version of Hsu's *General Principles.* "Weren't most of the pioneers on the generation ship crossmen?" Penn asked.

Gray nodded and led them up the first ramp. "Christians. Yes, most of them were. Also Moslems, whom you call alans, with a mix of other religions."

Penn could see Gray's expression only in profile, but that purged some of the embarrassment and passion from the conversation. It was difficult to speak seriously while walking side by side up a ramp crowded with women and children. Penn felt like a supplicant, hoping his native guide would divulge information that an Ahman of the Academy of Center was not supposed to want. "Have their beliefs survived?"

"I don't know what those beliefs were, so I suppose not," Gray answered reasonably. "Most lines celebrate the weekend family days, and there are line holidays, some of which coincide, like Year-End, Christmas, and Thanksgiving." He paused, then added, "I think some lines still follow old devotions, but they don't talk about it much. The Bridgers don't."

"Take me to a temple."

"Pardon?"

"Temple. A religious building. A church or chapel. I'm interested in archaic forms of religious belief." Penn tried to sound matter-of-fact.

"No one has asked to see anything like that before." Gray looked puzzled.

"Of course not. A good Jonist has no interest in religious superstitions." Penn winced at his own phraseology. "I'm researching Jonism's early years, and this is a perfect opportunity to uncover the belief systems against which Jon Hsu reacted, and to expose the myths and delusions he faced." It was a suitable excuse for both the natives and Governor Swan. "The Bible and the Koran are published here."

"So are *Aesop's Fables*. Bridger Dome sells a lot of copies of all of them."

Penn felt like a proponent of religion, and Gray Bridger was falling back into impudence. "Where do native religious zealots worship?"

"They would do it in their dome or family house, somewhere private. I couldn't take you there."

Sunlight was visible directly ahead. The temperature dropped as they approached the end of the underground city, and the air freshened. Penn squinted. Domes were outlined against the sky, echoing the harsher shape of the mountains beyond.

"Bridger Dome has a chapel," Gray said as they exited the tunnel mouth. "It's near the ossuary, in Bridger Underground. Sometimes they put bodies there first, for visitation."

Penn shivered in the cold. What could be learned in a neglected chapel? Then he remembered the street-corner oracle. *The Bridgers know something,* she had said. The answer was close; he felt it when he allowed himself to feel and not to think. He nodded. "Then take me to Bridger Dome."

Chapter 5

I. A Name on a Distant Wall

God was a fossil, according to Jonist dogma, a superstition superseded by Jon Hsu's principles. Gray couldn't reconcile Penn's status as an Ahman, one of Jonism's elite, with his explicit desire to track God down on Testament; Penn's professed reasons for exploring Testament's beliefs rang false. Jonists were supposed to care only about finding true order in the universe. Reed said Jonism was secular humanism deified. Once inside Bridger Dome, though, Gray felt remote from the Harmony and Penn's beliefs seemed irrelevant, something for precasters to worry about. The expanse of the vast rotunda diminished any single life, and ultimately, every offie was alone. Gray was a singleton, but he had a place here.

"You will stay with me this time," Penn ordered Gray. "And you'll leave when I do."

Gray bowed. Even inside the dome, performing the off-worlder courtesy was prudent; too much was at stake. Janet should have returned from her tests in the Exchange by now; she would be waiting for him. "There are stairways and lifts to the underground levels, where the chapel is located, but I'm not sure what you expect to find in an empty room."

"Isn't there a priest in the chapel? Are there worship services? Guided meditation?"

"No ..." Gray considered; he didn't want to disappoint Penn. "Not in the chapel. The mainline sepulcher is a quiet place. Since all Bridgers measure their lineage from its point of departure from the main line, Bridgers sometimes go there to contemplate their lives." Gray had done so the day he'd explicitly acknowledged himself as a singleton.

Penn nodded. "Ancestor worship is a part of several old religions."

A ball bounced past them. Nearby, a pack of rowdy children were playing Kicks, using two banks of lifts across from each other as the goals. Gray stepped aside for the sprinting girl chasing the ball. He smiled, remembering such games, and being scolded for playing them inside the rotunda.

Penn's attention was on the children, too, but he was frowning. "If Bridger Dome is an ancestor shrine, then your people don't show much respect."

"Most of our ancestors don't deserve respect, doubtless like yours, Martin, if you knew them as well as we know ours," Reed Bridger said. She had come upon them from behind.

Penn bowed. His face didn't show whatever surprise he felt at her arrival. "I understand that you've reconsidered your refusal to precast for me."

"I understand that you've threatened my grandson's freedom," she replied, mocking his rigid tone by repeating it.

Penn glanced at Gray. "Not if you precast."

"Later. I'm not refusing, Martin, so don't take this out on poor Gray, but I'm not ready. Go on about your business for now, my dears."

"That's not good enough," Penn said, offensively arrogant.

"Ahman," Gray reproved him.

Reed crossed her arms and shook her head at Gray. "A precast isn't a faucet, to be turned on and off. It's not fortune-telling, Martin, full of doublespeak hogwash and dire, enigmatic premonitions. There's no trick, and no necromancy, either. No communication with the spirits of our dead ancestors, the way the Edgemarket women do it. Just conversation. Sometimes that's all that happens—not every time I talk is a precast—and sometimes there's more, a drawing in of unconscious insights gathered from my mind and my memory, intuitive responses. A precast is the opposite of a mathematical proof; the reasoning can't usually be traced. It also can't be forced."

"Doublespeak hogwash," Penn said.

Reed grinned. "You've thawed, Martin. I suppose that if the Harmony made precasts, it would find an explanation, some pata-physical, quasi-scientific nonsense about chaos, brain-wave patterns, or random chance, but then, the Harmony would never invent precasts. They're too female."

"Lady Bridger," Penn said, in what sounded to Gray to be the start of a protest.

She laughed. "Just call me Reed, Martin. By the way, have you considered what a fine name you have for a religious reformer? And don't protest that Jonism isn't a religion when we both know that's exactly what it is. A religion without God, unless Jon Hsu is a deity. Yes, perhaps he is. What is more important, the messiah or his philosophy? How much do they depend on each other? Interesting questions."

Penn didn't reply, nor did he deny what she'd said. "Do *you* believe in a God, Reed Bridger?" he asked.

"I can't answer," she said. "We simply don't ask that question here, anymore. Our memories can't capture the experience of death, and whatever faith our mothers started with has faded through the generations, with their memories." She stopped. She glanced up through the Eye on the World, then back at Penn, and sighed. "Our true religion is our children. We worship them, not our ancestors. Or each woman is a creator god, producing new worlds in her own image." Reed walked a few steps away, then returned. Her movements were automatic; Gray had seen it before. Her body worked in rhythm with her mind. She came to rest intimately close to Penn. "What is missing in your grand Harmony that brings you to Testament to ask about God? You're not the first. Something is forgotten, a truth that Jonism ignores, or lost—questions we answer with memory and children."

"Your Alteration makes your beliefs different from those of standard humans?" Penn asked. He glanced into the dome rotunda, at the gathered Bridgers, with distaste.

Reed Bridger touched Penn's cheek, as she often had touched Gray's, with affection; she was focused only on Penn. He smiled slightly and bowed to her in some silent, shared communication. Gray was a forgotten observer beside them; he kept still. "No, my dear," Reed said. "Our Alteration only lets us postpone the final question."

" 'The final question.' Is there one?" Penn held out his hand. "I want a precast," he said gently. "Please."

Reed had already drifted into one, despite her earlier objection, and Penn didn't recognize it. "Ahman," Gray said softly. "She's telling you deep truth, as she understands it. That's how a precast starts."

Reed looked startled, then she nodded. "Martin and I need time together, and I think he'd rather be alone."

"Yes." Penn hissed the word, drawing a long breath as he spoke it. "Leave us alone, Gray." He bowed at Reed, and offered his arm to her. She placed her hand on it like a queen favoring her courtier, then she led him to a bank of lifts. Gray watched until they were out of sight on the tenth floor, and wondered what his grandmother would say or Penn would ask that he was not allowed to hear.

The children's game had brought them close again. The ball bounced out of bounds directly at Gray. He caught it by reflex, then scanned the children, searching for the proper one to whom to return it. There was a lone boy, about nine or ten, with big, dark eyes and an awkward, diffident manner. He was smaller than most of the girls, and stood on the edge of their group. Gray threw the ball to him. The boy missed, provoking catcalls from the girls. Gray walked quickly to the lifts.

He went to the highest gallery, where the floor space allowed just one room, clinging to the dome wall, and entered the only door for a hundred feet. No one was inside. The thick, whitewashed walls kept out sound from the rotunda. On this level there were no windows; electric light came from uncovered, frosted, hand-blown glass bulbs set high up into the walls. They were odd, twisted shapes which sent peculiar shadows where there would otherwise have been darkness. The furniture consisted exclusively of several rows of wooden benches which had been reverently made of onetime trees from the Earth garden below, an alien material in a quintessentially native room. On two walls were small engraved gold plaques, regularly spaced, with just one break near the bottom of the second wall; each plaque bore a single name. This was the Bridger main line sepulcher.

Small stones of various shapes and colors had been left at the bottom of each row of names, and a pile of additional stones had been swept into the room's corners. Gray felt in his pockets, but had neglected to bring anything. He went to the first plaque. JANET BRIDGER was inscribed on it in simple block letters. He traced them with his index finger and whispered the name. After scanning all the names of his mothers, he sat on the bench closest to the final plaque. It bore the name "Margaret Bridger." A space above, and an emptiness below, each waited for the succession to continue.

The bench was hard; the room was too warm. He wasn't sure why he was there. This place made him lonely.

The door opened. "Gray?" Janet said.

He smiled and turned to see her. She was framed by the much brighter light coming through the open door, making her body into a shadow, a dark angel. "You're back."

Janet nodded, looked backward into the gallery outside the door she was holding open, then came inside. The door shut slowly and solidly, finishing with a muted thump. She came to him around the benches on the side of the room away from the plaques. "What is this place?"

"The tomb for the Bridger main line." He had to force himself not to whisper.

Janet walked to the wall in front of him and read several names aloud. Her voice grated on his nerves as she mispronounced a name, and failed to use the conventional singsong style of a formal recitation. "Are their bodies actually here?" Delicately, as if some trick mechanism might expose a cadaver if she made greater contact, her fingers grazed the surface of the wall below a plaque. She was an outsider.

"Most, since the First Comers. Every Bridger can be interred in the dome, or in the catacombs underground."

"This place must be all bones." She went to the first plaque and looked up at it, but didn't read her name aloud.

"I won't be here," he said.

She returned to him. "Where do they put men?"

He shook his head. "I meant, I'll be a name on a distant wall from Bridger Dome, out in the Harmony." Unless, being Jonist and too rational for memorials to the dead, the offies tossed corpses out, like garbage. Gray sighed. Why, when he was so close to leaving Testament, had he come to the saddest, most sentimental place in Bridger Dome, the one where death was recognized as final? "Ahman Penn is getting his precast," he told Janet. "If your tests are all right, then tomorrow we'll buy tickets off-world. How did the testing go?"

"The man said I passed."

"Did he give you anything to show it?"

"No. Should he have?"

Gray stood and stretched. "It doesn't matter as long as Penn is on our side. My grandmother was at her best. The precast should satisfy him."

"I'd like to have seen it." Janet sounded wistful. "I'd like to know more about myself." She was looking at the plaque bearing her name.

Gray saw the dark mood developing; he hugged her. She clung to him, burying her face against his chest. Their bodies slid together naturally, like parts machined to fit. Her tension was palpable along the length of his body. There had been other women, ones he'd liked and even some he'd trusted—he thought of Melany Kane's easy acceptance of his occasional lapses in knowledge during their outland ventures—but his pride had created limits. He would not love anyone to whom he was inadequate; he would not accept the pitying affection a woman of Testament might feel for him. Janet was a woman who considered his defect to be natural, who would bear his children without fearing the results, whom he could love without wondering if she was ashamed of him. He needed her, for that; Testament needed her children, too.

"Sometimes," she said, "this world feels as unreal to me as I must seem to you."

"You're no less real than anyone."

"I've had waking dreams. I see things superimposed, different and the same, without knowing which vision is mine."

He clasped her more tightly. An emulation shouldn't reminisce.

"Mead says that's normal on Testament."

He pushed her gently back and held her at arm's length. "Mead? Did she hurt you?"

"No, she only frightened me at first. We came back together from the Exchange District. She bought me lunch in Edgemarket." Janet grimaced. "I don't entirely trust her, but she says she wants revenge against your grandmother, and I can understand that. She's outside; she wants to talk to you. To apologize, I think."

Janet had no memory of Mead's attack. "I have nothing to say to her." Gray released Janet. The door was solid. The walls were thick. Mead couldn't overhear them. "Janet, she's trying to charm you, like an icesnake charms a bury mouse before killing it. She can seduce anyone; that's Mead's special talent, but she only does it for a reason. Beware of her."

Janet put her hands on her hips. "I'm not a mouse. In the Exchange District, alone, I did just fine. I just think Mead's worth talking to."

"I know her. She can't be trusted." Gray was grim, wondering at the reason for Mead's latest twist. To be a link on the Bridger main line chain, to be remembered, and to pass down her mothers' memories had been vital to Mead's happiness. With the loss of that, she would be angry at everyone, most of all at Reed. That Janet was part of one of Reed's plans was dangerous, and yet he couldn't just discard Mead. She'd been hurt. Her long memory didn't prevent loneliness. Memories weren't friends.

"Give her a chance," Janet said. "It's only talking."

And Janet claimed she hadn't been charmed; but Gray nodded. He cared about Mead, and it was conceivable she wanted to make amends. "All right. Tell her to come in."

He sat facing the door. Janet opened it and called Mead's name, then held it open with one hand until Mead came inside.

Mead had changed from the provocative clothes of the morning into a green wool skirt and black silk jacket similar in style to those worn by offies. It was closely tailored to her figure, but without exposed flesh. If anything, she was more desirable than before because she was less obvious. He supposed she had dressed for Penn.

Mead didn't look at Gray. To Janet, she said, "Thank you. Thank you very much. But could you leave us alone together?"

Janet looked anxiously at Gray. "Why?"

Mead touched Janet's hand. "Please? It's family. Brother and sister. I need to explain myself to him."

"All right," Janet said. She left the room reluctantly, but she left.

Mead walked to the back of the room, tracing an invisible line among the plaques with her index finger as she approached Gray. She stopped once. "Elene," she said. "Remember Elene?"

"I thought I was getting an apology."

Mead smiled pleasantly at him. "Who said that?"

Gray lifted his legs to the correct side of the bench for watching Mead.

"The better to fight me, brother dear?" Before he replied, she crouched down near the nameplate for Margaret Bridger, their mother. Mead put her open hand on the blank place above Margaret's plaque. "I wish the old bitch was dead."

"You wanted to talk to me," Gray said. "So talk."

Mead lowered her hand to the empty place below Margaret's. She traced imaginary letters on the wall, spelling out her name, then shook her head. "Irene's a cow. I can't believe they'll let her carry the line. Even you would be better, if you weren't a man; at least you have some spirit under that virtuous veneer." She stood, leaning back casually against the wall. "You know, I can never hate you, however much I try. I remember mother, and the tug of her memory is recent and hard. Besides, there's that delicious disappointment written all over you. You struggle to be good, hoping that will get you what you want. It never has, and finally, you're leaving. Why should I be angry when you're doing what I want? Maybe I'll even miss you."

Gray raised an eyebrow skeptically. She had made conciliatory gestures before; he couldn't depend on her sincerity.

"You're supposed to say you'll miss me, too," she said.

He clasped his hands around his right knee and leaned back, to ease his tension.

"Ah. He doesn't speak. He knows he doesn't lie as well as I can." Mead laughed shortly. "Well. But I usually don't lie. I prefer the truth—unlike our grandmother. So, I've spoken with your little woman, and I know about your arrangement with Martin Penn. Don't be angry with her—I knew what I was fishing for, which made it easier to catch, particularly in such a tiny pond. I'm glad for you. You've fooled the chief bitch into letting you go. Since she wants you here, I'll help you get away." Mead fumbled in a pocket. "Once she knows you have tickets for the Harmony, your dear grandmother will cut you off from the drugs that help create your better half—or whatever fraction Janet Bridger is. So. A wedding present." She extended a box containing a handful of pale blue medical patches.

Gray didn't take them. "What are they?"

She laughed. "Don't you trust me, brother? I talk, but I've never really tried to hurt you; the other day was an accident. We Bridger women like our men. These patches awaken deep memories. This particular enzyme-protein mix activates the synaptic receptors in such a way that—at least in Bridgers—certain levels of organization are restimulated. The more often that same structure of related memories is used, the easier the receptors become to excite; a patch is the best way to begin the process. Look, it's too complex to explain to someone who doesn't have the background, but it works. You've seen the result in her."

Gray's suspicions eased; her explanation fit the framework of what Reed had, more briefly, described. "The other patches were a darker blue," he said.

"You're worried about the color on the plastic strip I chose? Don't take them, then." She withdrew the box.

"You don't believe that I fooled grandmother, Mead," he said. "Really, why would you help us?"

Mead sat down close beside him on the bench, closer than he liked. "You're not too stupid, Gray."

"I don't need you interfering with my life."

"I want revenge. Reed plans to spread the Bridger line out into the Harmony through your alia, doesn't she?" She smiled when Gray didn't answer and patted his hand. "I know she does. But if your alia stays Janet Bridger, a singleton, then it's likely that her descendants won't remember much of Testament. At best, there'll be a new line of *Harmony* Altereds. So I want what you want—more Janet. Unless you have an urge to cart a real alia around the Harmony? I bet Reed tries to discourage you from keeping Janet alert too much."

Reed had done exactly that. "The plan is important, Mead. It's not for grandmother, but for Testament." What about Janet, though, if Mead was right? Should he erase her to help Testament?

"You know that Reed killed our mother."

Gray came up off the bench. "The Shak killed her!"

Mead shrugged. "They pulled the trigger. But Reed had just become chief precaster. She could have prevented the attack if she'd tried."

"You can't look at life that way, Mead. If you hate anyone, hate the Shak." He sat down again, troubled. After their mother's death, he'd lived with Reed, a substitute mother, while Mead had been left home with their sisters, who'd had their own children to care for. No wonder Mead resented him.

"You're a man. How can you be loyal to them?" Mead slapped her hand against the wooden bench between them. "Do you want Janet Bridger or an alia shell? You decide— you don't have to take these patches." Yet she extended them once again, grinning. "Here's the way to your heart's desire."

Gray sniffed. The smoky scent was stronger than that of the patches his grandmother had given him. He didn't know what, if anything, that meant. He took them from the box; the patches felt oily. After putting them into his jacket pocket, he wiped his fingers on his sleeve. The slight pressure hurt; it was the arm Mead had slashed. He looked up. She smiled at him with deliberate exaggeration.

"I wish I could trust you," he said. "I hope you're telling me the truth. Remember, Mead, whatever plan you're making only works because I do have some faith in you." He expected her to laugh at him.

She didn't. Her false smile faded. "I know that." She went to the door, then came back and stood in front of him. He looked up and she kissed his forehead. "Be careful if you leave the dome tonight," she said. "The Shak have been sniffing around, eyeing the plaza. Virginia says they've got cousins in from Big Red, looking for men." As though embarrassed by her concern, she immediately hurried back to the door. She held it open a moment more before leaving. "Good luck, Gray. You're not so bad, except that you let them use you."

II. A Bedtime Story

He'd been too open. Like the bitter aftertaste of an otherwise savory meal, Martin Penn regretted the freedom with which he'd spoken during the precast. The knowledge that the Harmony would have no record of what he'd said, and that Reed was long past bearing children to remember it, had eased his inhibitions. Stupid. The woman could talk.

Guilt threatened to dull his intense satisfaction. He refused to let that happen. What had he said, after all, that was dangerous? They'd merely discussed Jonism, past and present. Reed had spoken heresy, were she a Jonist, when she said that Jon Hsu had been reacting not against religion, but against superstition, and baldly stated that the two were not the same. Privately, Penn had considered that himself, but her precast gave the concept almost the authority of an Elector's Ruling in his mind. At their best, religions sensed a higher principle than Order, a basis for morality, and even science; they weren't just the confusion of rites and rules that Jonism properly abhorred. *The Bridgers know some-*

thing. When Reed precast change for the Harmony, a new age, there had been a resonance inside his heart.

The precast had been inspiring. He couldn't say it was informative, because so much that Reed had said was a matter of insight, not knowledge, but the word "interesting" was too rigid and restricted. It had been a heady experience, to speak his secret thoughts aloud. He had been thrilled, had literally felt a chill down his spine, when Reed said—proclaimed, really—*There is an answer for you*—though she hadn't given it herself.

Penn was dazzled, and when he reentered Bridger Dome's rotunda from Reed's private study, he felt stunned. The clamor of voices and movement, the vivid colors, confused him after the close introspection and abstract glimpse of future history that had been his precast.

Bridger Dome seemed busier. Noise rose up from the main floor like steam from a boiling pot, up and out the dome's center hole. Penn clung to the railing and looked up. The Eye on the World was the telescope of an avid astronomer, watching the Harmony. Old Earth astronomers had used mirrors, and Reed had said precasters used memories as mirrors, enhancing their view of the world. From Penn's angle, only a sliver of dusky sky could be seen, but a single star was visible. It may have been Reed's offhand reference to the pleasures of children and family, but a nursery rhyme about the first star in the sky came into his head. His mother had used to say it; he hadn't remembered it in years. "I wish for an answer," he whispered.

At least Penn had been cognizant of the most basic quarantine restrictions and had not mentioned Elector Lee. *You have a friend,* Reed said early in the precast. *A friend in difficulty.* He'd stayed motionless and had avoided that topic.

"Sir?" Gray Bridger said. He came to the railing and bowed. Penn hadn't noticed his arrival. "Shall I escort you back to the Exchange?"

Gray was an intrusion, demanding time and attention, but after his prior difficulty, Penn wasn't inclined to return to the Exchange District alone. "Yes," he said curtly, and didn't acknowledge Gray's bow.

Penn followed Gray compliantly through the dome; he wanted to think about the precast, not where to go. Reed had implied—or had he only imagined it?—that the answers he sought were not incompatible with a broader Jonism. What, precisely, had Jon Hsu written in the *General Principles*? Something to the effect that convictions that left no room for discussion were superstition. Jonists were supposed to disdain all certainties, so how was it that orthodox Jonism—the product of the Electors—denied all validity to the belief in higher levels of Order than they were able to investigate directly, and dismissed such concepts as superstitious mysticism? Jon Hsu explicitly acknowledged there was gain from divergent viewpoints. What could precasters sense or know?

"Was the precast satisfactory?" Gray asked.

"Yes." Penn regretted not having a recording of the precast, so that he could review each aspect separately, rather than the gestalt.

"Then I've done what you asked."

Penn glared at Gray. "Yes. Quiet, and take me home."

Gray nodded, seeming finally to understand Penn's need to focus his thoughts. Outside, the wind-spiked cold forced Penn further into unwilling awareness of his surroundings. How much of the precast would be lost? Darkness had fallen, though the red, west horizon still glowed like embers from a fire, too low to radiate much heat or significant light. Gray procured transportation, and Penn couldn't avoid noticing the yellow sign and line of coaches he'd missed before. Gray sat quietly beside Penn during the ride to the Exchange District. "Should I come tomorrow morning?" Gray asked softly when their coach stopped at the rear vehicular loading entrance.

"Yes." Penn glanced around. Although outdoors, the area's environment was modified to conform to the standard inside the Harmony buildings. The warmth and relief from dryness were pleasant, but he would have to cross outside to reach the Gateways House. Inconvenient design. Penn left the native coach, neglecting to bow to Gray, or even to close the coach door.

Gray leaned out. "Is there anything in particular you want to do tomorrow, Ahman Penn?"

As a native, Gray probably had some experience with precasts, but Penn rejected the idea of discussing his with anyone. "No, nothing particular. Come at ten." Penn started to walk away.

"Ahman Penn."

Gray had left the coach and followed him. Penn turned.

"About Mead," Gray said, then apparently Penn's expression made him stop.

"What?"

"Should I tell her not to come tonight?"

Solitude was tempting, but thoughts of Mead were even better. "No." Penn walked away, shivering in the wind, and taking long, quick steps that were almost running, as if the cold chased him. Gray Bridger called a goodbye, which Penn ignored. The passage should have been underground, he thought, the way natives built their city. A guard at Gateways House opened the door manually for him. Penn hurried inside without thanking the man. Guards were unnecessary. Swan had made the Harmony's presence on Testament into a garrison, a vain reflection of Swan's attitude toward Altereds. What did the Harmony have to fear from women with long memories? Swan was a fool, intent on contriving a threat where there was none, except the possibility of reaching a new, unorthodox understanding of Jonism.

Upstairs in his suite, Penn went directly to the bed. It was the most comfortable place to think. Fully dressed, he lay atop the covers, staring straight up at the ceiling, and tried to remember the exact thought sequence of the precast. Their ideas had flowed and crossed and been overlooked, only to recur, a disorganized rough-and-tumble he wanted to separate and order into his own meaning. He set an alarm for a short while before Mead's arrival and got to work, but without using the Gateways utility. The only true privacy was a restricted mind.

Penn finished when the alarm pinged inside his head. He continued to lie quietly, luxuriating in languor until the last reasonable moment, then washed, changed to indoor, casual clothing, and went into the social room to wait.

She was late. It was clever of her, he thought, even as he became increasingly bored and irritated. He called up the psych test results from Gray Bridger's wife. She'd lied about who she was, as he had expected. Penn felt guilty helping Gray behind Reed's back, but it was unreasonable for his grandmother to keep Gray on Testament, where he obviously didn't belong. When the guards finally announced Mead's arrival, twenty minutes late, annoyance nearly caused him to refuse her admittance, and vanity made him turn on an entertainment. She arrived as he feebly pretended to be engrossed in a cyclone fiction of the worst type. He assumed a rapt gaze as a weeping woman clung to her lover and begged him not to leave—and that was only the opening scene.

Mead came around behind him, watching the cyclone without disturbing his attention on it. He felt the pressure as she leaned forward, against the back of his chair. She placed her hands on his shoulders; her hands were cold. Her breathing was audible, like that of someone who had run far and fast, but if she had an excuse for her tardiness, she didn't make it. He wanted to see her, partly for the danger he felt at having her out of sight, but also, she was beautiful.

"There is no science of storytelling," Mead finally said. "Or if there is, it's all familiarity; this is dull."

He glanced coolly at her, then returned his apparent attention to the fantasy, wondering why he was posturing. What fantasy was that?

"Everyone prefers variations of the stories they remember from childhood. For example, my brother likes 'Sleeping Beauty.' Do you know it?"

It was pointless to be drawn into inane chitchat, but staring at lackluster melodrama was equally pointless. The woman in the story raised her voice, sounding shrill and desperate. Penn paused the drama. It froze into a tableau of counterfeit emotion.

Mead pinched his shoulder. Penn was surprised, not hurt. "Shall I tell you the story of the sleeping beauty?" she asked.

He reached up and grabbed her wrists, twisting around to face her. She was voluptuous, but her wrists were thin. Her pulse was under his thumb, beating quickly. She was excited. Her cheeks were ruddy from the cold outdoors; her hair was windblown so attractively it seemed artful. "Tell me the story of Mead Bridger," he said.

She seemed surprised, then she grinned. "You actually care a bit about us now, don't you? I'll mention to my grandmother what an impression her precast made; I'll have to thank her for it. For your own sake, Martin, you should keep in mind that any cliché can seem profound the first time that you hear it. When it comes to religion, a Jonist Ahman is an innocent."

Did every Bridger on Testament know about his precast? Penn released her. Immediately, she walked around the chair and sat down on his lap. "Just think what the old crone could have done if, besides her other tricks, she had my body, too."

"Is your body a trick?"

She was light as a child on his lap, but her breasts were just above the level of his chin. If he looked at her at all, he seemed to look at them. She leaned close and whispered in his ear. "They all are. Didn't you know?"

The thick musk scent she'd worn that morning was gone, along with the titillating outfit. Her fragrance was that of a grown woman, a hint of sweat and pheromones, natural and entirely appealing. The conservative green suit was flattering. It made him want to take it off.

"So, you're curious about Mead Bridger," she said. "Well, Mead died somewhere between the ages of twelve and seventeen; that's the only thing that ever happened to her worth noting. Footnoting."

His hands lifted, then he placed them awkwardly back on the chair arms. Her perch on his lap felt precarious, but he didn't want to hold her without an invitation, and didn't want to move his legs to bring her closer against his body because, for all her provocations, there was innocence to Mead's flirtation, and true sadness that registered in the subtleties of her voice as she melodramatically counted herself among the dead. "And who took her place?" Penn asked in the same tartly playful tone she had used.

"A vampire. Every day the undead suck life out of the living here on Testament." She wiggled her bottom closer to his crotch.

Though it was discouraged by and in the Academies, Penn knew some folklore, from his mother's long-ago stories. "So you want to leave Testament to break the spell?"

"It's too late for that. I've changed my mind. I'll stay here after all, and retaliate. I'll make them pay for what they've done."

Mercurial, he thought, not taking her statement seriously. Mead's brittle brightness was reminiscent of Reed Bridger—how could it not be?—but she was skittish, where Reed was calm; she was cynical, where Reed was pragmatic; she was sensual, where Reed was affectionate; but most of all, Mead was vulnerable and Reed was not. Mead didn't trust him, or anyone, and that was the mark of a person who had truly been hurt. His own habitual reserve, a product of too long an involvement in the intrigues at Center, didn't waver, but his sympathies were aroused by her. Or perhaps, he thought, that was exculpatory justification for the other arousal she stimulated. He slipped his arms around her waist, but his touch was light. "Is that so?" he asked, as if her declaration was pure banter. "So you won't need my help after all?"

She snuggled closer. He guessed she was pleased so far by their flirtation, though it had been rather juvenile, and appealing for that reason. On Center, women were jaded, greedy, selfish, or unreflective; or as a respite from those superficial dalliances, there were probe girls, who had no real choice in the matter and with whom it was unwise to become attached. On Center it was no sacrifice to keep sex a matter of routine bodily maintenance, and that is what Penn had done. Marriage and even formal partnerships were discouraged in the Academies, anyway. Still, whatever memories she had, Mead was the youngest woman he had considered taking to his bed. Seventeen. Was he cradle-robbing? Inside the Harmony she would be counted a child, but in sixty years, without help from Harmony medicine, Mead would be as aged as Reed Bridger, nearing the end of her life, while he would not yet be considered old.

"I still need you," she said. "Shall I tell you how I'm going to fight them?" She was more absorbed by revenge for her supposed tragedy of infertility than by his seduction. "By telling everyone the truth." She grinned at her cleverness.

He sighed, reminded of the precast. "Truth is a slippery concept, Mead Bridger."

"You're feeling neglected. Poor Martin." She rested her weight against his chest and touched his cheek with her fingertips, making wide, slow, gentle curves on his face and neck. Her choice of an indirect, modest opening was a promise of a long, hedonistic night to come. "But I like slippery things," she whispered. Her full breasts pressed against his chest. As she kissed the ear into which she'd whispered, her other hand stroked his inner thighs, rubbing his genitals, when she encountered them, through the cloth of his pants. She settled into a leisurely exploration of his clothed body. From memory or life, every touch of her hands or tongue or lips was proficient. When he broke his initial passivity, he felt her smile as her lips pressed against his neck. Her body moved to encourage him.

Sex was no more a test of honesty between two people

than any other interaction, but qualities beyond her skill were apparent. In this, Mead was affectionate and generous; she was very easy to please and responded eagerly to every caress. He guessed at, or hoped for, an inner tenderness. He drew back slightly to see her better, and they looked at one another from a distance of inches. Her skin was without blemish, and had the perfect texture of a child's. So close, her eyes were startlingly beautiful and deep, without any glassy soullessness. Her physical loveliness made Penn uncharacteristically shy about what she saw in his face. He kissed her, in part to remove himself from her vision.

Her response was less passionate than he had expected. Only as he prolonged the kiss did she become genuinely involved. When he stopped, she waited, expecting another kiss, but not reaching for it. "How experienced are you?" he asked.

"Margaret was like a rabbit." Mead was snide about her own mother. "She'd do it with anyone, anytime. Reed, now, was more selective, and also more imaginative, as you might have guessed. And Tillie—she was . . ."

"I asked about you," he interrupted. "You, personally."

She lowered her eyes. "Three men," she said.

She wasn't backward, except, perhaps, by Testament's exaggerated sexual standards. Penn discounted the experiences she had in memory. Those were no more important than watching vids.

"The first was fun," she said. "But nothing happened, not even a miscarriage. I was careful choosing the second; he'd fathered six children. And the third was just work. I've gotten rid of him. Now I can have fun again." She initiated another kiss, a demanding one that asked to be responded to roughly. Instead, Penn softened the kiss, made it romantic, stroking her face, enjoying the smoothness of her skin. Her arms went around him, holding on. He wanted to touch flesh, but clothing covered her. He broke off the kiss and moved out of her embrace. "There's a more comfortable room, if you'd like?"

She nodded, her eyes very wide, and reached out a hand to him, then suddenly drew back and smiled more like her usual self. "I did come here for sex," she said.

Her reversion to the older-seeming, knowing Mead was a gratifying proof of the honesty of her prior responses; oddly, it also seemed childlike. He stood, bringing her to her feet along with him, then took her hand and led her to the bedroom he had been using. It occurred to him that Swan could monitor this, too, but there were rules, if Swan followed them inside his little stronghold.

Mead stripped quickly. He was disappointed she didn't make it part of the game of sensuality. He instructed the utility to provide a light meal, for later, and to close up the suite for the night. She came to him, naked and lovely, and began undressing him, or trying; she had difficulty with the closures of his shirt, pulling too hard and in the wrong direction. He smiled, feeling superior to his beautiful barbarian, took her hand away, and held it while opening the shirt himself with his other hand.

"Afterward, I'll tell you a bedtime story," she whispered. "Full of witches and princes and plans."

He dropped her hand.

"Martin?"

Of course she had a reason for coming—they didn't know each other—but he refused to feel he was paying for sex. "Tell me what you came here to say, then stay or leave; whatever you want."

"You're a funny man," she said. Her confused expression became a frown. "You don't want me?"

Penn couldn't imagine how she could wonder if she was desirable. "You mistake my point," he said. "*You* don't want *me,* you want my time and the favor of listening. I'm listening." He sat on the side of the bed, closed his shirt, and didn't look at her, the better to ignore her nudity.

"Actually," she said, "I do want you, but I admit I had other reasons for coming here tonight." She hesitated, but he didn't respond. "Martin, I don't want to hurt your feelings."

He looked up. Her expression was composed. She spoke with an adult's confidence, reminding him that Mead was more than she seemed. She was seventeen, but an Altered seventeen, with the surety that came from experiences which, if not precisely her own, still added knowledge to her life. "I'll listen with an open mind," he said.

She crossed her arms against her chest, covering her breasts, and turned away from a full frontal position. "You don't know the truth about Gray's wife."

Penn shook his head, relieved her revelation wasn't worse, or anything he hadn't already guessed. "I know the woman I've met isn't Dancer Bridger. I agreed to help them both leave Testament knowing that, and I won't change my mind."

"You don't know. The woman you've seen *is* Dancer Bridger, but Dancer Bridger isn't normal by any standards, including Testament's. She's what we call an alia, a person with a distinct mental defect." Mead glanced sideways, at nothing in particular, then looked back at Penn. "Only someone like my brother could care about an alia, and it seems he does. It isn't his fault, really."

She was utterly serious. "An alia?" Penn prompted.

"It's a name from an old Earth fiction. The hero's sister, Alia, is born remembering the lives of her female forebears. That is the perfect definition of alia syndrome—a body born with all the memories of its lineage active in its brain, without a childhood to become a person first. An alia *isn't* a person. The woman you met is an emulation, a stabilized memory rebirth—a kind of flashback—of Janet Bridger, the founder of the Bridger line, ten centuries ago on Earth."

Gray had called her Janet. Penn tried to reconcile the image of the attractive young woman Gray said was his wife with Mead's disclosure, and couldn't. "She seemed real enough. She passed our tests, showing she has a standard human psyche."

"Janet Bridger *does*. She's the line founder—a singleton, like you or Gray. The only one in the Bridger main line. Gray must have been overjoyed when she appeared, the perfect answer to his needs. He doesn't have a skeptical nature, like me. There's no such thing as chance when precasters are involved. I'm certain they made sure Dancer would emulate Janet Bridger. Why marry Gray to an alia, otherwise? We know the Harmony's rules well enough. *Any* marriage would have prevented him from leaving, and Gray's not ugly or bad-tempered. He's a singleton, but that's not usually inherited, and he *is* Bridger main line, after all. Lots of women would have agreed to help Bridger Dome and the Compound Council."

"You're saying it's a plan of the Compound Council precasters?"

She nodded. "Definitely. To get Dancer off Testament."

"Why such an elaborate plan to get one woman off-world?"

She shrugged. Her breasts rose and fell. "It's the way they think. Life here is children. I can't have life."

He thought back to the precast. *Our true religion is our children. We worship them,* Reed Bridger had said. He himself had proposed that Gray's wife needn't be sterilized. "They want to spread their Alteration into the Harmony?" His voice rose with disgust he should have hidden; Mead was Altered, too.

She studied him with sour satisfaction. "Yes. It's exactly the type of plan these women would produce. Their idea of taking action is spawning more of themselves."

Pain at her infertility was clear in her forlorn expression. She blamed the precasters and was angry, but she was also ashamed. However much she'd turned against her grandmother and her home, her decision wasn't freely made, it had been forced by her circumstances. Mead believed herself to be a failure. He reached out to her. She dropped her crossed arms and let him take her hands. They were tiny inside his. "They've hurt you very much," he said. Penn glanced at the bed in unspoken invitation. They sat down side by side. Her arms were tense, and she had goose bumps. Silently, he ordered increased heat.

"You're not so bad," she said.

He supposed she meant that betraying the precasters hadn't bothered her as much as she'd feared, and didn't take the tribute personally. There was another question he wanted to ask, but he decided to defer it. "You're cold," he said and put his arms around her shoulders.

Mead snuggled closer. "That can change. And this is awkward, one of us naked and one dressed." She had learned her lesson, and slipped her fingers inside the neck of his shirt, then slid them down, opening it. He shivered, and wondered who he now held: the Mead who schemed to seduce an Ahman the better to betray her grandmother, or the Mead in pain, who needed comforting so badly that even a stranger's touch was welcome. He grabbed her hands and used that grip to force her onto her back against the bed, and held her down. Her look was apprehensive, but she didn't protest or strain against him. Her dark hair was spread softly around her head. Her breasts had flattened; the nipples were hard. He guessed she would let him hurt her, if only to add that hurt to the others she held against the Bridger precasters. He had no desire whatsoever to do so, and her willingness made him particularly gentle.

He leaned over her, and kissed her. She relaxed, then rose

into the kiss, pressing herself up against him. Their tongues met and moved in each other's mouth, exploring, tasting together. When they parted, Mead smiled openly; Penn hoped her pleasure was real.

"When are you going to ask me about Gray?" she said, looking mischievous.

He laughed, surprised and truly pleased by his surprise.

"We can't either of us enjoy ourselves until you do."

He let go of her, but stayed close. "All right. Does Gray know about the precasters' plan?"

She shook her head—rolled it, actually, against the pale bedspread. "Gray doesn't know anything; he's too stupid. No, not stupid, just gullible, and insecure. He thinks they married him to an alia in order to insult him, or because no one else would have him, and imagines he's very clever to have fooled grandmother by using the Janet emulation like a singleton."

Penn didn't know how to respond. He wanted this woman, but didn't trust her. He wouldn't have thought so during their open argument that morning, but he now suspected Mead might protect Gray. That suspicion made him like her better.

She reached up and pulled his shirt down over his shoulders and arms, exposing his bare chest, then put her arms around his back, tugging him lower, to brush against her naked flesh.

He savored the brief skin-to-skin sensation, but pulled back. "What do you want me to do?" he asked.

"Isn't it obvious?" Her breath was warm against his cheek. "Sterilize the alia and fertilize me."

Chapter 6

I. An Intrusion

Gray was a woman. She lay on her side in the tunnel, listening apprehensively for any sounds that would mean the Shak were coming through the underground to attack Bridger Dome. She heard soft breathing and tensed. Someone was there. A Shak. Marie? No, she couldn't bear it, to kill a friend, a cousin! How had this started? Why had the outsiders come? Then she relaxed; the sound was too close. There was no attack, not yet.

Gray was a woman. Tense in her bedroll, she listened for the wild creatures, out in the night, and heard only the quiet sounds of her companions' breathing. They were asleep in the tent, as she should be. Genie Shak was on watch. They were safe. She stretched, and felt one of the others beside her.

Gray was a woman. She was too tired to sleep. The work was unending. Her sisters surrounded her, and closer, she heard the sound of her daughter's breathing. The children. The work was for them. Would they manage to survive here? She was too tired for thought. She listened to the relaxed rhythm of Anne's breathing, and let herself be lulled by the sound.

Gray was a woman. Vaguely apprehensive, she lay on her side, absently listening to Paul's breathing beside her. Paul had stayed, even though she was pregnant again. Finally she located the source of her discomfort—the sound of the ship was gone! The eternal harmonic that she'd heard from birth, and throughout every moment of her life, was stilled. Panicked, she stayed motionless, rigid, trying to comprehend what could have gone wrong. There were no alarms, no shouts for damage control. Abruptly she realized it was all right. She was safe, down on the planet, in the underground shelter they'd made to protect themselves from the wind and open sky. She sagged against the bed. Her body felt too large and too heavy, but that was the child—another daughter, she hoped—who would carry her memory on. She snuggled closer to Paul. He felt small, smooth, and soft. She straightened her back, pressing against his chest, and then recoiled.

Gray sat up, confused. He'd been half-awake, daydreaming in bed with Janet, unable to sleep because of dizziness and a pounding headache that had come on suddenly, late in the evening—but those hadn't felt like dreams. They weren't; they were reminiscences. He was a man who had remembered being a woman. Women: Frieda, waiting for the Shak, during the offie wars with the Dissenters; Lynn, out exploring the western part of the continent with the Fine Expedition; Alise, building Stone Town; and finally the earliest, Diane, a Bridger First Comer. He recognized them intuitively, with an automatic instinct, in the same way he knew himself.

He left the bed and stood, ignoring the indistinct wrongness of each of his movements, looking down on Janet in the faint starlight from the unshuttered window and hoping she would awaken as herself. They'd moved a few essentials from Mead's house, then eaten dinner in the dome and gone eagerly to bed together. He didn't want to return to bed, however, in case the aberrant memories recurred. He pulled on the pants he'd draped across the rocking chair. Janet moved restlessly into the place he'd left, as though her body was searching for him. He touched her head, feeling the curve of her skull and remembering the tender sensation of holding her newborn daughter, the skull curving within the palm of her hand. Gray jerked his hand away and hurried out onto the tenth-floor gallery of Bridger Dome.

He was disoriented, as if he'd been ill and napping and then had been suddenly awakened. It must be late, he thought, or very early, since no one moved on the rotunda floor. He saw the dome through a double vision, everything at a remove from his inner self, the watcher. The rotunda was empty, because she (Emma) was creeping out at night to admire its beauty, proud of her power and her son Jonathan's brilliant design. He shook his head, glimpsing the treetops of the Earth garden; she (Sarah) smiled and remembered planting the seeds, hoping for just such generous growth. Everywhere he looked echoed with strings of random associations from pasts he'd never known. He closed his eyes and held on to the railing, trying to stop the ghostly kinesthetic responses contact with the rail brought on.

This was nothing like the descriptions of the onset of memories told to him by friends. Adolescents reported an increase in *déjà vu*, then more and clearer flashbacks of actual events, but their recall was first from *recent* lives. The coming in of memory usually occurred over the four or so years of puberty, as personal memories gradually integrated with those from the past; Testament's memory was hormonally induced, however, and Gray had long since been fully a man. He had never heard of anything like this onslaught of undifferentiated sensory memorabilia, all at once and from the distant past, even among those few unfortunate prodigies who, like Mead, had fuller memories and became precasters too young. There was no single life he was reminiscing. One atop the next, all of his ancestors were inside his head. He felt as if his mind had been expanded to the size of Bridger Dome, and then had been filled with garbage.

He opened his eyes and stared across the dome to the other side of the tenth-floor gallery, to where his grandmother's rooms were located. He couldn't very well wake her in the middle of the night, demanding an explanation, so he walked to the nearest bank of lifts and took one down to the rotunda floor. There he stood, trying to regain control of his jumbled mind. After a moment, focusing on his physical self (too large!) and not his reactions, he took the path to the Earth garden and went deep inside, seating himself on a stone bench under a white oak tree.

For years, for all his life, Gray had craved development of a Testament-normal memory. Now that it, or something similar, was happening to him, he felt only revulsion. Without realizing it, he had adjusted to his defect and had replaced the dream of being a male precaster with another one, the dream of leaving Testament. What had once seemed positive, normal, and even enviable now was an intrusion. He *was* a singleton. He didn't want those women in his head. And if the Harmony discovered such a change, would it ever let him in?

"Gray?"

He jumped and turned, expecting Reed, if anyone, but it was Alcasta, headmistress of the Bridger Dome school, a woman of about forty-five and a member of the rival Bridger sub-line to his, the one descended by primogeniture, eldest daughter down through the generations. It was generally a friendly rivalry, though, with the "old" line claiming it didn't want the honor of so many precasters when weighed against the pain of so many daughters with last-line sterility syndrome—women like Mead. The Bridger old line was already on its fifty-first generation from Janet; she was the last common female ancestor between Gray and Alcasta, but everyone knew him, the notorious main line singleton.

"Didn't mean to startle you," Alcasta said.

Gray smiled and shrugged. "No problem. I'm just not quite myself tonight." It was the first time since childhood he'd used the family joke.

Alcasta didn't show that she read anything into it. "Quiet here now, before they release the bees for the flowers. It's a good time to be alone."

"Are you ever really alone?" he asked.

She smiled, more kindly than Reed would have been, and sat on the bench opposite his. "Memories aren't real. You learn from them, the way you learn to walk, then it's past; you go on."

"How?"

She observed him, then sighed. "Focus on the present; you'll master it, with practice."

Focus on the present. He studied her face, the incipient wrinkles, especially around her mouth and eyes—smile lines, not crow's-feet; there was a new slackness just beneath her chin and a slight heaviness about her upper arms, visible through her thin yellow blouse. Alcasta was younger than his mother would have been, but she was about the age he remembered Margaret Bridger best. "You know," Alcasta said, "not everyone believes that everything Reed does is right."

That wasn't news; there were always disputes within a line. It was the existence of outsiders—other lines, and especially Harmony offies—that kept a large lineage like the Bridgers from splintering. Gray grunted ambiguously, so as not to side with the old line against his immediate family.

"I was on the family council two years ago," Alcasta said, and stopped. She crossed her legs and glanced up into the Eye on the World, then looked back and studied Gray.

He was having difficulty concentrating. A kaleidoscope of images swarmed into his mind as Alcasta spoke. Some words were especially loaded: "family," for example, and "council."

"Something strange happened, that I've wondered about." Alcasta shifted on her bench, but her regard was steady on Gray's face. "Bridger Dome paid for an outsider's abortion."

That grisly word caught his instant attention. Alcasta nodded. "A Kane woman. A friend of yours. She was pregnant and wanted the child—we paid grief money, too—but the Compound Council ordered the Kanes to force her into an abortion, and they did. The Compound Council. It caught my attention that precasters were involved, and I asked the chief precaster of Bridger Dome about it." She sneered Reed's title.

"What did my grandmother say?"

Alcasta leaned forward. "I told Reed that some men want children, too; some men even want a family. I said I thought you were one; I remember you very well from school. I mentioned that a child would tie a singleton deeper into Testament. It was just a son; it wouldn't even have mattered if the child turned out to be another singleton, since a son can't pass his mothers' memories down. Besides, the Kane woman knew the risk and was willing to go ahead. Reed told me to mind my own business." Alcasta leaned back again, awaiting his reaction.

Gray shouldn't have been shocked by the news of Reed's interference, yet he was. He heard the echo of Mead's voice—*Don't you hate them?*—and his outrage drove away any nascent memories except those directly his own. He might have had a son. He would have had a son, except for their toying with his life, and Melany's. Melany. She'd wanted his child, even though he was a singleton. What *else* must she have thought was the matter with him, to cause Bridger Dome to pay money to abort his child? That he was the carrier of a recessive Bridger genetic disorder, perhaps a tendency toward incurable madness? Or an inheritable latent violence? That his children would be deformed monsters?

Gray's face was hot. Despite the fiasco, Melany had continued to include him in her venture plans, and had never mentioned it, nor had any other man's child. He hadn't called Melany to refuse her latest offer of a venturing position, or even to say goodbye. How alone she must have felt, with Bridger Dome and her own family condemning her child, and only casual neglect from him. He lived among women—Altered women, as Penn would have said it—and barely noticed they were as real, as individual, as essentially unique as he was himself, however many memories they had. He was ashamed of what must be Melany's memories of him. By refusing her affection for fear of pity, he had been selfish and arrogant—a stereotypical man.

Gray looked up. Through the wide oak leaves the sky beyond the Eye was lightening toward dawn. He had to awaken Janet; he had to meet with Ahman Penn and neutralize any damage Mead had done, but he pledged to himself that sometime today he would visit Melany and try to make amends.

"You weren't supposed to know," Alcasta said. "I thought you should."

Gray had nearly forgotten her. He stood and bowed, in the offie style, very low. "Thank you," he said, feeling awkward in his gratitude. In some sense Alcasta hadn't acted on his behalf, but to harm his grandmother.

"Do you understand why she did it?" Alcasta asked curiously.

He nodded. "I think I do." He hesitated, glancing up to the precasters' gallery, then back. "She thought it was necessary, and it probably was." He might well have stayed on Testament if Melany had registered him as father of her child. He would have wondered about life in the Harmony, but he would have stayed. There might have been other children, once Reed gave up on him as her guardian for Dancer. He could have been happy here. But not useful; they needed him for his special role, to protect Janet. His anger began to dissolve. "Thank you," he said again, and went back up to the room he shared with Janet.

Janet was still asleep. Her breathing was normal. He sat on the side of the bed and, softly, called her name. She stirred, but didn't awaken. His stomach tightened. He touched her shoulder and whispered, "Janet. Wake up. Before I see Penn, we can get my other things from home."

Home. Gray envisioned a tidy apartment filled with early-morning sunlight, pale yellow, not Testament's red-gold. A creature—he *recognized* it as a blackbird—flew across the open sky to a tree outside the window. A tree outdoors was fantasy, and this one was pure imagination: it had pink-and-white flowers over it, as thick as leaves. He *recognized* it, too. An apple tree. It was hard to go to work in spring.

Gray jerked his hand away from Janet's shoulder, as if her memories had jumped to him like fleas to a new host. There was only one other world a native of Testament could remember, and that memory was hers. "Janet!" he called, much louder, ineffectually shaking her. He remembered Mead's patches and reached for his jacket, on the seat of the rocking chair. The area near the pocket was stained, saturated with grease. He remembered the oil on his fingers. *The way to your heart's desire,* Mead had said. He flung the jacket to the floor. "The bitch!"

II. Imprimatur

"Now I understand why this world is quarantined." Penn lay quietly, watching Mead dress. She was in silhouette because the only light he'd raised came from the blanked screen behind her; he thought it was an interesting aesthetic effect. "Testament's women could destroy the entire male population of the Harmony through lack of sleep."

"Are you complimenting me?" Mead asked archly. "Or yourself?"

"You." Penn rearranged the pillows so he reclined higher in the bed, the better to admire Mead. "Definitely."

"Then I'm supposed to return the favor with a compliment to your stamina, if nothing else, but frankly, Martin, you're good but unremarkable. Maybe men on Testament have to be hardier, since there aren't enough to go around."

Penn laughed, at ease with Mead's ridicule. She didn't mean any harm. While he was occasionally offended by the license other natives took, he liked it that Mead seemed unimpressed by him. He was flattered enough at Center, and enjoyed the equality she assumed. "Why do you need to leave so early?"

"I have a job, you know," Mead said.

"I didn't. What do you do?"

She came back toward the bed. "Do you have a hairbrush? I work in one of the water control stations, minding boards of numbers and opening valves at long distance whenever a red light blinks. It's the kind of work they give adolescents to do, while their memories are still coming in."

The image of Mead engaged in busywork made Penn smile. "Why don't you resign?"

"I'm hoping to be fired. I didn't show up yesterday to sit

my boards, and I'm already on probation. If they fire me, then I'll get paid by Bridger Dome while they investigate. The water department is run mostly by Sheffields, so it'll take a while."

Martin Penn was both amused and discomfited. "What about your work record?"

She shrugged. "Martin, I already have a record as a troublemaker as long as your arm, and I intend to add to it, maybe with your help. What about that brush?"

"There's probably something supplied in the bathroom. Bring it to me and I'll brush your hair myself."

While she was gone he thought about her attitudes and behavior. Perhaps ambition was different among the women of Testament, more dependent on the communal efforts of family than on individual work. They were each an extension of their line.

The brush, tossed by Mead from the doorway, landed on his lap. She followed it into the room and sat where he could easily reach her. He positioned himself better and set to work. Her hair was badly tangled. She tightened her shoulders each time he pulled at a snarl, but didn't complain. The pleasure of touching her, the satisfaction in even a mindless job well done, and the intimacy of grooming Mead were unjustifiably satisfying. "Why not just stay, if you don't care about the job?" he asked.

She turned to him, forcing him to stop. "Because I don't want to see my brother this morning." She nodded at Penn. "This is embarrassing. You are an offie."

"Will you come back tonight?"

She ran her fingers through her hair, checking his work. "Why?"

Why, indeed? He didn't trust this woman or her stories of precaster plots, but he wanted her close. "For meaningless sex."

"I might."

He'd meant to make her smile, and hadn't. He wondered what he could have said instead that she would have liked better.

She took the brush from him, gathered up her hair, and twisted it into a rough bun, which she kept in place with several small black clips. They were immediately lost in the darkness of her hair.

"Come earlier, for dinner," Penn said. "At six."

"What will you do for me?"

Penn chuckled at her unabashed gold-digging. "Feed you."

"All right," she said judiciously, "if you invite the governor, too."

"That gross pig? What do you want with him?" Penn immediately regretted airing his feelings about Swan in front of the monitors inside the suite.

"I have lots more damage that I can do."

Penn frowned. "You could do some to my relationship with him."

"I don't make guarantees, but you're not on my shit list, and I take some care for people who aren't."

"I'll think about it," he said, fully intending never to allow Mead Bridger anywhere near Swan.

She smiled as though she read his thoughts. "Maybe I'll come, anyway," she said. She gave him a kiss intended as a chaste goodbye, but he encircled her waist with his arms and brought her down toward him. She allowed the kiss to develop a modicum of passion, but he felt her impatience and let her go.

"You're such a puppy, Martin, with your big feet and hands, always so eager. . . ." She shook her head, smiling, and left the bedroom. He heard her laughter from the suite's social room. "Martin," she called, "this woman is still clinging to the man's knee. Don't you think it's time she freed herself?"

Penn hurried after her. The entertainment from the prior evening was frozen among the suite's chairs, more ridiculous than ever. The tearful woman clasped her lover's leg in a humiliating attempt to claim him; the phantasm Casanova seemed satisfied by her self-abasement. Penn ordered the utility to rid the room of them. Mead clapped her hands together as the figures vanished. "Is that how your Harmony prefers its women?"

"Of course not," he answered, but she laughed again and went to the door. It was secured; the utility released it at his gestured command and she walked through the filter, waving her hand gaily to him as she vanished into mist.

As soon as Mead was gone, Penn missed her. He registered her on the Gateways House system, giving her full privileges to enter the building and his suite, provided he was present, without being stopped by the lobby guards,

then instructed them to warn him immediately upon Gray
Bridger's arrival.

The screen window still showed a view of Flute, but the
White Garden now looked affected. He switched the screen
to a jungle landscape from Sucre, site of the Harmony's capital city, Center, but that was ugly. Finally, he returned the
screen to a window, a real-time view of the foothills of the
Spine Mountain Range. It was very early. Testament's sun
had only recently risen, and its low light cast long shadows
across the landscape. Nothing moved. The cold, dry air, for
once, had lost its wind.

Penn was too restless to sleep. The Testament outpost received news, as well as facile entertainments. Penn called
up the most recent political display; the information was a
week old, from when the quickship carrying it had left Center. Elector Jeroen Lee was the first item, naturally. Lee
continued to cling to his position. The Grand Assembly
hadn't intervened; the current Marshal—a longtime ally of
Lee's—had claimed this was a matter for the Academies, so
Lee had avoided a vote on the weakest part of his case, citizenship. Few Ahmen had taken public positions regarding
Elector Lee, and his greatest support had generally been
from among them, Jonism's second tier. Two of the other
five Electors had publicly called for Lee's resignation. Unless some positive change occurred, it was only a matter of
time before Lee would be forced from his position, if he
was lucky and wasn't arrested first. Lee had agreed. *"It's
conceivable that I'll stay in office, but extremely unlikely.
The timing's wrong,"* Lee had said. *"In case I don't survive
this battle, I want you disassociated from me as much as
possible, Martin."*

"Elector," Penn had protested, but Lee had stopped him.

*"Be sensible. There is no reason for my fall to pull you
down. Go somewhere removed from Center's politics, perhaps your home on Flute. Or search out one of your Mysteries, but if you do, Martin, be discreet. You're probably too
young to be elected to my vacancy, but there will be others,
and of all possible candidates for the Electors' positions, I
consider you the best by far. I trust your humanity"*—Penn
remembered the Elector's smile—*"and I expect all future
candidates will need certified DNA testing. Probably in du-
plicate."*

Elector Penn. He shook his head. He didn't want the position, a fact Jeroen Lee never understood. Penn preferred being behind the scenes, as he was as Lee's chief aide. He didn't want the responsibility of determining Jonism's future when he was so uncertain of Jonism's soundness, when in his darkest thoughts he wondered if the search for Order was really an unending progression toward nothing. What was there to care about in a universe empty of meaning? How could a man ever find lack of faith to be deeply satisfying? There was something wrong with the message of Jon Hsu as interpreted over the centuries; an Elector's position was nothing but brute power. He didn't want to join them.

There is an answer for you. The Bridgers know something. His greatest hope arose from the unpremeditated words of Altered women, but these women centered their own hopes on ... children. Which made him think again of Mead.

Penn went into the bedroom and lay glumly on the bed. He couldn't sleep; the linens all smelled of Mead. Eventually he gave up, and found a medication in the bathroom for the pervasive fatigue he was sure to feel later in the day. He was dressed and waiting in the social room when Gray Bridger arrived, early. Gray looked tired, too, but he managed a proper bow. His eyes searched the room.

"Your sister is gone," Penn said, annoyed by the fact, not at Gray, but Gray winced at his sharp tone. So as not to put the young man in the awkward position of having to inquire into his patron's sexual adventures with a close member of his family, Penn added, "I enjoyed her company and I've invited her to dine with me tonight; she said she may come. Any distress this causes you or your family is unintentional."

"Ahman Penn, you misunderstand," Gray said. "No one cares where Mead rubs herself, or with who. She won't have children. But if she provokes you, then you could take it out on me."

Gray's lack of concern over Mead's carnal adventures seemed genuine, which was disturbing, since Mead claimed to believe otherwise. Apparently all native morals hinged on reproduction. "Is having children really so important here?" Penn asked.

"Yes," Gray said. "For Mead, it's ... everything."

That was the truth, Penn realized. Sex, and the story about leaving Testament, had been Mead's way of gaining access to him. Her scheme was working; the idea of curing her infertility didn't outrage him. He smiled; perhaps he would help her.

"Ahman Penn, as of last night, I've done everything you asked me to do, and my wife has passed her tests. I'd like the help you promised in leaving Testament."

Penn studied Gray, who glanced aside rather than meet Penn's gaze. Gray Bridger resembled his sister. He lacked her feminine delicacy, but he was a handsome man, better-looking than Penn knew himself to be. He was less highly strung than Mead, and only impertinent, where Mead was brazen. They both had impairments—Mead's infertility, and Gray's status as a singleton—and both had a prickly pride concerning them, which in Mead's case had caused her to single-handedly oppose the native Compound Council and her own grandmother. Whatever the truth of her accusations, Penn admired her independent spirit. Both needed his help, and they were equally willing to scheme to get it.

He should have been furious, but he wasn't. If Mead hadn't concealed her reasons initially, he would have sent her away and that would have been his loss, too; and perhaps it was vanity, but he didn't believe Mead had been faking the passion and warmth she'd showed during the night. Gray, trapped between the precasters and Harmony rules, had few other choices but to fabricate an acceptable wife if he wanted to leave Testament. Penn did wonder if Mead was right that there was a precaster plot, and that Gray didn't know about it. If she was protecting him, Gray was cooperating with precasters and was hardly an acceptable immigrant. Gullible, Mead had called him, but there was nothing wrong with Gray's intelligence. "Your wife's tests were interesting." Penn waited, giving Gray an opportunity to explain.

He didn't.

Penn motioned Gray to be seated. "Where do you intend to go, once you leave Testament?"

"Darien." Gray took his now usual chair.

"Why Darien?"

"They're supposed to be tolerant of Altereds."

"But you aren't an Altered man."

Gray shrugged, moved forward, then stopped, settling back into the chair. "No, but I'll never be ordinary inside the Harmony."

"I thought that being ordinary was why you wanted to enter the Harmony of Worlds." When Gray didn't respond, Penn continued, "The Altereds who are accepted on Darien are of a particular type, a type entirely unlike natives of Testament."

Gray looked at him. "Ahman Penn, are you reneging on your promise to help us?"

Refusal to help Gray and his unnatural wife was the easiest way out of the dilemma Mead's accusations had given Penn, but he felt some sympathy for Gray, too. By every standard, Gray himself was eligible to enter the Harmony. "I'm attempting to dispense advice," Penn said, not answering Gray's question. "Your information about the Harmony is limited. You would do much better on a less settled world than Darien. I suggest one of the Extreme worlds, such as Surf, or Sucre."

"Thank you, Ahman, but I'll try Darien first." Gray's lips compressed into a thin, stubborn line that reminded Penn of Mead.

"Fine," Penn said forbiddingly, although inwardly he was amused. Even if it existed, the precasters' conspiracy was flimsy, an ineffectual attempt to get one fertile woman off-world, though it was good that Mead had told him. "What skills do you have that will allow you to support yourself? Darien is long past needing manual labor in any quantity, unlike the Extreme worlds."

"No one else has asked; why are you?" Gray was defiant.

"Gray, you have less than even the basic education our poorest, most backward worlds provide to their remedial citizens, and since you are not a citizen you can never petition for economic assistance. Because of the information quarantine, these are not things you would know; it's to your credit you know as much as you do about the Harmony." Penn waited for Gray to absorb this—it was a lesson he'd learned from Jeroen Lee: cloak bad news with a compliment—then, just as Gray was ready to protest, he said, "By overruling the usual criteria and providing my imprimatur to allow your wife off Testament, I'll essentially be assuming responsibility for her, and through her, you. The bureaucrats here don't care, but if you starve, it's a blot on my judgment and my record. I can't allow it."

"Then we'll go to this place Surf," Gray quickly said. "I'll buy the tickets today."

"Good," Penn said. "That's sensible. The best choice of

the Extreme worlds is Sucre. Since Center is there, I'll be
able to keep an eye on you, and help if you're in trouble."
Idly, Penn wondered what it would be like to have Mead
with him on Center. Uncomfortably wild or wildly exciting?

Gray fidgeted in the chair. "Ahman Penn, we don't need
an overseer."

"I think you do." Penn imagined Cevan Swan watching
this and wished the discussion could have taken place in the
privacy of some public place in Stone Town. Knowing he
was being watched by a man who hated Altereds at least had
the benefit of keeping Penn scrupulous in regard to his own
protection. Since Mead had told him Gray's wife was a
freak, Penn had to take some action. "If you won't agree to
go to Sucre, and stay under my supervision, I'll need to examine your wife myself before I'll vouch for her fitness to
live inside the Harmony and give my imprimatur to the exception to the quarantine."

Gray stared out the window. When he looked back at
Penn, his expression was composed. He spoke carefully.
"None of this was part of our arrangement."

"Not explicitly, no," Penn admitted. "But I have to protect
myself and the Harmony."

"From one woman!"

"You lied to me, Gray Bridger. You told me she was a singleton, but I know now that's untrue. She's some other kind
of Altered. When I made my arrangement with you, I was
depending on the supposed fact that she was a singleton and
therefore she and her children would not have the native allegiance to Testament, even if her children did inherit her
memory. You should be grateful that I'm willing to overlook
your lie and deal with you at all; a conspiracy to violate the
quarantine could be construed as treason."

"Mead told you last night." Gray spoke so low that his
voice was difficult to hear.

Penn didn't deny it. "Another option is to sterilize your
wife. Then you both could leave without objection."

"No!" Gray jumped up from his chair and glared at Penn.
"Then we both could leave without your help. Why did we
need you? A woman wants children; is that so hard to understand? Mead would do anything for a daughter."

Penn believed there was a place for Altereds in the Harmony; he rather liked Gray and didn't perceive his wife as
a significant danger to the Harmony. Unfortunately, the

quarantine was an old, established Electors' Ruling and it was not a good time for Martin Penn, protégé of Elector Lee—the *Altered* Elector Lee—to contravene a law concerning Altereds. The repercussions to Elector Lee could tilt the precarious balance of his position. "Gray, you had planned to leave Testament without a wife; the marriage was made to trap you here. I can do this much for you: despite the registration of your marriage, and without waiting for the native council to dissolve it, I'll give you my imprimatur to leave for the Harmony alone. If your wife leaves with you, she must obey all quarantine rules against these freaks."

Gray hesitated a moment, staring out the window, then he started walking to the door.

"Where are you going?" Penn asked.

Gray stopped and turned around. "I need to think."

"You have a job with me."

They stared at each other. Gray's chin was up and his hands were clenched, as if Penn had become his enemy. "I quit," Gray said.

Penn suppressed a sigh. How had he become so entangled with these Bridgers? Gray would be a poor guide today, anyway. "Fine."

Gray nodded sharply. "You owe me a fee for yesterday, Penn, unless you've decided to deny that arrangement, too."

Penn grabbed some local currency he'd stuffed into his jacket for use during the day and tossed several bills—he didn't examine them—at Gray. Paper, they floated gracefully to the floor; Gray picked them up. There were at least two 100c bills; the agreement had been for much less. Without showing the least humiliation, or any remorse for his rudeness, Gray put all the money in his pocket, then walked out through the filter door. Penn watched him leave and wondered how it had happened that his native guide could make him feel ashamed.

III. Bad News

Elene's existence as an alia was like living inside a bad movie: there was no continuity. She was jerked from scene to isolated scene with only a hint of the travel and elapsed time between them. She awakened to an adrenaline-charged sense of danger and the memory of the incident in which she had been attacked, a memory as clear as any circumstance of her own, vanished life. She was in bed again, with the old woman from that previous awakening standing beside her. Not an active life. Warily, keeping an eye on the other woman, Elene sat up.

"Bad news, my dear," the old woman said. She examined Elene's face, then extended her hands, palm up, showing she had no weapon. "Bad news, Elene. You can't stay this time, either. I wasn't trying to call you, but you're strong in her."

"Who are you?" Elene asked. She was curious, but also hoped to prolong her awakening. It was all she had of life. She assessed her surroundings. Bridger Dome. From the curve of the outer wall, she wasn't too high above the rotunda floor. The room was plain, like those provided to overnight guests from outside Stone Town; the two women were alone.

"Reed, youngest of Tillie, twenty-fifth in the main line."

Twenty-fifth generation. The man—Gray, who called himself her husband—had been twenty-seventh, a grandson. Hundreds of years had passed since Elene's life, but people hadn't changed. This woman, playing games with alias and men, had to be a precaster. Elene didn't look directly at Reed Bridger; instead she tested her new body's strength and sensation with isometric exercises. Weak, but youthfully responsive. Existence as an alia was disorienting, no doubt about that, but it was more of an existence than she had imagined. She felt alive; she felt in control of this body; her thoughts were her own. To test herself, she mentally reviewed her life: dome school; summer work in Bridgerton; the rise of memory; her first daughter, Linni; a field command in the work of conquering the west from the Altons; her son and two later daughters—it all felt intact, but would she even know if anything was added or missing?

"You aren't useful just now," Reed said. "This war with the Harmony isn't your kind of fight, but if it turns physical, I wanted you available."

War. It was always best to know the full situation. "What kind of fight is it, then? And what is the Harmony?"

Reed shook her head, but didn't banish Elene into limbo. An alia was a harmless listener for someone who liked to talk. "A war of maneuvering for position, of watching and waiting for opportunities, of plotting freedom for our children. A slow war with a Goliath that doesn't even notice the conflict. Our weapons are their beliefs, our memory, and our children's lives."

Elene studied her. "That's a precaster's war."

The woman nodded. "The Harmony is an enemy from outside Testament. Those people imagine that they own us, like a man holding a woman inside a harem. They think that by ignoring us, they've made us disappear. They have an ideological aversion to us, which we have to change. And they have weaknesses. The lines have united to fight them. Most lines, anyway." She frowned and glanced out the window.

Elene followed her gaze. Shak Dome, Bridger Dome's nearest neighbor, was a jagged ruin, its walls collapsed into its rotunda. The edges had a worn and dirty look; the destruction was not recent, although some large pieces had never been cleared away. "The Shak! Did these outsider men attack our cousins?"

Reed walked to the window, looking out. "We did it."

Bewildered, Elene gaped.

"For the Shak, the world has always been too simple. They led the Dissenters. Like a sister who won't listen, they refused to understand we couldn't win a straightforward war with the Harmony, and shouldn't tempt them into destroying us. The Harmony has more *things,* more weapons, and men outperform women in battle." She looked at Elene as if waiting for a rebuttal, but none came. Reed was right. In physical prowess, men always had an edge. Even a woman's quickness couldn't fully compensate for brute power, and nothing could offset a male's desire to conquer, whatever the need and despite the odds. It was a good reason to bear few of them.

"They were good allies," Elene said quietly, looking sadly at the ruin.

"They were good allies, for a while," Reed agreed. "But they would have destroyed all of Testament, and died complaining that their way was right." She shrugged. "It's a harder time than yours."

Elene went to the window. For generations, Shak daughters and Bridger sons, and, less commonly, Bridger daughters and the scarce Shak sons, had blended and connected the two lines. In Elene's own time, their alliance had dominated Testament, as much as any line did. All that was lost. "Tell me about this war."

Reed came and stood behind her, looking out. "They call it a quarantine, but this is a siege," she said. "They don't understand that the longer it continues, the less likelihood we'll fall. We're learning from them, and they're learning nothing from us but what we want them to know. Meanwhile, we're safe from an invasion, and we're slipping out behind their lines."

Elene struggled to remember; an elusive thought nagged at her. "Gray. You told me to protect him." A surge of warm emotion directed toward him came from nowhere; she felt as if he were her lover or her son. "Why is a man important?"

"Men are part of a line, too." She touched Elene's shoulder. Elene turned, and Reed gestured toward the bed.

Elene shook her head. "It's more than that."

Reed glanced up at the sky and smiled as though she saw through Elene's attempt to stay alive. "To use the Harmony's metaphor, we're infecting them with our disease, our Alteration; Gray is a carrier. Protect him, and also his sister, Mead."

Elene remembered Mead—the one with the knife. "Her?"

"Yes. Both of them."

They'd been fighting with each other when Elene first entered this new life. "And if I have to choose?"

"If you must make a choice, protect Gray first." Reed glanced down at the floor and sighed. "I hope it doesn't happen that he needs you, but if he does, you may be protecting him against the Shak. Are you willing to do that? You were close to them, during your life."

"Why would they fight him?"

The old woman pulled her shawl closer around her shoulders, distractedly fingering the icesnake-skin. "The Shak have a story they want to tell the Harmony. It's been a hard job keeping them silent for so long, but now they're flooding into their ruin from Big Red. An important Harmony official has come—they have their sources, too. Gray is that offie's guide."

Finally, Elene felt she was getting hard information. "What story?"

"One that would tear the Harmony apart."

Baffled, Elene looked out again at Shak Dome. The ruin was awful; whatever was left of Shak Dome could only be underground. "Let them destroy this Harmony. Isn't that what we'd want?"

"We have our story, too. A better one. The difference between an atom bomb and a knife thrust. We don't want to die while destroying the Harmony; that wouldn't be winning."

"Are the stories true?"

Reed looked harder at Elene, then laughed. "Ah, Elene, you're smarter than I thought. But it's time to go. Will you defend us against the Shak?"

Unhappy, Elene still nodded. Bridgers came first.

"Good. The Bridger line could depend on you. Are you willing to die?"

"Again?"

They both smiled. Reed gestured at the bed once more, and Elene, feeling sour, went there and sat on its side. She didn't lie down, however. "What other emulation were you calling?"

"Your time is done, Elene. Lie down."

A mental heaviness like the quick, forced drowsiness of a sleeping drug, and a lack of pliancy in her gut-level affirmative response, told Elene she'd been subjected to an authority beyond her conscious control. "You've been tampering with my mind!"

"Not yours, my dear. At least, not much." Reed smiled and took Elene's hand as she stretched out on the bed. For a precaster, Reed had kindly eyes. "Sleep, Elene. Your time is done."

IV. Bad News

"Bad news, my dear," Reed said.

Janet's mind was heavy; her thoughts were slow, as if from fatigue, or alcohol, or drugs. She had gone to sleep for the night with Gray beside her, and now, from the light coming through the window, it was afternoon; Gray was gone. Why had she slept so long? The obvious answer made her gut tighten: she hadn't really been asleep. Then Reed's words echoed in her mind and captured her attention.

"Bad news?" Janet sat up in the bed. "Is Gray all right?"

Reed smiled—her bad news apparently wasn't too bad for *her*—and left the rocking chair. "He's fine; probably out guiding Martin Penn around Stone Town."

Gray had promised to awaken her, and he hadn't. He had left her, his wife, insensible and alone in the care of his hateful grandmother. Janet looked away from Reed, humiliated in front of her by Gray's disregard, and embarrassed by her wave of despair, so opposite to the euphoria of the day before. It was, in any case, impossible to be happy around Reed Bridger, whose eyes watched her with telltale disbelief in her reality. "What was the bad news?"

Reed joined her on the edge of the bed. "You and Gray won't leave for the Harmony together after all. I know you had some plan concocted, but it won't work."

Janet tried to bluff her. "I don't know what you're talking about. There is no plan; you married him to me to keep him here."

"We didn't marry him to *you,* my dear; we married him to Dancer. You're a vestige of another life, and an adulterated one."

Janet looked away from the triumph in Reed's eyes. "Whoever I am, I'm here."

"And he does seem to want you. He was furious at me this morning when I refused to give him the medicine to call you out."

Relieved and strengthened by the knowledge Gray hadn't willingly abandoned her, Janet smiled. "Then why wake me now?"

"Because we have to talk." Reed patted Janet's arm; her touch was unexpectedly gentle. "Penn is his only hope. Mead has destroyed your earlier plan, but Gray has one other chance. I need you to stop him from taking it."

"I won't do that!"

"Of course you will. Gray's last chance of leaving Testament is to desert you. Thanks to the precast, I know Martin, and I precast"—she chuckled—"that he'll offer Gray an opportunity to leave Testament alone. I need you alert to ensure Gray doesn't take it."

Janet's new life was like a bad movie. She was an actress yanked from scene to scene with no continuity between them. She might go to sleep again and wake up in advanced old age, or never wake up again at all. Gray was the anchor in her life, and she was an anchor, a burden, on him. He didn't deserve that. She stood and walked away from the bed. "I'll tell him to go, to run as far away from you and this place as he can get."

Reed clapped her hands. "How gallant. How selfless. And how naive. All that is necessary to persuade my grandson not to leave Testament is for you to exist, to be awake. I know him much better than I know Martin Penn. Gray won't desert you as long as Dancer is Janet, and, my dear, you don't control your reincarnations in Dancer's mind." Reed held up a blue patch. "I do."

Gray had told Janet about those patches. Everything Reed said made perfect sense. Gray would lose this chance rather than leave her behind. It wasn't necessarily love—she couldn't presume that Gray loved her after such a short time—it was the pledge of comrades, the honor created by mutual trust, Gray's kindness and his sense of justice, that would trap him now on Testament. There was nowhere to go to escape Reed, but Janet paced between the window and the door. "I'm willing to die for him," she said.

Reed nodded. "You could kill Dancer. I doubt that's what you meant, and I think it's unlikely, anyway. Perhaps you'd die to protect him, but not to give him leave to abandon you. I know you, Janet Bridger; I know you value yourself better than that. After all, isn't that why you left Jon Hsu?"

"Left him?" Janet didn't understand.

"Ended your affair." Reed sighed. "Don't play games with me, my dear." Her voice was hard. "Precasters, by definition, remember your life. We know about your secret affair—the great Bridger secret—but no precaster will talk. Except for us, you are the only one who remembers the almost-god of the Polite Harmony of Worlds. You know things the offies would want to hear, and, unfortunately, you don't care about protecting Testament or the Bridger line, but only about yourself and, possibly, Gray. A selfishness typical of your era. Which brings up the second topic of our discussion."

Strange to say, when she was nothing *but* a memory, Janet's recall of her own past was sketchy, more a matter of what she must have done than what she remembered doing. It had fed her fears that Reed Bridger was right that she wasn't real. But as she strained to understand what Reed was talking about, a picture of Jon Hsu slowly formed in her mind, a vision resolving itself out of shadows. Black hair and dark brown eyes, part Chinese and part Hispanic. Or was that the illustration from one of the Jonist tracts Gray had given her, for its information about the Harmony? "I don't know what you mean," Janet said firmly.

Reed laughed sarcastically. "Oh, of course you don't

know. Of course. You're already plotting some use for the information; you're going to tell it to Penn." Reed stood up and looked directly into Janet's eyes. "That won't happen, my girl. I won't let you out of Bridger Dome, even if I do have to keep you awake. You won't waste the Bridgers' secret knowledge on a bribe to Martin Penn. When the Harmony decides to eliminate us, then we need to have this to stave them off. Don't you think they'd like to know the personal life of their god, Jon Hsu? That he drove a red Mustang VII? That he liked pizza? That he liked *you*?" She chuckled to herself. "More important than the happy trivia are his ideas—especially his attitude toward the incipient movement to develop refashioned humans—Altereds. Yes, those are things the Harmony, especially a man like Martin, one who's searching for new meanings, might like to know. We won't sell it so cheap as a pair of off-world tickets."

As Reed spoke, Janet saw the memories she was describing as clearly as she did any other of her memories, as if they'd been dormant and had come alive. She had picnicked with Jon on the grassy slope by the Adler Planetarium. Jon, the only love of her life until Gray. Gray had saved her and kept her alive by his regard for her. But why hadn't she remembered Jon before? Janet sat slowly back on the bed.

Reed scowled at her. Janet opened her lips to ask, then didn't. She wouldn't give this woman any satisfaction.

"Don't protest that you won't tell Penn," Reed said. "I don't trust you. I can't afford to."

Janet's mind was racing. "You trusted me before. I could have told Penn at any time since I've been on Testament."

Reed shook her head. "Dancer, my dear, you've been here all your life; you're sick, not a traveler. In any case, I've never trusted you. Memory is peculiar. It rises, unbidden, with a whiff of smoke or a remembered song, or it vanishes, submerged by the everyday. On Testament, we're experts on memory. I knew that if you were being Janet Bridger, it would take some time for all your memories to appear—and we didn't expect Janet to become a semipermanent inhabitant of Dancer's mind. Who could predict Gray would become so attached to this particular association of chemistry and neurons?" She grinned, but glanced away.

Janet wet her lips, still trying to understand the explanation of how she had temporarily forgotten her affair with Jon, when now the reminiscences were so powerful. Details were returning, an avalanche of memory once the first stone had begun rolling. Jon's faint Peruvian accent. The ceramic pot he'd given her, its handle shaped like a stirrup, that came from his father's land. They'd both been so young. *Her* Jon had founded Jonism? She'd have to rethink its philosophy. Jon hadn't been a cultish man, no messiah, although he'd been profound, concerned with vital issues, like the deteriorating status of Western thought and scientific progress. That was why she'd left. She'd had her own life to live, and hadn't the temperament to cater to a zealot.

Reed Bridger started toward the door.

"Wait! What are you going to do?"

Reed smiled. "Keep you here, of course."

"You can't keep me a prisoner forever!"

Reed chuckled. "That sounds like the script to a bad movie. Of course I can." She opened the door. Sounds from the dome rotunda became audible, the background noise of hundreds of individuals. Her descendants.

Janet stood again. "We got off to a bad start, Mrs. Bridger. It doesn't have to be like this."

Reed turned back. Her expression had become milder. She looked out through the window wall, toward the ruined dome. Much more gently, she said, "I'm afraid it does, my dear." Then Reed left, closing the door.

Janet was a prisoner, trapped in this building, in this city, on this world, in this time. Her only way out was through Gray. He was her lifeline. If he made a separate agreement with Penn, then her life was over. He wouldn't, though. When he returned, they'd make a new plan.

V. Vultures of His Life

It was over. The precasters' plan had failed, and Gray was still trapped on Testament—uselessly trapped. Penn had said he could leave alone; if he did, guilt would sour his life forever. He'd promised Janet; he'd sworn to help his grandmother. He wouldn't leave alone, but if he took Janet, sterilized, the precasters' plan failed anyway. There had to be something else. It was all Mead's doing. Mead. He spat, forgetting he was in the pristine off-worlder lobby.

"Hey!" a guard shouted and came angrily toward Gray.

"Sorry," Gray said meekly. He felt a momentary panic, alone in their territory. They could beat him; they could even kill him. No one from Testament could help. This would be how it was inside the Harmony if he agreed to be watched by Penn; he would never be ordinary, just a worse freak than he'd ever been on Testament, and with no family, no line, and no purpose. He bowed low, hands on his thighs, held it a moment, then straightened. Submission posturing, Melany called it, sometimes necessary when they came into Exchange to sell their venture's skins.

Both guards were watching him, one from behind the desk, like a hunter in a blind awaiting the first break-and-run of prey. The other had stopped coming at him, but he held the handle of his stick gun, the heat weapon Testament's children held in awe and adults avoided mentioning. It could burn a hole instantly, clear through a person. The man behind the desk said, "That's Ahman Penn's guide."

"I'm leaving on an errand for the Ahman," Gray said obsequiously, and bowed again, more briefly.

"They're never any trouble," said the guard who'd approached him, supposedly to his fellow. "I told you. They live under a woman's thumb; they're not real men."

Gray was relieved, not insulted, by the simplistic macho disrespect. It was common inside Exchange, but an attack was unlikely if he refused to be provoked, which was easy, since he wasn't offended. To be subordinate to women was not a humiliation; whatever happened elsewhere, on Testament it was nature.

The two guards eased off, and Gray went briskly to the exit into Amity Square, suppressing the urge to run.

Once outside, he stood a moment under the shelter of the offie building. He should have confronted Mead about the drug first, instead of going to Penn, but he had expected to find them together. Reed might have advice, but could he trust it? He wished for a simpler existence, where it wasn't necessary to look for tricks and hidden motives, and thought with longing of Melany Kane, who had proved herself a good friend and who might have been more if he'd had his eyes opened earlier. What about Janet?

He started across Amity Square. The random flashes from his mothers' far past lives had slowed that morning as the drug Mead had slipped him wore off. He'd had no control over the experiences he relived, and hadn't assimilated them all, but many had involved Janet Bridger. He'd gained an intimate sense of her internal life, one deeper than any relationship would ever provide. He had experienced her memories inside his mind.

Janet was, perhaps, as honest and loving as anyone, but he knew her faults, her regrets, and her inadequacies from her own memories, as filtered through his mind. He couldn't ignore them as easily as he could ignore his own. Her faults weren't his, and didn't strike a chord of sympathetic understanding in him. She was ambitious to the point of selfishness; she was intelligent without being wise. She had no commitment to community or to anything larger than herself, as he did to the Bridger line. He remembered Reed, in the rotunda garden, and guessed the reason. Janet Bridger wasn't the product of a thousand years of selection for Testament and the Altered frame of mind.

There was a reason Janet had lived alone, an inflexibility. Her capacity for love had contracted into a tight knot that feared injury if it opened. Maybe that much of her had changed, or she at least saw her interests bound up with his, but the result of his reminiscence of Janet's memories was to tell him that he was bound to a woman who needed him, but whom he could never wholeheartedly love.

Mead had understood. This was her revenge. She'd changed his perception of Janet in the expectation that doing so would pervert Reed's plan. She'd done more. She had provided a proof that love depended upon lies. If sharing memories was anything like telepathy, and if ever an Alteration gave humans the ability to read minds, then humans would die out.

Children were the only genuine intermingling, the fusion of lovers honestly expressed in a new being, but in that, women won. Only mothers' memories were passed on. Even so, he ached for a child to love, who would extend some part of him into the future.

Gray approached the lifting lines and hesitated, not ready to return to Janet and the dome. He glanced out at the overlook. The Kanes had never built a dome. They were a modest, industrious line, no match for the Bridgers. He owed Melany a visit.

"You!" It was an offie voice.

Gray turned, not because he'd been expecting to be pursued, but since no one else was nearby. Three Harmony soldiers in spotless brown uniforms, each with a stick gun, advanced on him. Gray bowed. They weren't the guards from Penn's residence. All ignored his bow, but offies sometimes did. The one in front gestured. "You'll come with us, Bridger."

"Where? And why?" Gray asked, involuntarily glancing up at the tower building that dominated the cliff side of Amity Square. Inside Exchange it was called the Governor's House, but in Stone Town it was known as the Fort. Governor Swan did live there, but so did his troops, who, though they were rarely seen outside Exchange, constituted a formidable force, not so much for themselves as for their impressive weapons, periodically demonstrated in martial exercises. The Fort was also where the few natives arrested by the Harmony were imprisoned; no other natives were allowed inside.

The lead soldier smiled. "Move." He gestured with his thumb at the Fort. "You got it right."

"What have I done?" Gray was afraid that sounded like a whine, but he was alarmed. This seemed official, not a casual roughing up. He straightened and glanced around. There were Testament natives in the square, but none were close. None would intervene, anyway. He wouldn't have. The lifting lines were a short sprint to the left, but the offies would catch him before he made it there, even if they didn't shoot and incinerate whatever part of him they chose, probably a leg. "This is a mistake," he said. "Ahman Penn is waiting for me."

"Say his name all you want. Just move."

They were ready for him to make a break, even eager for it. These were Governor Swan's special guards, the Security force, with blood-red patches on their sleeves. Gray bowed again and complied, moving slowly toward the Fort. The soldiers must have been enjoying their role, because they didn't force him to hurry, although they crowded him like sheepdogs herding a stray lamb.

Native murderers and thieves who acted against Harmony citizens were punished—harshly—by the Compound Council; there were very few such incidents. The Harmony punished only those occasional natives they convicted of treason. Treason. Gray swallowed hard and glanced at the soldiers. That couldn't be. Penn hadn't been angry, and he didn't seem to be a vicious man.

The air chilled as Gray and his escort entered the shadowed area beneath the Fort. It stood on stilts, with restricted access through lifts in the massive supports and a landing site on top. No guards were visible, but the oppressive weight of the building above was demoralizing. Once he was in the lift, Gray's stomach tightened. He was inside the Fort.

Offie technology, what little Gray knew of it, played with gravity and light. The lift was smaller than that in Penn's residence, and every surface was a dark mirror. When the door opened, the room beyond was also filled with reflective surfaces, which shimmered. The front soldier pushed him out. His foot didn't sense hard floor outside, and he felt himself falling. The soldiers laughed as he stumbled. Two grabbed his arms and pulled him upright. "Walk," one said.

He tried. They seemed to have no difficulty, but the sensation he had was almost of floating through the space. His eyes didn't give many clues either. The walls, ceiling, and floors were of some tricky material, like fun-house mirrors. Some surfaces reflected his image; others did not. Distances were deceptive. There was light, but no source for it, although sometimes as he was half dragged, stumbling, through the maze, the light was so intense he had to close his eyes, and still he felt it burning through his eyelids.

"Here." The soldier on his right shoved him roughly at his own image. Gray thought he looked surprised and vulnerable, but not as frightened as he felt. He raised his hands to protect himself from impact with his mirrored image, but his hands slipped through it like falling into open water, then Gray was in another room. Just one soldier followed, and the doorway, if there had been one, reformed itself quickly behind them.

The room they'd entered had a brilliant light, strong enough to make Gray's eyes tear, which was centered only on him, so that he was unable to see the area beyond his spotlighted self. He felt buoyant, as if he were floating in the light, and couldn't get much purchase on the ground.

"A charge of treason on your record, Mr. Bridger, and even if it's dismissed, you'll never enter the Polite Harmony of Worlds."

Gray wiped his eyes and squinted. He knew that voice.

The soldier pushed Gray forward, into a flailing bow. Outside the narrow circle where he stood, the gravity was normal; then the near-weightlessness caught up with him, as did the light.

"You are part of a conspiracy to break Testament's quarantine," the same male voice said, as if it were issuing a Ruling. Then Gray finally had it—this was Governor Swan himself. The quarantine was a semipermeable barrier—in both directions—and it was Swan who calibrated the flow.

"Do you deny it?" Swan asked querulously.

Gray strained, trying to see something of the room into which he'd been brought, but the light's intensity prevented his eyes from adjusting for the darkness. The soldier was close enough, slightly lit by the spotlight, to be an uncertain shadow, but anyone or anything else was too far. Gray cleared his throat and bowed again, on his own. With care, he did it easily. This might be his only opportunity to clear himself; the Harmony, at least on Testament, did not consider that justice required public trials. "Yes, I do deny it," he said firmly. Gray took a step forward, hoping to get away from the light and gravity games, but they followed as effortlessly as a shadow. The soldier let his displeasure be known by moving closer to Gray's back.

"A quarantine violation planned by the Compound Council of Testament constitutes an act of aggression against the Polite Harmony of Worlds," Swan continued, as though Gray had agreed, or had not spoken at all. "Your sister has alleged it, but she is an Altered Person. You are not. Technically, at least."

Mead again.

"Also," Swan continued, "your sister apparently has no direct knowledge of the conspiracy, nor has she participated in it. Your case is different on both counts. With the direct, voluntary testimony of a standard human—I would give you the benefit of the doubt; you are symptomatically standard, whatever your DNA—it would be possible to charge the Compound Council with treason and finally take appropriate action on Testament. You, of course, can be charged with treason in any event. Whether you acted alone or with others, you definitely represented to Ahman Penn that your wife was symptomatically standard."

Gray tried to determine if Swan was alone, but the silence was empty of information. Gray guessed that Penn wasn't present; there hadn't been enough time, and this cowardly interview wasn't Penn's style. "My wife is symptomatically standard, just as I am," Gray said. "Ahman Penn heard this allegation. He didn't suggest there was any aggression against the Harmony." Taking a chance, he added, "Ahman

Penn didn't arrest me, and he would want me released if he knew of this; he employs me as his guide."

The silence lengthened, so that Gray imagined noises that weren't there and scuffed his feet to make some that were real, as well as to feel the ground. He was frightened, and afraid to show it.

"Ahman Penn," Swan said eventually. He sighed. "Ahman Penn and I disagree on the danger posed by Testament's Altered women, and the indulgence it is reasonable to give. His opinion of Altereds is questionable, and with regard to those on Testament, it is also inexperienced. I do not rely upon it."

Gray guessed the speech was made for his guard and felt hope for the first time. Penn was a more important man in the Harmony than Swan. "I am innocent," Gray said. If he admitted treason, then he would spend the rest of his life inside a cell, or, more likely, he would have one of the "accidents" that prisoners often suffered in the Fort. "Please contact Ahman Penn; he'll clear this up." Whether Penn would do that, precisely, or not, Gray would in any case feel more confident of his survival if Penn knew he was in Swan's custody.

The spotlight disappeared, but the sudden darkness was as bad; Gray couldn't see anything, and Swan's voice was just as disembodied. The gravity had become normal; perhaps the two effects were linked. "Mr. Bridger, Martin Penn is not the only individual with the power to free you from the confines of Testament," Swan said. "Certainly, a grateful Harmony would welcome a man who displayed his loyalty by discovering *and revealing* the conspiracy of Altered women to infiltrate their kind onto the Jonist worlds."

Gray was speechless, nonplussed rather than reticent. This wasn't an indictment, it was a negotiation.

"Think it over, Mr. Bridger. We'll talk again."

He'd been dismissed. Swan was offering Gray passage off Testament if Gray implicated the Compound Council, including his own grandmother, in a conspiracy against the Harmony, in treason. Gray stood motionless, absorbing the contemptible proposition. He realized then that, singleton or not, and however he'd been manipulated by the precasters, he was a Bridger and a native of Testament. In any choice between the Harmony and Testament, he'd choose his home. Enraged by Swan, Gray was also disappointed. He had once truly hoped to assimilate into the Harmony.

The soldier again pushed Gray into a bow, this time maintaining a steady pressure on Gray's back. Gray went lower than his escort intended and, moving suddenly, managed to sink down and out of the soldier's grasp. Though his feet seemed to slip against the floor, Gray ran straight to where Swan's voice had originated, intending to strike at Swan and hoping to do real damage to the governor by way of answer to his proposition. Instead, Gray ran headlong into a barrier. He couldn't see it, and the only sensation he felt was extreme heaviness. His hands, his head, and his torso seemed stuck in heavy glue. It hurt, compressing him wherever he contacted it, and squeezing his embedded flesh away from that which was not. Then it stopped, and Gray slid down to the floor, stunned.

"Come on," the guard said impatiently. "That was a marginal setting; think what we could have done." He came from behind, grabbed Gray's shoulder, and lifted.

Of course. Swan wouldn't face anyone, even in the dark, with only one guard present. Gray let the soldier pull him up. His head pounding, arms aching, and chest feeling as if a thousand-pound weight had just been lifted, he didn't have the energy to struggle as the man led him back through the twisty, dark, mirrored corridors and put him in a cell.

Once the soldier left, Gray cautiously investigated. The room had a smooth, utilitarian appearance, Testament-normal gravity, and Harmony standard lighting. The walls were dull, rust-colored, cool ceramic, as was the floor. The ceiling was out of reach, but it had a standard-looking Harmony sun-stone. There was a bed and toilet fixtures. Once the door closed, its seam was invisible. The arrangement looked more permanent than Gray liked.

Gray slammed his fist against the closed door, then was ashamed of his foolishness; he'd only let them know his frustration, his untargeted rage. The muted thud dissipated immediately, but his fingers continued to ache, along with the parts of his body that had been in contact with the barrier. Mead. This was her fault. Or was it? He didn't know. It was *them,* the huge shapeless mass of authorities and relations that, however individually they acted, had somehow combined to bring him to this cell. He was a bug pinned to their examining table, waving his arms and legs in useless misery while they waited for him to die. He was a pawn in a chess game who had been sacrificed. They watched him from beyond his reach—all of *them*, the vultures of his life.

Gray hunkered down, leaning his back against the rear wall rather than sitting on the bed, not that he expected the door to open, but from obstinacy. Besides, there would be time to sleep, later. Unless Penn rescued him, or his grandmother could do something, he might be in Swan's cell for a very long time.

Chapter 7

I. A Really Bad Idea

"Mission accomplished." Mead sauntered through the suite's filter door with her jacket slung over her shoulder like the pelt of a defeated beast. "I was fired."

Martin Penn stretched, then closed the portable screen he had been using. A stand-alone unit, it had limited usefulness, but it was reasonably secure from Swan. He'd passed the afternoon performing an in-depth analysis of his precast. "What did you do?"

Mead chuckled. "Don't go too near Wolf Underground tonight; your feet will get wet." She squeezed herself between the chair arm and Penn, nearly falling into his lap.

He was glad to see her and pleased she'd come early, and not only for the interruption. She smelled of Testament's outdoors. Her cheeks were still pink from the cold air. Her dark hair was loose around her shoulders, and it was mussed. Filigree jewelry dangled from her ears. She had painted glossy red color across her lips and fingernails, and her eyelashes looked unnaturally long. The effect was exotic and entirely delightful. Penn kissed her.

First she was rigid, apparently surprised, but when he would have stopped, she put her arms around his neck and pulled him back. As the kiss ended, she lowered her eyes; her reserve didn't seem calculated. "Don't start actually liking me, Martin."

"Why not?" Penn teased. "Because then you might start liking me back?"

Mead looked restlessly around the room, frowning. "I thought we were having dinner."

"Anywhere you choose." He wanted to leave the Exchange District, to have an opportunity to talk without the possibility of Cevan Swan overhearing, but he didn't want his desire for such privacy to be obvious. Penn stood. Mead slipped farther into the chair as his absence created more room. She twisted her head to look up at him. "Any restaurant in Stone Town," he said. "I'll pay. Unlimited funds, Mead, but make it good. The only native food I've eaten—lunch, yesterday—was dreadful."

Indolently, she extended her legs, pointing her toes at the closed screen. "I told you to hire me."

"I should have listened."

Mead smiled, then tapped the screen with the sole of her left shoe. "What were you doing?"

"Thinking about you."

She straightened in the chair. "Oh, stop it, Martin. I'm not really just seventeen. A little flirting is fun; too much makes me think you consider me a fool."

He watched her profile. A moue pulled down the corner of her mouth, but otherwise she seemed almost to be holding her breath. He wanted to say precisely the right thing and didn't know what she wanted to hear, so he said nothing.

"Do I frighten you?" she asked.

"Absolutely."

She grinned.

Gray, her own brother, had warned Penn that Mead was dangerous, but she could seem so cheerfully amusing that he forgot her humor wasn't lighthearted. He felt her danger, now. Though Testament was generally ignored, the Harmony would punish an Ahman's death. If she wanted to harm Testament, if the sweep of her revenge was that wide, there was little better she could do than kill him. *Do I frighten you?* Gray thought her capable of killing.

"I know where to take you." Mead jumped up enthusiastically. "Get your coat—you'll have to walk outside."

"Where are we going?"

"You'll see." She was putting on her jacket, then she looked at him—he hadn't moved—smiled as though she recognized his hesitation, and shook her head. "I promise not to hurt you until after dinner."

Penn bowed with mock solemnity, acknowledging her sardonic promise, then went to his bedroom; she didn't follow. He got his warmest jacket, but hesitated before returning to Mead. Among his personal possessions was a Neulander medical condition monitor. He picked it up, weighing it in his hand, then strapped it to his left wrist. Its gleaming black-and-glass exterior looked enough like a bracelet that she might not question it, yet it would warn him of poison; it could also begin a diagnosis of her medical problem, once it acclimated to her. The device expressed exactly his ambivalent attitude toward Mead.

She was quiet when he returned to the social room and barely returned his greeting; he extended his arm for her to hold, using an ancient gallantry he'd seen in vids. She held his arm while they stood side by side in the elevator. As they did, he set the Gateways utility to issue an alarm if he didn't return in six hours. The top of her head was lower than his shoulder. Even wearing a heavy jacket, she seemed frail. Was he a fool to distrust her, or a fool to go out with her at all?

The lobby guards, whom he barely noticed usually, smirked slightly as he left with Mead. Crossing Amity Square, he was immediately cold. She was a native, accustomed to the climate, while he had spent too many years inside Center's enclosure, breathing filtered air kept at an even temperature.

At the bottom of the lifting line was the usual row of vehicles for hire. Penn suggested that they ride. Mead grinned, but led him to the first in line, where she proceeded to haggle over the fare—he would gladly have paid the first one quoted—while wind drove frozen bits of dust against his face so that he had to listen with his back turned to them. Then, throughout the tedious ride, in a vehicle with frayed upholstery, a sickly scent of pine, and a suspension system that, even by native standards, must have been antique, Mead conducted a review of local news with their driver, sharing opinions about the construction of a new desalinization station, trading guesses as to the future of an outlands mixed settlement where a feud had begun between two dominant lines, and generally editorializing on events in an attitude of impromptu familiarity that, on repulsed reflection, Penn realized may have indicated actual familiarity in their past-remembered lives. She ignored him.

They were let out on a darkening street of large, detached private houses. "Welcome to my home," Mead said.

"Your home?" He shouldn't have been surprised, yet he was.

Her typical cutting response to a foolish question didn't

come. She smiled. "It's been in the main line for five generations."

Gray had shown Penn a representative native neighborhood; it was likely that Mead's every neighbor was a member of the Bridger line, which undoubtedly owned the land. Each building was a unit consisting of a woman and her children; occasionally sisters shared a home, all under the auspices of the family councils—in this case, that of Bridger Dome. The collective nature of Testament made Penn queasy; it was too reminiscent of a hive.

Mead took his hand and led him, like a child, on a narrow path through gravel raked into circular patterns that emphasized a few well-placed boulders. Penn paused to inspect it.

"My dry garden," she said. "I have a green garden in back."

"Ah." Penn struggled for something to say. "Unusual."

She shook her head and pointed. All up and down the street were more dry gardens. He bowed, annoyed by his stupid error.

The door had a doorknob, not an identifier plate, giving the private residence an aura of prestige to Harmony perceptions. They stood beneath a small overhang, which shielded them poorly from the elements, while Mead opened the door with a metal key. Penn was captivated by the primitive simplicity of home security.

"It's getting dark already," she said as she led him inside a narrow, stuffy entrance hall. She clicked a knob on the wall and the room filled with dazzling electric light from a hanging chandelier. Each cut-crystal prism was a bulb; each contained a filament that fired light into the air and to the others, producing a brilliant glitter.

"Beautiful, isn't it?"

The crystal splashed tiny rainbow colors across Mead's vulnerable expression. Penn considered the mechanism crude and the inefficient arrangement gaudy, but he smiled and agreed.

A stairway went only up. Two carelessly furnished rooms were open on either side of the hall. A hard, sharp noise was repetitively ticking; otherwise, the house was silent. Mead walked directly forward to a closed door and pushed it open with the palm of her hand. "Come on, Martin. There's work to do."

The rear room to which she led him was a kitchen. Large,

it also looked communal, with separate areas that duplicated functions. A long table with hard-backed chairs took up the side of the room with windows—blank now, because of the dark outside. Throughout, the kitchen gleamed with cleanliness, though the hanging metal pans and utensils showed signs of use. "We'll eat in," Mead said.

Penn hadn't come far inside the door. "I don't cook."

She laughed merrily. "I bet you don't garden, either."

"No, I don't." He should have pretended some polite enjoyment of her plan, but she wasn't even considering an alternative.

"What *do* you do in your spare time? Besides picking up native women?"

"You picked me."

She took a knife from a blue stone block containing others and tested its edge with her thumb. "You make a good straight man."

He frowned. "I don't understand your meaning."

"It's a left-handed compliment."

Her explanation required an explanation. It was pointless to inquire further, and her use of local idiom was as irritating as when they'd first met. "What are we going to eat? And when?"

"Leave that to me." She set her knife on the nearest counter, tossed her jacket onto a stool, then began bringing things—foodstuffs and utensils—from cabinets and a cold room. Penn watched; she didn't demand his participation. Several times she opened a cabinet or drawer, paused, and closed it again. Once she muttered, "A really bad idea," but when he offered that it wasn't too late to resort to a restaurant, she just chuckled.

Despite her occasional hesitations, Mead moved with the grace of a professional chef. She sliced with as much assurance as she spoke, and with more concentration. Penn sat on a stool and watched her deft hands as she cut into a pale yellow, fleshy object he didn't recognize; it smelled like trampled foliage: pleasant outdoors, but not directly appetizing. He felt increasingly confident that the product of all her industry would be acceptable, but this wasn't how he had intended to spend the evening.

"Anyone can clean," Mead said. She pushed on his back and steered him to a sink where she had discarded several bowls. Penn rinsed the dishes in cold water from the tap. His sleeves got wet. He rolled them up, but the dampness soaked through to his skin. He was working like the lowest sub drudge under the direction of an Altered woman. She was humming to herself.

Mead deposited more dishes beside the sink, critically inspected the bowls he had already rinsed, then glanced at him. "You're not happy." She seemed surprised.

Perhaps Mead had intended this visit to her home to be intimate and special, but he didn't care. "I'm wet and I still haven't eaten."

"Martin, you have a temper, even if it's on a slow fuse." She put her arms around his waist.

He turned back to the dishes. Mead laughed and walked away. Penn scrubbed at a greasy spot, then tossed the bowl down hard into the sink and turned the water off. Playing house with a seventeen-year-old native woman was disgraceful, even if Mead hadn't intended to demean him—although with her, one never knew.

"There were no Harmony tourists in Edgemarket this afternoon," she said. "That's what the Quinn driver told me. And coming here tonight I noticed a new moon in our sky."

"What?"

"I thought you'd want to know that Governor Swan is up to something."

Penn returned to the stool he'd used before, close to Mead. "What do you mean, 'a new moon'?"

"A ship. He brought it into low orbit from wherever its base is."

Testament was allocated a single cruiser. Swan was not only governor, he commanded the small military contingent posted to Testament. "He hasn't said anything to me."

"Would he?"

Mead's cooking hadn't slowed, and he remained unfed, but she'd detonated his anger in one burst—and directed it at Swan. The Governor had no *obligation* to inform an Ahman visitor of his plans, but . . . it was insulting for him to fail to do so. What was Swan planning, anyway? "Are you sure?"

She nodded. "Things have been tight ever since you arrived—extra security at Exchange's 'strategic' points—but this seems like more than just protecting you."

Swan disliked Altereds. He'd called Penn a liberal, and Penn was linked with Elector Lee. If Swan brought a credible Altered plot to light, and punished it, Altereds would be villains and Swan would be a hero, at precisely the wrong time for Elector Lee. "Thank you." He bowed quite deeply.

She smiled down at the thin noodles she was stuffing with a red paste. "Go ahead," she said, indicating the tray she'd been arranging with tidbits of food. "Have something while you're waiting."

He was less hungry than he had been a few minutes earlier, but the kitchen was becoming suffused with tempting smells. He ate one of the stuffed noodles, taking it from Mead's hand before she could arrange it with the others on the plate. It was excellent, a creamy, sweet cheese taste with a pleasantly sharp undertone he couldn't identify; the noodle was still warm. "Swan knows about the precaster plot, such as it is," Penn said. "He would have heard you tell me. That could be his excuse for extra vigilance, although it's very slim."

"He bugs your rooms?" For once, Mead sounded shocked. "I mean, he monitors them?"

"Probably. It's common on Center, at least in public places. Arguably, a tourist inn is public."

"Everywhere in your suite?" She stopped working.

Penn smiled. "I didn't know you were so modest."

"I didn't know you were an exhibitionist."

They looked at each other, and both laughed.

Her shyness seemed absurd, though sweet, since every descendant of a Testament woman remembered their mothers' sexual adventures. "A properly set monitor will edit certain things, including sex." Unless it was set at Security levels; she didn't need to know that. He took another stuffed noodle, and Mead returned to work. "These are very good."

"Your bracelet is blinking."

His medical condition monitor was flashing yellow. Abruptly concerned, he touched the "specify" site, then felt sheepish as it warned that the fat content of what he'd ingested was high. Penn turned the monitor off and waited for Mead to ask about it, but she didn't. He ate another, different type—it was yellow, originally part of the thing she'd sliced—but he didn't like it as well. "Are precasters really behind this situation with Gray's wife?" he asked.

"Of course."

Mead needed to believe it was the precasters, or else her revenge would have failed to hit its mark. "It seems so fragile; I expected better from them. And how could they plan that I'd let an Altered woman, even a supposed singleton, leave Testament?"

Mead wiped her hands on a cloth and stepped back, inspecting the plate of native delicacies. "She came here."

"Reed?"

Mead nodded and moved the plate farther from him, protecting her work. "To defend the alia, Gray's wife. She must have precast that I'd try to kill her. Gray doesn't realize the extent to which he's been manipulated by Reed, but I do."

Penn pulled his stool closer, wondering about that attack, but having larger questions. "I don't believe they're clever enough to know any human psyche so thoroughly. Even in the Harmony we don't."

Mead turned to him. Her eyes were angry; she had a deep frown that wasn't directed at him. "You're wrong. They don't know everyone as well as they know us, their children, but they can guess. That's precasting—they're excellent guessers. They call it informed intuition. And when they get hold of someone, there's always the possibility of confabulation."

"Confabulation?"

"False memory. You Harmony people act as if memory is an objective record, but it isn't. People revise their memories constantly in light of new experiences and new emotions. People are very suggestible, too. Precasters know tricks to make them even more suggestible. What you remember might never actually have happened."

"Precasters implant new memories?" It was a disturbing thought. He examined his memory of Reed's precast, but couldn't feel any change in his mind. Then he recalled Mead's statement that his attitude toward natives was more sympathetic. What distinguished confabulation from simply learning through experience?

"Precasters are experts at confabulation. They don't physically implant anything, although they sometimes use hypnosis and drugs. Repetition helps. They talk, ask questions, and shape new ideas and memories, or draw out stories programmed into the subconscious. It's easy to create a memory that's supposed to come from several generations earlier, since it doesn't have to fit as neatly into real life—our reminiscences of our mothers are never orderly or sequential—

but those old family memories can have compelling effects on people's attitudes and influence what they do."

"How can you know anything you remember is real?"

"The best way is by external confirmation. You can also check if it makes sense, and who gains from your holding that belief, but you can go crazy always wondering if your mind is your own. They don't do it often. Precasters aren't gods, setting our fates. Mostly, they put game pieces on the board, set things in motion, and only nudge one or another in the 'right' direction. Me, I just try to stay away from them." She sighed, picked up the bowl containing the remaining red paste, and took it to the sink Penn had left. He felt guilty as she rinsed it, and went to help, bringing a spoon and a few other implements she'd left behind. She washed those, too. "I have to clean the chicken breasts and stir-fry the pieces with the fruit."

"You've made enough food already." At first put off by her domesticity, so exotic in his experience, Penn was now enjoying her desire to please, and her pensive openness. He was also considering what to do about Swan.

"But there's no main course."

He hugged her, laughing at her agitation over a meal. She didn't hold back from his embrace this time. She laid her head against his shoulder, resting there, but as he encircled her in his arms, she pushed him away. "You *are* wet. I guess not everyone can wash dishes. Come with me upstairs; I'll get you something dry to wear."

Mead took his hand and looked up at him in a way that drove other thoughts from his mind. She led him upstairs, to a narrow hallway with a series of closed doors. The carpet was worn in the middle and the painted wall had a smudged line at about the height of a child's dirty hand. "How many people live here?"

"Just me, since I evicted them all yesterday." Her tone was leaden. She opened the second door on the left, and he followed her into a smallish, cluttered room. "Gray hasn't collected everything yet."

Penn wished he hadn't seen Gray's room. It was too personal a portrait of the young man, a dreamer's private place, filled with pictures of imagined other worlds. Jumbled items were scattered on most surfaces; nothing looked valuable. Stacked papers covered the desk. Despite the clutter, the room wasn't slovenly. It was an innocent place, reminding

Penn that Gray was one of the few natives who was truly young. Mead was not.

"I told you he's harmless," Mead said quietly. She picked up a hardcopy book and handed it to Penn. "He likes old stories about heroes."

Penn set it on the desk. "You wanted me to see this."

She nodded. "I suppose I owe Gray this much after all the tricks I've played on him. You see, despite being a singleton, Gray understands me pretty well; in some things, better than the rest. The Bridger main line are winners; they don't remember any important disappointments, except, maybe, the Harmony's arrival. In his own bungling way, Gray tries to be kind. I want to be rid of that, and him. I wanted you to see that he's safe to let into the Harmony." Mead opened a folding door. Clothes were hanging in a closet. "You're bigger, but not so much that something here won't fit." She ran her hand along the shoulders of the shirts, then pulled a blue one from its hanger, tossing it to Penn.

He caught the shirt and held it. The fabric was soft, but to wear Gray's clothing was distasteful. Certainly Governor Swan would make much of his wearing native clothes, if he was seen.

Mead noticed his hesitation. "Not good enough for you, Martin?"

She would be offended if he didn't put it on. Penn didn't examine why that was undesirable. "Gray probably wouldn't lend it, after storming out of my suite this morning."

Mead smiled as if visualizing the scene. "And what did you do to trigger that?"

"I said his wife should be sterilized, as you suggested. His reaction made me think he might know about the precaster plan."

She shook her head. "Gray wants children, although *why* is a good question. For most men, children are trophies; Gray wants them the way a woman does. The way I do. And Gray tries to be so noble, he probably intends to be monogamous. It must be part of Reed's plan, to keep him tied to the alia."

Penn took off his shirt, having to pull the left sleeve carefully over the medical condition monitor. Mead watched, then startled him by coming close and rubbing herself against his chest. He turned to face her more squarely, and she kissed him, almost attacking him with her intensity, thrusting her tongue into his mouth while her right hand urgently fumbled inside his pants. Her aggression was exciting. With quick, determined movements she undressed him, although she stayed mostly clothed, only pulling up the skirt of her suit while he stayed passive, enjoying her heat. She pushed him backward, onto Gray's bed, and climbed across him. She closed her eyes while she rode him, as if satisfying an impersonal lust. When she stopped, he had climaxed, but wasn't sure she had.

"Mead."

"Shh." She lifted her leg over and went off him.

She'd been ferocious, the way a man sometimes was. "Why?"

She glanced coolly at him. "You didn't like it?" She pulled down her skirt and started to leave the room.

"Where are you going?"

"I have to cook."

He watched her leave, then lazily got up. He was sticky, but wouldn't feel clean if he washed here. He put on Gray's shirt and his own pants; carrying his shirt, he went downstairs. Mead was working diligently with a knife, her lips compressed in concentration. He walked to her side, but she didn't look up. He unclasped the medical condition monitor. "Wear this," he said, holding it out.

She glanced sideways at him. "What is it?"

"It continuously checks your medical situation."

She hesitated in her work; the knife seemed to be pointed at him as she held it, but a grin spread across her face. "A poison sniffer! Thank you, Martin. No one has ever lacked that much confidence in my cooking before."

She thought he was only showing an increase in trust. He slipped it around her knife-wielding hand without telling her what else it could do. It was too loose for her wrist, and got in her way; she pushed it up her arm to her elbow. There was no reason for him to refuse to cure her infertility, or at least investigate its cause. As long as she remained on Testament, it would have no effect on the Harmony if one additional Altered woman conceived.

"Do you know why you can't have children?" he asked.

She resumed cutting. "Yes."

"Why?"

"I told you. Reed doesn't want my descendants on the main line, so she won't let me have any." Mead tossed the knife down onto the counter. "How do you people endure knowing that once your life is over, your memory is gone?"

Penn answered carefully, so as not to insult her. "I wouldn't be comfortable knowing that my memories would become the common property of others—especially freaks like Gray's wife. The mind is the only sure privacy a person has."

"Do you think you're so much better than us?"

He couldn't deny it. "The natural human state is, in most instances, the best form for observing the universe, and creating Order."

"Is that what Jon Hsu says?" Mead smiled as she said Hsu's name. "But you're the ones who come to Testament looking for God. That's how you get through your days—by looking for something beyond your life."

"Reed told you that." He was disappointed in Reed.

"I haven't spoken with the old bitch in days, and never about you. It's obvious. You people, you standard humans, are so lonely that you need to invent meaning for your lives."

"And you need to have children." He regretted that, but instead of becoming angry, Mead nodded.

"And I can't. I'm one of you, like it or not. Lonely." She extended her hand in the manner of a handshake. "A pledge," she said. "I'll always tell you the truth. We'll have a partnership."

He was astonished.

"Do you agree? Or don't you want me as a partner?"

In the Harmony, partnerships were formal arrangements just short of marriage. He'd never been asked by a woman nor had he offered partnership to one, but the thought of a partnership with Mead—temporary, of course—was exciting. "On Testament, we'll be partners," he said.

They shook hands. Mead's was damp and very tiny.

"Truth. The reason I can't have children is that Reed thinks I'm a precaster. The Compound Council doesn't want the rest of us to understand what it's up to, so it keeps us ignorant."

"*Are* you a precaster?"

She turned back to her work. In the corner of her eye, something glittered. A tear? She spoke without any ragged emotion in her voice, but her hunched posture and her grip on the knife showed that her words came hard. "Technically yes, but no, not really. A precaster is defined as any person who remembers Janet Bridger, the founder of our line. I've remembered a few bits of her life, but I can't precast; I haven't yet, anyway. I have no experience, and I don't know the things they *tell* each other. That's what makes a real precaster."

Confused by his feelings for Mead, Penn had nevertheless decided to cure her, if the monitor showed a cure was possible. He wanted to help her, but Mead was a precaster, or nearly one. She'd said herself that precasters weren't permitted to have children. A cure using Harmony facilities would provide more ammunition for Swan. Besides, although he was beginning to harbor a hope that Mead was not *just* using him, there was also the likelihood that once cured, she would vanish from his life. Her information was also valuable. It was expedient and entirely contemptible, but Penn decided to postpone an offer.

"Martin?" she asked, perhaps seeking reassurance. He hugged her. She looked up. Her tears, if she'd shed any, had dried, but her red lip paint was smeared, making her tentative smile seem off and somehow empty.

II. Unsuccessful Women

Janet was sure that Gray would return and free her from his grandmother; after all, Reed thought he would come, too. Janet paced back and forth between the window and the door, waiting for him, until her legs tired; then she rocked in the rocking chair, still waiting. It seemed to her that waiting for a man was a quintessential female experience, but it was not the existence of women on Testament.

Why only female memories, Dr. Bennett? Janet had asked Testament's real founder—not the men who'd sent off the ship, or even the people on it. It had been simple to justify the use of the relatively stable mitochondrial DNA, but now, a millennium too late, Janet saw Emily Bennett's ulterior motive. Subversive inheritor of the disreputable line of twentieth-century feminists, she had plotted the overthrow of men, taming them by harnessing the exclusively female ability to bear children against them. Men were transient mayflies beside Testament's women, who invaded their minds, tempering male dominance with the knowledge that men were only unsuccessful women.

Janet didn't like her descendants, didn't even like their city, Stone Town. A heavy name. Sticks and stones. Stone soup. The name rang of poverty and scorn, and that had been her experience of it. Reed Bridger, harsh and formidable, exemplified them. They plotted to possess their children, body and soul; they marginalized men, unable to make them wholly equal, unwilling to give them independence. Mead was just as bad. No wonder Gray ached to escape.

Janet intended to help him. She wanted to believe it was loyalty, or generosity of spirit, but suspected it was at least partly revenge against Reed Bridger. Reed was Janet's many-times-great-granddaughter, but it was a relationship so attenuated that Janet felt nothing for her but resentment. At every opportunity, Reed deprecated Janet, even calling her a "revision of a story" Reed was writing. Janet would give the story a new twist. There was a way off Testament. She would use her memory of Jon, if necessary.

Perhaps life in the Harmony was different. At least Jon's philosophy aspired toward greatness, although the unfriendly architecture of the Exchange District didn't seem promising.

She returned to the window, but it was dark. That afternoon there had been blue sky. The area between the ruin and Bridger Dome was wide, flat, bare, and open, a neutral field, not a park. The ruin itself depressed her, though she didn't know why it should. The rest of the city was an agglomeration of curved and angular shapes, as if a child's building blocks had been strewn in disarray across the land. There was nothing bold, arrogant, or arresting, nothing to marvel at or disapprove, only the monotony of an ugly suburb inflated into a metropolis and the beehive domes. Stone Town was the opposite of grand.

Gray was a product of this place, too. Away from him, her infatuation (that was the only explanation for the rush of emotion she felt in his presence) interfered less with her rational assessment; she saw his faults. He conceded too much to his grandmother, acquiesced to her as he would not to a man. He lacked the personal ambition of someone like Jon, and the breadth of Jon's mind. Of course, Gray hadn't had an opportunity to better himself, and, whatever his failings, she was tied to him. He was the only person who cared enough to keep her alive.

The door opened. Reed Bridger entered. "Gray hasn't returned," she said.

"No." Janet treated the statement like a question in order to have something to say. Though it was unsettling to acknowledge, Reed Bridger frightened her. Janet felt compelled to prevent her from dominating their conversation.

Reed came farther into the room and glanced out the window at the black hole that was Shak Dome. "Gray hasn't been in Stone Town today. Martin Penn left Exchange with Mead—they went to her house—but no one has seen Gray."

Reed intended to ask for Janet's help. Janet saw the signs with a pleasure tainted only by her concern for Gray.

"Our information from inside Exchange is limited." Reed went to the small pile of Gray's things they'd brought from Mead's house; she lifted a black ceramic vase modeled into the likeness of a woman, smiled slightly, and set it carefully down. "We do know Gray went into Exchange. It's likely that he has been detained by the Harmony governor, a hostile man named Cevan Swan. Either Martin hasn't protected him, as we thought he would, or Martin doesn't know. If Gray has been arrested, then it's because of you, because of your plan to hide your condition and enter the Harmony."

Guilt and panic were what this native woman wanted, but even knowing that, they were difficult to suppress. Her life depended on Gray. Janet took a breath and watched Reed. *She* wasn't panicked. "You don't know Gray has been charged with anything. It's also possible that he arranged with Ahman Penn to stay in Exchange until a ship arrives to take him off Testament."

"If that's the case, then he has deserted you."

Janet flushed, but held her head high. "If that's the case, I'm glad for him. He's free."

"That is the less probable of the alternatives."

Janet smiled. She was keeping up with this so-called precaster. "I don't think so. You refused to help him wake me this morning and he assumed I was gone permanently. You forced him to deal with Penn without me."

Reed sighed. "Gray is a singleton. Without our memories and caution, and because he had wanted so much to join them, he has always taken Harmony power, and Governor Swan, too lightly. It is treason to do what he tried. I doubt that Gray would desert . . . you. It's more plausible that he is being held. He'll be imprisoned and questioned by their Security, in which case, Gray may be better off dead."

Reed had whispered her oblique allusion to torture. Janet

looked away. However manipulative, Reed wanted her grandson safe. "How can I help Gray?" Janet asked.

Reed smiled with the closest look to approval she'd ever given Janet. "There is one thing you can do—go to Martin Penn. Ask for his help."

Something was wrong. "Why not ask Ahmen Penn yourself? You've given him a precast."

"Mead is with him; we don't get along."

Mead. "She's the one who betrayed us to Penn, according to you."

"My dear girl," Reed said, her tone once again expressing disdain, as well as her impatience. "Mead's relationship with Gray is a tangled one. Even I can't guess what she feels. I doubt, however, that she wants her brother dead. She'll probably be your ally in this; she'll never willingly be mine."

Mead and Gray. Janet had felt the electricity between them, although Gray himself seemed unaware of it, or that Mead wasn't. "This world is disgusting," Janet said.

Reed smiled with equanimity. "Don't take your opinions too seriously, my dear. They aren't necessarily intrinsic to Janet."

Sullenly defeated by Reed's implication, Janet said, "I thought you didn't want me near Martin Penn. Isn't that why I was locked in here?"

"Mead is a precaster, which makes her predictable. Her memories go back to Janet Bridger. What she hasn't thought about, she doesn't know, but the memory of the Bridger secret is available to her. Mead won't let him learn the secret from you, or tell it to him herself, while she still hopes to have children, and she'll be hopeful as long as she's with Martin. So if I were you, I'd be careful. You already know Mead's attitude toward you."

Janet had no memory of the attack. She'd been inert on the bed, which made it more unnerving. Mead would kill a helpless person. And later, Mead had tricked Janet, the better to betray them to Penn, but Janet straightened her back and assumed an air of confidence. "I'll free Gray, if he's being held," she said. If he wasn't, then she might be able to join him.

Reed nodded gracefully. "But say anything about the Bridger secret to Martin, and if Mead doesn't kill you, remember that *I* will." Without waiting for an acknowledgment, or to see if Janet was frightened by her threat, Reed went to the door. As she opened it for them, she said, as if she hadn't just threatened Janet's life, "I'll put you in a family car. One of the guards will drive you to Mead's house."

"I know where to go, and I have nowhere to run." Mead's house wasn't far; she'd walked there with Gray. Janet brushed past Reed, went out onto the veranda and along it to the lift. Reed needed her, and was afraid of that. Janet moved quickly, to make it difficult for the old woman, but she herself was weak and Reed managed to ride the same lift down.

"The car will be easier." Reed sounded worried, and the two other Bridgers sharing the lift looked askance at Janet. She stared stonily ahead. When the lift jerked to a stop, Janet strode out, again trailed by Reed.

Janet went to the nearest exit, not the one she recalled using with Gray. She could circle the dome outside, but she wanted to get away from Reed. She stepped through the entrance arch. Outdoors, the night was dark and chilly. A bustle of people—Bridgers, all of them, like some grossly swollen family reunion—passed to and from the dome. Many nodded a casual greeting at Reed. Beyond the lighted area, however, the city seemed empty as a graveyard at night, and as frightening. "Give me some money," she ordered Reed. "I'll take a cab."

"Good girl." Reed called one of the guards outside the entrance by name, then went to speak with her. Janet couldn't hear them, but the young woman, after a glance at Janet, handed Reed some paper money, which Reed brought back and gave to Janet. "The Quinns are honest," Reed said. "They've always been Bridger allies. Use one of their cars."

Janet started to walk away, but pride had its limits. There were no street signs anywhere in Stone Town, except Edgemarket's tourist areas. Memory was the usual guide. A ride would be best. Janet looked around for a cab, feeling Reed's attention, but not turning. There were cars in a line, quiet electric vehicles, smaller and quicker than the gas and electric models she knew from Before. She went to the first and got in without negotiating the price. She sat there, uncertain what to say. An address? Would asking to be taken to "Mead Bridger's house" be enough, even on Testament?

"Where to?" The woman cabby didn't turn around.

Janet knew Reed would rescue her if the cab stayed still long enough. "Just pull away," she said.

The car's motion was gentle. On the street, the view into the hills of the Spine wasn't blocked by the domes. The Exchange District was there, but it was dark, one of their technological secrets. In the Harmony, at least people had advanced beyond what she remembered.

Reed had said Martin Penn was in Mead's house, but that might not be true. He might have left. Mead could be alone, waiting; Mead might try to kill her again. Anyway, Penn was, at best, an intercessor. Governor Swan held Gray, if anyone did. Why not speak directly with Swan? Reed called him hostile, but that seemed a good recommendation, coming from her.

The cabby came to a corner, stopped, and turned around. "Where?"

Janet bit her lip. The people in the Harmony were more like her than these natives. She would be able to deal with Governor Swan, if Gray was a prisoner at all. The thought of arriving independently, of showing Gray she was responsible for herself, was attractive. Just as she thought she'd made up her mind to disobey Reed's instruction, her mind froze. This time she felt it, and even remained aware as, like jerking gears on a chain, something other than herself, or someone, struggled. She ached to expel the foreign presence. The feeling of being out of control of herself, of sharing her thoughts with an alien mind, the repulsive intrusion, was like mental rape. Then, as suddenly as it had vanished, her control over herself returned. Sickened, she knew Gray had told the truth about her condition. She needed him to keep her whole, and separate from those others. "Take me to the Exchange," Janet said.

Chapter 8

I. An Act of War

Swan had darklit all of Amity Square, from the funicular railway entrance all the way to Gateways House at the other end. Like anywhere darklit, the area seemed unnatural, and Swan looked ridiculous, a fat man in a quasi-military outfit, surrounded by rows of uniformed troops. Penn shook his head. "I don't believe this."

"Ahman Penn, you are the most important visitor this world has ever had. You set an alarm. How did you expect to be greeted?" Governor Swan bowed badly, using his bulk as the excuse for an otherwise disrespectful awkwardness.

"The alarm was precautionary," Penn said, "and the time hasn't expired yet, anyway—despite the difficulty you caused me by refusing access into the Exchange District to my only available transport, a native vehicle."

"Why, Martin, you really are afraid of me." Mead snuggled against his side, grinning.

Penn wanted furiously to slap her, but he smiled and pretended a passion impossible to feel in this situation, putting his arm around her and pulling her closer, which had the incidental benefit of concealing the medical condition monitor on her wrist, which otherwise glinted in the directed darklight beams.

"This is a hazardous world," Swan said. "You have consistently underestimated Testament's dangers. I am responsible for your safe return to Center; when you set an alarm, I set an alert. If you hadn't returned on time, we would have swept into Stone Town and retrieved you."

Swan was making a speech for the benefit of his soldiers, fussing over Penn's safety as a means of diminishing Penn; Penn couldn't allow that. "Governor Swan," Penn said loudly, so the formation of men would hear, not just Peter

Isaacs, captain of the Testament military detachment, who was standing at formal attention just to Penn's right, looking pained. "I alone am responsible for my safety here. Your opposition, had you swept down that hill into Stone Town, would have consisted almost entirely of women and children. Please do not embarrass the Harmony, or me, by attempting a rescue where there is no threat. Efficiency of that type is not regarded favorably on Center." Penn had used a tone appropriate for dressing down a subordinate, although as an Academic he had only moral authority, and no direct rank, over a civil service bureaucrat; Swan's position, though, had become absurd the moment Penn returned to the Exchange District.

Penn signaled Captain Isaacs to stand down. They'd assembled for his protection; he was safe. Isaacs might have chosen not to obey without an order from Swan, but Jonist soldiers were not robots; Penn felt proud as, with only a quick glance at Swan, Isaacs ordered his massed men at ease.

Swan scowled. "Ahman Penn, these Altereds are plotting against the Harmony, as you yourself discovered. This is a small outpost; they could attack us at any time."

Penn would not permit Swan to use Altereds as bogeymen. "Governor Swan, Testament is not a world that requires military remedies. The only plot conceived here—if it even actually exists; I have my doubts—involves getting one fertile woman off the planet. However much you might despise the nature of these natives, still, the Electors have Ruled that a quarantine is enough. Your duty is simply to enforce it until such time as the Electors and the Grand Assembly determine that these women should be allowed inside the Harmony with the rights of other Altered humans." Penn bowed politely, correctly, but turned away from Swan with alacrity, and tugged on Mead to follow.

"You certainly told him," she said, sufficiently loud to be overhead. "But Swan had cooked his own goose." She giggled.

The stupid woman was enjoying this. He stopped and shook her, roughly, under cover of their embrace. "Bow to him," he whispered as he thrust her slightly away. His association with a native woman did him no good in the eyes of this garrison; more important, there was a limit to the censure he would inflict on any Harmony official, and public impertinence from an Altered woman went beyond it.

Mead stumbled, making obvious his part in her motion, and therefore making it imperative that she do as he had ordered. She hesitated, and glanced at Swan, but Penn couldn't coerce her inconspicuously. Mead straightened, which underscored her small stature, and gracefully performed a perfect bow to Swan, one recognizing a definite superior. Then she waited, her demeanor requiring a response, unless Swan was blatantly discourteous. Given the context, to refuse would make Swan not only boorish, but disrespectful of Penn.

The soldiers were watching. Swan was damp with sweat, as if the darklit area were hot; his expression was stiff, but Swan bowed, if minimally. Only years at Center kept Penn from grinning. Mead had deftly turned a show of deference to Swan into a concession to her from him. Penn relaxed, and felt an ebbing of tension from the surrounding men.

Swan had just become his enemy. That was unfortunate, but largely irrelevant; Swan couldn't do anything to Ahman Martin Penn. Nevertheless, it was pointless to exacerbate the situation. Penn nodded at him. "Perhaps you would join us in my suite, Governor?" Penn asked. "We can discuss this contretemps better with some privacy."

"I would appreciate the opportunity, Ahman Penn." Swan signaled for the watching soldiery to disband. They complied reluctantly, peering at Swan and Penn as if they were actors leaving a play half-finished. Isaacs saluted, and hurried his men away.

Penn set a quick pace to Gateways House. Mead's hard-soled shoes tap-tapped like raindrops on steel. Swan would have been silent except for the huffing breaths from his grossly out-of-shape body. The Gateways House guards bowed deeply at them, and for once Penn bowed back. He walked directly into the open elevator and waited for his two companions to enter.

"Will this be private?" Penn asked Swan curtly as the door closed. "No monitors or snoops?"

Swan nodded, still trying to catch his breath, but he looked meaningfully at Mead. Penn didn't acknowledge the discreet question.

Swan was still wheezing when the elevator opened to

Penn's floor, but he kept up with Penn step for step as they entered the suite. Mead trailed behind the two men.

Penn tossed his jacket onto a convenient table, glad he had changed back into his own shirt. He wheeled around to face Swan. "What was going on out there? A suspicious man might wonder if his return was unwelcome, and think he was being made into an excuse to destroy Stone Town."

"Martin, no such idea entered my thoughts." Swan's gold buttons and epaulets looked absolutely silly, like something from the fictional drivel displayed earlier in this room. Still perspiring heavily, he opened the neck of his uniform jacket.

"With the current situation in Center," Penn began, then stopped, glimpsing Mead; circumspect for once, she was unobtrusively near the door to the private rooms. She had warned him Swan had called in his cruiser; Swan had hoped for trouble. "The subject of Altereds is sensitive right now. Cevan, I will not allow you to create an incident which could be misunderstood and affect the perception of Altereds."

"I would not *create* anything, Ahman Penn. There is a plot here, however much you discount its danger to us, and your safety weighs heavily on my mind." He glanced at Mead. "She told us about the precasters, but that doesn't make her harmless. You know it yourself; you set an alarm."

Mead was listening to more than she should hear, but Penn wanted to respond to that remark in her presence. "I set the alarm because of an incident with my guide; I trust Mead."

Swan grimaced. "You serve on the staff of one Altered, and assume the rest have his alleged distinction."

Swan was treading very close to the margins of his own quarantine, or else this was something he wanted Testament to know. Penn sat in the most comfortable chair and put his feet on the center table. He gazed impassively at Swan. If Jeroen Lee's descent from Altered Neulanders was still a secret, this pig would never have dared disparage him. "There is no similarity."

Swan sat in the nearest chair and gestured at Mead. "I notice she is wearing a Neuland medical monitor."

Penn didn't condescend to comment. "Mead, go into the bedroom."

Her only response was a bow, satisfyingly deep. Though

she looked interested, she left immediately, without a single sarcastic comment. Such good behavior was suspicious.

Swan sighed when Mead was gone, but didn't meet Penn's eyes. "A ship arrived direct from Center while you were out. An Altered is still an Altered inside the Polite Harmony of Worlds."

Bad news. Penn didn't let recognition into his expression. "There was a private packet for you."

"Where is it?"

"In my office. I took it for safekeeping."

"Still unopened?"

"Yes." Swan didn't pretend to be insulted, so Penn guessed they really weren't being monitored or recorded. "I'll send it to you. It has the Electors' seal. Would it be from him?"

"I have no idea." Penn kept his attention on Swan. The man squirmed. No wonder he was stuck on Testament; he wouldn't have managed the politics of any better post. It was too bad, however; Testament was no place for a man like him. "I expect all monitoring of this suite to stop immediately. The Electors are entitled to full privacy, as is any message they send to their emissary." Let Swan wonder about that.

"Of course, Ahman Penn, except when you have a native visitor alone with you here. Your safety demands a Security watch; the girl could do anything."

"And she does it very well, doesn't she?" Security levels. Penn was exasperated; Swan was doing all he could to be irritating. "I dislike being a source of entertainment. It will stop. I am responsible for whomever I choose to bring into this suite."

Swan leaned toward him. "You don't know these people. You think she's a pretty girl, and harmless, but their bodies are disguises."

Penn smiled. "You must be right; she said exactly the same thing."

Swan stood. He had nowhere to go, and sat down again. "Sex is an act of war here, Martin. It might as well be rape."

Penn laughed, thinking of wild and gentle Mead in contrast to Swan's own eccentric sexual scenarios.

Swan leaned back in his chair, trying to appear confident. The posture accentuated his belly. "Perhaps you should review the news. Four of the five other Electors have publicly stated that Jeroen Lee should resign."

Lee wasn't dead or impeached. He still could make terms for his departure.

Swan saw his relief. "You consider this good news, despite the fact that Lee has been your mentor?"

There was no use explaining that a demand for resignation implied the propriety of Lee's original election, or that the news was not that the Ahmen had voted to impeach. Penn stood. "Thank you for the news, Cevan. I wish this episode tonight hadn't occurred. I want to report only efficient conduct here; if there is no similar incident, then I will ignore this one and cast no aspersions regarding whether or not you are Flawed. Consider acting with more pragmatism. An attempt to make Testament an issue at Center will only rebound to your detriment."

"You don't expect Jeroen Lee to survive the revelation that he is Altered." Swan didn't state it as a question.

Penn hesitated, but responded. "No one with the pain-free Neulander Alteration could; perhaps another Alteration, but not that." The miracle Penn had hoped to find on Testament hadn't materialized. He glanced pointedly at the filter door.

Swan studied Penn and didn't move, despite the cue. "The selection of a new Elector is a rare event. This succession from among the senior Ahmen will be interesting. Particularly now, the candidates will need to be unblemished."

Faintly smiling, Penn waited for Swan to make his point.

"Any nominated Ahman will need to undergo DNA testing, but I doubt secret Alterations are widespread, and from what I hear of Center, a taste for exotic companionship is common; there are issues, however, on which the Academies are not complaisant."

Penn wanted to hurry Swan; the longer they spoke, the more antagonistic the atmosphere had become. Penn couldn't allow himself to be threatened by the obese custodian of a world of Altered women. "Many issues," he said. "But questions of curiosity versus belief are subtle. An accusation may harm the accused or not, but it rarely does any good for the accuser."

"True." Swan got heavily to his feet. "But, Martin, I think you are unwise on one subject. Too close an association with Altereds does not give the kind of impression I presume by your having left Center, you wish to make." He nodded in the direction Mead had gone.

"Don't presume, Cevan."

Swan hesitated, then walked toward the door. Penn had already mentally dismissed him when Swan turned back. "If a precaster plot was demonstrated by clear evidence, your position with respect to the menace posed by these Altereds must naturally change. It would be in your interest; your prestige on Center would be enhanced by uncovering it."

Penn was surprised by Swan's obtuseness. "The Harmony may not be ready for an Altered Elector, but a plot consisting of one girl's departure off-world is not a threat, it's an example of the quarantine's injustice."

Swan tapped his foot against the floor. "When you arrived, I believed an Ahman would see through these freaks, but you haven't. Their one ambition is to breed more carriers for their memories, to expand their lines. They are as bad as Altered Neulanders, alien to us."

"I've heard that said about every Alteration that exists," Penn said. "Men and women are individuals. If not for their Alteration, it's likely Testament's settlers would have failed, and it does no harm now. And Neuland . . ." Penn shrugged. "I can't defend them, but Elector Lee has the same genetic modification, and *he* is a fine man." Penn felt better for having said it.

"These women are conducting a war. They don't do things by ones. If we've discovered this plot, then there are others we haven't identified. They must not succeed; if necessary, I will stop them alone." When Penn said nothing, Swan bowed with precision, giving Penn's position its due, but no more, turned smartly on his heel, and strode out of the room.

Penn sat back in his chair. Only rarely on Center had he been forced to examine his beliefs as closely as he had on Testament. Though he had come to Testament for that purpose, doing it was uncomfortable, and left him feeling guilty, not about Altereds, but about his desire for a God.

Mead tiptoed into the social room. He looked up.

"I heard a bit." She sounded timid until she added, "You didn't say I shouldn't use my ears." She smiled provocatively, her face a delicious mask. "Let me show you what gratitude can make me do."

"Not now."

"Why not? Because I'm the living embodiment of everything that ugly man said?"

That was the exact source of Penn's discomfort; she was.

"Am I so bad?" Mead twirled around on her toes once, and ended in an elaborate curtsy. "Well, maybe I am, but I've never done anything to you. Nothing you haven't asked for, anyway." She flounced closer but stopped when he did nothing to encourage her by look, voice, or gesture. "Martin, I think your Harmony's problem with Testament isn't that we're Altered, but that on Testament women have an edge over men. In the Harmony, women are considered Altered men."

She'd made him smile. "That's ridiculous."

"Is it?" She giggled and sat down on the arm of his chair, leaned forward and whispered in his ear, "Are they listening?"

"Most likely, yes." It would be best if they both acted as though they were monitored.

Pointlessly, she spoke in a lower voice. "You need to protect yourself from everyone: the precasters, Governor Swan ..."

"You?" he interrupted.

She nodded solemnly. "We're partners, but yes. I owe you the truth. Swan hates us, but even so this quarantine is a sieve for minor bits of information; it has to be as long as there are tourists. I knew who you were before I came: Martin Penn, senior Ahman on the staff of the most liberal Elector. The Compound Council would have known more, and guessed how to manipulate you. Swan is right; you can't afford to be their stooge."

Penn took her arm and reviewed the readout on the medical condition monitor. "You really hate them," he said.

She pulled out of his grasp. "Yes, I do. They juggle our lives; they breed us and train us like animals. Precasters." She spat coarsely at the floor, shocking him. "Gray is strong enough, but he's tame. He knows what they do, but he doesn't get angry. The rest are too stupid. I'm the wild seed."

"They've kept you from having children."

She looked at him, blinking too much. "Yes. They're weaving a pattern in the cloth of their descendants' lives, and I'm not a part of it; I know too much. They want us ignorant."

He tapped the medical condition monitor. "I can correct that. This shows there isn't anything substantially wrong, just blockage of the fallopian tubes; it's a three-minute procedure to correct, using a properly calibrated laser scalpel. Isn't that the best revenge?"

Tears filled her eyes and spilled over, running down her cheeks, but she didn't wipe them, or make any sound. "So easy?"

He nodded, held her hand, and waited for her to smile. "I'll do it tomorrow."

"Why?" she asked. "Am I that good in bed?"

He was puzzled by her reaction. "Does why matter?"

"It shouldn't. I didn't intend that it would when I first came to you, but now it does."

"Good," he said, pleased by the honest confession of her plan. "I'd like to see you happy." It was the closest approach to truth he could express.

She stared. Smudged darkness around her eyes made them look even deeper and larger. She got up and went to the window. From Penn's position, the naked window looked black. "Thank you," she said, facing away from him. "I should go home."

"Mead?" The image of Mead wandering her empty house alone was gloomy, and if she didn't stay here, under his protection, Swan might do something to harm her. "I thought you'd be happy. Isn't this what you want?"

She turned around. "I am happy," she said. "Truly, Martin. And grateful. I just wonder why the cure is so simple. Is there some other plan? And after you do it, will they let my child live? A precaster's daughter?"

He shook his head and went to her at the window.

"You think I'm making this up, but I'm not. I'm afraid. There's a reason for everything they do, and they're ruthless."

Penn looked down at the top of her head. She seemed like a child herself, but Mead would be a mother soon; she wouldn't wait long. And the father? Penn was repulsed by the thought of fathering an Altered child, yet a worse image was Mead with another man. He pulled her close. "You can come with me to Center, into the Harmony." He adopted a teasing tone. "You asked for that once."

She smiled impishly, craning her neck to look up at him,

letting the somber mood be changed. "Only if you tell me that you like me."

"You said I shouldn't."

"I changed my mind."

So close to the glass, it was possible to see faintly the black-on-black shapes of the mountains against the night sky, but not the stars. Mead was reflected there. "I do like you," he said.

II. An Interesting Night

Nothing changed. The light never went off. If not for his watch, Gray would have imagined days had passed. He lay supine on the bed, eyes closed. Swan would want him to brood on his captivity, so Gray tried to use the self-discipline he'd taught himself in the outlands, the concentration of awaiting an icesnake in silence, so as to prevent his prey from becoming his predator. He couldn't. Hunger distracted him. His stomach growled; no food had been provided, and he hadn't eaten since breakfast. His thoughts kept turning to Swan's malevolent intentions toward Testament. Offies were methodical. Testament didn't provide anything essential to the Harmony. Swan could do as he liked. Gray told himself that his fear was natural in these circumstances, but he hated being dominated by it and was glad whenever he dozed, which wasn't often enough.

The question of loyalty obsessed him. *Don't you hate them?* Mead had asked. He didn't hate the precasters. Was that a flaw? Loyalty was as simple as their need and his connection to Testament and as complex as his relationship with the Bridger line. He envied Penn. Whatever fungible Harmony world he was from, Penn, like Gray's memory of Janet, had only himself to consider.

They'd left him his clothes and possessions. He fingered the stained spot on his jacket, which he'd rolled into a pillow, and sometimes probed the inner pocket, where Mead's patches awaited his further investigation. A monitored cell wasn't the place for that. Gray didn't understand Mead, but had always believed there were limits on her behavior, and reasons for it. Why give him the drug? Had it only been revenge?

His horror at the memories had cooled, along with his anger. Whether intended or not (*The way to your heart's desire,* she had said; he wondered), Mead had provided a gift, a chemical substitute for what he'd been denied when they made him a singleton, and another reason for loyalty. Partaking of their thoughts wasn't pleasurable, but he now knew that his motherline was in him. His fathers, too. There were men in every memory: Paul, for example, and Emma's son, Jonathan, the architect of Bridger Dome. Gray belonged to Testament, just as they had.

He was napping when the door to his cell opened. A guard entered. "Come," he said.

Gray had decided to refuse to cooperate, but as he received the order, he changed his mind, despising himself for doing so. Was it only fright? But the futility of direct opposition was obvious. Gray grabbed the balled-up jacket, unwilling to abandon the drug, and came.

It was dark outside his cell. The warped reflections were gone, but Gray was confused by the absolute blackness and the feeling of sliding along lighter ground than Testament's. He thought he heard other guards. His guard kept a hand on Gray and used it to direct him, like riding a horse in the Eastlands, except he was the dumb animal here. Eventually, they stepped through a doorway. There was normal gravity and light.

"Gray! You're all right!" Janet's voice said.

"Janet?"

"As I said," Swan told her affably.

As Gray's eyes adjusted, he saw a fuzzy shape that resolved itself as Governor Swan, seated at a desk. There were two guest chairs facing Swan's desk. Janet was in one of them.

Gray took a step closer. His guard was the only one in the room. There were no obvious barriers. Janet seemed to be visiting, not a captive, but she was inevitably also a hostage.

Cordially, as if Gray were a guest, Swan waved Gray toward the second chair. Gray looked around. His guard had retreated to the rear of the office, his hand on his gun. No one else was in sight. Gray looked at his watch. Three a.m. Janet smiled encouragingly. He nodded and sat down.

Janet touched his hand. "I came to find you," she said. "Governor Swan understands that *I* am a singleton, but one with an unusual disorder, and that you only wanted to protect me. Your arrest wasn't his idea, anyway, but Ahman Penn's, and your sister's."

"Really?" Gray hoped to sound noncommittal or stupid. Swan had apparently not threatened Janet. Keep it that way, he thought, trying to understand Swan's game.

"Martin became fond of your sister rather quickly," Swan said. "Although she does have certain energetic qualities, I suspect there is more at work; she is Altered. In any event, Mead Bridger told Martin your wife was not a singleton; he believed her and arranged for your arrest."

The reference to the supposed sexual prowess of Testament's woman was a common offie fantasy. As a guide and a man, Gray had often been asked about the special erotic powers of native women. He didn't, however, understand the obvious slight to Ahman Penn, or why Swan was playing at the edges of truth by pretending he still thought Janet was, in some sense, a singleton. Certainly not just for Janet. Then Gray remembered the unremitting monitoring inside the Harmony district. Swan was creating a record. His attention was that of a careful liar in full performance, and he was looking for dirt on Penn. Never, since his seizure by Harmony guards, had Gray been more certain Penn had no role in it, but Gray felt no particular loyalty to Martin Penn.

Swan smiled at Janet, but spoke to Gray. "You haven't been charged formally because of my own doubts; her tests showed your wife to be a singleton, like you."

"I see," Gray said cautiously. "Then you don't believe there is a precaster plot? Or that I'm involved in cheating the quarantine?"

Swan blinked. His smile looked as if it had become more of an effort, but it didn't fail. "Unless I am mistaken."

"You're not," Janet said confidently, glancing sideways at Gray. He smiled at her, knowing—remembering—how she must feel, proud of her achievement in dealing with Swan, in manipulating the situation, false though her assessment was. Fortuitously, Swan wanted information on Penn, and was willing to overlook Janet's true nature, at least for now.

Swan had kept his attention on Gray. "Perhaps if you tell me more about Ahman Penn's activities on Testament I will be able to determine the truth. You are his guide here; I understand he inquired about gods."

"I wasn't present during his precast," Gray said. "Just at its beginning." Swan apparently wanted information casting doubt on Penn's Jonism.

Swan nodded. "Even that might provide valuable informa-

tion regarding his reliability. And what did he discuss during
the day you spent together?"

Gray leaned back in the chair and glanced up at the ceiling as if trying to remember. He had spent an entire day with
Penn beyond Swan's monitors. This was almost a comfortable situation; only Penn's future was at stake, not Testament's.

"I have staff who might help jog your memory," Swan
said, giving every appearance of making a constructive,
practical comment and not a threat. "If you can't remember
on your own."

"I'm just tired," Gray said immediately. "Let me go home
with my wife; I'll return tomorrow morning, fresh."

Swan shook his head. "Impossible. Ahman Penn would
never approve. Until his charge against you is refuted by
proof he is unreliable . . ." His words trailed off. "I can't release you."

Janet looked at them both as if she finally suspected more
was at work than her maneuvering of Swan. She nodded
sharply. "I'm certain that Gray has valuable insights into
Ahman Penn's reasons for coming to Testament, but his
grandmother, who performed the actual precast, would know
even more. Let the two of us return to Bridger Dome and
discuss the matter with her."

Gray started to object—he would never do anything to
send Reed into the Fort—but Swan was already shaking his
head. "Testimony by an Altered isn't acceptable," Swan
said. "Only Gray and, perhaps, you could give credible confirmation of Ahman Penn's interest in faith and his allegiance to Altereds."

Allegiance to Altereds? Gray wondered what Swan was
fishing for there, but the important thing was that Janet was
awake, which meant she must have been awakened, undoubtedly by Reed, who therefore knew that Gray was in the
Fort. But why send Janet to Swan? Now Janet was trapped,
too. Maybe Reed could do something. Go to Penn, perhaps?
If Penn suspected what Swan was after, then he would want
Gray and Janet freed. The important thing was to delay, and
to get Janet out of the Fort. Gray rose slightly from the
chair, and had the pleasure of watching Swan tense. "Sir,"
Gray said, and bowed deeply. "I'll be glad to help in any
way I can. Perhaps my wife should go to the dome to talk

to Reed Bridger. And tomorrow, after some sleep, when I'm more alert, I can make a formal statement."

Janet looked at Gray and smiled. She understood now. "Yes," she said to Swan.

"There's no need to leave in the middle of the night," Swan said jovially. "I have comfortable rooms right here, where your wife can stay." He stood and signaled to the unobtrusive guard. Janet looked at Gray. She was biting her lip, waiting for him to do something.

"It will be all right," Gray said helplessly. "How did you come here?"

The guard was close, but Janet ignored him. "I walked, when the cab couldn't bring me. Your grandmother said you were here. She's worried about you."

"Ah," he said meaninglessly.

She stood, and he did. She suddenly pressed herself against him. Her body was trembling. "I'm sorry," she whispered in his ear.

She was a lost soul. He'd belittled her loyalty because it wasn't the same as his, but she'd come to Exchange only out of loyalty to him. It had been a mistake, but she'd tried. He hugged her, mindful of Swan watching them.

Swan cleared his throat. Janet moved away from Gray. "I'll see you in the morning," she said firmly.

Swan, like a gallant gentleman, bowed to her. The guard ushered her out, but didn't treat her as a prisoner, not quite.

Just the two of them, Gray and Swan, were left in the room, with no obvious barrier between them, but Swan had Janet. Besides, there was certainly some of his tricky offworld magic weaponry deployed. Gray sat back down in his chair. Swan stood motionless, probably giving orders through the Exchange's invisible network, the telepathic system.

Swan jerked back to life and took his seat. "An interesting night." He tapped his fingers on the desktop and didn't look at Gray. "You cannot bargain with me, Mr. Bridger. You can only cooperate, or not. Your wife is evidence of one intrigue, if your sister's accusations stand, and even if not, she ensures your cooperation. Neither of you will ever leave this building if you fail me. I need detailed information and credible proof that your answers are true. The stakes are higher now. The reputation of one of the foremost Jonist Academics in the Harmony is at issue, not just Altereds, and your evidence must be incontrovertible. That means under Security's seal. You will talk with them, not me. Now."

Someone was nearby. Gray turned. Another guard was waiting to take him, having slipped in unnoticed. "Talk?" Gray asked. Exchange's Security had gained its unpleasant reputation from activities other than conversation.

"If they believe you, if you cooperate completely, then talk will be all there is. Again, good night, Mr. Bridger." He gestured to the guard and returned his attention to his desk.

Gray had misjudged the strength of his bargaining position. "Why do you want me to denounce Ahman Penn?" he asked to delay the trip to Security.

Swan never looked up. The guard put his hand on Gray's shoulder. "All right," Gray said, "I'm coming." The guard let him shake off the hand. Gray bowed very deeply to Swan, who didn't acknowledge it, then left, as the guard directed him.

Outside was a return to the black maze. Gray let the guard guide him, while he remembered Swan's mention of his disagreement with Penn about Altereds, and Penn's "allegiance" to them. Though it had done Gray no good, Swan said Penn was "fond of" Mead. In all the years of his administration of Testament, Swan had certainly never been fond of any native. Swan was behind Gray's arrest. He had wanted information sufficient to indict the Compound Council, but had dropped that angle in favor of an attack on Penn. Unless there was a personal feud between the two offies, the only reason Gray saw for the switch was if Penn was an obstacle to Swan's desire to hurt Altered Testament. Penn didn't matter, but Testament did. "Do I get to rest?" Gray asked the guard. He wanted to think this through.

The man didn't answer. The difference between a singleton and other natives, which Gray had always been so quick to explain to offie tourists—I'm like you, not them—had no meaning inside the Fort. There were only natives and Harmony citizens.

He had to delay. Gray had no objection to incriminating Penn unless it would hurt Testament. It seemed that it might.

Mead had furnished a way of deflecting questions, though it would be obvious. Noncooperative. Gray reached into the inner pocket of his jacket, felt the patches, wrapped by him in a plastic bag, and opened the bag, careful that they didn't spill out. He need only touch the greasy, drug-coated patches and his mind would become a confused, capricious history book, tripping from memory to memory. The plastic slipped between his fingers, but he didn't expand the opening to make contact with the drug.

Eventually, the guard manhandled Gray into what seemed to be a corner. "In there," he said, as if Gray could see through the nearly tangible darkness, as somehow these Harmony soldiers could. Gray moved in the direction the man pushed, and banged into a wall. He tried to turn, and couldn't; there were walls close on both sides. He'd walked into a trap like a rat walking into a box. "Hey," Gray called and tried to retreat. The guard was gone and another wall had formed behind Gray. He shuffled slowly back and forth in a very limited space, discovering he was alone in a box too small even to spread his arms. He raised them and encountered a ceiling about a hand's breadth above his head. It was a featureless, dark, coffin-sized container. He'd heard of them: a Safe Box—safe for his questioners.

He leaned against the back wall, the one he knew had once been open, braced himself with his feet against the other wall, and pushed, hoping pressure could move it and expand his space, but there was no elasticity in the closure. Neither wall moved.

He reached for the plastic bag, but didn't touch the drug. He smelled it, though, a smoky scent, very strong in this enclosed place.

"Gray Bridger." The voice spoke just at his ear, a murmur that reverberated in his head, but didn't originate there. The proximity was intimate, like a lover's whisper. The voice was female, which was clever. Security understood Testament.

"Yes." Gray continued leaning against the back wall. "Look, I'm tired. I need to sleep. I'll answer everything, just give me a chance to rest. Otherwise I might make a mistake." He thought he sounded reasonable and cooperative.

"Put your palms flat against the forward wall."

Gray hesitated. They weren't going to let him delay. Instead of doing as the bodiless woman (if she was real at all and not a computer figment) commanded, he opened the bag containing Mead's drug. It had taken hours to act before, but he hadn't had much on his fingers then, or been sensitized by prior exposure. How long would it take?

Pain started in his head and ratcheted slowly from his

temples down and backward toward his spine. It was a bad headache, not agony, but by its sudden occurrence and its steady spread, he understood the point; Security didn't need his hands on the wall to deal with him.

"Put your palms flat against the forward wall."

"All right!" Speech increased the pain, and as it advanced down his spine the misery increased dramatically. Lights seemed to burst inside his head. His arms shook. He pressed his right arm, already inside the jacket, against his chest, trying, through the pain, to feel into the bag. He was losing tactile sensations rapidly, drowned out by the pain. Before perception was entirely gone, he wiggled his now scorching fingers, hoping they had reached the drug and that it would act quickly enough to make this effort worthwhile. "Stop! I can't move now!" he tried to shout, just managing a whisper. He kept his hand in the bag.

"Put your palms flat against the forward wall."

Pain raced up and down his back. Pressure in his head increased, and he gritted his teeth as though to prevent it from exploding. His ears rang with the echo of muscle tension and pain. His skin felt as if it were on fire. Tears were streaming from his closed eyes. His knees collapsed.

It would have to be enough. Gray slapped the palm of his left hand flat against the wall in front of him. Immediately, the pain lessened, but didn't stop. His right hand was encumbered by his jacket. In pain and darkness, he couldn't disentangle himself one-handed. He twisted his right hand outward so that, through the jacket, his palm was against the wall.

The pain began ratcheting upward, a snail's path of relief, but like a snail the reprieve left a trail of slime, the residual vibrations of the pain. He felt shrunken.

"Put both palms flat against the forward wall."

Gray seized on the order as approval to readjust his position. He pulled his right hand free of the jacket and pressed both hands hard, flush against the forward wall. He managed to stand again; the narrowness of the Safe Box had prevented him from slumping very far. Only as the pain ended did he feel the strain on his arms as he crushed his hands into the wall. The silence lengthened and he lightened the pressure on his hands, but he didn't stop touching that wall. Security had taught him his first lesson.

He had been tested and had failed. Despite his unspoken

vows of fortitude and courage, when pitted against a stronger force, he had broken, rushing to obey the offie voice. Yes, he'd reached the drug—he felt the grease on his hand and forearm—but if the voice had asked him to betray his grandmother, Gray was uncertain he would have refused for long. He was unworthy of Testament, and her. Disillusioned and disgusted with himself, Gray also recognized the worst: the pain he'd felt had been imaginary, and he had known it then. Now that it was gone, he was unharmed.

Tears trickled from the corners of his closed eyes, self-pity at his new self-knowledge. At least the offies hadn't asked. He had no confidence that they couldn't break him, but there were many ways to fight. He told himself that now, forewarned, he would do better. He was weaker than he'd thought, but he'd never been more certain of his loyalty. These offies would get nothing from him. Gray lifted his head. "I don't deserve to be treated like this." He had no difficulty with a whine, only in finding his voice again. "I'm innocent; I'm here to cooperate."

No one answered.

The silence was peaceful. Let them leave him alone as long as possible. He leaned on the forward wall—always keeping his hands there, flat—and turned his head to wipe his cheeks on his shoulders.

"What is the substance on your right hand?"

They did need the wall for some things, then. He was afraid not to answer; he was afraid to lie. "Medicine."

There was another long silence. He was grateful there was no pain, then stopped himself. Grateful? Swan had imprisoned him, wanted to harm everything Gray loved. He had seized Janet as insurance, and had set his Security to torture Gray. Gray could be glad there was no pain, but not grateful.

"What kind of medicine?"

"For memory." Without any patches to recall her to life, the offies would see Janet's true condition as an alia, but he hoped to delay that knowledge, so he tried to distract them. "I need to sit down," he said. "I've been here all day without anything to eat. My shoulders ache; can I take my arms down?"

There was no response. He sighed and leaned his head on his extended arms.

"What does the medicine do to memory?"

He shouldn't have mentioned memory; it was a touchy

subject on Altered Testament. "It enhances it," he said. It wasn't a lie, exactly. "I thought it would help during this interrogation." Neither was that, strictly speaking.

"Were you bringing this medicine to Ahman Penn?"

Gray almost smiled. They were trying to get on track. "No," he said, and added, "But my sister, Mead Bridger, gave it to me." True, and a red herring.

"Why?"

"I have no idea why she does anything."

"Gray Bridger," the womanly voice whispered beside his ear, "you are teasing me with misrepresentations and distorted truths. This is your only warning. Now, tell me clearly and succinctly about this medicine."

Teasing me. The voice made it sound personal, but the voice was false. Afraid of saying too much, he decided to protest his innocence again. "I spoke the plain truth," Gray said. "Mead gave it to me. I don't know why she did; I haven't seen her since. She claimed it was to help me and my wife."

"What quality of this medicine caused you to suffer pain in order to absorb it?"

Good question. He didn't have a ready answer, but the voice sounded exasperated, and there'd been no punishment. "I hoped to postpone the questioning," he said. "I'm tired."

There was another of their long pauses. Gray pictured bored offie bureaucrats evaluating his responses, or maybe not so bored; this was important enough to get Swan out of bed in the middle of the night.

"What specific effect does this medicine have on memory?"

He finally understood their dilemma. Security *seal,* Swan had said. Poor offies. They couldn't seal his answers until they first established his state of mind; the drug was an outside influence. He hadn't done so badly, after all. It was in his interest to tell them the worst about Mead's drug. "I only had contact with this *drug* once before, when my sister handed it to me," he said, "but that time, its effect was to confuse me. It enhanced memory by randomly creating associations between what I was seeing or hearing, including spoken words, and buried memories from my ancestors. It was disorienting. I couldn't function." That told them he hadn't wanted to cooperate, but also that he couldn't, once it began to work.

"Do you remember more than your own life?"

"I am not Altered."

"Specifically, do you remember more than your own life?"

"I never have, except for brief fragments after I first came in contact with this drug." One by one the questions seemed innocuous, but they led him into telling more than he wanted them to know. If they learned he had some of his mothers' memories they might not let him into the Harmony. He still wanted to go, not for himself, anymore, but as Testament's proxy and Testament's revenge. "The effect was temporary; I'm not really sure if it was memory or hallucination."

"Are you presently experiencing that effect?"

"No," he said, but quickly added, "Not yet."

"Strip, Gray Bridger. Remove all your clothing."

He took his hands away from the wall cautiously; they didn't chastise him. His muscles burned and he was stiff from time spent in the awkward position. His right hand felt as if it had been rubbed in fat. He wiped some of the grease on his already contaminated jacket and slowly moved to comply with the order, making a neat pile of his clothing, working entirely by touch. When he had finished, the rear wall of the Safe Box opened. He caught a glimmer of light as hands reached in and removed the piled clothing. Then he was pushed away, the opening vanished, and he was alone. He slumped against the wall and waited, glad for the illusory privacy of the dark. "Can I go to my cell?"

For once, they answered. "You will stay here until the fugue begins," the woman's voice said softly. "If it does. You will be quite sorry if you've lied."

Chapter 9

I. Souvenir

Read quickly, the letter said. *This paper will dissolve shortly after its exposure to air—August's idea of extra security. I think the boy reads too much.* Penn smiled, and adjusted his position beneath the bath table to ensure that no part of the page was visible to potential monitors. He had no faith at all in Swan's promise.

> *Be certain you have some scrupulously noble and ethically defensible reason for your stopover at the Protectorate of Testament. Martin, it is a decidedly odd choice of destination. Avoid the spectacular; don't become absorbed in any Altered Mysteries. August's research indicates Governor Cevan Swan is no friend to me—or likely to you, either. He is a fanatic purist who has twice petitioned the Grand Assembly for permission to involuntarily eliminate the native Alteration; be wary of him.*
> *The situation here is unstable. I survive, but don't dare issue any Rulings for them to challenge. It is time for you to return; perhaps I can get something for you from my resignation after all. You're young, but are you interested in a new red hat—mine?*
>
> *Lee*

The edges of the paper disintegrated as Penn began to re-read the letter, then a pinpoint hole spread and quickly engulfed the word "unstable." In less than a minute Penn was grasping a few shreds of grayish-black string, and then only dust. He wiped his hands on his pants leg. He hadn't realized Jeroen Lee could ink-write—Penn had expected a keyed recording or print—but it stood to reason; Lee enjoyed theatrics.

Lee considered Swan a real danger; if he was right, then Penn might have underestimated Swan. Penn had been blunt. He had discounted anyone on this remote outpost as a threat, but Swan might have support on Center, and Testament was more like a fiefdom than a sinecure. Well-liked or not (Penn suspected the latter from the guard captain's actions), Swan ruled as an autocrat, with all Harmony communications screened by him and the few arriving ships under control of the quarantine he administered.

Be wary, Lee had written, and Lee would certainly have avoided making Swan an enemy. Lee was a consummate politician, but Penn had become introspective, and less cautious, as his doubts grew and ambition waned. Did he want the red hat of an Elector? His usual lack of enthusiasm was increased by knowing that if he was elected now, it would be as Jeroen Lee's puppet. They shared many opinions, but Lee was only tolerant, not a seeker after Mysteries, metaphysics, or God.

Penn crawled clumsily out from under the bath table, feeling comical, glad Mead wasn't watching. He used the table edge to help himself stand, stiff after crouching in the cramped position. The suite was eerily silent, with a middle-of-the-night coolness in the air. Swan had waited until early morning before delivering the packet.

Penn returned quietly to the bedroom. Mead had insisted on "real" light in the window screens, but Testament's pale sunrise washed the room with gray, not gold, giving everything a dingy, faded cast. Its wintry look cooled her body, outstretched across the disheveled bed, and made her the color of a marble sculpture, detached from life. She was beautiful, but no more so than other women he had known. She was intelligent; so was everyone at Center. She was lively, impudent, angry, and Altered; all true. Nothing he knew about her explained her effect on him.

He had been careful not to wake Mead when the utility had called him to the door, and yet most women would have awakened anyway; she slept with a child's concentration. Asleep, she had a softness that her daytime turbulence hid. He came farther into the room and watched her slow breathing, then sat in a large chair; stuffed too full, it felt hard as wood against his incidental aches. Mead's face was in profile against the sheet, her lips slightly open. The graceful curve from the tip of her nose to her forehead was a single, sleek line. Her masses of dark, curling hair formed a shadow behind her. She appeared relaxed and even happy, then a stray dream made her lips tighten and she frowned.

To restore Mead's ability to conceive children would require use of Exchange's facilities and would further antagonize Swan. It was stupid to goad an enemy that way. Elector Lee would not have done it, but Penn had decided he would. However trivial a problem infertility was inside the Harmony, he couldn't be indifferent to her pain. His physical infatuation had expanded, he wasn't sure into what, but he would remember Mead Bridger.

Penn entered the Gateways House utility. A pile of messages had been set outside his mental gate, but he stepped over and past them and summoned a schematic of the Exchange District. "Medical," he called up from the utility, and immediately the relevant data—the personnel, their specialities, the available facilities, listings of common medical needs of Testament's Harmony visitors (foremost was serum treatment for a local variant of a minor sexually transmitted disease), records of quarantined medical knowledge unavailable for citation to natives, and more, an ever branching information tree—was accessible as adjunct memory to him. After a cursory review, by his own authority as Ahman he added himself to the local medical roster, then used his new position to slate a treatment room for his exclusive use that day. Then he withdrew and watched Mead. He wanted company. When she stirred, he called her name. His voice was loud in the dawn silence.

She stretched, yawning; her eyes opened, and she was immediately awake. She lifted herself onto an elbow. "Why are you up so early?"

"Swan finally sent the packet." He indicated the outer wrapper, lying where he'd tossed it, on the table beside the bed.

"You look serious. Bad news?"

"Good news, actually." He answered as if he were speaking to Swan. "I'll be returning to Center on the next ship." This would be behind him, then: Swan. Testament. And Mead.

She sat up. "I'm sorry to hear it."

His pleasure disturbed him. "I'll keep my promise first," he said, purposely misunderstanding.

"I knew you would."

He left the chair, but even when Mead made room for him, he didn't join her in bed. He studied the curve of her hips through the bedclothes, resenting the way knowing her had compromised his judgment. "You could come with me to Center."

She gazed up at him like a worried child. "I thought you were teasing last night."

"There, you wouldn't have to worry about precasters. I can't violate the quarantine by curing you, then bringing you into the Harmony, but since you're infertile now, I could use my imprimatur to allow you into the Harmony without a hysterectomy. I'd take care of your problem when we reached Center."

"Martin, you wouldn't like me on Center. I'd embarrass you."

"Probably." He smiled as he thought of all the ways this was a bad idea, much worse than any conflict her cure would cause with Swan. Mead wouldn't remain politic for long, even if she began inoffensively at Center. *Avoid the spectacular,* Elector Lee had written, and bringing exotic, sardonic Mead with him to Center was embracing it. "The more I think about this, the more I want to do it."

Mead sat upright, letting the sheet fall away from her upper body. "Why?"

The question hung between them, unanswered. Mead broke the silence. "This is sweet of you, truly, but I can't leave."

"Why not? What do you have here but an empty house and a precarious future?"

"Martin, you'd be my only reason for going. I want to win, not run away."

Martin Penn had avoided serious romantic entanglements with women. A life lived without them had given him a warped view of women. He had assumed the choice was his and had expected that despite her tart condescension, Mead would do whatever he wanted. He wasn't ready never to see her again. He had not envisioned rejection. "You can be very tiring, Mead," he said.

"Yesterday morning you said something like that, but in a much nicer tone of voice," she teased.

"You could be an ambassador for your people," he said. "An advocate for them at Center."

"That's your job."

"What?"

From the foot of the bed, she picked up the shirt he'd worn the night before. The wet area was now dry, but stained and wrinkled; she put the shirt on, rolling the drooping sleeves over her elbows. "You like us now. I know Reed—I *am* her—and I don't know where her plans begin and where they end."

"That's ridiculous." The reference to Mead's Alteration disturbed him. How much of this woman was herself, and how much was a product of her mothers' memories?

"Of course it is." Mead left the bed. His shirt hung well below her hips. "The Harmony is Gray's dream, not mine. This is the only place where you and I can be comfortable together."

There was some truth in what she said, but he was disinclined to acknowledge it.

Mead came close, taking one of his hands between her two smaller ones. "You would be ashamed of me, and I couldn't live with that. Besides, you don't really want me to come. You're only angry that I refused."

He pulled his hand away. "I'm not angry, Mead. A bit disappointed. No one at Center has met a native of Testament before. You would have been an interesting curiosity."

She stepped back and glared. "A souvenir. As bad as that, Martin? Surely someone has said no to you before?"

He was glad to see her emotion and to know his own appearance was under strict control. "Who are you, Mead? Is there any part of you that's a seventeen-year-old girl?"

"You mean a part you can push around? Isn't that what a woman is to you people?" She looked down at her red-painted toenails. She was trembling.

He *had* expected her to bend to his will; he couldn't admire independence and not allow it to be exercised. "I'm sorry," he said and bowed to her, wanting to comfort her but afraid that to do so would also be to condescend. "I didn't ask you to the Harmony as a curiosity. I wanted you—want you—to come because . . . I like you." He motioned at the bathroom. "Wash and dress. I'll get breakfast for us from the provider."

"You'll still help me?" She gestured vaguely at her abdomen.

He had the power to say no, to deny her most fervent wish. She knew it. He wondered where she would draw the line between dignity and desire. Would she beg? Did he want to see her do it? No. "Of course," he said. "I've already arranged the facility. Anytime today."

Mead's release of tension stopped her trembling. She sighed. "You really are all right, Martin. I like you, but I need more than that before I'd go into the Harmony." She looked down. "The truth is, I'm afraid. What would I be out there? An Altered freak."

"No, Mead," he began, then wondered why he'd automatically denied it. She was right.

She hugged him, pressing herself hard against him when he didn't pull her close himself. "If you were staying longer, I'd let you father my first daughter."

She meant well, despite how his stomach roiled at the thought, proving her point. Better if he didn't bring her to the Harmony. He stepped back from her.

"Are you going to let Gray leave?" She giggled. "He'll make a much better ambassador."

Penn considered Gray Bridger's desire to leave Testament entirely reasonable. "Yes, if he asks."

"I'm surprised he hasn't come back already; he's good at swallowing his pride." She shrugged, dismissing Gray, and left for the bathroom. Penn listened to her movements and then the running water through the partially open door. What did she think about, as the water played against her body? Did she relive other lives? How different was her mind from standard? He'd never know.

Penn stretched out on the bed and entered the Gateways utility, intending to read his messages, but she had reminded him about Gray. He was sorry the young man had left angry. Using the open utility, he called the downstairs guards. (Let me know immediately if Gray Bridger enters the Exchange District) he ordered, and had almost cut the line to return to his mail when the senior guard relayed that Gray was already present.

(Where?) Penn asked. Coexistence with the guard through joint connection in the utility felt abrasive, like a high-pitched background whine or a bug crawling on a bare leg; emotions leaked into the utility from the guard's undisciplined mind, coloring his answer. (In custody, in the Governor's House) the guard answered. There followed an automatic map overlay with Gray's position pinpointed in the detention area.

(When?) Penn asked, careful not to leak emotion himself. (Yesterday.) The guard exuded pride in his service.

Penn was gracious as he left the connection. He had made mistakes enough underestimating this garrison and overemphasizing his own importance. Swan was detaining Gray Bridger for a reason. That he'd kept silent about imprisoning Gray meant Swan was hunting information about him, hoping to discredit an Ahman.

II. A Twenty-first-Century American Lawyer

"Remember me," a voice murmured just beside Janet, either an order or a question, but when Janet turned, no one was there. Something bad was going to happen. She sensed it in the stink of smoke she smelled, in the bitter taste of her own dry mouth, and in the falling sensation she couldn't escape. Her phantom self couldn't run.

There was danger. She had to protect Gray.

"A man," a voice said in a skeptical tone, talking from beyond her sight.

Janet was no longer in Grandma Tillie's house (was that where she'd been?) but in a large room, like a concert hall lobby, or the Bridger Dome rotunda, crowded with women. She couldn't identify anyone because they all had her face. Several pointed at her and laughed, repeating in overlapping echo: "Damn her, damn her, damn her."

Janet sat up, her heart racing. Panicked, she wasn't reassured by her surroundings; she didn't recognize the red-and-gold room. Another nightmare awakening. "Not again," she whispered. How many more centuries had elapsed?

As her breathing slowed and the fear lessened, she realized that she remembered Gray; she knew what and where she was, as she would not in an entirely new awakening. Besides—she turned her head, searching for something familiar—she did recall this plush room. She was in the Governor's House, in a much finer accommodation than her plain room in Bridger Dome, but a more dangerous one. The bed was immense, with a gently yielding mattress and satiny sheets; a day bed in a soft ivory fabric was luxurious; every chair was deep and comfortable. The armoire was the largest wooden piece she'd seen on Testament. It was heavily carved with flowers and birds. The room was itself calming, like eating a big meal.

"Dancer. Dancer?" a soft, warm, feminine voice asked. "Are you finally awake?"

Dancer. That was her name here. She was Gray's wife, Dancer Bridger. The unfamiliar name hadn't awakened her as effectively as her own would have done. She looked around, but no one was present. It had to be an intercom. She spoke loudly and said, "Yes, I'm awake."

"Governor Swan wants to ask you a few questions."

"Of course. But first, can I dress?" The woman didn't answer. Janet hoped that meant agreement, and that observation of her—visual or aural—had stopped, though Gray said inside Exchange everyone was monitored. "Long live Big Brother," she muttered, and kicked the covers off. There was nothing else she could do.

Outside the window was a very European flower garden, one that should have belonged to a castle, with boxed hedges and a gorgeous fountain. Unable to open the window, she then realized it was one of their window screens, its realism flawless.

She washed and dressed hurriedly. She didn't want Governor Swan to enter while she was naked; she remembered his leer as he'd checked on her just after she'd climbed into the bed. She was in a precarious situation. Clothes had been provided in the armoire, arranged on a mannequin: a provocatively styled red outfit. There was nothing else; her own clothes were gone. She had a wonderful body now, but it had become a burden.

Immediately after she finished dressing, Governor Swan entered, followed by another man pushing a cart; the fragrance of food coming from the cart was delicious.

Swan bowed. "You'll breakfast with me?"

"Of course," she said, and, tardily, she bowed, holding her hands to cover her otherwise exposed decolletage. Swan wasn't handsome—in fact, he was fat, with a pudgy, plain face and a wart on the side of his nose—but he held her captive, along with Gray, so she smiled to flatter him, and told herself her fears were groundless.

The servant who had brought the cart opened it into a dining table, arranged the dishes, and set two chairs at opposite ends, all while Swan looked smilingly at her body. Janet didn't dare object. The servant bowed and left, closing the door. It seemed heavy, but she didn't hear it lock her in with Swan.

"May I help you?" Swan held a chair for her.

Put slightly at ease by the courtesy, Janet sat. Gray was solicitous, but his manners were different. Testament lacked chivalry. Small talk was a necessary tool in a stilted situation. Janet nodded at their surroundings. "This is a beautiful room. I hope I didn't displace anyone?"

He smiled, which had the unfortunate effect of narrowing his eyes. "Not at all. My last guest left several months ago; I've been hoping for company."

Stop looking for menace in innocuous remarks, Janet told herself.

He took his place and removed the cover on his plate. The aroma of grilled meat and cooked fruit with cinnamon made Janet's mouth water. He smiled down at the meal, then looked across the table at her. "Please. Eat. You are my special guest."

Janet set aside the cover on her own meal. It looked wonderful, and richer than the food she'd had on Testament, but "special guest" had unsavory implications. "Is it possible for my husband to join us?" she asked.

Swan had begun eating. A greasy sheen made his lips shine pink. "Other arrangements have been made for him."

"Is Gray all right?"

Swan frowned and set his fork down. "I hoped we could discuss him later, but this is probably best. Your husband hasn't cooperated. That's one reason I came this morning. The other is you. We tried to wake you when the problem arose with your husband. We couldn't. You had fallen into a non-responsive state our medics still don't understand. They finally tried a medicine that was found in your husband's possession. It worked; I hope you will explain. But first, enjoy your breakfast."

Janet stared down at the food, unable to take the first bite. Swan had no such trouble. She heard him chewing, and the clink of his silverware against the plate. They would know exactly how fragile her existence was. She wouldn't be able to claim to be a singleton again. She'd let Gray down. "Gray wants to leave Testament," she said quietly. "His grandmother interfered to keep him here. He was only trying to leave despite that."

Swan continued his meal.

"He was uncooperative because he was protecting me. If

I tell you everything about this, will you let him leave? Please!"

Swan smiled. "That depends on what you say. I want to know more about this medicine."

She nodded, gathering her thoughts. As she understood the Harmony requirements, the worst charge against Gray was that he—they—had tried to get her off Testament without complying with the quarantine regulation against off-world travel by fertile women. "First let me say one thing, Governor Swan. I'm entirely willing to be sterilized. I have no interest in bearing children."

Swan stopped eating. He leaned back, still holding his fork.

"I am not really a native of this place. I don't think the way they do, or want what they want," Janet said.

Swan put his fork down on his plate. "I've never been more convinced of that than I am now."

"My name is Janet Bridger. I was born a thousand years ago. They tell me I'm not real, but all my memories are intact, and what else is a person but the sum of her memories? I don't have any memories of other women. I *am* a singleton."

Swan dropped his gaze. "You admit Mead Bridger's claims are true, that you are a—what was her word?—an alia."

It was irrefutable. "Yes."

"And the medicine causes you to ... appear?"

She nodded. "Gray said it activates memories laid in the mitochondrial DNA."

"It has a peculiar effect on him, as well. He is in what my medics believe is a deranged, possibly hallucinating state." Swan used his spoon to pick up some of the cooked fruit; steam rose as he held it, waiting for the fruit to cool enough to eat. He glanced at Janet, less interested in gobbling food than he had been. "None of this is helpful to me. It tells nothing about Martin Penn. All you've done is confirm that you and your husband engaged in a scheme to deceive the Harmony about your true condition." He ate the fruit and took another spoonful.

Janet stood up, gathered her thoughts, and smiled at this horrid man who held her fate, and Gray's, in his hands. "Governor Swan, I come from a time when legal nitpicking was a highly developed art. I don't know how carefully the

Harmony hones its niceties, but I do know that Gray and I never made a formal application to enter the Harmony together, or bought tickets to leave, so we haven't done anything whatsoever that is technically wrong. Ahman Penn had us arrested, but you can let us go—if you want."

"Why would I want that?" Swan smiled at her, but his eyes were still on Dancer's excellent body, not Janet's face.

Janet stepped away from the table. She was a "special guest" unless she could prove her value as something else. "You wanted information about Ahman Penn that you thought—hoped—my husband had. But Governor Swan, how likely is it that an eminent man like Penn would confide any secret to his native guide? You are grasping after straws. I mean," she amended at his inquisitive look, "that it isn't likely at all. Anything he may casually have said would not be enough for you to make a clear-cut case against him, as I think you really want. But if you sterilize me, and don't let Penn know; if you release Gray and me together—then perhaps you can catch Penn violating the quarantine rules by arranging for us to leave Testament." She took a step, then returned, an abbreviated pacing. Swan was watching her, but she could not read anything in his expression.

Swan sighed and stirred the fruit, then set down his spoon and picked up a muffin. As he nibbled, he said, "Interesting, but unworkable. A medic like Penn could realize too easily that you are no longer fertile—or claim later that he had. I'm impressed, however. I hadn't expected you to propose any gambit at all, especially one so devious and . . . delightful."

"Delightful" was in a category with "special guest," a category she didn't want to inhabit. She smiled, though it was difficult. "Governor Swan," she said, standing very erect before him, at the opposite side of the table, "I am a twenty-first-century American lawyer. From what did you imagine those Altered descendants of mine in Bridger Dome developed?"

Swan chuckled, and his belly moved against the table. "Then you approve of your descendants?"

She took a deep breath and looked into his eyes. Swan disliked Altereds. She had to play this absolutely right. "No one intended the memory mutation to create these motherlines of women. I dislike every native I've met, except Gray. He is a normal, standard man."

"He has the memories. The effect of this medicine shows

it." Swan tapped his fork against the plate, making an irregular tinkling sound, but he seemed to have forgotten about eating.

"The drug caused a hallucination, not a memory revival. You said so. And he only took it to protect me."

Swan set down his fork and raised a glass of fruit juice, as if toasting her, then sipped it while watching her over its rim.

Janet crossed her arms, then sat back in her chair, observing Swan warily, from a greater distance. "What can I do to free us? Gray, and me?"

Swan shook his head, smiling, and raised his glass at her again. "Nothing. When Martin Penn returns to Center, I want his opinions regarding Testament discounted. Apparently you can't help with that." He shifted in the upright chair as if it restricted him. "You have only one use left."

Her chill was instinctive, the reaction of a woman to a large, threatening man. Jon Hsu was the only card she had left to play. Reed had claimed their affair was important information. Perhaps to Penn, but to Swan? Reed had also claimed it was too valuable to waste, but the Bridger secret belonged to Janet, not Reed, and Janet felt no loyalty at all to Testament. Reed had seen to that. "Suppose I knew something interesting?"

"Useful?" He'd returned to his meal.

"Not specifically useful to your problem with Penn, but something you might like to know. Information that could make you famous."

"Tell me."

"I want some assurances first."

He stood, pushing the table away, and into her. "Tell me, and I'll judge its value. You have no other choice."

She faced him, pretending calm. "I can't agree. My information is valuable, and remember, your methods, whatever you use to force information, might not work on me. I'm different."

His jaw moved, causing his jowls to flutter. "Tell me what you know and I'll put you with your husband."

"I need more than that."

Swan slowly nodded. "If your information is valuable, and *after you are sterilized,* then I'll allow you and the singleton to leave Testament. So, what is this about?"

Janet studied him, appraising his honesty. Swan wasn't

giving up much in freeing her from being one of his "special guests"; she wasn't the passive woman he'd expected. The rest of the bargain was dependent upon his goodwill, of which she had great doubt, but she was under his control, as was Gray, and this was probably the best she could do. The nature of her information was such that there was more than she could give all at once. That gave her future bargaining power, assuming he was interested at all. "All right." She smiled and picked up a muffin. "I knew Jon Hsu personally. I remember him quite well."

III. The Memory Plague

Gray was awake. With the tiny part of his consciousness able to stand back from the nonstop force-feeding of random memories, he wished he could drown himself in sleep, but awareness was an unavoidable symptom of the sickness infecting him, the memory plague.

He was in his cell. The legitimate sensations he occasionally felt from his own body (so large, so wrong) gave him little idea how he had managed to walk, or when he had been transported back, but he was on a bed. A guard was present.

His mind was never alone. It absorbed a few reminiscences, but they came so quickly and so hard that most were lost. He must look as Dancer did when no emulation controlled her, but he guessed his condition was improving, because enough of his personal identity was continuously present that he could form coherent thoughts.

Periodically the offie checked on him. Gray (who was that?) tried to keep her eyes tightly shut, hoping to reduce the insinuations of foreign memories into his mind by minimizing the triggering perceptions, but she felt her arm raised to take her pulse, which set off spreading waves of overlapping mental imagery and nearly swamped the small boat that was Gray Bridger, lost in the depths of his own mind. He opened her eyes to look for mom. She didn't know the uniformed man bending over her, but he remembered other men, remembered Harmony soldiers bringing him into the Fort. Gray turned his head, his first conscious control over his body in hours. A woman stood behind the man; he knew her: Janet.

Then he was trapped again in the smallest prison possible, lost in the memories of Janet's life.

IV. Truce

Swan leaned across his desk toward Penn, resting his bulk on his forearms, the informality declaring an otherwise unacknowledged truce. "She's with the husband now. It's a detention cell. They're safe there, and I needed time to digest this."

Swan's news—the claim made by Dancer Bridger—rendered Penn's questions about Gray Bridger's confinement insignificant. The woman could have the knowledge he'd yearned to discover. She'd known Jon Hsu intimately, as an individual, a scientist, and an Academician; she'd recall his opinions and beliefs. Had he truly rejected everything for Order? Her memories might show the distortion Swan's brand of blind orthodoxy had done to the true meaning of Hsu's *General Principles*. The new age of Jonism Reed had hinted at might begin that afternoon. *The Bridgers know something; they always have,* the street-corner oracle had said.

Penn kept his tone neutral. "The sensor information indicated she believed what she was saying?"

Swan's acknowledgment was a sigh. "Ahman, do you think it could be true? That Jon Hsu had an affair with the progenitor of these Altered freaks?"

Swan had used Penn's title. Jonist doctrine, and anything having to do with Jon Hsu, was the exclusive jurisdiction of the Electors and their Academies. Provisionally, at least, Swan was relying on Penn's opinion, despite their other disagreements; Penn needed to maintain their new accord. He wanted unfettered access to the woman, so he tried to address what he assumed would be Swan's concerns. "It's impossible to say if this is true just yet, but remember, Cevan, the original Bridger woman wasn't Altered—only her descendants. An affair between the Bridger progenitor and Jon Hsu won't necessarily affect Harmony policy regarding Altereds."

"Not directly, but we'd have to depend on these Altered women." Swan scowled and turned around to gaze out the window screen behind him. Abruptly, the window screen went naked: the restful view of Amacuro's highlands vanished and Stone Town spread out below them. The golden domes, the sparking sea, the hills and twisting blocks of houses made the native city into a version of the crossman Eternal City, ancient and mild. "Do you know," Swan said, without looking back at Penn, "that this world would be nearly impossible to destroy by conventional means? These women are like ants; they've built half their structures deep underground. A sweep wouldn't touch those. The only possibility is a biological weapon."

"The Electors ban use of biological warfare against humans, even non-Jonists," Penn said immediately, alarmed by their opposite reactions to the same information. Penn's instinct was to preserve the carriers of this new knowledge, while Swan contemplated their destruction.

"I know." Swan turned around. "And I have none. The best I could do is a cruiser-based gravity wall to confine and crush a small area, with soldiers to keep their reinforcements at bay, and to tackle survivors. It might work. These motherlines are tribal, and don't often cooperate."

To distract Swan from thoughts of destruction, Penn said, "Cevan, if this is true, it completely overturns the Alias Hypothesis. If she knew him as *Jon Hsu,* clearly that was not an alias; the HSU acronym of the Hard Science Underground was coincidental."

"That outrageous heresy should have been suppressed anyway."

Penn nodded, although he'd considered the Alias Hypothesis interesting. "Still, she may tell us why there isn't significant independent verification for portions of Hsu's life, if what she says is true."

"If it's true." Swan studied Penn. "Ahman, does it matter if it's true? Think of the harm to the integrity of Jonism that this will cause. The divisiveness. Some will believe it; others will not. And there's the grotesqueness of an association of Jon Hsu with Altereds."

Truth was never evil, no matter how inopportune or unpleasant. To Penn, that was an essential part of Jonism, one he wholeheartedly embraced, but not to men like Swan. "Those concerns are premature, Cevan. If this isn't true, then it's meaningless, a scrambled memory distortion from a freak. And I didn't detect any indication of a gentle attitude toward Altereds in the recording we just watched. It seemed the opposite—she dislikes the Altered natives. Her retained memory of Jon Hsu might actually create a more hostile atmosphere for Alteration. Our first step is to investigate."

Swan nodded. "I'd like Security to peel away the layers of her memories like onion skins, but with her unstable mental condition—requiring drugs even to stay conscious—her mind would collapse."

"Security is entirely unnecessary." Penn's smile felt unnatural. "There is no period of old Earth history better known than the Great Mentor's generation. We'll see how her memory agrees with known facts. Another matter—if this is true, how did they keep it secret for so long?"

Swan went back to the window. "You don't understand these creatures. Although every female of the Bridger line is a *carrier* of this offensive secret, most natives know nothing farther than five or six generations back. Only precasters remember their remote past, and they know how to keep their mouths shut. This girl is a fluke."

Penn went to the window and stood beside Swan. The governor smelled of false sex pheromones and sweat, an unpleasant mixture of unnatural ardor and tension. "You believe it, don't you, Cevan?" he asked, very softly. "You think it's true."

Swan looked up at Penn respectfully; he bowed. "I fear it, Ahman. The woman volunteered to be sterilized. No healthy native woman of her age would. Her memory is that of Janet Bridger. But I'm also afraid in case it is a lie. There are rumors that precasters can make others believe lies, and even make themselves believe untruths. Imagine the spite, the depth of hostility, of these women if this is a precaster plot. They would be attempting the destruction of Jonism, the very substance of our civilization."

For a moment, Penn did imagine it: precasters like patient spiders weaving a web of lies to trap something much greater than themselves. Confabulation. Mead hated the precasters; he hadn't believed her accusations, or that women would work their damage through their own descendants' lives. "Revenge," he whispered.

"You do understand." Swan wasn't gloating, but welcoming another carrier of a great and terrible burden.

Penn walked away from Swan. "True or false is for the Electors to decide, not us," he said, relieved that was the case. "Our role is to investigate and determine if this is something worth passing on to them, not to judge the matter ourselves."

"No, Martin," Swan said, approaching Penn more closely than Penn found comfortable. "Now that they know their secret is out, these women will try to spread it. Our duty is to manage this situation on the Harmony's terms, not those of the precasters. True or false, this story must not leave Testament."

"We have to know it, first." Penn rapidly was losing faith in Swan's analysis. When truth and fiction had the same result—suppression—something was wrong. "I need to interview the woman. The Electors will want a report. We can't take this all upon ourselves."

Swan hesitated. It was only luck that Penn had arrived at the Governor's House shortly after Swan's interview with Dancer, or Swan might not have included Penn in the secret. Although Swan could not prohibit an Academy investigation, he could delay Penn until Swan had taken preemptive action. If not for that brief moment of congruence, when Penn had seen the possibility of a massive precaster fraud, Penn suspected his request would have been immediately refused. "You reserved a medical facility," Swan said slowly. "I understand you have *that woman* in it now."

Penn had forgotten Mead. This was not a good time to cure her. "That can wait. We need to resolve this."

Swan appeared at least partially satisfied. He went to his desk and created a screen, oriented on the medical department. Penn nodded, as if he'd asked for Swan's help, and used Swan's access to instruct the medical facility to hold Mead, pending his arrival or other instructions. "Good," Swan said. "She's involved in this somehow, Martin."

"I don't believe that."

Swan smiled. "They're lovely creatures, aren't they? I remember my first one. But the singleton said that the medicine used to create 'Janet Bridger' came from this sister."

For all his sometime distrust of Mead, Penn never doubted that her hatred of her grandmother and the Compound Council was virulent and real, and still did not. "I'm sure she's not working with them. She only knew that Gray's wife was an alia, nothing about this."

Swan's shrug was a skeptical denial. "If you must make her fertile, consider using the technique I mentioned, to convert her offspring to standard humans. She needn't be told the full extent of the cure before you leave Testament."

That would be dishonest and cowardly, but Penn bowed as if Swan had suggested a brilliant solution. "I'll consider it," he said. He was considering something else. Mead was a precaster, an errant one. Her memories of Janet Bridger were few and scattered, but if she confirmed this story, he would know it was true. Already, he sensed that it was. Intuitively, aesthetically, and unconventionally, Penn believed that the universe had a larger design; he'd been drawn to Testament for a reason: to discover Janet Bridger and learn about Jon Hsu. Reed had said it: *There is an answer for you.*

"I have a few matters to attend to, then we'll see the woman together," Swan said.

Penn smiled and bowed.

Chapter 10

I. Encounters with the Past

Gray was bewildered. His mind had cleared, but he had no idea why Janet, Martin Penn, and Governor Swan were gathered in his cell. He was settled comfortably enough on the bed. Less would be expected of him if he maintained the fiction of his mental incapacity, so he observed in silence and with what he hoped was a vacant expression as guards brought chairs and arranged them in a semicircle facing him.

Janet dragged hers around so she sat beside him, looking out at the offies. "Go ahead. Ask whatever you want," she said.

Alarmed, Gray sat up. Janet smiled and patted his hand reassuringly. "It's all right," she said. "We'll be able to leave Testament once I tell them everything."

Her attitude was wrong. "I don't think you should," he whispered, avoiding focus on the offies and hoping they would disregard him, as they had during his encounters with the past.

"It's all right." She squeezed, then released his hand.

The mind-echo, gentler now and fading, reasserted itself at her tone, and involuntarily he remembered many such reassurances, mother to daughter, a series extending through twenty-seven generations. Disconcerted, he lay back on the bed.

"I'm ready," Janet said, and bowed to Swan.

Swan looked grim, but Penn seemed eager. He leaned toward Janet, then glanced at Swan, as if for permission. Swan gestured at the guards to leave, then nodded when they had. Penn cleared his throat. "When were you born?" he asked Janet.

"1984." She smiled at Gray, sharing the joke. "Like the book."

"That's 49 BJ," Swan interjected.

BJ. Before Jonism, which counted the publication of Hsu's *General Principles* as year zero. They knew exactly who and what Janet was. Gray had suspected they might, but didn't understand Penn's enthusiasm, or Swan's dismissal of the guard.

Penn ignored Swan's help. "There's a book of your life?"

Janet rolled her eyes at Gray. "I saw it in your room," she told him.

"Restrain yourself," Swan snapped. "Your future and that of your world are in the balance."

"My world?" Janet chuckled. "I don't have one."

"We live on Testament," Gray quietly pointed out to Janet.

"I was born in 1984," Janet repeated. "February 17th. In Chicago. Its suburbs, anyway. I grew up in the heartland of *Oprah* and *Donahue,* a land of navel-gazing and declining expectations as people became more concerned with angels and devils than progress. I understand what Jon wanted to accomplish. You need to know if I'm telling the truth, so you're checking my references? Ask anything. I'm real."

Penn hesitated before continuing. "Chicago is a jurisdiction? Oprah and Donahue were your parents?"

Janet winked at Gray, then looked back at Penn. "If you're going to check my credentials, you should study my era better."

Gray realized that, unlike the offies, he had understood exactly what she said. Like calling up his own memories, he saw Oprah's changing waistline and Donahue's white hair on a TV screen in his—*her*—mother's house.

"Explain yourself." Penn's tone was as harsh as Swan's.

Janet gazed at Penn with aplomb. "Yes, Chicago was a jurisdiction, a major American city, and Oprah and Donahue were famous personalities, not my parents."

Gray closed his eyes against the visions as Penn asked more questions and the answers Janet gave appeared first inside his head. The experience was like his first contact with the drug in Bridger Dome, uncontrollable reminiscing but with the ability to separate himself from the memories. Not only were images conjured up out of the Bridger tribal past, but he also felt the flavor of remembered sentiments. The alien emotional palate was glum. She hadn't been happy, his

Janet, however giddy she was now. She'd been too much alone.

Penn sounded less argumentative with each question. "What year was the Hong Kong Massacre?"

"What year?" Janet was puzzled, and so was Gray. The years ran together seamlessly, with events sometimes out of sequence, their time frame misremembered, but the image conjured by the name was horrible and clear: bodies dumped from the Central and Kowloon Star Ferry piers, floating in the water as if macabre loggers had been hard at work cutting human trees. Jaded with miseries, the disgusted world did nothing, saying the problem was an internal one, entirely Chinese, except that the ocean should not be polluted by the tens of thousands dead. "I was still in school," she said slowly as Gray traced through her memories, too. "Law school. And I graduated in 2009, so around then?"

Penn gave no indication as to whether her answer was wrong or right. "What was made in Hollywood?" he asked.

She laughed, a bit shakily after the prior memory. "Is that supposed to be obscure?" she asked. "Movies, the best in the world, the largest export product of the U.S.A."

Penn seemed to have a list. "Who was Nathan Singh?"

Swan stood up, cutting off yet another of Gray's dizzying reminiscences. "This is pointless," Swan said. "Anything you can know, so can they, possibly even better. It would take forever to find significant inconsistencies, and even so you couldn't be sure whether it was her memory or our information that was at fault. Ask about what's important; ask about Jon Hsu."

"You're right," Penn told Swan.

Jon Hsu. Gray sat up; if trouble came he didn't want to be flat on is back to greet it. Questions about Jon Hsu sounded dangerous. The others glanced over at him when he moved; only Janet smiled. "Are you better?" she asked gently.

"Yeah," he said hesitantly, hoping that he seemed weaker than he was. His arm muscles burned when he rested his weight on them in getting up, his back ached, and he was wearing an outfit like a hospital gown, loose and easily opened, which lacked dignity, but in spite of having had little sleep and having an aggressive hunger that made his stomach rumble as he thought of it, he felt remarkably well. It was adrenaline, or Mead's memory drug contained a chemical substitute for psychological composure.

"You're not jealous, are you?" she asked him tenderly.

Confused, he noted the suggestiveness of Janet's dress and looked at Swan. "Jealous of what?" Gray knew Swan's foul reputation.

She blushed and shook her head slightly. "I had an affair with Jon Hsu. Back in my own time. Of course." She giggled nervously. "That's what they're interested in, what this interview is about. My relationship with Jon."

Amazed, he stared at her.

"What do *you* know about this, Mr. Bridger? What have you hidden about Jon Hsu?" Swan stood and loomed over him, close in the cramped room.

"Nothing," Gray said blankly, in perfect honesty. "I don't know—I don't remember—anything about Jon Hsu, except what the Harmony has told us." He looked curiously at Janet, reciting the name over and over in his mind. Jon Hsu. But there was no memory, just the fleeting insinuation of a joke: *They'll have to catch him first.* Why was that funny?

Swan stared blankly a moment, then looked at Penn, and nodded significantly at the nearest wall. "Truth."

"Of course," Penn said testily. "He's normal. It's medicine for her, but it only sent him into a delirium, Cevan. He has no information relevant to this. Even Altered natives don't know the Bridger secret, just precasters and our discovery, Dancer." He bowed slightly, and corrected himself. "Janet."

"You're not upset?" Janet asked Gray again.

Her question was like Penn's desire for permission regarding Mead, offie sexual game-playing; she wasn't from Testament. He was more concerned that Penn was calling her Janet, and with his phrase: *the Bridger secret.* He'd never heard of a Bridger secret, nor anything whatsoever about any affair with Jon Hsu, although it might not be something a singleton would know. "It was another life," he said with a graciousness made disagreeable by his understanding that for Janet jealousy was a sign of affection; was he supposed to apologize for Melany, and the others?

"Mrs. Bridger," Penn said, calling her attention back from Gray. "Tell us when you first met Jon Hsu."

She sighed, glanced again at Gray and took his hand, then fixed her attention on Penn. "He was a fellow at Argonne National Lab, outside Chicago. I took some training there when I was hired by the University of Chicago. My job was to be sure we complied with the regulations limiting experimental science."

Penn scowled. Even a millennium later, those hard science restrictions seemed personally to offend him, although they'd led directly to Jonism's growth. "How did you meet?"

Gray, meanwhile, was visualizing Argonne. It had reminded her—him—of an impoverished prairie college. Inside deteriorating buildings, tiny offices had lined gray-tiled halls. The grounds were overgrown; the adjacent forest preserve would have blurred into the laboratory precinct except for the fence, electrified to keep out the anti-science protesters who had become routine at every experimental science institution. The fence regularly killed some of the area's unique albino deer, provoking further protests. "You will be called an apologist for science," her supervisor had said, "and therefore will be unpopular." She hadn't remarked that she was accustomed to unpopularity.

She. Gray came back to himself. No one had noticed his slip into a reminiscence. The offies were engrossed in Janet's fictitious tale of how she and Jon Hsu had met— fictitious because, although Gray remembered Janet Bridger from the deepest recesses of his DNA, courtesy of Mead, he did not remember any encounter whatsoever with Jon Hsu. He was certain there had been none; he had easily remembered everything else she'd said about her life. There was no affair with Jonism's founder. The Bridger secret was a lie. Yet Janet seemed sincerely to remember and believe it. He looked at the small hand holding his own and wondered: who was this woman he had called his wife?

II. Virtual Truth

Janet smiled at Penn. Gradually his questions had ceased trying to provoke a mistaken response from her. He'd become enthusiastic, greedily seeking understanding of what she guessed were some of the central issues of Jonism. Sometimes she didn't know the answer, but it would have been foolish to lie. The interview was fun, like reliving a very important, exciting portion of her life. The memories were crystal-clear. Gray was quiet, but however much he protested that he didn't mind, Janet supposed a man could not enjoy details of the earlier intimacies of his wife. Governor Swan had also fallen silent, but unlike Gray, Swan looked sullen. He was standing, his hands thrust into his pockets, scowling at the floor.

"Genetic modification was a frontier of science when I knew Jon," she answered one of Penn's questions. "The Human Genome Project had successfully completed its map, despite the constant pressure by conservative extremists to end its work—the science restrictions weren't originally so bad, but they got worse. Of course, we never discussed this memory Alteration, because it didn't exist then. From what we did discuss, Jon would have approved; he considered all knowledge to be progress."

"Yet he wrote that altering the human genome *wasn't* progress, that it was unnecessary," Penn said like an acolyte seeking an answer from his master.

"Well, I don't know what he wrote later. There were popular pressures, even on someone who opposed them, and he would have been edited. I only know what he *said*." She lowered her voice. "He said reforming some elements of the genome could be useful."

Penn nodded and pulled his chair closer. "Did you discuss it with him before you agreed to provide genetic material?"

Janet's continuing friendship with Jon had been the bright spot in her drab life, but they'd never been truly close after he'd left Chicago. "No. By then we were just exchanging Christmas cards."

"I don't believe this!" Swan shouted.

"You're saying Jon Hsu was a crossman?" Even Penn sounded shocked.

Gray had tensed, and pulled away from Janet. Obviously, this was a delicate topic; Janet wished she could consult Gray privately. "No. Not really," she said. "Everyone exchanged cards; it didn't mean anything but 'Seasons Greetings.' I know this is a lot of information to take in at one time. I'll be glad to talk with you again later."

"You'll talk with us whenever and wherever we want, if we want you to say anything at all," Swan said nastily, but he was looking at Penn.

"Of course." She bowed her head, but watched the two men through her lowered eyes. They were glaring at each other.

"Why are there so few records of Hsu's life?" Penn said, turning away from Swan and changing the subject to one less momentous than Christmas cards. "We know very little about his training, his research, or his personal life."

Janet was puzzled. "I don't know. I didn't know there was a problem, of course." She pondered the question. Penn had implied that Jonism's early years, the years subsequent to her departure as a speck of mitochondrial DNA in her descendants' cells, had been difficult. "They might have been erased," she suggested tentatively. "His followers could have needed to protect each other and Jon, if the government's attitude toward hard science degenerated." She remembered the Jonist tract Gray had given her. It said Jon had been martyred, and she shuddered, thinking of that.

"How?" Swan seemed incredulous. "Records would have been protected from tampering. They've only been lost."

Janet laughed, and was sorry when Swan advanced on her; she bowed at him. He hesitated, then turned his back on her without acknowledging the bow and went to the portion of the cell behind the chairs. She spoke to Penn instead. "No computer record was really secure in my time, despite the fact that all records were on computer. Software taps, data theft, record invasion and tampering—they all were constant problems. There even was a name for suspicious records: virtual truth." She saw their blank looks. "Like virtual reality, a popular entertainment—you know, holograms."

"I've heard of that." Penn nodded, encouraging her to continue.

Gray was seated on the edge of his cot. His head hung down, as if he were tired and aching, but his attention was fixed on Governor Swan.

Janet wished she could make this easier on him. His attitude had changed since she'd begun discussing Jon. "Jon's disciples could have erased him from the Internet," she said. "It would have been simple."

"Enough," Swan interrupted, turning back and speaking to Penn. "We're no closer to a resolution than when you and I first spoke."

Penn stood and turned his back on Janet and Gray, so he could see Swan better; he seemed more confident than when he'd first begun. "I disagree," Penn said. "The Electors will be interested; they'll want more. Testament has been an overlooked source of information. There may be other hidden memories. We'll need to be gentle; only with the trust of these people can we learn what they know. This will be an important world."

Janet noted the challenge to Swan inherent in Penn's tone. Her bargain was with Swan, but Penn seemed more accommodating. Uncertain where her best interests lay, she was silent.

"Where will it stop?" Swan asked Penn. His question was rhetorical, spoken with more weariness than anger. He held the back of his empty chair like a cane and studied Janet without seeming to see her. "If you think this will help *him,* then consider: will a Bridger woman someday be made an Elector?"

Swan's question hung in the air between the two men; Janet needed to distinguish herself, and Gray, from the rest of Testament. "We want to live in the Harmony, free of this place."

Swan's intake of breath was a hiss.

"I'll take them back with me to Center," Penn said.

Gray stirred, and Penn frowned as if daring him to speak; Gray didn't.

Swan looked down at the floor. "She'll need to be sterilized before she leaves Testament," he said.

Gray got up from the bed, moving as if motion were difficult, but when Janet tried to help, he brushed her away, partially behind him. "No," he said clearly and uncompromisingly. "My wife stays whole."

"It's all right," Janet said. She spoke quietly, to soothe him. "I've already agreed. Children aren't important to me. You could say that I already have my fair share of descendants." She smiled, but it faded as Gray faced her.

"You don't understand," Gray said, grabbing her shoulders, then releasing her. "You need children!"

"I'm not a native here. I don't want children." Janet pictured a squalling, red-faced, clinging brat. Gray had been obstinately fixated on this issue all along. "I never have. It's you who wouldn't compromise. Decide: the universe or a child?"

Gray was rigid and unfriendly. Janet cringed; he was necessarily a creature of his own time and culture, which valued child-bearing excessively, but harshness from Gray was frightening. What did she have without him? "Why do you care so much?"

"Why does he?" Swan looked back and forth between

them. "Another lie from his witch sister," he said gloomily to Penn.

"I don't think so." Penn stepped between Gray and Swan. "It's a good idea that your wife be rendered infertile, Gray. Then there is no question as to her ability to travel with me into the Harmony, no question but that she's in compliance with the quarantine—as it exists for now."

Gray sat down hard on the side of his cot, as if his legs had given out. Janet sat next to him. He turned and seemed to look through her, as if she were a window into an unpleasant reality. "It's over then." He rested his head in his hands.

"The precasters' plan?" Swan asked sharply.

Gray didn't answer, and Swan shrugged and turned away. He and Penn began to argue, off at the other end of the small room, away from the bed. Gray dully watched them.

"Gray?" Janet whispered.

He raised his head and touched her left cheek with his index finger. "You're not real," he whispered without meeting her eyes. "You're her reformation of Jonism, not her scout." He dropped his hand.

Janet flushed and felt tiny. She wasn't real. Reed had said it over and over but Gray's belief had kept her doubts at bay. *Who am I?* she wondered. Desolate, she saw the weight of her thousand dark years reflected in Gray's dark eyes, and felt warm tears on her cheeks, cheeks on a body that was Other than Janet. Even now, though she'd adjusted to it as one adjusts to too large shoes by cramping the toes to keep them on, she sensed herself trying to keep the truth from her awareness. She wasn't real, not to the only person who'd thought she was, the only one who mattered. Not to herself. Gray watched her, but didn't wipe her tears; then he turned aside to listen to the offies. He seemed to get farther away. It didn't matter; she wasn't real. She didn't belong here. She sank into herself, withdrawing from all the Others.

III. Wishful Thinking

"Clearly," Penn told Swan, "Janet Bridger's memory of Jon Hsu is something the Electors must judge for themselves. From this moment, Dancer Bridger and Gray Bridger are under the protection of the Academy of Center." Penn wanted to get along with Cevan Swan, but couldn't permit

Swan to take matters into his own hands, as he had threatened. Dancer was vital to a complete understanding of Jonism. He, an Ahman of the Academy of Center, was now in charge. Gray was irrelevant, but Penn intended to protect him from Swan. Fairness required it, but there was also Mead's erratic affection for her brother; he was the only person she had ever mentioned fondly. It went without saying that Penn intended to fully protect Mead from Swan.

"You did an exemplary job of discovering this information, Cevan," Penn said. "The Electors may well authorize a tribute." Particularly Jeroen Lee, Penn thought. This broadminded vision of Jon Hsu, the connection with and toleration of Altereds, was precisely the miracle the Elector had needed. Relieved, Penn realized he would be able to pursue the Bridger investigation and let *Elector* Lee manage Jonist politics.

Swan waved away Penn's compliment like batting at a fly. "She said nothing that we can confirm as true, and probably never will."

Penn hardened his tone. "I believe her. You believe her. I'm sure the Electors will, too."

"You want to believe her; you came here searching for gods and you just found the path." Penn began objecting immediately; Swan held up his hand and spoke over him until Penn stopped. "What is more fundamental in Jonism, the prophet or the philosophy?" Swan said. "I've always believed Jonism is a philosophy, that it is distinct from cults of personality or godhood, which is what—I thought—distinguished Jonism from superstition, with its emphasis on holiness and gods. But now I see I've been blind to the weak-minded who can't look into clear light without a colored lens, and to the mystics who see light in unexplored shadows. I've been blind to the power of wishful thinking. You are an Ahman of the Academy of Center, Penn. Open your eyes. She tells anecdotes about the man Jon Hsu, carefully aimed anecdotes that will tear the Harmony apart. We must not allow that. Nothing she says can ever add one bit to the philosophy of Jonism."

"We must listen, if her *anecdotes* are true," Penn said firmly. Swan was a bigot who would never acknowledge anything good that came from Altered Testament. "Jonism can survive, and will be enriched. This will add depth to

Jonism. It's the *source,* not the content, that disturbs you. You're Jonist. Open your mind."

"The source *is* the content." Swan gestured at Gray. "This man doesn't believe her. While you were entranced with her stories, I watched him. She believed what she said, but he didn't. She's admittedly a freak even among freaks, and he is at least symptomatically normal. What does that tell you?"

"It tells me that Gray Bridger is ignorant," Penn said, more quietly, to Swan. Penn glanced at Gray, who was seated, watching and listening intently. It was emotionally disappointing that Gray couldn't provide confirmation of his wife's memory, but Penn would have been suspicious had he done so.

If only Dancer had come to him privately. He could have freed Gray, and brought them both off-world before Swan knew the truth. Penn smiled. Now he would have to persuade Mead to come. Swan hated her as much as she claimed the precasters did, making Testament doubly unsafe for her. "This is a matter for the Academies, Cevan, and certainly inappropriate for discussion here." Penn nodded at the two natives. Janet looked dazed and withdrawn, but Gray was balanced on the edge of the bed, learning too much about the divisions inside the Harmony. Despite administering the quarantine, Swan was much too loose in his own conduct.

Swan was inattentive, which meant he had entered the Governor's House utility, from which Penn was excluded. It was rude to do so at such obvious depth while Penn was talking; nevertheless, as soon as Swan's attention returned, Penn continued as if he hadn't noticed. "There is one way of verifying the accuracy of Dancer's memory, and that is by means of a Bridger precaster."

Swan laughed sourly. "You have an Altered living in your suite: Mead Bridger. Isn't she a precaster? Security can take her mind apart this afternoon."

"No. Absolutely not." Penn focused tightly on Swan as a way of steadying himself from his rush of anger. Swan wanted him to lose self-control, to seem an emotional fool regarding Testament. From the corner of his eye, Penn noticed Gray. He'd risen unsteadily to his feet and was watching Swan. Mead, after all, as his sister. Penn gestured at him to keep silent and stepped around the chairs, into the small open area of the cell, closer to Swan. "I am *not* suggesting that we 'take apart' anyone. Mutual cooperation must be the foundation for our new relationship with Testament. We will talk with them."

"Talk is all you'll get. I've had some experience with Testament. One family, the Shak, make it a practice to kill women who become too friendly with my personnel. They make no secret of their hostility, and that is their only difference from the others. This Janet memory is bait; I only wish I saw all of the Bridger trap." Swan hesitated; he put his hands into his side pockets and looked down again. "Martin, to preserve the Harmony we must destroy this information, whether it is true or false. Destroy it utterly, destroy it as if it never existed, and then forget what bits we ourselves have heard. Janet Bridger's memory is not necessary!" Swan's face was red, as if he had climbed higher uphill with every word. He waited for Penn's response with obvious tension, staring at Penn with beady eyes gone wide and a body become motionless.

Penn took his time replying. Something wasn't right. Destroy, Swan had said. To be so open in the presence of natives could not be in character for Swan. He was attempting to convince Penn to acquiesce in the destruction of Janet Bridger's memories, in the killing of Gray's wife. Swan had the power to do it. Penn was alone; there was no Academy on Testament. "The investigation on Center won't be token or sympathetic," Penn began.

Swan shook his head. "I can't allow any investigation, Martin, token or otherwise. To begin one at all is unthinkable. This is an act of war against the Harmony."

Gray lunged at Swan, knocking two chairs aside. A physical attack was idiotic; they were inside Swan's own Security cell. Penn did nothing. He expected the cell's protective grid to descend, separating them from each other, and to punish any motion against the confines of its grid, but seconds passed and no grid fell. Despite that, Gray had stopped.

Swan was holding a weapon; it was aimed at Gray.

"Cevan! What is this?" Penn bumped into Dancer, who was still seated on the cot, as he stepped away from the weapon. It was a stick gun, a lethal flesh-burner carried by soldiers in actions beyond the Harmony borders. Oriented on Gray, the thing still could be set wide; its usual use was in open areas, not indoors, but it was a good choice for an untrained man.

Swan chuckled, but he was sweating. "You are a short-sighted man, Martin Penn, but I regret this. At least you are human." The weapon shifted, targeting Penn, while still covering Gray.

Never underestimate anyone, Jeroen Lee would have admonished him, Penn thought, *especially a man you consider a fool, if he's in a high position. You probably are wrong.* Lee might have talked his way out of this, but Penn stared down the shaft of the stick gun, unable to think beyond the fact that Swan was serious; he intended to murder an Ahman.

"There will be an inquiry if you kill him," Gray Bridger said calmly as he sidled away from Penn.

"*You* will kill Ahman Martin Penn," Swan said, "not I. Then I will execute you and your accomplice with your own weapon. That is the beauty of this gun; it leaves so little evidence behind for analysis."

"Why would I do anything like that?" Gray seemed to be discussing the plotting of a play. "Where would I have got the gun? It isn't reasonable. There will still be an inquiry. They will know it's a lie." He took a small step forward, as if for emphasis, but stopped immediately when Swan rotated the gun's tip in a tight circle, warning him back.

"An investigator will be from Security. He'll understand that the Bridgers are a treacherous brood of Altered scum who need to be eliminated; he'll conclude that a Bridger boy, who was already being held for treason, attacked and murdered one of the Harmony's finest men, and then was executed along with his Altered, freakish wife by a man who is above suspicion, the governor of this disagreeable place."

Penn sensed the girl's restlessness beside him, but didn't turn. "What of the monitors?" he asked. "They'll recognize your tampering."

Swan's aim didn't waver. "You're in a Security cell."

Penn gaped. Security occasionally did things it didn't want recorded, so monitoring of such cells was under manual control, presumably subject to Swan's ultimate command. He'd turned it off. "You underestimate the scope an inquiry will take. They will send probes. They will interview everyone. They will dissect your life and your lies. This fiefdom of yours will be opened to public view and the truth will come out eventually. You will be disgraced."

"It will have been worth it, if my disgrace saves the Harmony." Swan used the gun like a pointing finger and indicated Gray's wife. "You, come away from Penn."

She didn't move.

"I can as easily kill you there," Swan said, sounding oddly rational as he extended the weapon to shoot.

"We'll leave," Gray pleaded. He stretched out a hand in appeal to Swan, incidentally blocking Swan's aim at his wife, then left his arm extended as he took a weak step forward, hugging the wall on the far side of the cell from Penn, away from the overturned chairs. "You'll never hear from either of us again. It's safe to let us go. Say we escaped; it makes more sense than our killing Penn in your presence. Plus, if you send us back to the precasters alive, they'll know you discovered their plot. They'll know you won."

The native was babbling, groveling to save his life, but Penn was grateful for the temporary reprieve. He was frozen in place, with no options.

"The precasters will know anyway." Swan eased the gun back, closer to his chest.

Gray shook his head and shuffled closer.

"Get back!" Swan raised the gun and stretched out his hand, pointing it at Gray.

Gray leapt at Swan and screamed.

IV. Extenuating Circumstances

Gray tackled Swan low, at the knees, counting on the time the startled, inexperienced man would take lowering the gun to give him his chance to survive. He connected as Swan shot, knocking Swan backward at the same time Gray's lower legs ignited in fiery heat. He screamed.

"You Altered scum!" Swan shouted.

Skeptical of whether Penn would help, Gray forced himself to hug Swan's plump legs tightly as Swan kicked out. The gun went off again, warming Gray's back. He had to get that gun. Penn did nothing; he would have stood talking while Swan burned the three of them into dried bone. Gray's legs were dead weight behind him, stiff. He couldn't get leverage to pull Swan all the way down. The man was kicking, struggling to get away. Soon, he would remember to aim the gun and discharge it into Gray. "Help me!" Gray called to Penn.

A woman shrieked a war cry as she vaulted forward.

"Janet!" Gray had wronged her, dismissing her ability to fight, or react properly in a crisis, but she was magnificent. She yanked Swan sideways, jerking him out from Gray's grasp, and cracked Swan's head against the cell floor while bringing him down. Efficient. Gray rolled to the side; pain sliced through his legs as he moved them. Meanwhile, Penn only watched, though he had been threatened by Swan, too. Janet wrestled Swan's obese body, shoving him against the wall with strength disproportionate to her size, then the gun was in her hand and Swan was limp, his hands slack against the floor, his head lolling to the right. Her eyes met Gray's as she started wearily to get up.

She wasn't Janet.

"Stay on him!" Penn shouted.

Gray glanced up at Penn, disgusted with the man. "Swan's out."

"We're not being recorded, but this room still has sensors!" Penn stared at Swan's inert body, and then at Dancer as though he'd never seen a woman fight and win. "They'll gas us if the security parameters are breached. I presume they haven't because she's a woman. Swan has an unusual . . . appetite; this is a crude system."

"The gun went off." Dancer's voice was professional as she discussed their situation. Gray recognized Elene. "No one is watching us." She stretched, unkinking her shoulders, but stayed on the floor with Swan and kept a firm grip on the gun, holding it without threatening anyone, but ready for use.

Penn knelt beside her and examined Swan, taking his pulse, lifting his eyelids, checking his injured head. "Swan's program expected the gun discharge." Penn sounded composed; it seemed that his failure to aid them had been a choice, not timidity. "No human is monitoring us or you two would be dead. Swan didn't want witnesses to your memories."

Elene glanced at Gray.

"I think he's right." Pain made him grit his teeth, but he managed to move to a seated position, slightly twisted but better than a sprawl on the floor. From the calf down, the skin of his right leg was singed. The burns on his left extended over a larger area, and went deeper.

Penn turned from Swan to examine Gray's burns. "That's

not too bad." Penn gently touched the flesh of Gray's left leg, but removed his hand quickly when Gray winced. "Lucky he had the thing set so wide. It's all superficial; not much muscle damage. A skin sack and topical anesthesia will do it. A few minutes in a surgery."

"We don't have a surgery," Elene said snidely. "Can you walk?" she asked Gray.

"Maybe. If I have to." Elene was an uncomfortably distorted version of Janet, a rearrangement of the features that should have made Janet. She had appeared once before when there was physical danger. Had his grandmother arranged some trigger for her surfacing? She had saved his life, and Penn's, though, so he forced a weak smile. "Yeah, I can walk."

"We're safe as long as he's unconscious," Penn said. "The minute he's awake, he can alert the military system. Isaacs is a reasonable man, though; perhaps Swan would only use Security."

The telepathic system. Tying Swan up would be useless. Gray tried to stand, using an overturned chair for support, but didn't manage it.

Elene patted Swan's cheek. "I'll kill him."

"No! We can't," Penn said. "That's certainly in the system parameters. We'd have Security here immediately. They'd arrest you both and possibly even me." Penn sounded convincing.

Gray exchanged a look with Elene. She nodded, acknowledging him as their leader. "Get him on the bed," he told her.

"Good idea." Penn got up from the floor and stood, uselessly, watching Elene. "If you could undress him?"

She said something low, under her breath, that Gray didn't need to catch, but she tugged at Swan's collar awkwardly, with only her free hand.

"Give me the gun," Gray said.

Penn raised an eyebrow. "That might not be acceptable to the system. Give it to me."

Elene ignored him and handed it to Gray. It was heavier than Gray had expected, with a solid, comfortable fit to the handgrip. To mollify Penn, he said, "The system already let her hold it."

Penn didn't respond. Gray wished he knew what the offie

was thinking. So far it had been "we," and he'd been informative, but Penn's interests weren't the same as theirs.

Elene opened Swan's tunic-jacket. The man had loose, pasty flesh and an ugly, hairless chest with flabby breasts. He stirred. Without waiting for instruction, Elene knocked his head against the floor again and maneuvered him toward the bed.

Gray grasped the nearest chair, forced himself not to anticipate the pain, and hauled himself to his feet. Surprisingly, once up, staying upright wasn't difficult. It hurt to bend his left knee, but Penn had been right; it wasn't bad. "We've got to get out of Exchange before he wakes up," Gray said. "Any ideas?"

Penn was staring at Elene. He shook his head. "She's not the same woman."

"Alia," Gray said. He was sweating, his hand on the chair was slick. Elene was looking back at Penn, frowning.

"Are Janet's memories gone?" Penn asked her quietly.

Elene looked questioningly at Gray.

"Temporarily," he said. "Ahman, can you get the door open?"

"Yes. The minute it's open, though, we'll be under direct observation. We've got to know what we're going to do."

Elene wrenched Swan's inert body up off the floor and into her embrace, lugged him the last short distance to the bed, then dropped him onto it. Immediately, she sat close beside Swan, but she would not have fooled any human observer into thinking she was engaged in a seduction.

Still holding the chair, Gray took a step forward. He *would* be able to walk. Penn and Elene were watching him, awaiting a decision, it seemed. Gray was surprised by the offie's failure to try to take charge. "What do you suggest?"

"It's vital that Janet Bridger's memories be safe," Penn said. "We should stay in the Exchange District, perhaps go to my suite. I'll make her discovery known off-world. I am an Ahman; Swan can't harm me in public."

Penn was still heavily influenced by Janet's figment memories of Jon Hsu; they were why he was helping them. Both offies had believed Janet. It was possible Gray had forgotten Jon Hsu, while remembering some other of Janet's memories, but Gray had instinctive, grave doubts and a Testament native's willingness to trust his intuitions. However, this was not the time to mention Reed's suggestion that Jonism was ripe for a religious reformation. "Ahman, you have no real authority on Testament; you're just a tourist. Governor Swan doesn't have to harm you publicly. He can do it in your suite, with the recorder off again, or he can deport you under the quarantine, and if we're still in his custody when he does, available to him in the Exchange, he'll kill us, destroying your evidence of Janet's memory. He's already accused us of treason. We'll be safer in Bridger Dome, and then out in the countryside. We'll get free of this cell, and you'll say you're escorting us away from Exchange on the governor's orders."

"You realize . . ." Penn said and stopped. He cleared his throat and began again. "You realize that up to this point I am entirely within my rights and proper role as an Ahman of the Academies, but if I help you escape, and without a record of his attack on me, Swan could accuse me of treason, too."

They absolutely needed Penn. The telepathic system inside Exchange made Penn an essential accomplice, and one who, because of it, was impossible to intimidate, although Gray's hand tightened around the gun. "What are you going to do, Ahman?" He was glad he'd stayed polite.

"There are extenuating circumstances for my actions, obviously, if Swan's attack could be proved, but in any event, Swan is a fanatic. Once he awakens, you're right, he'll attempt to kill her, and perhaps even me, unless I make Janet Bridger's memory known immediately in the Harmony. Then it would be too late; he'd have to give up. We must broadcast this news."

"You still need Dancer alive. Otherwise Swan could kill her and say you were mistaken or tricked."

Penn studied Elene for a moment. "Any precaster . . ."

Gray was tired of trying to convince the offie of the obvious. "They would deny everything. Their lives, and maybe the entire Bridger line, would be in danger from Swan if they spoke about Jon Hsu. They've kept the secret this long already—I'd never heard of it. First end the quarantine, then you'll get information from the precasters. Maybe. And until it's safe for us, my wife and I will stay away from Exchange. Right now, we're going to the dome. The precasters will know what to do."

Elene had listened, as much an outsider to this time and

situation as Janet had been, but she nodded at Gray. "We'll go to the dome."

Gray gestured at the door with the gun, watching Penn to see if he would agree.

Penn smiled wryly. "You've forgotten, Gray Bridger. If you don't give me the weapon before we leave this room, the sensors will spot it."

"That's easy. You're my hostage." Gray pointed the gun directly at Penn. His hand was steady; it felt good.

"They'd gas the whole building before they'd let a native threaten an Ahman. Face it, there is no rationalization that will explain your carrying a Harmony gun, or let it continue."

"He's going to wake up sooner or later," Elene said, jerking her head toward Swan. "Maybe we should just kill him and run."

The idea was appealing. Swan was the problem. Gray was sure, however, that Penn was right; they'd never leave the Fort alive if Swan died, and in addition, it would be an easy twist to make it seem like a Bridger assassination plot, with possibly disastrous consequences to his line, and to all Testament. Swan might have left just such a directive. His senior aides were not fans of Altereds, either.

"If you want my help, you can't kill him," Penn said. "Murder is no way to introduce your ancestor's memories to the Harmony, and it would be difficult even for me to explain."

Gray hesitated, considering the possibilities. He'd never had so difficult a choice rest entirely on him; he didn't like it. They needed Penn. Killing Swan was dangerous. "All right. We'll leave him. But once we're outside, you go your way, and send your message into the Harmony. The two of us will go to Bridger Dome, and from there, out of Stone Town. I'll keep Dancer safe, and Janet's memories outside of Swan's reach."

Swan groaned. They all looked at him, then Penn turned back to Gray. "Agreed." He held out his hand for the gun.

Gray hated trusting an offie, but there was no choice. He gave the gun to him.

Chapter 11

I. Academy Business

"Ahman Penn," the clerk said, smiling with the falseness apprehension adds to a face, "I'm so sorry, but this message is for off-world. I can't send it because of the expanded quarantine restrictions."

Martin Penn had been worrying about Mead. On any normal, civilized world, he could have sent a coded, secure message to the Electors (this was too important to direct only to Jeroen Lee) through the local utility. Swan's quarantine forced him to attend to it in person, leaving Mead back in the Governor's House, ignorant of events, while he performed this unfortunately more urgent duty. The clerk's refusal jerked his thoughts away from concern for Mead's safety. Word of Janet Bridger's memory had to get off Testament in order to defuse Swan. Penn straightened to his full height and wished he were wearing his robes of office. "How does a quarantine on natives prevent an Ahman of the Academy of Center from communicating with the Electors?"

The woman looked befuddled and resolute, a dangerous combination, then she bowed abruptly and stayed low, taking refuge in propriety and regulations. "Ahman, Governor Swan ordered a communication shutdown in both directions early this morning. No messages are going out."

"Except mine." Penn thrust the input pad at her. Swan must have ordered the shutdown even before he divulged the news of Janet Bridger's memory to Penn. He'd already planned his purge, and had only hoped for Penn's cooperation. "This is Academy business," Penn said.

On Center, probably anywhere but Testament, that would have been enough, coming from an Ahman. Her voice quavered, but again the clerk refused. "It'd mean my job," she said.

"Yes, it will." Penn glared at her, an unnecessary cruelty, but anxiety for Mead and fear that Swan might have thwarted him made Penn vindictive. "If you don't send this, then your name will be on the next Flawed List issued by the Academy."

The woman blinked rapidly, holding back tears. "I'll contact Governor Swan for an exception," she whispered.

"No!" An inquiry into Swan's whereabouts might cause some efficient Security man to remember the unmonitored cell that Penn had left with the Bridger prisoners, but which Swan had not. "Take it and hold it. The moment—the instant—that the shutdown is lifted, you will immediately send it, without checking with anyone at all. Do you understand?"

She nodded, then bowed.

"All right. Do it, and we'll see." He stormed out of the office. He'd seemed petty and unreasonably belligerent, but he hoped the woman would do as he'd instructed. He had to get word off Testament. Penn could announce the Bridger information to the bureaucrats stationed on Testament, but Swan would just stop the information from leaving Testament.

It was still difficult to believe that Swan, a Harmony official, had attempted Penn's murder. Since he couldn't prove it easily, the best thing Penn could do now was vanish, go into hiding with the Bridgers. He wouldn't be safe anywhere in the Exchange District, if Swan was as determined as he'd seemed. An inquiry from off-world would come; an Ahman's disappearance couldn't go unnoticed. The investigators would be men Swan couldn't coerce and Penn could safely contact.

There was Mead to consider. If Swan had awakened, Mead would be in his custody, and Penn could be walking into a trap if he returned for her. Nevertheless, Penn hurried across Amity Square to the Governor's House, holding the gun in his pocket to keep it from protruding. Gray had asked for it, once they were outdoors, but Penn had refused, certain Swan's guards would stop an armed native, while a weapon in Penn's possession was merely peculiar. Gray and his wife must be safe by now—Janet's memory was safe—and that was vital, too.

The lift guard bowed as Penn reentered the Governor's House. At his order, they'd turned off the light and gravity camouflage used for prisoners—he'd complained because he

wasn't attuned to Swan's house system, and found it personally annoying. Without it, the protected zones looked drab.
Their brown corridors needed renovation; not much money
was allocated to Testament by the Grand Assembly, and
Swan hadn't put it into comforts for his men. "Back already,
sir?" the guard asked.

His hurried movements might well appear suspicious if
anyone was watching. Swan might well have assigned some
Security man to track Testament's important visitor. Penn
smiled and returned the guard's bow. "There's one more
Bridger," he said, letting them presume he had a plan. Security wouldn't inquire into an Ahman's meaning unless Swan
directed it, and there were limits on what even Swan could
do to him, *in public*. Penn tried not to hurry. No one stopped
him as he went to the medical facility; a medtech directed
him to the room Penn had reserved.

Mead was resting in the bed. An officious medtech had,
for no good reason, hidden her hair inside a blue cap; it
made her look pure, spiritual, and young. Without their usual
paint, her lips seemed pale. Her face was drawn, with dark
circles beneath her eyes. Penn coughed, making his presence
known. She smiled and her eyelashes fluttered, but she
barely opened her eyes. Medicated. "I thought you would
never come," she said.

He touched her forehead with his fingertips; she was cool.
He lifted her right hand, holding it so as to feel her pulse. It
was rapid, and though he counted automatically with a fixed
time from his autonomic clock, it was her thin wrist, her soft
skin, and her attention on him that he felt. Her eyes were
trusting.

He set her hand gently back at her side. A medtech was
hovering behind him, overanxious to help. Without turning,
Penn ordered, "Neurodorphin. Three-fourths standard dose."

"But, Ahman," the tech protested, "how can you perform
the surgery, then?"

"I've changed my mind."

Mead struggled against the drug, trying to sit, but she
moved like a groggy child. He wanted to support her back,
and didn't. "Martin?" she whispered, letting herself fall limp
against the white sheets.

The medtech handed Penn a skin patch, and Penn pressed
it on her exposed neck, holding it against the vena jugularis
interna for the requisite count of ten while Mead stared up

at him, eyes wide and still not truly wary. "Get her clothes," he snapped at the medtech, thinking of Gray's robe, flapping ridiculously in the wind.

"I'm sorry, Mead," Penn said. Despite his real regret at disappointing her, his voice was stiff and unconvincing. He removed his hands from her neck and gave the used patch to the medtech. She would be alert within a few minutes. He wished he could speed the process, but medications that would have done so were also dangerous. "You're going home."

"Home?" She seemed to be trying not to cry.

Her home was a heartache. With its vacant rooms and empty kitchen, it was a hollowness like her unfilled womb, a physical reminder of what she couldn't have. He turned away.

"Why, Martin?"

"Because you've lied to me." It was an excuse he hoped would tell her this was a ruse to get them away from the Exchange District quickly. He willed her to understand that he would keep his promise as soon as it was possible, yet even as he did, he watched her for a guilty reaction, and wished he fully trusted her.

She closed her eyes, then opened them and studied his face. "No, I haven't," she said. "Martin, please?"

She sounded stronger already. "Do you have her clothes?" Penn asked, turning to the tech, who was across the room, fumbling for them in a cupboard.

At least he hadn't performed the conversion of her children to standard that Swan had suggested. Before he'd interviewed Dancer/Janet there had been a possibility he would. The need to accommodate Swan. . . . What difference did the *content* of an Altered's memory make? Logically, none, yet he would never reduce a Bridger's memory now, knowing that he was also destroying transmission of the memory of Jon Hsu.

The tech handed him Mead's clothing. "Get dressed," Penn brusquely ordered her. Her lips trembled. A tear rolled down her cheek. She must imagine she'd been betrayed by him. She brushed the tear away against the pillow and sat up, jerking her clothes from his hand in a gesture that tried to show contempt, but the drugs warring in her system only made the gesture sloppy.

"I should have known better," Mead said bitterly. "Let it

be a lesson to you, Martin. On Testament, be suspicious whenever your wishes seem ready to come true."

"Mead," he began, then stopped. She looked up at him, and when he didn't continue, she kicked off the covers that had hidden her slim bare legs and began dressing. The medtech shut down the medical sensors and monitors that made the medic room suspiciously like a Security cell.

When would Swan awaken? Penn tried to arrange his arguments against a charge of treason—it wouldn't stick, not with this news—but his thoughts returned to Mead and her dagger looks at him, which were only marginally better than her sorrow. He had to make her understand, despite Swan's ubiquitous monitors. "As a precaster, you must remember Janet Bridger's memories of Jon Hsu. I've just been hearing about them."

The medtech stopped working.

"What are you talking about?" Mead asked.

Mead was only technically a precaster. She might not remember Janet Bridger, but she could understand the urgency of getting away from Swan. "Gray's wife told us the truth this morning. Her memories were verified by sensor readings. The Bridger progenitor had an affair with Jon Hsu on old Earth. Your line has direct memories of Jon Hsu."

The medtech gasped, then looked down, pretending to work.

"The Bridger family holds the key to some important questions," Penn continued. "Unfortunately, Governor Swan is displeased with these new memories of Jon Hsu."

"Memories of Jon Who?" Mead chuckled like the villain in a cyclone drama, or like herself. She swung her legs over the side of the bed. Color had returned to her face, and she showed no dizziness. "They've given you exactly what you wanted to hear, Martin. And you say *I've* lied. You really are a fool."

There was a sudden dryness in his mouth. What if Janet Bridger's memories were false? Mead had mentioned confabulation, and Swan said precasters could convince themselves of lies. He needed to ask Mead about it, but not here. He grabbed her hand, holding it too tightly. "Let's go. I'll escort you home."

She yanked her hand away, then pulled the blue cap from her head, shaking out her luxuriant hair. "Don't bother. You won't get anything more from me, meaningless or otherwise.

Apparently Reed lies better than I lay." She hopped down from the bed and laughed her sulky, seductive, joyless laugh.

She didn't understand. "I'll take you home," he insisted, and walked out of the room. Her soft-shod feet, still wearing hospital slippers, made an almost inaudible padding sound he listened for behind him. Inside Swan's Governor's House, she had no choice but to follow.

There seemed to be a great many guards in the corridors. They nodded a brief salute as Penn passed them, but he felt their eyes lingering on his back, and on Mead; they weren't friendly, as most of Testament's Harmony personnel had been. It was like waiting for someone to leap out at him and yell, "Boo!" Would Swan have remained unconscious for so long?

Instead of going to street level in Amity Square, Penn decided to exercise the privileges of his position. He needed speed. Stopping the next man he encountered who wore the livery of a Harmony soldier, not Security, he said, "I want a coach on the roof, on the governor's landing pad. Now. No driver, a manual."

The man gazed blankly at Penn.

"Academy business. A coach. Now. Lead me to the roof. I'm unfamiliar with this place and don't have access into the system."

"Sir." The guard bowed.

Mead finally must have sensed something beyond her own unhappiness. She took longer steps and came to his side. "What's going on?" she whispered.

"Nothing that concerns you."

Silence made Penn's flesh prickle. He was straining to hear pursuit, although it wouldn't come charging down the corridor, shouting. Both of them were strangers to this place and outside its system; they could be directed into a trap. The bureaucrats and soldiers bowed, but too many men were armed. Penn felt again for Swan's gun as the soldier he'd commandeered opened a door onto the roof. The light outside was dimmer than that in the corridor, but Penn heard the hum of a Harmony coach setting down, a noise so routine at Center that the sound, here, seemed foreign.

"Ahman Penn, is this coach satisfactory?" another of Swan's men—not military—asked as Penn hesitated across the deck from the waiting coach. The situation was unreal: an Ahman and an Altered native running from the Harmony;

it couldn't be happening to him. Swan's fear had driven him to insane lengths, but the Harmony shouldn't have become unsafe to a prominent citizen. Penn recalled the young officer of the previous night, who'd used his own judgment, without waiting for Swan. "Can you contact Captain Isaacs?" Penn asked his escort, who was also military.

"He's inspecting the ship," the man said, pointing at the sky, though the cruiser wasn't visible. "Should I call, Ahman?"

"Martin." Mead tugged on his sleeve.

The guard frowned slightly as he glanced at Mead, then his expression changed. At the same time, Penn felt a shift in the connect in his mind. It was the mental equivalent of a shadow passing overhead, not strictly tangible, yet real. That subliminal sense told him that Swan was awake and checking on his whereabouts. "Get in the coach!" he ordered Mead.

They were several paces away. She hesitated, then Penn pushed her.

"Ahman?" The expression on the face of the soldier who'd led them to the roof was incredulous, but he began to extend his hand. "The governor orders . . ."

"Not now! I'm on Academy business."

Briskly, Penn followed Mead as she climbed into the coach. His one hand patted the weapon in his pocket, assuring himself it was there; his other hand reached for the open coach door.

The soldier followed. He had a gun, too, but he didn't seem to be considering it an option in dealing with Penn. "Sir, the governor says he must speak with you first."

"Later," Penn said.

Mead grabbed Penn's arm and pulled him inside.

"No, sir. I'm sorry, but please, Ahman Penn."

The driver had left the coach. The steering mechanism, a track ball, was in front of Mead. Penn reached across her for it as the soldier grabbed the still-open vehicle door.

"Get lost," Mead said in a deadly serious tone. She pointed the gun at the soldier; she must have taken it from Penn's pocket. "Move away from the car or I'll hurt you, and then maybe Ahman Penn."

"Mead!"

"Get this car up, now, Martin!"

"Get out of the coach," the guard said.

Penn wasn't certain if the guard was talking to Mead or to him. Penn's hand was on the track ball. He pressed down, activating it, and pushed the lift cue on the side with his thumb. The coach rose and hovered a few inches off the Governor's House roof, but the safety wouldn't let it rise higher with the open door and a man clutching it. "Let go," Penn ordered the guard.

"I won't let her take you, Ahman," the guard said protectively.

Mead shot him. The stick gun's heat, outdoors, wasn't intense in the area beyond where it hit; it was silent, except for a greasy sizzle from the affected flesh. Penn smelled the foul, burnt meat odor. The man didn't scream; he couldn't. Penn saw him as he reached to close the door, which the man had released. The guard's face was a melting mess; he couldn't scream because his mouth was gone. He was beyond hope, dead. Mead had killed him. Penn's thumb was still pressing the lift; the coach shot skyward, then out and over the side of the cliff, down into Stone Town.

II. A Word to the Wise

"A word to the wise, Gray," Reed said. "The first place Swan will look is not the best place for you to hide."

Gray didn't stop eating to reply. A mug of onion soup, a hunk cut from a cheese round, and half a loaf of crusty white bread: those, and being home, were heaven.

Reed sighed. "I like to watch you eat. It must be instinctive." She scooted her rocking chair closer to where he sat on the floor, using the low table to hold his meal, as he had often done during the years in which Reed's tenth-floor apartment had been his home. This wide, windowless front room—its width equaled that of the two back rooms combined—was reminiscent of a cavern, as were many Stone Town rooms. Reed had told him they felt safe, like those on the slowboat. A painting Gray had given her—an imagined old Earth scene—hung on one wall. Another wall had a generation portrait, a formal photograph of Reed's mother, Reed herself, her six sisters, all of Reed's children, grandchildren, and great-grandchildren; it had been taken shortly after Gray's birth, and before Mead's. He—an infant—and three cousins were the only males in the picture. Behind this room, against the exterior dome wall and lit by windows, not lamps, were an airy study (which had doubled as his bedroom, because it contained a folding guest bed) and Reed's bedroom, with its tiny personal bath, a privilege of power inside the dome.

Gray mopped up the soup with the end crust of bread, then finished the cheese. He stretched. Familiar surroundings had allowed him to relax. It was good to be able to rely on someone else to think. He closed his eyes. Reed's rooms weren't as insulated from the dome's noise as Janet's. He heard voices of women he didn't know, but they were half-familiar anyway because their rhythms belonged to his family. The tenth floor, containing most precasters' residences, had some activity, but the rest of the dome was deserted. Nothing was going on, no work groups or classes, no doctor visits or children's games. The stores had closed. The mood was one of tense anticipation, but the atmosphere was calm.

"Don't fall asleep, Gray."

"Why not? I trust you to take care of everything." He opened his eyes, though, in order to catch her grin.

Elene walked in from the bathroom. Her hair was wet, but neatly brushed, and pulled back with a red barrette, showing her high forehead and accentuating her long neck; she'd dressed in a loose gown Reed had given her.

"He looks terrible, doesn't he?" Reed asked Elene. "Unshaven, glassy-eyed, and haggard."

"And burned," Gray added. The greasy salve rubbed onto his burns by one of the dome doctors smelled like tar and itched. "Plus, there's Mead's cut. Don't forget that."

Reed cocked her head at him. "A precaster? Forget?"

Elene looked from Reed to Gray. "He's not so bad."

It was pleasant to pretend that this was a lazy-day conversation; Gray was reluctant to end it with hard questions, but he would need to leave soon and there were things he wanted to understand. "I told you about Governor Swan, and that he was angry because of Dancer's memories," Gray began, "but we didn't discuss what she said." He felt awkward mentioning Dancer/Janet in front of Dancer/Elene. To him they were separate people—Elene seemed as alive as anyone—and yet they weren't. He didn't know how Elene felt about it, but a certain delicacy prevented him from asking Reed to help recall Janet. He needed to see Janet again, though, soon. "Are Janet's memories true?"

"Truth is what you believe when you need to believe it."

Reed began rocking her chair, keeping one foot on the ground.

"You had Dancer in your care for a long time."

Elene sat on the newly reupholstered sofa—now a vivid floral print. She moved much differently from Janet, as if she were heavier; her demeanor was vigilant, not continually surprised. Having seen her in action twice, Gray was impressed.

"Of what, precisely, are you accusing me?" Reed asked him.

Confabulation. A superstitious part of Gray didn't want to say the word aloud. Reed smiled, knowing him, and that smile drove him to speak. "Is Janet real, or a confabulation?"

Reed tried to share a grin with Elene, but Elene looked away. "Janet is as real as anyone," Reed said. "Isn't her desire to be sterilized an example of an independent mind?"

"Is it?" Gray got up from the floor, having difficulty bending his left leg, but managing it without help. "Is this a plan of yours to set parts of the Harmony against each other?"

"Schism. Use the proper word, Gray. And I don't plan at all; I just act confident."

Gray shook his head, simultaneously amused and annoyed.

Reed slowed her rocking. "Yes, we'd like a schism in Jonism, but you haven't said why you suspect Janet's memories are wrong."

He hadn't previously admitted the effect of Mead's drug on him. "The Janet I remember isn't much like the Janet I know."

Reed bounded out of her rocking chair on the forward stroke of the runner and hugged Gray. "I do love you, my dear; I even love Mead. You don't believe me, but I do."

Startled by the unexpected embrace, Gray was also leery. Reed was probably just changing the subject. "I believe you, grandmother, I just don't think it matters to you. You'll do whatever you think you need to do for the Bridger line."

"Shouldn't I?" When he didn't have a quick response, she stepped back and said, "So you want to know the truth because your memory of Janet Bridger doesn't include Jon Hsu. First, it seems your sister has given you your wish.

Congratulations! Let me welcome you to the ranks of Bridger precasters."

Gray stared open-mouthed. Reed was serious; she wasn't teasing him. He'd never considered that because he had memories of Janet Bridger, he was therefore a precaster. Would Mead have intended that? "I don't know anything," he finally said. "I'm not a real precaster. A chemical . . ."

"Exactly." She nodded decisively, satisfied. "Memory is overrated on Testament as a source of wisdom. Good judgment is impossible to pass down. We do our best. Mead has given you the tools; I gave you the training. Use both and you'll do fine."

"We were discussing truth."

Both Gray and Reed stared at Elene, startled by her unexpected interruption, then Reed waved a hand. "Let Gray decide it."

"A man," Elene said, with the conservative Testament condescension toward men.

"We exclude the other side of the human race from our memories," Reed said, lecturing Elene. "We make our own schism. Not one of us remembers being a man. That's plain stupid. The Harmony is full of men. There were men on the slowboat." She smiled at Gray. "We must return men to the lines."

He'd never be able to keep up with Reed's shifts of topic. "What do you expect the offies to do?" he asked.

"It's careless to speak of groups, my dear, where individuals are the relevant factor; it's rude for you to be careless just after a compliment." She clucked her tongue.

"What will *Governor Swan* do, then?"

"Cevan Swan is a fanatic. If he survived, having heard Janet's memories, he'll try to kill Dancer first, and every Bridger precaster, then all members of the Bridger line. He could succeed; stop him, any way you can. It's also crucial that he be kept away from the Shak. If they provoke him now, it could put all of Testament in jeopardy."

"The Shak?" Gray asked. "What do they have to do with this?"

Reed shook her head, as if answering were too much trouble.

"We should have killed Swan when we had the chance," Elene said. "Our lives, against the lives of all the Bridgers." She frowned at Gray, but didn't make a verbal accusation.

He flushed anyway. She was right. He'd botched it. He'd listened to Swan's vitriol; he'd seen the gun. If Swan was willing to kill an Ahman, he would have no qualms about the destruction of the Bridger line, and every native on Testament.

"Never mind," Reed said. "Spilled milk. I want you safely out of the dome. Both of you. There won't be much time." She gathered up her icesnake-skin shawl and shepherded Gray and Elene out onto the gallery. Elene went ahead, walking toward the lift as though she knew the dome well, moving independently. Gray hung back with Reed. The dim light obscured her wrinkles, giving her a false youth. She'd once been beautiful; that was what everyone who remembered her said. He had unthinkingly assumed she'd been a classic Bridger beauty, like Dancer—he couldn't call his wife Janet anymore, not with Elene there—but he realized that she hadn't. Except for being taller, in her youth Reed must have looked a great deal like Mead. He wished he could have known her then; he wished he knew her better now. All his life it had been Reed he'd yearned to satisfy. He'd hoped to be a precaster, thinking that would please her. When it had become clear that staying meant being a permanent disappointment, he'd tried to run to the Harmony, away from the trap of her affection. "I won't let you down, again," he said.

She turned her head to look at him, then took his arm. "You never have."

"I should have killed Governor Swan."

"Don't brood, Gray; be glad, as I am, that you're alive. You did a fine job covering for my error. I should have taken Janet to Martin Penn instead of trusting that vixen to get there herself." She put her arm around his waist in another quick hug, while he thought, *Her error?* "You don't kill easily; it's why you hunt, I imagine: to push your envelope. The rest of us remember too much death; I hope you never do." Just before they reached Elene on the rotunda floor, Reed pulled him close, the way a lover might. "I've said it before, but you've never believed me. I'm proud of you."

Elene was surveying the empty galleries. The only people in sight were the honor guard, at their posts, and even they were irregulars, older than usual. "You're taking a defensive posture," Elene told Reed with the authority of a general.

"How else?" Reed said. "Here's where he'd come first, if Martin doesn't stop him."

So the desertion of the dome was a strategic evacuation. The guard were all veterans. Reed's calm acceptance of Gray's news had been the kind of gentle ruse adults used on children.

There was a commotion at an entrance arch. Gray looked. Someone was insisting that he not be turned away. A moment later, Gray spotted Martin Penn being escorted toward them across the rotunda floor by Virginia Bridger, his aunt and chief of the guards. Mead trailed them, her attention fixed on Reed. "Grandmother." Gray touched Reed's arm and pointed.

"Ah. Here's our bishop now. And the black queen." Reed hurried toward them, followed by Gray and Elene. "You should have stayed in the Exchange District, Martin," Reed said heatedly, as soon as they were in earshot. "You must return there."

Penn shook his head. "The governor is berserk; he doesn't even care about the consequences of killing *me*. Since my life is all that protects yours, I expect you to help me stay safe until I can contact the authorities off-world."

Reed pulled her shawl close around her shoulders. "All the more reason for you to leave. We can't be drawn into Harmony politics. Besides, I'm sure you overestimate your own danger."

Penn frowned and turned to Gray. "You've explained that I know the Bridger secret?"

Reed laughed. "The Bridger secret? Gray told me about the nonsense his alia was spouting. Did you believe that freak?"

Gray glimpsed Elene, watching at ease, detached as if the word "freak" had referred to another person.

"Those weren't lies, lady Bridger," Penn said. "I saw the sensor readings."

Reed advanced on Mead. "Look at the trouble you've brought. Has it gained you what you want?"

"Leave her alone," Penn said, moving to Mead's defense.

Mead looked up at Penn, then walked away, disassociating herself from him. "No," she said. "But at least I've stopped you from sending this thing"—she indicated Elene by a quick thrusting out of her chin—"off-world, and with my brother as its keeper." She glared at Elene, who stood in a posture that kept her ready to defend against a physical attack, but who seemed only bemused by the spoken one. Virginia Bridger went closer to her mother, Reed.

"Lady precaster," Penn said in a conciliatory tone. "Reed. All that I've endured today has been because I believe the Bridger family holds information vital for the Harmony to know. It's time you came forward with it. Testament will benefit; the quarantine will end; you will be safe under my protection."

Reed grinned. "A fugitive tells me that."

Penn looked startled, then sheepish, then stubborn. "The truth about Jon Hsu, the things he discussed with your ancestor, everything you know, as well as the association of that information with Altered humans, can help Testament and save the career of an important man."

Reed crossed her arms. "So, Elector Lee is in trouble?"

Penn smiled sourly. "It has been publicly revealed—inside the Harmony—that Elector Lee is himself an Altered human, although not with your Alteration, obviously. If you didn't already know."

"I didn't," she said. "I only knew you worked for him. But how unfortunate for Elector Lee that Janet Bridger's memory is the imagined product of a mentally ill freak."

Gray had never heard his grandmother use the word "freak" before, and she had just done it twice. It struck a discordant note, as had her calling Mead the "black queen." He dismissed the obvious interpretation, that Mead was a "black" enemy, a hostile destroyer, because every time he'd played chess with Reed, from his first lessons until their last battle a month earlier, Reed Bridger had given him white. Black was her color. Always. Coming just after the recognition of Mead's physical likeness to their grandmother, he noticed more similarities. Mead's mannerisms, her voice, her turn of phrase were Reed Bridger again. It was more than the commonalities all close members of a line shared with each other, it was a way of thinking, an approach to the world that was greater than memory, a mixture of tendencies and tone. A freak and the black queen. Gray wanted to mull his insight, but events were distracting him.

Penn turned to Mead again, as if for confirmation, but she wouldn't look at him. "Lady precaster," Penn said, as if using Reed's name were disrespectful, "I understand that you need to be discreet, but you protest too much. Mead doesn't have the memory yet, but you do. Don't be afraid to tell me the truth."

"You're really good," Mead said emphatically to Reed. She walked past Penn to confront Reed. Virginia, by a hard look and slight movement, intercepted her. Mead looked over her shoulder at Penn. "She's playing you, Martin. You would have been suspicious if she instantly confirmed this so-called Bridger secret, so she's making you fight her to get her to yield it." Mead shook her head, crossed her arms, and faced Reed. "It won't work."

"How can I win with logic like that?" Reed raised her arms up as if entreating help from the Eye. "If I say it isn't true, then I'm trying to trick you into believing it is. I suppose if I said it was true, Mead would just claim I was lying. This granddaughter of mine is crazy, Martin."

Gray heard the pride Reed tried to disguise with humorous frustration. The next moment, in an intuitive flash of insight, he understood Reed's real plan. Everything, all of this, was for Mead. Not Janet. Not him. They were feints, distractions. The Compound Council wanted *Mead* inside the Harmony, fertile and in the arms of an Ahman of the Academy of Center, Martin Penn. She'd be a much better scout than Gray. Mead hadn't realized it yet, but the moment she did, she'd begin to remember Janet's affair, too.

"I want all four of them out of here," Reed told Virginia. "Now. Use force if you must." She turned to walk away from them, and her eyes met Gray's. She nodded, as if confirming his new knowledge, then had almost turned away when an instant of shared memory passed between them, their minds running simultaneously down a single track, like a retrospective telepathy, and for the first time Gray shared a family reminiscence: the pride Emma had in her son. He gasped at the joy of partaking of that memory with Reed. He'd never felt closer to her, or safer. She felt that pride for him.

Daylight vanished inside the dome. A loud, harsh vibrating sound shook them. Light returned with a whine as Bridger Dome's backup generator started, bringing up the dome's interior lights, but outside, through the Eye on the World, the sky was black.

"Too late," Reed said.

III. Finite Resources

They reacted like amateurs. It was obvious to Elene that Bridger Dome had been cut off, that a siege had begun, but they babbled like children rather than taking action. Even the guard captain listened to Penn instead of safeguarding the dome's approaches.

". . . deployed an atmospheric cruiser," Penn said. "It's a police weapon, meant to contain riots or to separate a criminal enclave from the general population. It isolates an area while other forces are brought in."

"Isolate how?" Mead—Elene's first nemesis in this new life—had a gun hidden in her pocket; she'd put her hand on it as she spoke. Elene moved closer to keep an eye on her.

"It's an impermeable artificial gravity barrier—a gravity wall. Nothing can cross it. Not light, radio, or any similar wave; not people or other matter."

"Swan's quick," Reed said. "He knew what he wanted to do."

"He can reposition the barrier or make the perimeter larger or smaller," Penn said. "Larger to bring his troops inside; smaller to divide us. He also could run a series of continuously smaller barriers, destroying everything by slicing it to ever smaller shreds. Or he can just wait. There are finite resources of food, water, and even air in an enclosed space."

That wasn't what they needed to hear. Shaken as she was by Penn's grim explanation of the outsiders' technological virulence, Elene said, "He can't do that, if he knows you're here. You're too important, aren't you? And this is public."

Penn shrugged. "Probably not." The tension eased, although their helplessness hadn't changed.

The guard captain, Virginia, tapped her ear, indicating a comlink source for her information. "It's a dome around our dome. It ends about twenty feet outside our entrances. There's no break."

"How deep does the wall go?" Gray asked. "Can we get out through the catacombs?"

He wasn't stupid, Elene had to admit. She'd been about to ask that question herself; she would have already, except that she felt like an observer.

"We'll check," Virginia said.

Penn said, "He's aware of your underground. He would set the barrier deep."

If the off-world governor decided to shred them using the barrier, there was nothing they could do, but meanwhile they were being psychologically overwhelmed by the technology. This was no different from any siege. They needed two things: supplies to withstand it, and a way out. "We should investigate the catacombs immediately," Elene said.

They looked at her as though a dog had begun giving advice, then one by one they accepted it and nodded, Mead last of all. Elene wondered at that. Mead had seemed intelligent. Something had recently disturbed her, and made her slow.

"Mother?" the guard captain asked Reed.

Reed nodded. "Of course. Now."

"The connections with Shak Dome were always the deepest," Elene advised, "unless you've dug something new since my time. We should try there first. If they're blocked, everywhere is."

"*Shak* Dome?" Gray sounded as if she'd suggested dealing with the devil. The reason the Shak connections were deepest was the longtime alliance of the two lines. Gone, now.

Reed drew in a breath. "The Shak are our best choice for an escape route. Virginia, keep your people up here, ready in case the offies expand the wall and try to get their soldiers inside to attack, or send in a bomb. Gray will go down with Elene, Martin, and Mead. If anyone gets out of here, I want it to be them. Put them on a comlink and we'll know they've gotten through, either if they tell us, or on the passive signal, if we're cut off. Give the link to . . ."—Reed looked at the four she'd named—"Elene."

Elene nodded. "I'll do my best."

"There's no sense waiting here for Swan's attack," Mead said irritably. "Let's go, Martin. We'll start; I know the way."

"Come with me and I'll get you a link, Elene." Virginia said Elene's name gingerly, as if she feared being scalded by the sound. Elene could imagine feeling the same way about an emulation of an alia.

"What do we do if we get out?" Gray said, stopping them all from departing.

"I'll go to him," Penn said. "I'll tell Swan I don't intend

to pursue the matter of Janet Bridger's memory, that it's a lie."

"Martin, don't be ridiculous," Mead snapped. "Then he'll just kill us all for treason. We have to kill *him* first."

Penn frowned at her. "You do that easily enough."

"He was hanging on the car! He would have stopped us, and we had to get away!"

Elene understood. Mead had used the gun and Penn was in the grip of a fit of conscience. Men were fools.

"Mead's right," Gray said. He looked at Reed for confirmation, but the precaster's face was blank. Elene recognized the signs; the precaster was forcing Gray onto his own resources. He needed the push. "Mead's right," Gray repeated, frowning. "We have to kill Swan, or he'll kill us." To Penn, he added, "If there is a Bridger secret, then some Bridger precasters have to survive."

"Yeah, and I want to be one of them," Mead muttered.

"Is the Bridger secret true?" Penn asked Reed. When she didn't speak, he gently added, "There might never be another time, lady Bridger."

Reed looked up through the Eye on the World, but inky blackness covered it. She gestured at it. "Governor Swan believes it, Martin, and he's not a fool. Ask me again when this is over; if we both survive, I'll tell you everything."

Implying it was true. Elene didn't know what the Bridger secret was supposed to be, although it apparently involved one of her emulations, but Gray had seemed dubious. Precasters. Elene caught the guard captain's attention, pointing with her thumb toward the storage area where guard uniforms had been kept in her time. Virginia was mumbling instructions into her comlink, but she nodded and started walking, although in a different direction. Elene followed. When she'd gone a few steps, she remembered Gray and looked back. He was watching Mead quarrel with Penn.

Elene caught up with Virginia. "How much trouble can we expect from the Shak?" It hurt to say that; Elene remembered her almost-sisters from Shak Dome with more affection, in several cases, than she had for her line sisters.

"You're Elene, nineteenth?" Virginia asked.

If Reed was Virginia's mother, she was main line, too, and carried Elene's memory. "Yes."

Virginia paused and extended her hand; Elene shook it,

pleased by this level of acceptance. She wasn't real. Was she?

"Expect the worst," Virginia said. "We betrayed the Shak when the offies came. We aren't proud of that. We protected the offies from our cousin Shak when they had a plan to attack the Harmony at its foundation. We didn't kill them all, though, and the remnants hate us."

It was essentially the same story Reed had told Elene. "Why *didn't* we kill them all, then? It would have been safer."

Virginia opened the door into her office. Eight generations earlier, it had been Elene's for a while, before her field command; not much had changed, not even its warmth or the yeasty smell of bread. The main dome kitchens were below. "They were our brothers' children," Virginia said. "It didn't seem necessary, and they fought hard. They still do."

Elene raised an eyebrow. "Shak are dangerous enemies. We'd better arm ourselves, in case we do get out from behind this wall."

Virginia unclipped the gun at her side—a magnum not substantially different from those in Elene's time, or even from Earth—and handed it to Elene. "You should know one other thing about the Shak. We bribe them for peace with men. They steal a few extra now and then, but most of the time we tell Hela Shak, their chief precaster, which men they'd better not touch and there's an informal quota on the rest. Not many of us know about it, but it goes through my office."

"An unpleasant business." In part to avoid discussing such a dishonorable matter, Elene examined and loaded the magnum, noting the inlaid hing-shell handle. The gun was a decoration; Virginia hadn't expected to use it often.

One of the honor guard brought a uniform and pack with a comlink into the office. Virginia had her put it on the desk and leave. When she was gone, Elene inspected the uniform for size. It looked as if it would fit her new body and would be better in the underground than the precaster's dress, so she changed; already nearly ten minutes had passed since the barrier had come down.

"Hang on to the offie Ahman," Virginia said. "You'll need him in dealing with the Harmony. You might be able to trade Gray Margaretson to the Shak for passage into Stone Town. From there, you can organize help for the rest of us from our local families, and from Bridgerton. If the Shak want more than just one singleton, tell them on my authority that we'll let them have whomever they want this year, extra men, in exchange for their help."

"That's shameful," Elene said, feeling the intense, congenital protectiveness toward Gray that she'd had since her first awakening. "Gray made some mistakes today, but I've had worse companions. Your precaster puts a high value on him." Besides, Elene knew the Shak; if their hatred ran deep enough, they would rather watch the destruction of the Bridgers than get a few extra men.

Virginia watched as Elene clipped her pack to the belt. "She's sending Gray to meet the Shak," Virginia said. "Reed can't expect him to get through. Singleton or not, they'll want him because he's main line."

"She also sent me. It's my job to make sure he does survive, and I intend to do it." Elene shivered as a surge of pleasure went through her. She frowned, thinking it was something programmed by the precaster, but it hadn't been quite that. She'd had a memory along with it, a reminiscence of sex. Virginia was waiting for her to leave. Elene nodded pleasantly and went out of her old office, to where she'd left Gray. She would warn him about the trading in men, and possible Shak expectations. It was only fair.

He was alone, gazing around the rotunda like a visitor, or as if it might be his last time inside. His grandmother had left. Elene clapped him on the back as she would have any comrade, and instantly, as she touched him, the sexual reminiscence replayed in her mind. She remembered sex with *Gray*. Impossible, unless there was leakage between emulations. If so, then she, Elene, was dying from this mind. She scowled. "Get going, boy. There isn't time for sentiment."

IV. Just Like a Woman

Women are aliens, Gray thought. Just when you think you know them, just when you're almost comfortable with them, everything twists.

Elene led the way down into the lowest catacombs as if the short cut were her special route. He knew it, too; he'd lived inside the dome more recently than she had, yet she was the leader because she was a woman. She wore the uniform of the honor guard, a casual recipient of just another of the things denied him, a singleton and a man. Honor guard. He spat in the tunnel, heedless of the disrespect it did the dead. Some honor the guard had. They were trading in men's lives; Elene had told him the truth about the Bridger honor guard. *Don't you hate them?*

In its upper levels, the Bridger Underground's walls were smoothed with plaster and painted, usually white. Besides the ossuary and chapel, there were storerooms, offices, and shops, all of them now closed, but their signs and a few glass windows made the family area look like a staid Edgemarket. In a few places, the ceilings were low, so that Gray sometimes had to stoop, but there were also larger open areas, remnants of natural caverns. Children's playgrounds, most of them. Empty, now.

Lower, in the catacomb proper, tunnels narrowed and were unpainted. They were called the "offices of the dead" because they formed a grid of corridors and closed doors like an office building. Behind the doors were rooms of shelves of bones. Throughout, small plaques on the doors numbered and named the dead, including their sub-lines. The main line was a convenient yardstick, not nobility, and the plaques were no different in style from the ones in the main line sepulcher, except that more names were engraved on each. Lower still, the tunnel corridors were lined with scattered, disjointed bones on shelves, but even here there were names engraved on plaques and signs of visitors: stones left behind or a faded, handwritten note from someone who had remembered something meaningful to her, to be read by the next. Testament's dead were never entirely forgotten. At these depths, there was a distinctive odor of clay, dampness (the Stone Sea wasn't far and formed the absolute limit on a tunnel's depth), and decay that Gray associated with all death.

They played leapfrog with the lights, turning on, then off, each bank of electric lights as they passed through, in the way every Bridger was taught, and hurried to catch up with Mead and Penn. Elene stopped abruptly and snapped off a light, plunging them into underground darkness, which reminded Gray unpleasantly of the Safe Box. "There's light ahead," she whispered.

"Mead and Penn?"

"Probably," she said softly against his ear. He smelled her breath. In the dark, intimately close and whispering, she reminded him intensely of Janet. "But we're fairly close to the end of Bridger territory. The Shak Gate could be open, or some other way they've made."

The Shak could be just ahead, the women who had killed his mother, and would be glad enough to kill or capture him. These were the women on whom the Bridger line's future rested. "We have to make this work," he said. "They were your friends. How do I get the Shak to help us?"

She touched his shoulder. "Apologize," she said. "Sincerely. It may help, and we were wrong. Don't be weak in front of them. They despise it. They have memories of when we were friends. Use that."

He nodded, then remembered the dark, and said, "Thanks." He waited for her to go on.

"Gray," she said, "she wasn't lying about loving you. Your grandmother."

Just like a woman. With the possibility of death ahead, the likelihood of death behind, she had to set things right between him and the Bridger line. He hadn't expected such softness, though, from Elene. "Neither was Virginia lying. Reed can't think much of men."

He sensed her shrug as a gentle movement of the stale air. "That's life. The good and the bad. Choices are made. But she wants you safe."

Her voice was wrong. It wasn't merely the enclosed, underground space. This wasn't Elene. "Who are you?"

"Who am I?" She sounded puzzled. "Dancer?"

There was no woman named Dancer. Dancer was an alia; this must be a new emulation. Someone unpredictable. "Turn on the light." He wanted to see her face.

Instead, Dancer moved stealthily forward, signaling him with a hand on his arm to come. With no real choice, he did, walking as quietly as he knew how. The silence of the outlands was different from this, fuller and wider. Voices ahead resolved into Mead's complaints, then Penn's gruff, affectionate response. Gray relaxed; they turned a corner. The bank of lights spotlighted Penn and Mead. They were alone. Gray went ahead.

"You took your time," Mead said by way of greeting.

Gray went past Penn. "Mead, give me that gun."

"Why should I?"

"I'm a better shot, and so we'll all be safer," Gray said, for want of a better answer.

Penn frowned, trying to understand. "Are there animals in these tunnels?"

"Just women." Gray held out his hand.

Mead studied him thoughtfully, then looked at Elene—Dancer. "Is she scaring you, brother? Your wife?" Mead grinned. The light was barely adequate and threw shadows across their faces. Mead's grin was horrible, a skeleton's, but she gave him the gun.

He stuck it in his belt and looked at Dancer; she gazed back at him with just the calm, competent expectancy he associated with Elene, and she was, or seemed to be, Elene again. He walked ahead, turning on the next bank of lights. They let him lead. He kept alert, listening for the Shak and feeling foolish doing so. The silence was complete. There were no Shak ahead, or anything to get them beyond the perimeter of the gravity wall.

They walked through six more short banks of light. At the seventh, the light stopped too soon, and its last length flickered in distress. Gray approached the light's end painstakingly slowly, with the others hanging back. Even in the tunnel, this darkness was another dimension of black.

"That's it," Mead said.

The other three came closer.

No one had touched the barrier. Maybe it could be breached. Curious, remembering the one in Swan's office, Gray delicately reached out. Penn pushed forward past Mead and slapped Gray's hand away. "Don't. The surface is dangerous."

"Gravity," Mead said. "Why doesn't it suck us all in?" She glanced around. "Or pull in the things it touches?"

"It's not the same as natural gravity." Penn moved back from it, drawing Mead with him. "I'm no expert on these things. They're used for battlefields and riots. I only know what I've heard, that it's a gravity shell. Things can get stuck in it, but not pulled in. If it passes through something, the object is severed. There are different amplitudes. I don't think it's wise to experiment."

"What do you suggest we do, Martin?" Mead asked acidly.

He didn't answer.

"Might as well go back," Elene said. "I've told them we've found the wall and can't pass it." She patted her ear, as Virginia had. The comlink.

"We'll wait." Gray hunkered down, looking at the barrier. "Elene—Dancer—tell them to send people down here with shovels. Maybe we can dig under it."

The corridor walls around them trembled. Gray held his hand against the rough, dusty stone wall. The trembling became a gnashing sound. A thin layer of grit, finer than sand, spilled from the air on all sides except the barrier, as if the encircling walls had sprinkled them with powder. There was a creak, a snap, and silence. The gravity barrier hadn't changed.

"What was that?" Gray removed his hand from the stone; his handprint was obvious, like that of a prehistoric cave painter from old Earth.

"They changed the amplitude," Penn said uncomfortably. "Or they moved another part of the barrier."

Gray imagined the apex of the dome being crushed under the weight of fifty gravities. Swan could lower the barrier's height bit by bit and pulverize Bridger Dome. "He'll grind us into dust."

"Let's go; maybe we can help." Elene took a few steps back the way they'd come. Her feet left footprints in the new dust. She snapped on the next bank of lights and waited for them.

The stone walls shook again, harder, and made a sound like the tunnel crushing in on itself. Dust and small bits of rock tumbled from the ceiling. "Gray!" a woman called. Someone screamed. Dust choked him. He covered his mouth and nose with his hands, wondering if they would be buried in it, or squashed by a collapsing ceiling.

The trembling stopped. The dust drifted onto them, unseen in the absolute darkness.

Chapter 12

I. An Expendable Hero

"Did anyone bring a light?" Mead said, speaking from Gray's right and above. She was still standing, then.

No light appeared; no one answered. Gray calculated that he had been less than three feet from Swan's gravity barrier, but he could not be sure it had not moved. That was, in fact, the likeliest explanation for the loss of light, that the wall was now on their other side, cutting them off from Bridger Dome's electrical power grid. They were free, beyond it, and thus into Shak Underground. Gray touched the handle of the offie gun. "Are we all here?" he asked.

"Penn," Penn said.

"Elene?" She'd been the farthest from the gravity wall. "Dancer?" He heard breathing, but it could have been Mead or Penn. "Janet?"

Nothing. He stood, keeping careful contact with the stone wall behind him so as not to become disoriented. His feet scuffed the floor.

"Are there rats down here?" Mead asked.

"That was me. Mead, Elene was nearest to you. Can you feel for her?"

"I'm not moving until I can see."

"Are you going to stand there until the Shak come, or the offies?" Gray couldn't blame her, though. If Elene's silence meant she had been cut off from them, the black wall was close. "Here, I'll come to you. Start talking, to guide me."

"Wait. I have an idea," Penn said. "Swan's stick gun generates heat in whatever it contacts. We could create a glow."

"You'd need an awful lot of heat to make stone shine." Gray didn't trust uncontained heat or flame. In the outlands, they'd used lanterns or the moons and stars for light; with so little fuel, campfires had been only an occasional atavistic thrill.

"If the gravity wall is still ahead of us," Penn suggested, "the heat might cause a reaction."

"Reaction" sounded unsafe. Gray didn't understand the science, and wasn't certain Penn did, but they had few choices. "I'll try it. I'm forward of everyone." He extended the gun, using two hands to keep it steady in case there was a recoil, and pushed on the recessed button. Nothing happened. He held the button down again, longer.

"Is there a faint shine?" Mead asked.

"I don't see anything." Gray stopped, put the gun back in his belt, and felt for the stone wall, relieved when he touched it. Standing in utter darkness, shooting blindly ahead without detectable effect, he'd had to fight the sensation he was on a cliff's edge, about to fall. "If I aim it in the other direction, I could hit one of you, or Dancer, if she's there."

"Well, I am. Don't," Mead said. "Try making light by burning clothes."

He imagined holding his shirt outstretched while shooting Swan's heat gun. The gun shot wide; he might ignite his hand. "No. I'm coming to you, then looking for Dancer. Talk to me."

"You always were obstinate," she said. "What more can I say? This would be a real adventure for my daughters to remember, if I were going to have any. Alone in the dark. An offie, an alia, a singleton, and me. None of us smart enough to have brought along even a match."

Gray reached Mead. She grabbed onto him, resting her head against his chest for a moment. She was trembling. He bit off the remark he'd been about to make: *I'm the singleton; what's your excuse?* "I'm here," he told Penn, who couldn't be far. "There might be something useful in the guard uniform, if Dancer is on this side."

Mead straightened, but kept her hand on his forearm, in constant contact with him. "If she is, then your alia sure has lousy timing in changing her minds."

Mead was right, and Gray didn't have any of the drug with which he could revive Janet. "Penn, how do I tell if I'm close to the black wall?"

"I'm not sure. Try pushing something forward, then bringing it back. If it doesn't come, maybe it's stuck in the alternate gravity. Be careful."

Mead giggled. It sounded loud in the darkness. "We forgot matches, but at least we remembered to bring an expendable hero."

Coming after the news that Bridgers doled out men to the Shak as bribes, Mead's candor stung worse than usual, probably worse than she intended. She must have felt a twinge of conscience. "Oh, here," she said, balancing herself against Gray. "Use my shoe." She thrust it into his hand and took a small step toward Penn.

Gray knelt, to be more stable, and, without leaning forward, slid Mead's shoe ahead and brought it back. So far, so good. Gray scrabbled onward. On the fifth trial, Mead's shoe couldn't be pressed farther, but it came back. Something blocked it. He raised the shoe to knee height and moved it carefully ahead without finding any barrier. "I think I've found her," he told the others. He inched his fingers along the dusty floor, and sure enough, he encountered a warm body. "Janet?" he called; she was the person inside Dancer that he wanted most to see. He called her name again, and then Elene's. There was no answer.

"All right already," Mead said.

Penn hushed her.

Dancer was warm and had a pulse, but the only way to determine if she was injured was by touch, slowly. Gray grasped the cloth of her guard uniform and, taking care to lift her head, pulled her back to where he knew the area was safe. She groaned as he moved her. Carefully, he let his fingers roam over her. Everything felt normal. "She seems fine," he told the others.

His hands encountered the holster and Elene's gun. He took it, without mentioning it to the others. He didn't trust Penn or Mead enough to want them armed. Elene's guard uniform also had a pack. He opened it slowly, mindful of the possibility of spilling and losing the contents in the dark. He fingered them one by one. They were difficult for Gray, who was effectively blind, to identify. She could have been given anything: food, medical supplies, ammunition, or tools.

"Find anything useful?" Penn asked.

Gray wasn't sure. He held the object he hoped was a flashlight, pointed it ahead, then pushed the toggle. And there was light. He focused it on Mead and Penn.

"We're back in business," Mead said. She squinted; her face was coated with dust, giving her a ghostly look.

"Good job, Gray." Penn looked calm, except for his rapid blinking in the sudden light.

Gray examined Dancer. Her eyes were open, but her mind was clearly vacant. Bad timing, as Mead had said. He ran the light over her body, immediately seeing what his hands had missed. Her left foot and the part of her leg just above the ankle were missing, cleanly severed.

Penn saw it, too. "She's in shock." He came forward and knelt beside Gray, feeling Dancer's pulse, then telling Gray to aim the light so he could examine the wound. There was no blood, as if the gravity cut had cauterized it. Penn looked into Dancer's eyes, and sighed. "We don't have anything to treat her, but she's stable and at least she's not losing blood."

Mead had shuffled forward to join them; she touched Penn's shoulder.

Penn looked at her. "She's young; she'll be all right."

Gray took Dancer's hand in his own. Like an infant's, her fingers tightened around his.

"Check behind her," Mead suggested.

Still holding Dancer's hand, Gray did. The light didn't extend far into the featureless tunnel before dissipating.

"Throw a coin out there and see if it comes down," Mead said.

"It doesn't matter what's behind us," Gray told her. "We have to go on." Dancer's injury proved the barrier was there.

"We're not sure if we can," Penn commented. "Shine the light ahead."

He did, although it was useless. It lit an unmeasurable expanse of darkness before fading. From the amount of walking they had done, they could have been across the plaza between the Shak ruin and Bridger Dome, but they'd turned many times, and the underground was a notoriously difficult place to keep one's bearings. "Is there any way up to the plaza now that we're past the gravity barrier?" Gray asked.

Mead tried to be helpful. "No, there's nothing. We're past the ventilation grids. The Shak may have some new connection into our underground. That's possible; they try it now and again. Come on, Gray, give me back my shoe and let's get going."

Gray released Dancer's hand and returned the shoe. "Penn, you and I can carry Dancer."

"She's safe where she is," Mead said. "If we get out, we'll send back for her."

"That does seem best," Penn reluctantly agreed.

Gray shone the light in their faces. They couldn't see his. "We're bringing her." He couldn't let Janet, or even Elene, awaken in the black underground tunnel, alone and injured.

"What do you think is going on in Bridger Dome?" Mead asked. "We have to hurry. We can't, carrying her."

Mead had a point. Gray understood his grandmother better, feeling the dilemma of decision-making when there were several critical, contradictory interests. He sniffed the air. It was fresher now, and seemed to be improving, although Mead said they were beyond the Bridger ventilation system. He felt a faint breeze against his face. It must be Shak engineering, and Shak Dome ahead, women whose enmity he took for granted. "Mead, exactly how do we get into Shak Underground?"

Her indecision was clear in the flashlight's beam. "I'm not sure. I've never explored the underground in this life, and since their dome was broken, the Shak tunnel like bury mice." She turned away from his light. "I'm sorry, Gray. I didn't think we'd really get out; I just figured on hiding from the offies when they broke into the dome."

"So much for Bridger precasters," Gray said.

"Is that what you are?" jeered a woman's voice from the dark tunnel ahead. "I thought you were Bridger ghosts."

Gray snapped off the light. "Who's there?"

"Dr. Livingston, I presume," Mead said. "Hey, you. Shak. Take me to your leader. We come in peace." She giggled nervously.

"What?"

Gray thought that was Penn. From the Shak, there was silence. He doubted there was only one; one alone wouldn't have spoken. He tucked the flashlight into a pocket and took Elene's bullet gun from his belt. It required aiming, but he was more familiar with weapons of that type and wouldn't make a mistake as easily.

"We require your assistance," Penn said. His off-world accent was pronounced. "Governor Swan has . . ." He stopped abruptly as Mead hissed at him to shut up.

"So you need help, Bridgers?" the contemptuous voice

said. "No wonder, if you let a man lead you. Turn on your light, Bridger boy."

"Turn on yours," Gray called back. They were close enough that he heard separate voices ahead, but couldn't distinguish words. Shak. His hand tightened reflexively on the gun.

"We don't have one, Bridger boy," she said. "We see in the dark. We see that gun in your hand. You're a handsome boy. What a pretty face my next daughter will have."

"Cut the crap," Mead shouted. "So you've got infrared or heat-sink. We want to talk to your precasters. It's important."

"We don't care what Bridgers want. You're dead, Bridger bitch."

"She's under my protection." Penn's statement was ludicrous, but at least he hadn't abandoned them in favor of the Shak.

The women laughed. "We'll make a bonfire from your skin, you Bridger snake, after we help you shed it. Your boyfriends can watch."

Gray shuddered. He'd never known, precisely, how his mother had died, and Reed hadn't allowed him to see her body. He had always told himself that his nightmare visions of it must be worse than any actuality, but Shak imagination already seemed as bad as his worst fantasy. He could not let that matter. He had to get Shak help; they needed passage through the Shak Underground. Elene had said not to be weak. He strained to distinguish how many Shak were present and their movements. The tunnel was narrow; no Shak could have gotten past them, and if any had, they would have struck Swan's barrier. Gray stepped to the side, closer to the protection of the tunnel wall. "We have a common enemy," he said, keeping tight hold of the gun. "The offies. Let us talk to your precasters; let them decide how to treat us."

"We don't want to *talk* to you, Bridger boy. You'll burn differently."

Too close, much closer than the Shak woman keeping them busy with insults, Gray heard a sneaking footfall. Without thinking, using outland instincts, he shot at it, but low, to wound and not to kill.

Someone fell. Someone came forward to help. Gray stepped back from where he'd been, but no one returned his fire. "Not bad," a woman whispered at his ear. The timbre of her voice reminded him of the voice in the offie Safe Box. Two strong hands closed around the wrist of his hand holding the gun and yanked his arm backward and down. As he bent in response to the forced movement and pain, she grabbed his other arm, twisted it too, holding him captive. "But not good enough," she whispered. He dropped the gun. Another Shak picked it up, and removed the offie weapon and the flashlight from his possession, after patting him down. "Let us talk to your precasters, to Hela Shak," Gray said. "There's always time later to kill us."

They didn't answer. He heard scuffling as the Shak captured Penn, and then Mead, who swore vigorously. The Shak, though, were experienced at stealth and kidnapping.

"Thanks for the gift-men," a different woman—near Gray—said, apparently to Mead. She gave orders to the others; this was the real leader, not the one who'd stalled them.

"Is the woman I shot all right?" Gray asked. His shot had been impulsive, because they were closing in and Elene had counseled him not to appear weak. Maybe it had been ill-advised, since they needed Shak help, or maybe it made no difference. There were at least ten Shak women, from the voices and footsteps, enough to do as they liked.

"You didn't kill her," their leader said. "Did you want to?" His captor held him in a clever grip that didn't let him move while another—the leader, he guessed—bound his wrists.

Gray didn't try to escape. "No. Listen. Maybe Bridgers are your enemies, but *we* aren't. We need to talk to Hela Shak."

The woman hesitated, while Gray listened to Mead's invective and the sound of her struggle to break free. "Stop it, Mead!" he said. Unexpectedly, Mead did stop fighting, but not swearing, so they gagged her.

The Shak leader, or someone, patted Gray's arm. "You'll see Hela soon enough," she said. Gray thought she sounded pleased. Unlike the woman who had taunted them as her companions crept close, this one was nearly friendly.

"Laris, what about the bitch on the ground? Kill her?"

Dancer. "Please, no," Gray said, twisting in a futile attempt to see faces in the dark. "She's injured and harmless; she's my wife."

Laris, the leader, slapped Gray's buttocks good-naturedly.

"You'll have plenty of *wives*." But she ordered the others to carry Dancer with them, while ignoring Penn's attempt to persuade her to help them to the surface and away.

The group set out, moving more quickly through the underground than Gray liked. He was disoriented by the darkness, and the Shak occasionally prodded him with slaps and shoves to hurry him through their sloping, twisting tunnels; nothing was lighted. Laris stayed nearby; he knew it from the ribald jokes the others made, linking her with him. "You're making a mistake," Gray said. "Reed Bridger sent us out from Bridger Dome to beg your help. We can offer good terms. I'm a singleton, anyway; I'm no use to you."

"She's not prejudiced, Bridger boy," another woman called from behind. "She likes all men." The Shak giggled as if liking men were peculiar.

Gray hesitated. "The offie really is important."

"Martin Penn," Laris said, stunning Gray into silence. "Ahman of the Academy of Center. We know. The offies have been screaming for an hour, over every broadcast, that the Bridgers kidnapped him, and that now Swan is destroying Bridger Dome."

II. Bridger Truth

Hela Shak was a younger woman than Reed. Red-haired, thin, with a scarred face and a blind right eye, all white but for a tiny black pupil at its center, her savagery frightened Penn; she was viciously satisfied by their capture. "Reed Bridger's own grandchildren," Hela said. She leered at Gray, who tried to ignore her, turning aside when she strutted close and patted his cheek, to the encouraging shouts of her relatives, then she smiled down at Mead, who was much smaller. Hela suddenly spat in Mead's face. Hands bound behind her back, gagged and closely guarded, Mead trembled, furious and frustrated. Penn's own fists were clenched.

To distract her, Penn bowed awkwardly, out of balance because of his bound hands. "Lady Shak, I guarantee you a rich reward if you release us unharmed."

Hela turned away from Mead. "You keep poor company, Mr. Penn," she said.

He didn't correct her failure to use his title, although it grated. "Off this world, I am an important man, an Ahman

in service to the Electors. Once I contact the proper authorities, you will profit from your help to us now."

She smiled in disbelief and shook her head with amusement shared with the small gathering of Shak. "Helping you
means helping Bridgers," she said. "I won't do that. Ever."

Except for a few women close-guarding the captives, the
girl-gang who'd captured them stood around the periphery
like a barbarian tribe of Amazons, with oddments of weaponry and ammunition crisscrossing their bodies and little extra clothing. The others were apparently precasters, like
Hela, since they were older as well as more fully and tradi-
tionally dressed, in the rustic, brightly colored clothing Penn
had seen throughout Stone Town.

The narrow, windowless room to which they'd been
brought was too large for their gathering. Most of it seemed
permanently unused. It was a scene of ruined splendor, a
masterpiece composed of shadows and cracked, broken rock.
The jagged walls had been painted in abstract, patternless
colors that emphasized the devastation, as if they wanted
constantly to be reminded of it. The room's far end, where
they'd been brought, was an office. Its plastic chairs and
desk had a cheap, worn look that was absent in Bridger
Dome. There, things were old, but never battered or poorly
made. The room was apparently also a bedroom; behind the
desk was an unmade bed, partly concealed by a narrow cabinet from which peeked the green sleeve of a shirt. Hela's?

Shak Dome's odor was of old food and human bodies; it
was clean without being fresh and smelled as Penn imagined
a barracks would smell. Barracks: the word described Shak
Dome, although "dome" was a formality for this wrecked
place; it was an armed camp.

The Shak were poorer than the Bridgers; they gloried in
their grievances. They were women, though; so far, they had
threatened and humiliated but had not harmed anyone. However, Gray's fears about sexual slavery no longer amused
Penn, though it was at Gray that the Shak directed most of
their attention.

Gray's wife, while still unconscious, had been separated
from them. Penn worried about that; she was the only sure
vessel for the memories of Jon Hsu. First, though, they had
to survive.

"Governor Swan has offered a reward for you, Mr. Penn,"

Hela said. "There's a bounty on these Bridgers, too. Should I deliver you to Swan?"

If the delivery was public, and Penn could use the occasion to declare the Bridger truth to a large assembly of even the local Harmony citizens, while casting doubt on Swan's conduct, it might be the best alternative left to them, but if his return was private and unseen, Penn would be killed, and native Bridgers charged with his murder.

"You should help us get away from Swan," Gray said loudly. "Only traitors would ally themselves with him. What he wants can't be good for Testament."

The girl-guard standing next to Gray, who was the leader of their captors, shoved him hard, sending him staggering, but he managed to stay on his feet.

Hands on her hips, head thrown back and slightly tilted so she could see him with her good eye, Hela Shak stared threateningly at Gray. "Since when have Bridgers"—she spat—"been known for statesmanship? What have they done for the Shak?"

The armed women whispered to each other, their tone as hostile as mood music in a cyclone drama.

"You have one use, Bridger boy, and it's a trivial one beside the reward the offies will pay for you. Dead or alive."

"Then sell me to the offies," Gray challenged her. "I know that the Shak have been wronged by the Bridgers." He hesitated as the Shak, including Hela, waited in breathless silence and Mead squirmed in distress, trying to free herself. "I apologize," he said. "You killed my mother, yet I say that the Shak are more wronged than I am. I apologize." All eyes were on him. Beneath her gag, Mead tried to express outrage, and she stamped her feet in futile protest, but Penn stayed quiet. Gray was doing a good job of swaying these brutalized primitives. The attitude of the Shak women had softened considerably, and his guard even smiled at Gray. "This is my sister." Gray indicated Mead, who'd stopped struggling, although her dark eyes were wild. "But some of you are my cousins. I recognize it in your faces and see my family in your eyes. We're in your line. The Bridgers have given you their sons."

"Not willingly," Hela said. Other women murmured the same sentiment.

"Don't you think the Bridgers could have come here, together with the other lines whose brothers and sons you've taken, and stopped you? We haven't; you're in us, too. We've hoped that someday we can be friends again, and allies against the offies."

Women shouted, arguing with each other. Penn felt lost in a costume drama from one of the alan worlds, where different customs made human interactions inscrutable.

"Help us," Gray yelled over the voices of the crowd of women. "For everyone on Testament. Please! The time is now."

Hela Shak raised her hands above her head. The women quieted. "Have we already forgotten Bridger promises? Have we forgotten how those deceitful *cousins* talk and talk and twist the truth? Even their singleton boys can do it!" She dropped her hands, but the Shak didn't move. "Get those two Bridgers out of my sight," she pronounced like a death sentence. "Leave the offie here; I want to explain Bridgers to him."

Gray and Mead were taken from the room. The Shak were harsher with Mead, half-dragging her when she attempted a detour to pass closer to Penn. "Wait!" Penn called when Mead stumbled and a pregnant Shak woman kicked her. Mead looked at him as they yanked her up. Her hair was loose and fell across her face. She brushed it away with her shoulder. Her eyes held his. She couldn't talk, but her look spoke to him. Mead was afraid. They had escaped the destruction of Bridger Dome only to fall into the clutches of tribal savages who taunted Mead with torture and death, which they'd actually carried out on Mead's mother. Penn was her only hope. With a sinking despair, Penn knew that Mead could be killed, that he might never see her again, then the Shak wrenched her forward, out the door, away.

Hela Shak had stayed near her desk, watching. She beckoned Penn to her. He went, because cooperation was his only chance to save himself and Mead. She turned away for a low-voiced discussion with two other, older women. Penn stared down at the desk. It was cracked, its broken edge darkened by an accumulation of dust and dirt. An aged computer station of the type used throughout Testament was on one side of the desk, and a small pile of hardcopy bound books, such as those he'd seen in Gray's bedroom, was on the opposite corner. After a glance at his inattentive guard— there seemed to be no concern that he might escape or attack—Penn craned his neck to read the book titles. They were journals of an old-fashioned biology, no doubt descended from the ancient work done on old Earth, a good source for some medic-in-training's research project into folk medicine, if Penn found a way out of this situation. Since Swan's attack, the world had gone insane.

Hela's companions glanced at Penn, nodded at Hela, then left the room. At her signal, Penn's guard also left. They were alone. Hela continued to scrutinize him. Penn bowed.

"You should have spoken, not the Bridger."

Encouraged by her calm tone, Penn said, "Gray told the truth."

"And what is Bridger truth this time?" She chuckled and sat on the corner of the desk nearest to him.

There was a sudden ear-shattering sound, a thunder much louder than the roar he'd heard from inside the gravity wall. Hela Shak smiled and glanced in the direction of Bridger Dome. The booming noise slowly vibrated to a halt. Swan had repositioned his gravity barrier again.

"They need your help," Penn said. "So do I. You'll be very well rewarded if you release us."

Hela cocked her head so her one seeing eye gazed at him directly. The blind eye was disconcerting. She ignored his plea. "Were you kidnapped, as Swan says? Did the Bridgers kill an offie soldier?"

"No. I left the Exchange District on my own, accompanied by Mead Bridger. She shot a Harmony soldier so we could get away." By doing so, Mead had helped Swan's case, but it had been necessary. Hadn't it? Mead wasn't like the Shak.

Though also a precaster, Hela had a different demeanor from Reed, a plain, artless style. With all her eccentricities and apparent informality, Reed maintained her reserve, and allowed one to others. It was the difference between a peasant and a patrician, and made Reed seem more civilized than this spartan woman.

"She's your lover? Is that why you're helping them?"

It seemed risky to refuse to answer, however intrusive the question. "Yes, she is, but I'm trying to help the Bridgers because it's right. Also, they have certain information that's valuable to me."

Hela grinned, and in her expression Penn saw what Gray had stated, a family connection between the Bridger and Shak lines. "What did the Bridgers say—they love to talk—

that made you want to help them, and infuriated Swan?" Hela asked.

"The Bridgers haven't said anything directly, but Gray's wife . . ."

"The alia?"

"Yes. She emulates Janet Bridger, the founder of their line." Penn wet his lips, deciding how much he should tell Hela Shak.

"The emulation remembers valuable information?" she prodded.

"Yes." Penn told her about Dancer's revelations, stressing for this audience the positive effect that Jon Hsu's remembered attitudes toward Altereds and this new connection with Testament would have for all natives, not only Bridgers. He spoke quickly, aware of the mayhem being done nearby. Hela listened, quiet except for annoying clicks as she tapped her fingernails against the desk. She didn't ask questions. When he was finished, she stood. "When the Bridgers tell a story, they do a good job."

"The Shak line would have different memories," he said.

"Indeed we do." She grinned again. "Do you trust the Bridgers, Mr. Penn?"

It seemed to be a serious question. He considered his answer, recalling Mead's inconsistencies, her tales of precaster plots, and her avowal of honesty, remembering Gray's generally honorable behavior, his wife's certainty, and the sensor proof of her memory, and lastly, reflecting on Reed Bridger's vitality and conduct. "I don't doubt that they are capable of fraud," he said, "but I fully believe that what I've learned is true, and that the Bridgers I've met are people whose indiscretions have been reactions to unfair circumstances."

"You're very generous in judging them. They're your friends."

The Shak hated the Bridgers; he shouldn't have been *generous*. "They're my proof," he said. How could she ignore what was going on across the plaza? "Janet Bridger's memory will dramatically change the Harmony's attitude toward Altered people everywhere, including here on Testament."

"As it changed Swan's attitude?" she sneered.

He shook his head. "Swan has always hated Altereds. This is just his excuse. He won't stop with the Bridgers; he'll fabricate proof of a larger plot. I can prevent the destruction of Testament—that's what it will come to—if you let me go. If I arrive publicly, safe and unharmed, then I can attest that I wasn't kidnapped and I'll stop him."

"You'd have to kill Swan to make him stop now," she said.

Mead had said the same thing, but Penn was convinced that in a public confrontation, he would be able to persuade Swan's small military detachment to stop; Swan could do nothing without them. What Penn didn't understand was Hela's unconcern in the face of a dire, immediate threat to all natives.

"And what if there really is a Bridger plot?" Hela asked. "Maybe Swan is right. Will you stop him then?"

"If there is a plot, then the perpetrators need to be punished, but there is no justification for random destruction. Lady Shak, the physical structure of Bridger Dome is being weakened, and there are people inside who needn't die, and shouldn't. Will you let us go?"

"Maybe," she said. "But not for them." She walked away, looking into her messy bedroom area, then turned to face him from a distance. "I'll keep the Bridgers. The boy has his uses; I already have bids on stud for him, singleton or not. The alia is an abomination. The bitch would die appealingly."

"No." Mead, tortured to death. Mead, burning on some primordial funeral pyre. These Shak were *alien.* "I need them all alive."

Her lips curled in a derisive smile. "Listen to me before you decide, Mr. Penn. No Shak ever met Jon Hsu."

"I've told you that it doesn't matter. The Harmony will lift the quarantine for every native once Janet Bridger's memories are known."

"A lie never becomes the truth, no matter how well told, or useful. The Bridgers are lying to you."

She waited for him to ask for more. He didn't, having expected her to try to discredit the Bridgers when he told her their secret. Finally, she continued on her own.

"Lana Shak, the founder of *our* line, was a contemporary of Janet Bridger. Our two lines were sisters and friends—cousins, as the boy said—trading brothers to build our families, sharing a background memory that was a generation earlier than that of most other original lines." Her blind eye seemed to stare at him, a horror from a story. "Lana Shak

never met Jon Hsu, but she knew him. Lana was a member
of the Hard Science Underground. I see you know that
name."

"I've heard of the Hard Science Underground," he said
warily. "They were early followers of Jon Hsu."

She shook her head. "They *created* him. Jon Hsu is an ancient lie, a virtual man. He existed, but he wasn't real; he
was data fed into machines. He was virtual truth—computer-
generated imagery, holograms, and ghost-written text. A superficial existence in records that were deliberately . . .
enhanced with him."

"Nonsense." The enormity of her accusation made Penn's
protest feeble.

"Jon Hsu was created to protect the rest of the Hard Science Underground; he was their symbol of rational, scientific objections to the mystical nonsense they felt was
perverting and destroying human progress. His name went
on the monographs no one felt safe authoring; he was the
one on whom fundamentalist venom was heaped. His existence sheltered the rest of the underground, and he was a
joke for those who knew the truth: the authorities want him,
but they'll have to catch him first."

Penn turned away from her. She was a lying savage, he
told himself, bent on destroying Jonism, plotting a revenge
against the Bridgers and the Harmony so corrosive and enormous it made him physically ill. Did she expect him to help
spread this hoax?

"After our ship left Earth," she said, "apparently Jon Hsu
became a popular figure. No one could deny him. Who
needs God? Men can create men, too." She grinned. "Funny
that a nonexistent man is the founder of your religion.
Makes you wonder about all of them."

"Jonism isn't a religion," he said automatically. "It's a
philosophy and way of life."

Hela Shak snickered.

Penn forced himself to be composed and speak reasonably
despite the urge to kill. "I can believe that the Bridgers
might—and did—keep secret an affair between Jon Hsu and
Janet Bridger. It's knowledge that could be useful if they
were ever persecuted, something not to be wasted while they
got along fairly well with the Harmony administration. But
it's known that you Shak hate the Harmony, and wanted to
fight us when we came. I don't believe that you would keep

a secret of these colossal proportions, going to the fundamental fabric of the Harmony, for so long. I don't believe you."

"Oh, we didn't keep it secret, Mr. Penn. We told our partners, our sisters, our friends—we told the Bridgers. It was our great and former allies in Bridger Dome who protected you offies from the truth. They said silence would save us—all of Testament—from what telling you would cause you to do to us. They said the Harmony would exterminate the bearers of such news, that we were on shaky ground with you already, being Altered. The Bridgers said to wait. This is a slow war, they told us. The time will come when truth can be a lever to pry the Harmony apart, and let us stream out through its gaps. *That* is the Bridger way; that is Bridger truth—whatever is useful. The Shak disagreed, along with some others."

She indicated the shabby room, by its dimensions obviously the site of a lost grandeur, and seemed to study it anew herself, turning her head from side to side because of her blind eye. "Look what the Bridgers and their new allies on the Compound Council did to us." She gestured at her scarred face. "Look what they continue doing, to keep us away from you. And now they've made a story that's better than truth, seemingly so trivial, yet carefully crafted to polarize, then rupture, your precious Jonism."

"You aren't convincing."

"Is that a prayer, Mr. Penn? The Bridgers tell a better tale, but mine happens to be true. I think you know it; you strike me as an honest man who's going to be very angry as he realizes the depth of Bridger lies." She pulled a long, thin knife from her boot. He tensed as she walked behind him, but, with a quick slice of the knife, and without nicking his hands, she cut away the cord binding him. His freed arms dropped to his sides; his muscles stung. He made a sound, then gritted his teeth and rubbed his upper arms. He would not give this woman cause to scorn him.

"Come with me to visit your Bridger friends. The singleton won't know, and the alia's mind has been muddled by Reed Bridger, but the bitch precaster, Reed's granddaughter—your lover, as I recall—she knows. Come along, Mr. Penn, and let us discuss Bridger truth with her."

III. Remaking History

There were rumors of how the Shak treated Bridger men, stories of brandings, cages, sawed-off limbs, and suicide, but the room where Gray had been brought, together with Mead, was obviously just a storeroom converted to their use, and the guards were firm but not malicious. Dancer was already there, unconscious on a stretcher. Her wound had been treated; the severed stump was bound with clean bandages and a blanket had been thrown over her. Gray nodded at Laris Shak. "Thanks."

She shrugged, then flushed as her troop made ugly kissing sounds. "Your arms have to stay tied," she said.

Laris looked a little like Gray's sister Irene; she seemed to share Irene's congeniality. Gray guessed he could push her. "Can you take off her gag, at least?" He indicated Mead. Laris smiled at him—he recognized that kind of smile, one that would want a reward later—but she did as he asked while joking to her troop about the hard job of freeing such a big mouth.

Mead worked her jaw, but didn't speak until the guards had gone, closing the metal door solidly behind them and sliding a bolt into place with a definitive sound. *"Thanks,"* Mead said, mimicking his show of gratitude to Laris, and batting her eyes in a parody of flirtation.

Mead was always at her worst when she was afraid. Gray ignored the sarcasm. "Now it's up to Penn," he said. "There isn't much time."

"Relax. At least you'll live. You're already collecting more admirers than a wild dog does fleas. The next generation of Shak will have your dopey smile."

"Shut up, Mead."

She smirked. "A fate worse than death."

He kicked the door so hard that his toes felt crushed, but the noise was just a dull thud and his shoe left no mark.

Mead sat carefully on the floor, slumping her shoulders against a stack of boxes to protect her tied hands. "At least you'll have children. You might even have some now."

"No. None." He remembered Melany Kane. How many choices had been stolen from him, lost in the Bridgers' great game? "Bridger Dome even paid the Kanes to abort my son. I might as well be infertile, too."

She observed him until he looked away, suspicious of the intensity of her scrutiny. Because of her youth and acerbic attitude, it was easy to forget Mead was a precaster. He didn't like that thought; she knew him better than anyone, even Reed. He walked away from her to investigate the protruding contents of a stacked pile of woven reed boxes. Rags, ready for recycling, one of the lotech industries the offies allowed. On the fringes of the eastern Spine Range, around Big Red, where some Shak remnants lived, they milled rags into paper, which they sold through intermediaries and some of which the Bridgers eventually crafted into books. The Shak would let Bridger Dome be compressed into dust, and lose their market. Cousins.

"Four hundred years ago," Mead said slowly, thinking through some reminiscence, "the Shak tried to breed hermaphrodites, as a solution to the man problem, but they died too young."

He had no response to that unsettling piece of old news.

"Men are a waste of womb time, a waste of energy, for their mothers. They don't pass on memories. Reed claims men are important to a line, but I notice we don't have any uncles."

"Reed just happened not to have a son," Gray said, stung by the slight to his sex implied to Reed.

"Why did Margaret bother having you? Why did Reed tell her to have a son? What changed?" Mead stared moodily at Gray. "There really is a man problem, and it's much worse since the offies came, but the real problem is with us, the motherlines. If the Shak don't care about the Bridgers, well, we're enemies. But do you think the other lines have lifted a finger to save any of us? Have the Wolfs tried to stop the offies? The Kanes?" She shook her head. "There are *social* reasons for having two human sexes, not just biological ones. Maybe our Alteration isn't such a complete success. Motherlines are insular and selfish."

That was a depressing and largely irrelevant thought. Mead was precasting something, but only as a way of hiding her head in the sand while, just outside, Bridger Dome was being destroyed. Swan would reduce his barrier, as he already had at least once, collapsing the bubble, like tightening a belt. Was it lower now than the full height of the dome? Swan could grind the diamond glass into powder and squash the helpless defenders inside; he wouldn't want any

Bridger precasters left, and unfortunately, many of them were there. If only Gray had let Elene kill Swan.

"We have to get out of here!" he said.

"Sure. I'll just untie your hands with my teeth," Mead said. "Wasn't that why you had them get rid of my gag?"

"I shouldn't have bothered." Gray went to Dancer. She looked well, without the grayish pallor she'd had when the Shak had first brought her into their dome, but there was the vacancy he'd seen too many times, the look of a body with no one home. His bound hands prevented him from touching her. Janet Bridger. He whispered the name, knowing there was little hope of rousing her. Whoever she was. His memories of Janet Bridger didn't jibe with the woman who was his wife, but that only meant that, however it had happened, Janet, his Janet, was unique. She wouldn't pop into existence in some other alia. And Elene? Or the woman he'd met in the tunnel? Gray sighed. He didn't know the answer to the puzzle of Dancer's existence, except that she was a miracle, an entire motherline in one body; they all were, all the women in his life. That was the tragedy of infertility, that the line would end. That was the tragedy of being a man. "Janet?" he whispered again.

Mead settled less uncomfortably against the boxes. "Why not call Elene? At least she was useful. Unless you consider being the *pièce de résistance* of the precasters' plan a use."

"Janet wasn't the center of the precasters' plan," he said, without looking back at Mead. "You were."

She chortled. "Yeah, right."

Gray bent over and gently kissed Dancer's smooth cheek. "Janet volunteered to be sterilized by the offies. That's when I was certain there was something wrong in what Reed had told me."

A huge vibration and a sudden explosive sound reverberated through Shak Dome. It brought tears to Gray's eyes. The noose around Bridger Dome had tightened again. He turned to Mead. She had rested her head against her upraised knees. Gray couldn't see her face until she lifted it after the echo died. Her eyes looked haunted and her mouth was grim.

"I'm nothing," Gray said. "I don't have any part in the precasters' plan." It hurt to admit it; belief that he had a special purpose for the Compound Council, and for his grandmother, had provided confidence. "They *know* you, Mead.

They can predict you, and they can't predict an alia or me. Grandmother works by indirection—you know how she likes to say she doesn't plan, only sets things in motion—but she doesn't work blind. The Compound Council wouldn't use a singleton and an alia as off-world scouts. They can't trust people they don't understand, and they never understand a man. Besides, Reed knew Janet's loyalty to Testament was questionable; I think she encouraged that attitude. And any scout of theirs would want children."

"You want children more than any man I know," Mead said thoughtfully. "A singleton."

He shrugged. "So what? I'm a man. But do you really think that Reed didn't know you'd want revenge? She'd met Penn; she knew I'd have more contact with him because he wanted a precast. She *knew* you'd go to him to try to stop her supposed plan. Janet was a red herring, to give you something to trade, so he'd trust you." Gray paused, feeling his way through ideas and memory, certain this was true. "If we get out of here, Penn can take you off Testament. He'll cure your infertility. They even gave him a motive to want your children—Janet's memories, which mean so much to him, and which will have a secondary effect on Jonism. He'll never understand that your children will always belong to Testament."

She nodded at the locked door. "If Reed created Janet Bridger's memory to help me, why are we stuck here now because of it?"

"Something went wrong; grandmother even told me so. Janet was supposed to tell only Penn, not Swan, but she was too independent. She went to Exchange looking for me instead of doing what Reed told her to do."

"A precast by a singleton. And not half bad." Mead laughed, shaking her head, stopped, then laughed again. "I guess that drug worked pretty well. I'd almost believe you, Gray, but I know better. You're so good. Top of the line. Reed's favorite toy. You've got to have a part in any plan of hers, and that means you've got to be useful."

Gray glanced at Janet and wished he could ask his grandmother. Janet stirred on the stretcher, and her hand dangled at its side. Her fingers wriggled.

"They don't want my children," he said.

"Or mine," Mead said quietly.

"Not yet, anyway," Gray said. "I'm sure I'm right."

"You're just guessing."

"Precasting."

She grinned, and for once they shared a joke.

Muffled voices came from the corridor outside. Mead stared at the door as if she could force it to open. "Now everything depends on Martin and what Hela has said to him."

The door was unbolted and opened. Hela Shak sauntered into the room, trailed by Penn. His arms were not bound, and there were no longer any guards surrounding him. Gray glanced at Mead, while keeping his attention on the Shak precaster. Mead was watching Penn with a tentative smile. Penn, however, didn't look at her immediately, and then did so with stony, distant reserve.

Hela smirked at Mead, gloating. "Nothing nasty to say, Bridger?"

Mead smiled innocently at Hela. "I'm speechless. You're finally showing some common sense. Martin, tell them to untie us, too. We'll make a public entrance into the Harmony camp. There isn't much time to save the dome."

Penn looked away.

Hela kicked a bit of dust in Mead's direction. "I've told him the truth. He knows Jon Hsu didn't exist, that he was a virtual man."

"What?" Gray asked.

Penn was watching Mead.

"I don't know what you're talking about," Mead told Hela. Mead, always impatient with tricks, was not a good extemporaneous liar. She struggled to her feet, tottering slightly when she got there. Penn didn't help.

"Is it true?" he demanded. "Did the Bridgers conceal a truth like this? Was Jon Hsu a joke ... ?" Penn cleared his throat. "Mead, you promised me the truth. Are your promises worth anything? Was Jon Hsu a fabrication of the Hard Science Underground, a thousand years ago? Tell me."

Gray was stunned. With the clarity of a gestalt intuitive vision, he understood what the Shak had told Penn, and knew it could be true. *Why are there so few records of Jon Hsu's life?* Penn had asked Janet. *They'll have to catch him first:* a joke. Gray's own instinctive rejection of Janet's memory gave the Shak claim an immediate logical allure. Except for a Jonist. If Swan had been so alarmed by Janet's affair with Jon Hsu that he wanted to destroy the Bridger line, how would the rest of the Harmony react to the news that Jon Hsu was a fiction? How was Penn taking it?

Penn was motionless, staring at Mead. She still hadn't answered.

"You see?" Hela Shak was smug.

"Mead?" As though it were a great effort, with his shoulders first slumped, then resolute, Martin Penn went to her. He touched her arms in a spare embrace, and when she didn't look at him, he raised her chin. "Tell me the truth. I'll believe you."

He was begging to be told by Mead that Jon Hsu was real, and that the Shak were liars, but Mead stayed silent.

The events of the last few days, even given Elene's revelations about Bridger trading in men's lives, had taught Gray that when offie truth and Bridger loyalty were incompatible, loyalty prevailed. "Ahman Penn," Gray said, turning their attention on him. He assayed a bow, despite his bound hands. "The Shak are lying. Cleverly lying. This is something that will be impossible to prove. Meanwhile, you turn on us—the Shak's enemies—and permit the continued destruction of Bridger Dome."

"What does a singleton boy know?" Hela stepped between Penn and Gray.

Apparently, Penn agreed. "How you must all have laughed at us," he said bitterly to Mead, and released her.

Finally, Mead spoke. "I don't know the truth, Martin. It's not from the Bridgers' memory. Janet Bridger was a lawyer, and never a member of the Hard Science Underground. She didn't know science, or computers; I can't even judge if it could have been done. Wouldn't some outsider have wanted to meet him?"

"We told the truth to the Bridgers," Hela Shak said.

Penn observed Mead with no change in his stern expression.

"Yes," Mead continued, speaking more quickly, "the Shak did tell us Jon Hsu was a fiction, but as for whether what they said is *true*—I don't know. They mentioned it for the first time after the Harmony found Testament and told us about Jonism."

Hela Shak came forward, away from Gray; she scowled at Mead. "We didn't mention Jon Hsu before the Harmony's conquest of Testament because until then it was irrelevant.

No one here cared. There was no Jonism. But what I've said is true."

"Every line rejected their story," Mead said. "We all thought it was a Shak fabrication, a weapon in the war they wanted to wage against the Harmony, a war we rejected. We did our best to prevent the Harmony from hearing about it for fear of what you'd do to non-Jonist troublemakers, and Altered ones."

"Didn't you *know*?" Penn asked. "Didn't the Bridger precasters have Janet Bridger's memories of Jon Hsu?"

Hela Shak smiled.

"I don't know why the Bridger precasters didn't belive the Shak. Precasters—everyone, once they remember Janet Bridger—stop having children; there's no memory of the reason for their doubts. I don't have a complete memory of Janet Bridger, either." Mead turned her head aside. "I've never claimed that I had any memory of Jon Hsu, Martin, and I've told you the truth. I'm your partner, not this Shak scum."

Hela Shak came at Mead with her arm raised, but Penn nodded briskly and glanced at the door. Hela stopped. "Thank you," he said impersonally to Mead, and studied Dancer without approaching her, frowning as if the Bridger secret she'd told was a stigma visible on her forehead.

"Memory isn't truth, Martin," Mead said, coming close to him again. He looked down at her, still frowning. "Even the Shak can't know. After a hundred years of telling the story to each other, even a lie becomes a belief by force of repetition. It's remaking history. Memory isn't real; it's just memory." She shrugged, and it made her sway slightly, off balance because of her tied hands.

Penn didn't touch her. He nodded at Hela Shak. "I've heard enough from the Bridgers. Let's go."

Gray's heart sank at the way Penn pronounced the Bridger name. "Ahman," Gray began. "Just because Mead doesn't know . . ."

"Quiet, Bridger," Hela said triumphantly. "This offie has had enough of your lies."

Penn didn't correct her. They left the room together.

Chapter 13

I. My Memories, Myself

Janet had faded out, and now she faded back into existence, lulled into awareness by the sound of Gray's voice. She smiled, pampering herself by keeping her eyes closed while she reminisced recent happy memories: the night of her awakening and the intimacy of sex; her first meal with Gray, a quiet breakfast in her sun-filled room. She remembered light shining on his dark hair, so that she wanted to touch it and then had; startled, he'd smiled at her. Best of all was the evening after her test, when everything had seemed ready for their departure. Yet her last memory was the one she didn't want: his pique over the matter of children and his subsequent denial of her reality as Janet. He couldn't have meant it.

As she awakened further, Janet realized they weren't in Gray's cell. Time had passed, unperceived. Her bed was a hard slab; the air was stagnant and smelled of old clothes. She felt a dull pain in her left leg. It wasn't really her leg; it was Dancer's. *She shouldn't think that.*

"But why didn't you just tell him you remembered Jon Hsu?" Gray sounded angry. "The Bridger line is at stake."

No one answered. Gray's voice was too distant for him to have been talking to her. She opened her eyes. They were in an ill-lit storeroom with cracked and dirty stone walls. Janet rolled to her side to see him better, and gasped as pain shot through her leg.

"Elene?" Gray called. He came to her, then looked down with an astonished smile. "Janet! Are you really here?"

She laughed at his surprise while wondering who Elene was. The sting of the other name was lessened by his pleasure. His earlier rejection dwindled into a bad dream; perhaps it was one.

"How's your leg?" he asked. Gray looked terrible. His hair was whitened with dust; his eyes were bloodshot; his face was drawn and pallid. He worked his shoulders as though unkinking them, grimacing, but his arms were drawn behind his back.

She struggled to sit—he didn't help her—and then she looked down across the length of her body. A bulky bandage covered the area where her left foot should have been, except that her left leg ended too soon. She felt independent of her body's plight, not merely numb to it. "Not so perfect anymore," she murmured to herself.

Gray shook his head. "It doesn't matter. You're awake, and without the patch." He grinned. "A miracle." He bent forward like a precious child, with his arms behind his back, and chastely kissed her forehead.

She gaped. "Your hands are tied! What's going on?"

"We're prisoners in Shak Dome."

"Shak?" The name conjured up overlapping meanings. For an instant she recalled her almost-sisters, Nellie and Kathleen, then lost the memory in favor of an impression of the ruin outside her window.

"Are you all right?" Gray asked.

"Of course she is. Her hands are free." Mead was on the floor. She clambered to her feet, moving with difficulty because her hands were also pulled behind her back. "She can untie us," Mead said to Gray.

"We still couldn't open the door." He shook his head, his anger at Mead seeming to revive. "Our real hope is Penn. Why didn't you say you remembered Jon Hsu? He was begging."

Mead walked to the door, turned, and answered Gray from a distance. "Because I *don't* remember, and Martin wouldn't have believed me if I lied. This way, at least he trusts me."

"You think there's hope, after what you said?"

"He dislikes the Shak. He's Jonist, however much he looks for deeper meanings, and he was controlling an extreme reaction to their story." She shrugged, then winced. "He's a good man; even if he believes them, he won't abandon us."

"You actually do like him." Gray sounded surprised. "You try not to disappoint him."

Mead looked poised to make a derisive response, then

didn't. "Gray, we need to help each other," she said. "You asked before; you wanted to be friends."

Gray had forgotten Janet's presence; Mead had put her in second place again, and stolen Gray's attention with a plea to which Gray was certain to consent. Janet wanted an acknowledgment that she was real and alive, and needed to forestall Mead. "What are you talking about?" she asked mildly.

Gray turned back to her. His smile was apologetic. "Swan didn't want your memory of Jon Hsu to get out into the Harmony," he began, but Mead interrupted.

"Why bother? Are you going to retell the story forty times, when each one of her past lives awakens?" Mead chuckled. "Then again, what else do we have to do?" She turned to Janet. "You're either a lie or you're not; either way, Swan thinks you're dangerous. Because of you, he tried to kill Martin, Gray, and one of your alter egos, and he's attacking Bridger Dome right now. He wants to kill everyone who might have your memory of Jon Hsu—if anyone does. We escaped the offies, and then the Shak captured us."

"I told the truth." Janet saw pity in Gray's face. She already felt worse than she had at any previous awakening. It wasn't just the injured leg, although as she focused on it, the leg began to throb. Her mind felt heavy and slow. Her thoughts weren't crisp, as though some were siphoned off into barren channels. She remembered bad dreams, full of repressed terror, pain, and violence. She suspected that those dreams were real, part of the other life she led as someone else, a woman who had managed to get Janet's foot cut off—because it *was* her foot. It had to be, if she was real. "What I told them really happened," she repeated. "Do you believe me, Gray?"

"It doesn't matter to my feelings for you," he said.

"You don't." What was a person except her memories?

He hesitated, and glanced back at Mead. "I have some memories of Janet Bridger, because of a drug Mead gave me, but . . . not that."

"You remember me?" It was worse than his going through a private diary; nothing could be worse.

"A bit."

Janet wiped tears from her eyes. At least if he remembered her, then she was real. He must remember Jon. "We picnicked near the Adler Planetarium," Janet said. "Jon brought ceviche and I brought cheese and French bread. I remember it. Do you?"

Gray didn't meet her eyes. "No."

"Who am I, then?" Janet whispered, turning away. Mead was watching her, looking very strange, as if she'd choked on something hard and raw.

Very firmly, Gray said, "You're my wife. You, Janet, and no one else."

"Not Elene?"

"Definitely not Elene."

Janet felt a slight release of her tension, then Mead took a quick, hissing intake of breath and thrust herself into the discussion.

"She could loosen the knots," Mead said. "Ease the pull on our arms. The Shak might not notice, and it could come in handy later. At least we'd die more comfortable. Oh, I forgot. You're not going to die, you're going to be put out to stud."

Gray sighed and rolled his eyes at Janet, but Mead was grinning. "Don't pay attention to her," Gray said. "She's afraid, and that makes her nasty when she has an audience. She doesn't mean anything; she just wants us to contradict her so she'll feel safer."

Mead took a step away.

Gray worked at unkinking his shoulders again. "My arms do ache," he said. "Do you think you could get this untied?" He turned his back to her, displaying the rope securing his wrists. Brown, it looked like braided leather. She sat up, carefully lowering her injured left leg over the side of the stretcher. The pain intensified. She gritted her teeth and studied the complicated knots of the binding, wanting to help Gray, to show her usefulness. "It looks like something the Shak would do," she said. "To loosen it, you have to pull it tight."

Mead came close and stood beside Gray, also looking at the knot. "Don't think," Mead said. "Let instinct take over. You know the trick."

"What?"

"You have the memories of women who could do it. Use them."

Gray turned, removing his bound hand from Janet's direct view. "She's an emulation, Mead. She can't remember."

"Maybe she can. She woke up on her own. She remembers more than Janet Bridger; she recognized Shak work."

Gray appeared excited and pleased. "Do you remember being in the underground, alone with me?" he asked. Before she answered, he spoke again to Mead, as if Janet were irrelevant to her own life. "Grandmother mentioned something called a 'pseudo-personality' that comes from integration of emulations. Do you know anything about it?"

She—Janet—did. She shouldn't have, but she understood what it meant to integrate, knew it with a clinical detachment that came from somewhere outside herself, and made her quake. Information had been purloined from another woman and added to her. It was indecent. She was *Janet;* she wasn't Dancer.

Mead inspected Janet as if she were a mannequin in need of new clothes. "She's been conscious quite a bit. Janet and Elene. Reed must have fooled with them for a while, too, before you met them. First a pseudo will repeat thoughts, have the same ideas and images, then discrete memories spill over, influenced by actual events. Finally, the memories intermingle, fused together by the dominant personality. It's possible Dancer is being created—not the same as a true person, but a distinct personality, unlike any one emulation, and capable of living a normal life."

Gray grinned at Janet. "We'll get out into the Harmony together."

"First, let's get out of Shak Dome," Mead said.

Janet looked at the closed door with the Shak beyond it. "No. I don't want to become part of someone else."

"You can't stop it," Mead said unsympathetically. "Their memories will seep into yours like rainwater into soil. Mud. And a new plant will grow. Dancer."

Janet stared at the knotted leather strip around Gray's wrist, seeing only a tangle. That memory was hers; she knew nothing about knots. She touched the leather, pressing Gray's slightly reddened hands, and closed her eyes for a moment, then tugged in two places on the knotted leather, tightening, then loosing it, nearly freeing him. "There," she said.

Gray kissed her gratefully, but who was he kissing? Not Janet.

Who am I? A body and a soul? Her body was different from the one she remembered, and if ever Janet Bridger had possessed a soul, it must have departed with her death a thousand years ago. Only her independent memories made her separate and real—and Gray thought some of hers were false. She didn't want imported thoughts or foreign memories. She didn't want to integrate her mind with anyone else. She would refuse to be invaded. Inside her self, she wanted solitude.

Gray was smiling, moving his arms almost freely, flexing his fingers; Mead asked for the same to be done for her, but Janet, the real Janet, the transient who was inside Dancer— Janet knew nothing. "I don't want to die," she whispered as she undid Mead's knots anyway, without having to think.

Mead didn't answer or thank her. To Mead, she'd never been real.

Janet looked at Gray.

"It'll be all right," he said reassuringly. Hollow words.

Who am I? she wondered. If I'm not myself, I'm no one. Gray would hold another woman, using this same body. He would call her Janet, seeing Janet bits, but Janet's memories, and Janet, would not be the same. The creation of a new woman meant Janet Bridger's death. And who had she been to begin with? Were her own personal memories real? Gray rejected her truth, and accepted Dancer; he had killed her, the woman he'd claimed as his wife.

II. The Black Dome

"You can have one of them," Hela Shak told Penn, "provided you keep your promise. You choose which Bridger you want."

Penn recognized this as a test of his conversion to the Shak cause, but didn't know the correct response. He feared desperately for Mead; he needed Janet Bridger's memory, but definitely couldn't admit a desire for Dancer; Gray was a pointless choice, but Penn didn't want to leave him behind either. "You'll give me all three of them," he said forcefully. "The Bridgers will be punished by the Harmony, not you."

"You don't give orders to me, Mr. Penn."

Penn wondered if her consistent failure to use his title was a calculated insult or merely evidence of Shak inexperience with the Harmony of Worlds, but now, when he could reasonably have done so, he didn't correct her. Despite the gross provocation of her avoidance of his Jonist title, he needed to be reminded of Hela Shak's opposition to the Harmony, her contempt for it and her venom. The reminder would help him take the only possible action that furthered Order, although it was a necessity he abhorred. "I think I can," Penn said. "You intend to use Harmony resources to defeat your enemies, the Bridgers. You expect to use me to announce the nonexistence of Jon Hsu and expose the Bridger lie. I *will* complete our bargain, but lady Shak, I think I have some leverage here. I want all three of them brought with me to meet with Governor Swan."

She stared at him as though reading his intentions in his eyes, but he knew she couldn't determine anything from his Center-hardened facade. Perhaps Reed would have known, but this woman was no Reed Bridger.

"You still care for that Bridger creature. You want to keep her safe despite her lies." Hela tapped her hand against her side in a gesture that reminded him of an impatient, overbearing schoolteacher, but he was unable to be amused by this vicious, Altered woman.

Penn attuned his reply to native expectations. "I never cared if Mead was telling the truth. I don't want her for her memory or her mind."

Hela laughed and slapped him on the back. "You sound like a man. But no."

Penn tried to judge her obstinacy. Apparently, her fears had been eased by his response, and she believed he accepted the Shak's great lie, but she still wanted to win something. He needed Mead. Her long last look in the Shak cell, which he had been unable to return without alerting Hela Shak, haunted him. Mead was a new precaster; she could also hold the secret of Jon Hsu. She must be freed. Then again, that might be rationalization for lust. Her hair had been loose, tangled, and dusty; in the yellow light of the Shak underground cell, her skin looked sallow. Her bedraggled posture did nothing good for her figure. He'd never wanted to hold her so much as when he turned away and left with this Shak hag. "All right," he said, frowning. Gray Bridger, to his misfortune, was the easiest sacrifice. He remembered Mead's poor joke: the expendable hero. A precast? "Give me two of the three. The two women."

"Is that offie chivalry? No, Mr. Penn. One. I'll give you the Bridger boy as a gesture of good faith. I have a bad feeling about him, anyway; he's long-term trouble or I want to know why Reed Bridger spent so much energy on him. But I'll keep the alia. She's the one Reed used in creating this imaginary affair with the nonexistent Jon Hsu. I want the Shak truth to be told, not Bridger lies."

Penn bowed as if the barbarian woman were an Elector. There was a chill along his spine. Dancer Bridger was, indeed, the only one who had volunteered the Bridger secret; Reed, while hinting at it, had delayed committing herself. Other Bridger precasters would know the truth. *The Bridgers know something.* There was only one Mead. "If you won't give me Dancer, give me Mead. You don't need her for anything. I do." He leered, though it sickened him.

Hela Shak shook her head. "You care for her; I want insurance of our bargain."

Resolution of the Shak problem was too important to let his personal feelings intrude, but he tried one last time. "We don't have a bargain unless I have Mead." Not even a probe could have guessed he was bluffing.

Hela turned her head to regard him better with her one good eye, and he sensed her defeat in her hesitation. "All right," she said finally. "But I'll be there when you tell Swan."

He nodded. "You'll accompany me outside?"

"Why not?" she said gaily. "I want to see Swan's face when you tell him there was no Jon Hsu. You, an Ahman of the Academy." She looked at him suddenly, as if his relief showed. "Don't think, Mr. Penn, that you can double-cross the Shak."

He smiled falsely and bowed. "I don't. I fully intend to tell Governor Swan about my discovery here."

Then he stood to the side, near a fissured wall, as the Shak women bustled about Hela's room, making arrangements for the meeting with Swan. One of the girl-guards stayed near him, but he wasn't confined or shackled, and when tension caused him to forget himself and pace a short distance along the side of the room, they allowed it. He stopped when Mead arrived.

Head held high, she looked like a queen among the dirty, ill-clothed Shak, despite her own disheveled appearance. Gray walked sullenly beside her, head down as if lost in thought.

Hela paused in her conversation. "Mead Bridger," she

said. "*Cousin.* Would you like to apologize, too?" Her gaze went to Penn, then back to the two Bridgers.

Mead didn't answer. She'd noticed Penn; her eyes dropped.

Hela laughed and assembled the group, giving instructions on the order they should keep. "The offies have been contacted," she said. "They're expecting us. There will be soldiers, as well as the Governor; I want no incidents." She turned to the Bridgers. "You two stay silent or you're dead." She glanced at Penn for approval. He didn't contradict her.

Gray glared at him. "I saved your life, Martin Penn. My grandmother got you out of the dome. You owe us something."

His girl-guard kicked him.

Penn turned away. Gray was right, but there was nothing Penn could do for him now.

Shak women lined the underground corridor their procession traveled. The pitiable, Altered rabble looked odd, out of balance; Penn realized there were no men. The fathers of the Shak were captives, another reason to despise them. Like all natives, these were mostly young, and many were children, who called bellicose insults at Mead and Gray. Some adults tossed bits of garbage at them. Gray kept his head down and suffered it silently, but Mead called them cowards and jeered at them, though it caused more of the dirty missiles to go her way.

"Can't you stop this?" Penn asked Hela.

"Why?"

Shak were easy to dislike. He avoided looking at the young mothers holding babies, at the red-haired youngsters or dark-haired ones with solemn eyes that reminded him of Mead; he ignored the fractured walls that witnessed Shak poverty and trouble. As they went up, the mob dispersed. There were gaping holes opening the ruin to the sky. Penn looked straight ahead until they were outside. There, everyone stopped, without a command to do so, overwhelmed by the black shroud over Bridger Dome.

The plaza and street had been cordoned off by Swan's military contingent. No natives, except their own small group, were visible from the tumbledown entrance of Shak Dome. The exterior of the gravity wall scintillated, glistening like an oil slick in sunlight, as if a viscous fluid slid continuously over the surface of the dome. It was fascinating to watch, beautiful and destructive at once, like an open flame. The spherical cruiser hovered above what would have been the open Eye. Penn couldn't recall Bridger Dome well enough to know by sight whether Swan's barrier was lower than the summit of Bridger Dome, but the great chunks of rubble scattered around the rim of the barrier showed that it was.

The soldiers had erected a square, squat makeshift military command post on the plaza, an angular counterpart to the dome. There was little movement outside. Harmony personnel could do their jobs from screens, except when the barrier's periphery changed. Two rows of motionless covered figures lay on the ground, attesting to an engagement of some kind; they were too distant to determine whether they were Bridger women or Harmony soldiers. Guiltily, Penn hoped they were Harmony men.

They were spotted shortly after leaving the shelter of the Shak ruin. A company of armed men marched double-time across the area while Penn's Shak escort wavered to a halt at their border, on the empty street. Hela held that position as the Harmony soldiers surrounded their group.

"Sir. Ahman Penn. You're all right? You've been released?" the commander—Captain Isaacs—anxiously called as he came up to them.

"I'm fine." Penn was impatient. "I understood we would meet with Governor Swan."

"Yes, Ahman. He'll arrive as soon as I report that you're here and there is no trap. Sir, have you been coerced?" Isaacs eyed the Shak suspiciously.

"Absolutely not. I was not kidnapped by the Bridgers, and I'm not coerced now by these people, the Shak." It took a few minutes to convince the soldiers, and Hela Shak's agreement that her women be disarmed—although she kept her own collection of archaic weapons: two knives and a projectile-shooting gun—but it wasn't long before Cevan Swan plodded out of the command post. Penn had assumed, correctly, that Swan would be there, personally directing the attack on Bridger Dome. If only Penn had been integrated into the local military utility, he could have conversed privately with Swan, but there had been too much antipathy between them, and Swan had never provided the connect code. Penn attempted to access the general Exchange District utility, hoping the military system would have a hookup, but there was nothing. He would be limited to speech, plain and simple, all overheard by the Shak. Meanwhile, Swan's last contact with him had been an attempted murder.

"I'm pleased you've survived," Swan said to Penn. "Knowing these natives, I didn't expect it." He bowed properly, doubtless conscious of their audience of soldiers.

Penn ignored the false pleasantry and the bow. "Call off the attack on Bridger Dome." Hela shifted position beside him, provoking the soldiers to place their hands upon their guns. Gray and Mead were still within the cluster of Shak girl-guards. "I need to have some words with Reed Bridger; charges may be made." Hela warily subsided.

Swan smiled. "I'm afraid it's too late, Martin. The structure is weakened to the point that if we withdraw our gravity shell, the building will collapse upon itself."

Gray shouted something furious and wild, which was ignored. Mead whispered, and he quieted.

Penn looked to Captain Isaacs. "Is that so?" he asked.

Isaacs glanced at Swan, obviously distressed at being ordered to declare whether his civilian superior was lying. "It is, Ahman Penn," he said earnestly, coming forward. "The materials they use to build are weaker than ours." He shrugged. "Steel and stone. If they don't take shelter, some of those inside will die."

"You've destroyed that grand building and killed its defenders over a kidnapping that never occurred?"

Isaacs was speechless. Behind him, Penn heard the Shak chatting with each other, gladdened by the destruction.

Swan nodded. "Unfortunate, but you see, Martin, there's nothing to be done. Now, come inside. You'll want to bathe, and eat. You look terrible. You can tell me about your ordeal."

"I intend to, from right here." Penn paused a moment to look around. Mead and Gray were to his right and behind, among the Shak. Swan appeared unhappy, probably fearing Penn's public revelation of his criminal conduct inside Governor's House, but Penn no longer was concerned with that, and what he wanted from Swan was exactly what Swan was: a Jonist bigot who lacked belief in justice for Altereds or in any morality greater than Order and advantage.

"Mr. Penn?" Hela Shak prompted him.

He still delayed. Penn had almost believed Hela Shak. Her story, so bizarre and perverse at first that it made the Alias

Hypothesis inconsequential, had fit into the doubting corners of his mind, the places left bare even after the reassurance that Reed's precast had given him—*There is an answer for you.* He had waited for Mead to deny the Shak's claim—Gray had tried—though he had suspected that if she did, she would be lying. He had searched for meaning in life, but God was a delusion, and Jon Hsu was a lie; the universe was empty; the Shak were right.

Then Mead had spoken. Calmly, sensibly, wanting desperately to deny the Shak, Mead had told the truth. She had brought Order back into life. The Shak were enemies of the Harmony and had always been. They had pursued their war for a hundred years, using their memory as a weapon, waiting for an opportunity to destroy the Harmony's foundation, its brain and its heart, by denying Jon Hsu and Jonism. Their memory was their revenge. They had told themselves, and had perhaps come to believe, a great lie. They expected him and others to believe it, and spread it into the Harmony, merely because it was memory. But Mead had told him over and over, memories could be lies.

Memories were forever entangled within the minds of their vectors. Lana Shak's false and clever memory was inextricable from the bodies of the Shak. Penn cleared his throat and raised his voice so the Shak could all hear him recite their lie to Swan.

"Governor Swan, you are aware that the natives of Testament have memories that span generations, even a millennium. I told you I came to Testament in part to seek new knowledge of Jon Hsu. I have found something, in the memory of the Shak." As he spoke, Penn watched the glint of afternoon sunlight across the black gravity wall that made the interior of Bridger Dome essentially another world. His statement became an oration, and his repetition of the phrase "the memory of the Shak" became the notation on a litany of insults and errors that he stated as truth, provided there was truth in "the memory of the Shak." He carefully explained the great joke that had been played by the Hard Science Underground, according to "the memory of the Shak." He embellished the story when he bitterly described the glee with which the makers of Jon Hsu, according to "the memory of the Shak," had written Hsu's seminal *General Principles.*

Swan tried to silence him at first with objections, which

Penn ignored. In a public forum, Swan had no authority to stop the Ruling of an Ahman. Swan became silent, watching Penn's eyes. Captain Isaacs, in earshot, gaped and stared squeamishly at the Shak as though they'd become poisonous amphibians. "It's true," some of them called out from time to time, relishing their victory.

"I am an Ahman of the Academy of Center," Penn said. "I have heard the report from the memory of the Shak. I have one other piece of information. The Bridgers, and the Compound Council of Testament, have kept the Polite Harmony of Worlds from learning this great secret, protecting us from the truth in the memory of the Shak. This is an Academy matter, Governor Swan, and in the name of the Academy of Center, I ask that you make these women comfortable, as formerly you did the Bridgers; they are our honored guests."

Penn finally glanced at Hela Shak. The foolish woman had tears in both her good and blind eyes, victorious, satisfied tears. He turned to look behind, at Mead. She met his glance, and nodded.

"I understand," Swan said carefully. "Then shall I also withdraw the gravity shell from Bridger Dome, Ahman Penn?"

"I'm sure you can deploy it more suitably," Penn answered. He hoped that Swan would realize that whatever mitigating steps he could take to preserve Bridger Dome were worthwhile. The Bridger memory needed to be preserved, now more than ever. It was the best defense against the Shak, who would not all be in their ruined dome.

"I have misjudged you, Ahman." Swan bowed at Penn, then bowed just as deeply at Hela Shak. He turned to Captain Isaacs. Whatever his unvoiced orders, Isaacs nodded graciously at the Shak, with the obvious intention of escorting them away to the Command Headquarters.

"I'll go alone," Hela said. She seemed to have become more suspicious as Swan spoke. "My people will return to the dome to wait for me. If I'm not back in an hour, they'll know you're not honest and this is a trap." She turned a puzzled look on Penn, then hand-signaled her women. "I'll keep my gun."

"As you wish." Swan bowed to her. "This is great news you've given us," he said. "What is more important to Jonism, the philosophy or the man? Would crossmen wor-

ship their God if they knew their Messiah was a lie? Would
alans follow a Koran that excised the life of Mohammed?
Yes, Jonism is a philosophy, and not a religion. It can exist
without Jon Hsu. I have never felt this to be more true than
I do at this moment. Still, not everyone will be as grateful
as I am."

Hela softened. She nodded at Penn, then started toward
the headquarters, although her girl-guard did not. Penn
bowed slightly to Swan, truly impressed that he had been
able to retain such calm and a ready explanation for it.
"Bring the Bridgers, too," Penn said. "We'll need them."

Hela laughed and pointed at the black-clad dome, a funeral casket surrounded by a fringe of stone rubble. "The
Bridgers are dead."

III. Through the Heart

Swan's gravity wall had become a brace shoring up Bridger
Dome from the destruction Swan had begun. Gray watched
it shimmer like a bubble of polluted oil, beautiful and
wrong. He would have killed Swan—Reed had told him to,
and even if she hadn't, he owed it to the Bridger line—but
he knew he couldn't succeed here and now, and so didn't try.
A delayed win was better than a premature defeat: Reed's
philosophy.

Mead sidled close. "I did it," she whispered. "He doesn't
believe them."

Gray listened more closely to Penn. The fragile structure
of their salvation depended on this man, and he droned on,
reciting the Shak story to Swan like imparting gospel, always referring to its source. Gray didn't see how Mead had
managed anything. Then it struck him: Penn was openly telling it to *Swan*.

Once upon a time, Gray had admired the Harmony for its
power, its wealth, and the freedom of its men; he had wanted
to belong to it, imagining it was like a line, with reality, continuity, and depth, a community of which he might become
a full member. He had been wrong. The Harmony was a
bully.

Gray listened to Swan give Penn a veiled compliment and
observed Hela Shak with near pity as she smirked and
smiled and reacted to the offies' meaningless, decorous

bows. The Shak guards, previously disarmed, returned to
their dome, pleased with the proceedings.

Bridger Dome was still under the spell of Swan's gravity
barrier. Gray inched forward, intending to remind Penn of it,
but two Harmony men moved closer to Gray, and he hesitated.

Mead leaned close and whispered, "Stay in the background; we're not part of this."

"Bridger Dome is still under siege." Most eyes were on
Penn and Swan, but a uniformed offie looked hard at Gray.
He nodded his head in a slight bow meant to placate the sol-
dier. The man frowned, but did nothing more.

"She knows we got out," Mead said softly. Between the
two of them, "she" had only meaning. Mead put her chin
down to her throat like a guard activating her comlink to
transmit.

Reed must have known, when the wall moved and Elene's
comlink went dead, that they'd gained the other side of the
barrier. "We need to free the dome," Gray whispered.

Mead nodded her head at the sky. "He only has one ship."

Gray turned to the cruiser hovering above the black half-
sphere of Bridger Dome. One ship. Mead expected Swan to
attack Shak Dome next, and soon. Not only had Mead persuaded Penn that the Shak story was a lie, but she thought
that Penn was sufficiently inflamed, although to Gray he
didn't show it, that he would take immediate action against
the Shak.

"Penn!" Gray shouted. "My wife is still inside Shak
Dome!"

A soldier rushed at Gray, then stopped when Gray stayed
still. Gray ached to pull his arms free of the Shak rope and
rush at Swan, but it would be futile. He bowed at Penn instead.

Swan had been motionless, staring into the distance at his
cruiser, probably using the telepathic system to convey orders. He rotated slowly to look at Gray and smiled. "I'm
sure Ahman Penn knows."

"We do need Gray's wife," Penn told Swan.

"What is it?" Hela Shak was not a stupid woman, only ignorant of offies and men. She set her hand on the handle of
her gun and glared at Penn. "Is this a trick, Mr. Penn?"

Penn bowed at her. "She's direct evidence of their fabrication. Have your women send her out immediately; she need

to be interviewed by Security." He turned to Swan. "We'll wait, Cevan."

"No." Hela was adamant. "I'll keep the Bridgers' living lie in Shak Dome, to protect you from confusion." She grinned like a winner.

"I'm going to get her." Gray started back to Shak Dome.

"Stop!" The soldier who had frowned now had his stick gun targeted on Gray.

Mead stepped in front of him, blocking the soldier's aim. Penn quickly shouted an order not to shoot, and called to Mead to come away. "She's depending on us to survive, Gray," Mead said in an urgent whisper. "It's both of us. You and me. The alia is nothing; you can remake her anytime inside your own head."

"You know that's not true." Still, Gray had stopped. The best hunters sensed death before it came, according to Melany Kane. Gray looked around, tasting death in the wind. Penn was approaching them; the soldier hesitated uncertainly. His captain was near Swan, who seemed oblivious, engrossed in his silent commands.

The gravity wall around Bridger Dome dissolved with a sound like breaking glass, but so loud it seemed the sky was shattering. There was an anxious pause, long enough so that everyone had time to turn, to look, to gasp. Bridger Dome still stood—for an instant. Its walls looked strong, though there were breaks in some of the bands of diamond glass. The summit, though, where the Eye on the World had been, was cracked. Pieces had fallen away—explaining the rubble outside the barrier periphery. At the top of Bridger Dome, jagged peaks like crenellation replaced what had been an opened sphere. They turned the dome into a crown. An unsupported crown, one that had not been engineered.

Falling inward from the top, Bridger Dome began its collapse. Dust rose, obscuring sight, as polished stones crashed down from the jagged rim. Like knees giving out on a tired man, a broad band of diamond glass was crushed; the stones above it slid down, shattering and bursting their former boundaries, dropping onto the plaza. Tumbling, boulder-ized blocks rolled far. In one final retaliation, a corner of the offie headquarters was squashed.

At the far side of the plaza, nearer to Shak than Bridger Dome, their group was untouched.

"They would have gone to the underground," Penn said

like a prayer. He stood with his legs apart, hands clasped behind his back, watching in exactly the posture he had used a few days earlier while surveying Bridger Dome's interior.

Swan recovered first. "I'll send in troops," he said.

Penn turned and spoke commandingly to the soldiers' captain. "You won't harm anyone, and you'll provide medical aid to survivors."

"Hold them all," Swan ordered. "Don't let any precaster slip away."

Swan had destroyed Bridger Dome. The top third was sheered off, unevenly, and the lower portion of the walls drastically weakened, with irregular portions broken away. Though it still stood, new entrances had been exposed by the partial collapse. Some of the chunks of stone must have fallen inside. Penn spoke of survivors, but there were no immediate stirrings of life.

"Ahman Penn," Gray called. "Let me go there and search for my grandmother."

"He's a prisoner," Swan said. "Charged with treason."

"We need the Bridgers, Cevan. And there is no justification for your action against Bridger Dome. None." Penn sounded grim. He had turned on Swan with clenched hands, but he took a deep breath and did nothing. Swan backed a careful step away.

Gray thought: *Now. Do it now.* Yet he couldn't move.

Mead stared up into the sky.

Hela Shak turned to Mead. "Well, Bridger. Now we're almost a matched set." She gestured gleefully at the ruined domes.

"Not for long." Mead pointed.

The Harmony ship had moved away from the wreckage of Bridger Dome. Its damage there completed, it floated in midair above the Shak, preparing to drop death.

Hela shaded her good eye and stared up. "No!" she screamed. "Penn, you know the truth!"

"We should wait for the Bridger girl," Penn muttered, but not strongly enough to constitute a real intervention.

It was Swan who answered Hela. "I've often wished for an uprising," he said, "so I could put it down. But you natives are shadows. You bend with the ground and the light never doing anything that will quite justify the use of force. Until now. There won't be more memories of the Hard Science Underground or Jon Hsu. Anyone who considers it wil remember the Bridger Tomb. And now, the Shak Hole." He smiled and raised his arm in a broad gesture. When he brought it down, there was a burst of light and an overpowering sound. A dark, burnished barrier appeared with the flash and thunder, as if Swan wielded a giant magician's wand and had brought black sorcery down around Shak Dome.

Hela Shak yanked her gun from her weapons belt, aimed at Swan, and was herself immediately shot. Two Harmony soldiers burned her simultaneously, while the rest watched with their weapons aimed. Though she had been ten feet away, Gray felt the heat on his face as they shot out her chest, melting her through the heart. She saw him as she died, her eyes alert, then fading. She dropped, or tossed, the bullet gun, then toppled onto the hard pavement. The gun skidded toward Gray.

Two soldiers kept their weapons drawn as the other four examined Hela Shak's corpse, as if it were possible that she could have survived, then they all eased off.

Gray pulled his hands out of their ineffective bindings, but kept them behind his back. They tingled, but he could move his fingers.

There was another booming sound as the Shak barrier decreased in size; Gray barely noticed. His attention was fixed on Hela's gun.

"Wonderful," Swan said, and bowed at the soldiers directly, ignoring their captain. "You'll be formally commended."

Gray knelt, as if from weakness, or to examine Hela's body, though he was too far. The Testament-made gun was being ignored for the moment by the offie soldiers, as they might have ignored a spear or arrow as too primitive to be a real weapon.

There was another huge, vibrating sound as the barrier decreased again. Coming so soon after the last one, it almost made an explosion. Distracted, the offies glanced over at the Shak Dome gravity wall. Swan spoke, and the soldiers laughed. Penn was conferring with their captain, looking unhappy.

"Gray," Mead said. "Dancer's job is over; she's dead."

Because of the gravity wall vibrations, Mead was hard to hear; he didn't strain to listen. He knew Janet was still alive. She'd been underground, and she'd be safe there, but only for a little while. He could reach Hela Shak's gun. The offies were standing over her corpse like tourist hunters posing for a picture with their kill.

Mead knelt beside him, talking rapidly in a soft, low voice. "Swan couldn't pulverize Bridger Dome because the military thought Martin was inside. This is different. No one wants the Shak to survive. Gray, Reed made her expendable. Let her go."

Expendable. That was him; Mead had said it first. He wished she'd leave him alone. Once the Shak and Bridger lines had been allies and cousins. Gray was a hunter, a good one. He'd killed beasts before. He studied the offie soldiers: well-armed men, but innocents, with no blood memories for guides. They were frightened by the kill they'd made, and excited. To kill an offie, he'd have to shoot him in the head, where their medics couldn't repair the damage.

Another thunderclap sounded as once more Shak Dome was compressed by the gravity shell. It was being crushed much faster than Bridger Dome.

Gray aimed the gun with his eyes, grabbed it, and shot Governor Swan. The Harmony had taught him something: how to kill.

"No! Martin!" Mead threw herself across Gray, screaming for Penn.

IV. Self-Doubts

Martin Penn stared at Swan, glad the man was dead.

"I take full responsibility for underestimating the danger posed by the natives, Ahman Penn." Isaacs's face was pale and his expression fixed. "I'll send him to Security." He gestured vaguely at Gray, who was physically restrained by two soldiers, although he'd been silent, and hadn't made any trouble after shooting Swan.

Penn didn't look at Mead, but felt her attention. She'd protected Gray from being shot by the soldiers, depending on Penn to save her; he'd barely managed it, and now wondered what that sequence said about their relative relationships. "No. Your first priority is to stop the destruction over there." He gestured, without looking, at Shak Dome. Enough was enough, and his scapegoat was dead.

Isaacs shook his head. "Ahman, as I told you, Governor Swan cut me out of the command loop to the cruiser."

"There must be other ways to communicate with them outside the system."

"Sir, it's too late." Isaacs looked at Shak Dome, and Penn followed his attention. The rapidity of movement of the gravity barrier made the swirling motion of the black surface more pronounced. It was like looking at moving stormclouds over a dark planet, beautiful and remote. Shak Dome, because of its ruined state, hadn't been as large as Bridger Dome, and it was already only half its original size. "When the shell's that small, it starts tearing into things inside. They'll just pop it, soon."

" 'Pop it'?" Gray Bridger asked.

"You. Quiet." Isaacs glowered at him.

Penn was tired. Everywhere he looked, there was death, and these most recent killings had been caused by him. He knew Isaacs would be determined to pursue the matter of Gray's punishment. The highest Harmony administrator of this world had just been murdered by a native. Penn was only grateful Swan was gone. No one was alive in there, by now. "All right," Penn said. "We'll let it run its course. Release your prisoner into my custody."

"Ahman Penn, I can't do that. You're not officially appointed here." Isaacs's independence, which had been helpful once in dealing with Swan, now was a detriment. "I have to hold him. This is treason, and I understood from Governor Swan that this man already had one charge of treason against him."

"There was no such charge." Penn stared at the young officer. Though the man began to sweat, he didn't cringe. "Gray Bridger was held by Security while Governor Swan was trying to implicate the Bridger family in a conspiracy that didn't exist. Meanwhile the governor made an attempt on my life." Penn tried the ploy that had not worked before, while Swan was alive. "This is Academy business, Captain Isaacs. I am taking charge of Gray Bridger. There is a message that must be immediately sent to the Electors, and then I will remove him, with several others, from Testament and take them with me to Center."

Isaacs looked at Swan's body, then bowed very low. "Ahman. But I must make a full record of events, and file appropriate charges." He turned toward his men.

Penn glimpsed Mead. She'd moved, abortively, toward

him. "Captain Isaacs," Penn said loudly, "you will come with me." He walked away from the others.

Isaacs followed after only a brief hesitation. Penn went out of earshot, but an otherwise easy distance from the group of soldiers and the two Bridgers. "Captain, if you believe a *local* investigation regarding Governor Swan's death is necessary, please also be certain to investigate Governor Swan's action in attacking Bridger Dome, while I was inside it." Penn paused to let that sink in. "Swan's activities here, in which you participated, were totally illicit. I was never kidnapped, as you heard me state to him. That was information of which he already was aware when he launched his attack and of which you, as military commander here, should have been, particularly given my earlier confrontation with the governor, which you witnessed. He had also tried to make an unprovoked attack on Stone Town then." Penn waited for Isaacs to object or comment, but the soldier only lowered his eyes.

Isaacs had defied Swan once, and Swan had not trusted him; Penn hoped that indicated a philosophical disagreement. "You know the memory trick these Altered women have. The Bridgers remember Jon Hsu. The governor did not want their memories known. The Shak story was a lie designed to discredit the Bridgers, but they didn't deserve this." He gestured at the black shroud over the shrinking Shak Dome just as another huge boom occurred and it was reduced again. "These are Academy matters; there will be an Academy investigation." Penn softened his tone. "Do you want a career, Captain Isaacs?"

The man looked up.

"Until the Academy reviews this matter, Captain, it would be best if there was no local, possibly inaccurate, report. There are two corpses: the governor, shot with a native gun, and a native, shot by your men. The precise sequence of events is presently unimportant. I am taking Gray Bridger with me to Center. Release him to me."

Isaacs bowed, but didn't move. "Is this right, Ahman?"

Penn heard the echo of his own doubts in Isaacs's question. He glanced at the ruin of Bridger Dome and quickly looked away. The sight was painful. "Yes, Captain, it is."

Isaacs sighed and signaled his men. They released Gray.

Penn walked back with Isaacs. He needed to talk with Mead. He needed to touch her and hold her and know that what he'd done to the Shak *was* right, but Mead didn't meet his glance. As they approached, Gray stepped forward and bowed mechanically to Penn; his courtesy was formal and distant. His face was already ashen, but he flinched as yet another resounding boom marked a further reduction in Shak Dome. There was a discharge that shook the ground like an earthquake. Penn turned. The gravity wall over Shake Dome was gone; so was any trace of the dome itself. Rubble the size of gravel was strewn over sunken ground. Penn quickly looked at Isaacs. "No one survived at all?" Penn asked.

Isaacs shook his head.

Penn expected some show of anger from Gray, or even Mead, but neither of them spoke. The soldiers began removing the bodies of Swan and Hela Shak. Everyone was very quiet.

"Ahman," Gray mumbled without looking up, "with your permission, I will join your people helping survivors in Bridger Dome."

There was justice in letting Gray rescue Bridgers. "Go on. In fact, Captain Isaacs, I suggest you solicit Mr. Bridger's advice when it concerns the rescue of his family. I will hold you personally responsible for any further adversity experienced by them. Help him find Reed Bridger. When you do find her, bring her immediately to me."

Janet Bridger's memory was gone, unless a precaster agreed to provide the information. Reed was his best hope. Without a living carrier of the memory, he might as well give up. Elector Lee, too. The Janet Bridger memory would be impossible to prove without one of the Bridger descendants as a witness, and sensors identifying the statement as true.

Gray left with Isaacs. The soldiers dispersed, leaving Penn and Mead alone. Neither spoke. Penn waited, needing her to begin, but finally she outlasted him. "Swan must have had an office in the headquarters; let's go inside," he said.

She was avoiding his eyes. "All right." Her voice was low; she sounded miserable. No matter how she condemned the Bridger precasters, there must be a sense of loss.

"It's over. There's nothing to be afraid of," he said.

She nodded, and kept enough distance between them that he didn't touch her, though they walked side by side into the temporary building.

With Swan dead, Penn could do as he wished. There was

no authority on this world strong enough to challenge him until another governor was appointed, if one ever was. The protectorate was a doomed institution. Some functionary would administer the Exchange District. Swan's death was convenient. Penn hadn't liked Swan. He hadn't liked the Shak. The blood of both was on his hands, the price of the Bridgers' memory. He wished he knew that the deaths were meaningful; he wished that, like Captain Isaacs, he could ask someone if what he'd done was right.

"Here." He opened the door to an office marked for the commander. It looked pristine and smelled new. Swan had never used it. There was nothing on the desk. The window screen wasn't activated, only the sun-stone. Mead sat on one of the two chairs—a chair faced each side of the desk—but Penn didn't want to go so far from her and sat on the desk itself, near her. "I intend to keep my word to give you the ability to have children."

"I know you do; you're an honorable man." Her voice was cool, but with no hint of sarcasm. No hint of their former intimacy, either. She ran her fingers through her hair once, then seemed to decide it was hopeless. She shivered, but he hadn't the ability to enter this system and warm the room.

"Mead?"

"Yes, Martin?"

He stood, feeling restless but having nowhere to go. "I'm sorry about Gray's wife."

"Ah. You want Janet Bridger's memories about Jon Hsu."

"I didn't mean it that way." Though that was so. Even through the horror and fatigue, like a tracker on a recent trail, he knew the Bridgers' memories held the secrets he wanted, the answer Reed had promised, and from inside Jonism itself and not from an alien religion. Jonism—really, the Bridger memory, expanding it—was the only justification for what he had done in manipulating the destruction of the Shak. If he couldn't account for those deaths in his personal moral ledger, he'd be haunted by them. "Will Reed tell me the truth now?" he asked.

She brushed her hair aside and looked up at him. Her lips were cracked. The Shak hadn't fed her or given her anything to drink, as they had him. He had nothing to offer. "Do you still believe in memory?" she asked. "Despite the Shak?"

The memory of Jon Hsu's lover would make Alteration

acceptable, and deliver Elector Lee from disgrace. More than that, the questions that Hsu's memory could answer might tell Penn the part Mystery played in Hsu's original search for Order. But looking at Mead, he could not help but consider that Janet Bridger's memory would make *her* more acceptable at Center. "I believe in truth, Mead," he told her. "It's fundamental to Jonism. I see that memory can be distorted, but that doesn't make all memories into lies. You haven't had Janet's memories, and you say they're not true, but I believe them. I listened to Gray's wife; it wasn't a lie." He couldn't tell her his other, capricious reason: a street-corner oracle, randomly met, had said the Bridgers knew something.

She leaned forward, resting her head in her hands. Her wrists were reddened and scratched from the Shak ropes. He suppressed the urge to treat them, knowing it was an excuse to touch her. She sighed, got up, and walked to the door. She moved without her usual grace. He was afraid she would leave him and searched desperately for words to make her stay. "Mead?"

She stopped and looked back at him, waiting.

He took a hard, deep breath. "Will you come with me to Center?"

She didn't react. "Pity, Martin? There wasn't much I cared about in Bridger Dome."

Her hand was raised to open the door. "All right, Mead. I give up. What do I have to say to keep you?"

She stared at him. "Keep me?" She seemed confused, not angry.

"I misspoke," he said stiffly. "I meant . . ." What had he meant? "I hope you will accept my invitation to come with me to Center."

She stared, then shook her head as if bewildered. "I'm sorry, Martin. I'm not entirely myself. . . ."

"Mead. Do you know something?" It was intuition; perhaps there was something in Testament's air. Penn jumped off the desk and went to her, but didn't touch her.

Mead looked up at him. "I'm a precaster, Martin, but I don't know anything the old ladies *tell* each other once they move into Bridg—once they join the precasters formally. In my own way I'm as unique as the alia, Gray's wife."

"You've remembered Jon Hsu." His happiness was enormous, drowning out the horror of the earlier bloodletting.

"Janet Bridger's memory of Jon Hsu is the best possible defense against the Shak story; I'm suspicious of luck like that."

"That's backward, Mead. It's the Shak story that was the lie."

She sighed and shrugged wearily. "Am I real, Martin?"

"I don't know what you mean."

Suddenly, Mead was sobbing. He pulled her close and put his arms around her. It was wonderful to hold her, to feel her body pressed against his; his fingers tightened around her. "It's all right," he repeated until she stopped trembling.

Still within his arms, she said, "Is this a coincidence, or was I deliberately made by Reed? Am I another cog in their hundred-year plan? Did they cause my infertility, to make me go to you, asking for your help?" She wiped her eyes on the loose fabric of his shirt, although it was dirty. "Remember? You said the cure was easy?"

"Of course you're real. Precasters aren't magicians; they can't mold anyone."

She pushed him away. "I don't remember everything, but it's coming. It started when the Shak made me think about whether he was real—or just a bit after, when I was talking to Gray's alia. Am I part of a plan to destroy the Harmony? Or to save it from the Shak? Maybe I'm just your confirmation of Jon Hsu's memory; maybe I'm no more real than the alia."

He wanted to shout with joy, but she needed him to seem dispassionate. "There is no one who is less likely to have been manipulated by them than you."

She smiled cautiously. "I remember Jon Hsu."

He grabbed her shoulders and twirled her around, then hugged her against his chest. He kissed her wild, filthy hair and savored it. He hadn't known, until then, the depth of his unacknowledged uncertainty, but Mead's memory was the best source he knew. Whatever Reed said was potentially tainted; she'd been the person most likely to have manipulated Gray's wife, if Janet Bridger's memory was false. Mead, however, was honest. Her own self-doubts, her open pondering of the possibility of deception, only confirmed that there was none.

Mead looked up, her beautiful, precocious eyes searching his for truth. "Martin, what if I look at Reed, and she's laughing at me?"

"Jon Hsu lived," he said firmly. "Your ancestor knew him. There is nothing wrong with your memory; no confabulation. You'll tell all the worlds of the Harmony about Jon Hsu, the things that didn't get written down, but were preserved only because you're Altered. You'll come with me to Center; you'll be my partner there, no matter what anyone says about it."

She grinned, and his joy stopped. It was no use telling her that by accompanying him to Center she'd help Testament, or the Bridgers. She'd care even less about Jonism, the Harmony, or Jeroen Lee. "I need you," he said. "*Will* you come with me, Mead?" Her children would be his daughters. Altered, but with Jon Hsu's memory. It would be all right. The Harmony was changing; it would have to.

Her eyes were luminous, with unexpected tears in their corners, and a view that looked back a thousand years. "I like you more than I should, Martin."

V. Testament

Dry rain—a fine white stone powder mixed with larger bits of stone—sifted down through the shifting debris. It coated everything, as if a dust storm had just moved through, and wrapped the cooling bodies of the Bridger dead in a blanket made of the substance of Bridger Dome. Gray walked carefully over the uneven surface that had been the rotunda, looking for Reed.

"My men have found more survivors," Isaacs said. "They're bringing them outside." The offie had, at Penn's suggestion, attached himself to Gray, and never let go. Gray wondered when Isaacs would start asking pointed questions, but Isaacs never did.

"Reed?"

Isaacs hesitated, consulting what he called his "utility," as if it were power or water to his mind. "No. Not yet. But I'm sure we will. Everyone who went into the underground levels survived, and most of those aboveground in the lower levels."

It had been essentially the same answer for an hour, but Reed was nowhere to be found. With their usual efficiency, the offies had laid out the dead they located in a neat, straight row that bisected a relatively clear area in the center of the shattered dome. They were careful to arrange the dead women's clothing so that they were dignified and decently covered.

Gray had expected the dead to have vacant faces, as Dancer did—had—between emulations, but these women's personalities were stamped on them, like their memories, continuing beyond death. Each time he came to one he knew—Virginia was there, looking dour—he hesitated. Often their eyes were open. He wondered what their last moments had been like, and if they'd been afraid of death. Like so many other memories, no one could share that; everyone died alone. He thought of Janet's brief life, just budding into someone new, then casually destroyed along with the Shak. Gray had no regret at having killed Swan. It wasn't only revenge; Swan would have hurt Testament again, and destroyed the Bridger line.

"We won't harm them," Isaacs said. "Why do so many run away from my men?"

Gray hadn't the patience to pamper him. "Maybe they lack confidence in your goodwill."

They continued down the row in silence. Gray had been sure Reed would be in the rotunda, not hiding underground, but the offies hadn't found her.

"More people, claiming to be relatives, are at the buffer line," Isaacs said. "Should we let them in? My men say there are too many amateurs already inside. It's dangerous."

Daughters. Sisters. Mothers. Sons. Brothers. Gray imagined their helpless anguish as they watched the destruction, not knowing why it was happening, if their loved ones survived, or even if the Harmony would make them targets next. He glanced at Isaacs. The offie looked smooth, shallow, and competent. Shak Dome was a crushed hole in the ground, with no identifiable bodies left, and Bridger Dome was a ruin because of this man and others like him, men more disturbed now by the mess than they had been by the deaths. Offies and Jonists.

"What right do you have to say no?" he asked.

Isaacs hesitated, and when Gray turned away, the offie touched his arm, restraining Gray from leaving. "I'm sorry," he said.

"Leave me alone." There might come a time when he could listen to sympathy from an offie, but just now he doubted it. He hated them; he hated knowing that on their scale, this was a trivial action. Gray shrugged Isaacs off and studied the destruction, trying to get his bearings in the new geography of the dome. He noticed the garden. Maybe the offies had missed Reed among the broken trees and dying flowers.

Trailed by his offie shadow, Gray went there, and he'd guessed right. She lay under the branch of an oak tree, on the ground beside a crushed bench. A limb had fallen, sheered off when a chunk of the dome had struck it, and the dusty green leaves had hidden her. Gray knelt in the space between her body and the tree limb. He hit his fist into the dirt, imagining how she would have sat there listening for the next crushing reduction of Swan's gravity wall, waiting for it to destroy her home. He took her hand, expecting warmth, but she already felt cool. For the first time, he wished for the comfort of religion. Testament's substitute, memory, eluded him. He had no memory of Reed but his own.

Precast for me, grandmother, he thought. *Tell me how to live my life, how to be useful. Don't make me go on alone.*

"Who was she?" the offie asked quietly.

Gray didn't answer, but, from behind, Mead did. "Our grandmother. Reed Bridger."

Gray turned to see her. She looked better than she had earlier; she'd washed her face and straightened her clothes, although like everyone inside the dome, she had acquired a shrouding of white dust.

"I'm sorry," the offie said again. Polite like all of them when they weren't sure if you were above them in status. Gray turned back to Reed's body before he'd have to watch Isaacs bow.

"Go away," Mead said fiercely. For her, Isaacs did it, or maybe he just wanted to report Reed's death personally to Penn.

Mead knelt beside Gray. "She was a wicked witch, Gray, and a house fell on her."

"That's not what I remember." He put Reed's hand back gently at her side. She was smiling slightly; any pain couldn't have been bad.

Mead touched Gray's arm. "She bet that we lived, and she won. It was a good time to die, a useful time, or she would have fought death harder. Lots of sympathy from the offies, and now she doesn't have to explain anything to us or tell

Martin about Jon Hsu. You and I are the only ones left that Martin will trust."

"There was no Jon Hsu." He didn't turn his head.

"Stupid Gray. Of course there was. I remember him quite well, now that I've thought about it. Better and better."

So Mead had become a real precaster, guiding memories and people. He glanced sideways at her.

She grinned. "You and I will take the Harmony by storm."

He looked up. The highest gallery, which had held the main line sepulcher, was gone. "I'm not going anywhere. I'll help rebuild Bridger Dome and spit on the offies if they offer aid."

"No, you won't." Mead covered his hand with hers. "The dome won't be rebuilt, Gray. The time for it is over." She sounded very sure; she studied him awhile in silence while he wondered why Reed hadn't gone to a more secure place. She'd spoken of useful lives. Had she believed in useful deaths?

Mead removed her hand from his and nodded. "You'll leave for the Harmony with Martin and me. It's what Reed wanted; you were never meant to stay on Testament." Mead gestured around the dome. "She would have known you'd never go, after this, if she were still alive."

"Leave me alone, Mead." Was he to blame for Reed's death?

"Just be glad Martin likes me enough to keep you from being executed for treason. That was stupid, Gray. You should have let someone else do it. You're too important to risk yourself like that."

Exasperated, Gray sat back on his heels and stared at her. "You're crazy. I'm expendable. A singleton and a man. The Bridger line doesn't need me." He supposed he should thank her for saving his life, after he'd shot Swan, but didn't. Reed's eyes stared, as sightless as glass, and her body was twisted under the tree limb. He couldn't imagine life without her.

Mead touched his arm again. "Gray, those old Assenters didn't want to be conquered, they only recognized that in a direct fight, the Harmony would win, and we'd be worse off for trying. They didn't give up; they fought a different kind of war, one that required patience, planning, timing, and luck."

"A hundred years' war?" He shook his head. "I never saw signs of it."

"Do you think Reed Bridger would ever be a willing captive? Of course not. For a hundred years the offies have kept fertile women out of the Harmony. Meanwhile, they've let men drift off Testament, more of them recently. *Fertile* men. Men like you. You thought your alia was supposed to be a scout for the Compound Council, but Gray, why send a scout when you can mastermind an invasion?"

He saw her implication. "That's ridiculous. Males don't pass their mitochondrial DNA."

"Offies don't test the DNA of men. There are other ways the Alteration could be done." She smiled and touched his cheek, exactly as Reed had often done, making him feel, just for a moment, that Reed wasn't truly gone, and reminding him that she wasn't. A part of her was in Mead, in Eris, in all his sisters and all his near cousins. Even in him.

"Gray, you want children as badly as I do. You love Testament, no matter what they've done, and yet you've passionately wanted to leave. I *know* this. I precast it: you'll establish a Bridger fatherline."

Fatherline. Sure. It was like Mead to ridicule him over their grandmother's corpse, but her expression was serious. A more elaborate joke, then? "I won't fight with you here, Mead, but I don't believe you. It's not something the Compound Council would do."

"You know them so well? I don't. No one does. Women in their afterlife; who can guess what they think and they plan? But I know this. Reed truly cared for you. She wouldn't have cared about anyone who wasn't also useful. And there's been an increase in sons throughout our generation; lots of them have been leaving. There are other Testament men out there, Gray. Reed molded you to be *her* emissary into the Harmony, and she was ready to let you go, but then Martin arrived on Testament. She couldn't resist the opportunity to establish Testament's best pedigree in the Harmony's highest echelon. So she reeled him in—for you—with Janet's memory and me."

"She wanted you with him; I told you."

"And you did a good job, but it wasn't quite convincing. I know who her favorite was; she told everyone often enough—which was bound to get you disliked by me, and all our cousins. I'm an afterthought, a supplement that was added when the opportunity with Martin arose, but you, you're her special boy. You've been in her plans since before you were born."

Testament's memories spilling out into the Harmony on the seed of men. Men remembered by their children; real fatherhood. It was too close to his secret dreams to be real. "No," he said, "it's another of your tricks. They didn't want my children."

Mead nodded eagerly. "I started to understand Reed's plan when you told me about Melany Kane. They just didn't want your fatherline here, on Testament, where it could alert the offies too soon." She clapped her hands together. "What a good trick your children would have been on the Shak!"

Gray turned away from Mead and looked around the dome. Offie soldiers were calling to each other. They wanted to clear some of the larger dome fragments from the rotunda center, where they blocked an entrance to the underground. Their off-world accents, peremptory manner, and assumption that their presence here was their right made Gray bitter. He looked back at Mead. She was staring at Reed's face as if waiting for her to speak. "Gray, this isn't just good against the Harmony; we need men's memories on Testament, too. If it works, men like you will have children on Testament. Then the motherlines won't be so tribal; there'll be more cooperation. We'll have men between us, men in common, as more than some quickening device for producing daughters."

Reed had told him that he would be remembered: *I swear it,* she'd said. He'd thought she'd only meant fame. "You really think she planned this?" Gray spread his arms wide.

"Yes, I do. She set everything in motion. It's a war, Gray, a siege. You're the escape route, you men. Call it a precast, or whatever you like, but I'm *certain.* The embedded Jon Hsu memory is another front of the war. The Harmony has to change, if we're going to be more than barely tolerated. Your alia was a soldier. They activated the Jon Hsu memory earlier than they'd expected because, through Martin, they decided the time was right."

Gray believed Mead. They were all parts of the precasters' grand design, carriers of Testament's memory, warriors in the battle against the Harmony. This was Reed's kind of plan. They were expendable, every one of them, but Testament and the Bridger line were not.

Mead reached out and rearranged Reed's shawl. Gray hadn't noticed his gift around his grandmother's shoulders because the bright icesnake-skin was covered with dust. Mead sighed. "She makes me crazy, even dead. How much did she really know? How fully do they actually plan?" Mead stood up and dusted off her clothes.

Bits of Gray's life were falling into place. Janet had agreed to be sterilized because she didn't share Testament's craving for children. Perhaps that was innate in the original Janet Bridger, and yet, perhaps Reed hadn't wanted him to be monogamous, if Janet had survived to get out into the Harmony. The precasters would have preferred that he have children with several different women, the way most men did on Testament—the usual male scattergun effect, the children disseminated widely. He remembered his schooling, his shattered expectations, the distance he'd felt from his family, particularly the difficulty with Mead.

"You remember something," he said, intuitively knowing it must be true.

She nodded. "I remember mother. At first she didn't want a son. She was remembering so much, she thought she'd have a last daughter. Reed had to convince her, so Reed told her about you. Hinted, anyway, to get her to bear you. You're our testament, Reed said. Margaret speculated on what Reed meant, but never really knew. Neither did I until today, but I've always envied you. Margaret was so proud." Mead's voice had turned bitter. She walked a few steps away and continued speaking from there. "I was an impulse, an afterthought, the way I've always been. Mother wasn't a precaster yet, not quite, so she decided—what the hell—to have me. Reed didn't have any hand in *my* conception, and had no interest in my life. I was the one they'd have to sterilize, because she might know too much. They must have felt so merciful, leaving me my own life!"

Gray had gotten to his feet during Mead's account. He had always innately known her heartache without understanding why he was at its source. "They changed their minds, Mead," he said. "When Penn came, they pushed you at him, knowing who you are and what that would do. Reed was glad. She was proud of you; you're so much like her. Maybe she even decided secrecy was a mistake in this war, and that it would be good to have a precaster out there in the Harmony who would have children."

Mead frowned. She seemed not to have heard him, but when she spoke, he guessed she'd taken what he said into account. "We need men. To change the Harmony, we have to change, too."

Four Harmony soldiers were coming in their direction with tools and a stretcher. They clearly intended to remove Reed from beneath the tree branch and place her in the row with the other Bridger dead. Gray couldn't watch, and it was unreasonable to stop them from doing what had to be done. He looked one last time at his grandmother, but under the shroud of Bridger Dome's dust, she was a statue, not real. Finally, he understood his use. He was the culmination of a hundred-year war, Reed's plan for the future, living proof that on Testament, war was biology. "Thank you, Mead," he said. He started to walk away.

Mead hurried after him. "Women *do* need men. We need partners. Look, Gray, stop. I need you, all right? Brother and sister? Throughout everything, we've always helped each other. You helped me just now. We'll have a partnership, a real one."

He stopped walking and waited. "What's the catch, Mead?"

"There's none. Gray, I never really lie. I do need you. The thing is, now, suddenly, just when it's convenient, I truly remember Jon Hsu."

Gray stared.

"Is it something *she* implanted?"

He understood her disgust at having falsehoods inserted into her mind, then thought guiltily of Janet.

"You can keep me honest," Mead said. "I want to know the truth; she wouldn't have bothered tampering with your memories, since *you* wouldn't have remembered anything. And I don't want to be alone out there. Please, Gray?"

The offies would bring him to Center anyway, and she needed him; the Bridger line did. In whatever capacity he could be used. "Penn?" he asked.

She smiled. "Martin believes everything I say is *true*. All's fair in love and war."

"Or both," Gray added.

She didn't answer that.

He extended his hand. Mead grasped it and they shook. "*Do* you remember Jon Hsu?" she asked.

"Maybe," he said slowly, wondering at the most useful answer.

"Good." Mead nodded. "You, me, and Janet Bridger's memories, infiltrating the Harmony, all according to Reed Bridger's plan. What do you think of Testament's revenge?" She grinned. She was speaking too quickly, exhilarated and frightened at the same time. "They may check your DNA; they're compulsive researchers. There were men aboard that slowboat. Could there have been a direct male memory of Jon Hsu? Something repressed, a recessive? Maybe your children will be direct descendants of Jon Hsu's son, or even have Jon Hsu's memories?"

Gray shook his head and looked up at the open sky. In a way, he would be following Reed. He imagined his grandmother soaring out into the universe beyond. The Eye on the World had opened wide and become a mouth. The Bridgers were going to talk the Harmony to death.